The Villages

Books by Dave Hutchinson

Thumbprints
Fools' Gold
Torn Air
The Paradise Equation

The Villages

Dave Hutchinson

Cosmos Books, an imprint of **Wildside Press**
Pennsylvania . New York . California . Ohio

The Villages

Published by:

Cosmos Books, an imprint of Wildside Press
PO Box 301, Holicong, PA 18928-0301
www.wildsidepress.com

For more information, contact Wildside Press.

ISBN: 1-58715-399-8

for you abide, a singing rib within my dreaming side,
you stay

Contents

Part One

Tim in Bloomsbury

One

1

On the morning two bodies, burned beyond recognition, were found lying in front of St Paul's, I woke up with the worst hangover of my life.

I tried not to move too quickly as I wandered downstairs; my stomach felt as if it was moving independently of the rest of me. In the kitchen, I downed two paracetamols and half a bottle of Evian I found in the fridge, then I sat at the table waiting for them to make me feel better. Outside, the sun was shining and the birds were singing. I rubbed my face and wondered if it was safe to try and shave.

Eric came in while I waited for my eyes to stop hurting. He was smoking his morning cigar and carrying his morning pint-mug of coffee. He looked at me for a couple of minutes, then he sat down on the other side of the table.

"By the way," he said, "George Romero rang. Says he wants you for *Dawn of the Dead Four*."

"You bastard," I muttered.

"No makeup necessary," he said. He took a puff on his cigar, blew smoke at the ceiling. "Save a fortune in special effects."

"Put that bloody thing out. It's making me sick."

He looked at the end of the cigar. "This? Making you sick? Nah."

"If you need proof, I can always honk on the table," I said.

Eric shook his head. "No, what's making you sick is the booze you had last night."

"I thought you decided not to do medicine."

"I did." He put the cigar in his mouth and grinned around it. "I couldn't stand to look at sick people all the time."

"From where I'm sitting it looks like you enjoy it all right."

"Oh, this isn't professional curiosity. This is just sadism." He took the cigar out of his mouth and stubbed it out in the ashtray in the middle of the table. He looked critically at me. "All right. What you need is Eric's Hangover Cure."

"Will I regret it?"

"Not as much as you're regretting last night." He got up and started to search through the cupboards.

I wasn't regretting last night. I couldn't actually *remember* much of last night. What I *was* regretting was how it had made me feel this morning. I did remember deciding to blow what little money I had left, on the grounds that it wouldn't last much longer anyway and I might as well enjoy it. I remembered a pub in New Barnet, and an Indian restaurant somewhere else, and that was it. Which did nothing to explain the traffic cone I'd found in the hall when I came downstairs.

Eric's Hangover Cure turned out to be a pint of coffee so strong I should have been jumping all over the house, but in my present condition all it did was return me to a semblance of life. Then it made me sick all over the kitchen table.

I managed the walk to Oakleigh Park station all right, and I survived the ten-minute train journey down to Finsbury Park, but I was sick again the moment I stepped onto the platform. The paracetamol hadn't even dented my headache and my eyelids felt as if they'd been lined with sandpaper.

The connection from Finsbury Park to King's Cross took only four or five minutes, and from there it was one stop on the Piccadilly Line to Russell Square Underground station. By the time I got into the lift at Russell Square I actually felt marginally better. I didn't think I had much left to throw up, anyway.

On the way to the interview I bought a roll of Extra Strong Mints from a newsagents' to try and hide the smell of stale whisky and vomit I was sure I was exhaling. I was reasonably sure I was going to screw up the interview, but it couldn't hurt to at least try and make a good impression.

It hadn't been much of a year so far. I was twenty-three and had only just managed to scrape a pass in my Finals. Whatever career prospects I had vaguely considered had more or less evaporated.

I would have gone back home to Nottingham, but there wasn't much there for me either. I'd decided to stay in London instead, and had watched my meagre savings vanish like faery gold. I did interview after interview, failed to get job after job.

Then one day I saw an ad in *Private Eye*. "Leading independent filmmaker urgently needs researchers. Must have a clean driving licence. Foreign languages an advantage." I replied to the ad, and here I was, carrying my hangover and my clean driving licence and my O-level German and what Polish my grandmother had managed to teach me up a narrow twisting flight of stairs above a sandwich bar in Bloomsbury.

The office was six floors up. On each landing there was a tiny window that looked out into the foliage of the trees planted in the pavement outside. The window on the top landing looked over the trees to a corner of what I assumed was the British Museum.

Opposite the window was a door. There was an index card pinned to it with the words "Lonesome Charley Productions" printed on it in black felt-tip. The door wasn't closed properly; when I knocked it swung open.

Inside, the loveliest woman I had ever seen was sitting at a huge IBM golfball typewriter. She looked up and smiled at me and my hangover disappeared.

"Yes?" she asked, still smiling. "Can I help you?"

She was small and she had long blonde hair and the most beautiful, flawless skin, the sort of skin you only see in makeup advertisements or dreams. I stood stupidly in the doorway. "I'm, er . . . My name's Tim Ramsay. I'm supposed to see Mr Dean at two."

"Right." She turned away from me and shouted, "Harry, there's someone to see you!"

On the opposite side of the room was another open door, through which I could see a table piled up with files and folders. Beyond the table there was a further doorway, and through that I could see a grimy window.

A man wearing baggy cord trousers and a white shirt walked through the third doorway and came towards me down the length of the office. He was in his middle forties and his short brown hair was thinning on top. In one hand he had a long brown envelope and a folded sheet of paper. As he reached me I put out my hand to shake hello and he put the envelope and paper into it.

"Take this to the address here," he said, "and then take what they give you to the second address. Then come back here." And he turned and started to walk back into the far room.

I looked dumbly at the things he had given me, then stared at his retreating back. "Excuse me?"

He stopped and looked over his shoulder. "If you need an *A to Z*, Sophie will let you use ours." He carried on through into the third room and closed the door.

"So," said Sophie to me, smiling brightly. "Will you need the *A to Z*?"

The first address on the piece of paper was an office over a photocopy shop just off Ladbroke Grove. In the outer office, an alarming-looking young man with a Mohawk haircut was sitting at a desk slitting open envelopes with what appeared to be an old infantry bayonet. He looked me up and down and said, "What?"

I held out the envelope. "I was told to give you this."

He took the envelope from me, slit the flap, and looked inside. He extracted a folded invoice and looked at it. Paperclipped to the invoice was a cheque. He snorted. "It's a fucking miracle."

"What is?" I asked.

"Fucking Harry Dean paying us, that's what. He have a win on the horses or something?"

I shrugged. "Something like that." I had no idea what he was talking about.

He stood up. He must have been nearly seven feet tall. He held out a hand about the size of a sandwich plate. "I'm Martin."

We shook hands. "Tim Ramsay."

"Well, Tim, let's see what we've got for you. Bob!"

Bob came through from an inner office. She was almost as tall as Martin, wearing an ancient pair of dungarees and a black teeshirt, and she was completely bald. I'm afraid I stared.

"Guess what?" Martin said. "Harry Dean's paid us."

She gasped and clutched her chest theatrically. "Can it be true?" she exclaimed. "Has it all been just a bad dream?"

"Have we got anything for Harry?" Martin asked.

"I think something came in on Friday morning," she said. "I'll just check."

While she was in the other room, Martin said, "I haven't seen you before. You new?"

"Sort of."

"Been working for him long?"

"I'm not even sure I *am* working for him."

"Well"—he waved the envelope at me—"I'd say thanks, but we thought we'd have to sue Harry for this, so tell him it's cash on delivery from now on."

"Right."

Bob came back and handed me a flat film tin about the size of my hand. "We'd appreciate prompter payment from now on," she said.

"I know. Martin was just saying."

"Well, just make sure Harry knows it."

I looked at the film tin. "It might sound like a stupid question, but what is this?"

"Belly camera film from an ME-109 over London," said Martin. "April the seventh, 1941."

"You're kidding."

"No shit," said Bob.

The second address was an electronics shop halfway up the Tottenham Court Road. The window was haphazardly stacked with various items of audiovisual gear and surveillance equipment. Inside, a thin, morose-looking shop assistant walked over and asked if he could help me.

I took the film tin from my pocket. "Mr Dean asked me to bring this here."

He looked at the tin as if its presence in the shop only made him feel more woeful. "You want the boss."

I looked around the shop. We were the only two people there. "Could I see him, then?"

The shop assistant sighed and walked to a door at the back of the shop. He knocked and the door opened. A small Asian man in shirtsleeves looked out. "What is it, Roger?"

"Something from Harry," Roger said.

The Asian looked at me. "Brought me some film?"

I held up the tin.

He nodded. "Okay, tell him I'll do it as soon as I can. I'm busy right now."

"Fine," I said, handing the tin to Roger. "I'll be seeing you, then."

2

There was nobody at the office when I got back. Tucked into the keyboard of the typewriter was a note which said, "Gone to lunch. Back soon. Wait."

There was a visitors' chair beside the desk the IBM sat on, and a stack of old *Independent on Sunday* colour supplements on the floor next to it. I sat down, picked up one of the supplements, and waited.

An hour later I was halfway through the pile of magazines, most of which I had already read anyway, and there was no sign of the return of Lonesome Charley Productions.

I got up and walked around the office. There were little windows at one end but they were so grimy it was hard to make out anything outside.

In the second room a couple of battered filing cabinets stood against one wall. I tried the drawers but they were locked. The files and folders on the table were mostly empty. I wandered on.

The walls of the third room were occupied by rough home-made-looking shelves supporting ranks of video and audio tapes. What wall space remained was covered in photographs. Some of them had been torn from magazines; others were yellowed and curling and looked like original prints. Most of them depicted bombed buildings, smashed roads, people in boilersuits or the uniforms of the wartime ARP carrying blanket-covered stretchers out of rubbled houses. There was one shot of a team of firemen hosing water at a burning building; another was Herbert Mason's classic photo of St Paul's, seemingly adrift on a sea of smoke. I walked from photo to photo. It was like being in an exhibition about the Blitz.

I heard the door close in the outer office and a voice called, "Hello?" I walked back through the office. The secretary, Sophie, was standing beside her desk. She favoured me with that ethereal smile. "Good. You made it back. Did everything go okay?"

"Martin and Bob say they want cash on delivery from now on."

She sighed and nodded. "Harry's a bastard when it comes to paying his bills." She took off her coat and hung it on a rack behind the door. "He's gone up to Viren's to look at that bit of film you brought back."

"Viren's?"

"The shop on Tottenham Court Road. Viren does film-to-tape transfer for us." She dropped her shoulder-bag on the desk.

"Oh," I said, suddenly remembering. "He says he'll do it as soon as he can. Does that mean anything to you?"

She was fiddling with some papers on her desk. "It sounds familiar, yes."

"Look," I said, "no offence, but I was supposed to come here for an interview. I didn't expect to do a day's work."

"I know." She checked her watch. "But I make it only about three hours' work. We'll reimburse your travelling expenses, of course. Wait here a second." She went into the far office and came back a few moments later with a bundle of five-pound notes. "Did you take a taxi?"

I shook my head.

"In the normal course of events, getting expenses out of Harry is a complicated business, and you can't always be certain he'll pay you," she said, counting off six fivers. "He always demands receipts if you take a taxi, but I think just this once he won't mind." She held the money out to me.

"I just said I didn't take a taxi," I said.

She shook her head. "I think you may be too honest to work here. Possibly too honest to work anywhere. Take it. It's only petty cash. Harry never keeps track of it."

I took the money and stuffed it into my pocket before she could change her mind. I wasn't *that* honest. "I don't understand. Did I get the job?"

"I don't know. That's up to Harry." She smiled at me. "Do you want the job?"

"I'm not so sure any more." But I did. I wanted to work with her. "Have you had many interviewees?"

She looked thoughtful for a moment. "I don't think it would be fair to answer that question. You should ask Harry. Go home—there's nothing else to do here. Harry won't be back again today."

"So what should I do? Wait for him to call me, or what?" I was starting to get confused and angry in about equal measures. "Should *I* call *him*?"

She took her coat down from the rack and put it on. "I think you should do what you think is right," she said. "Also, if you want to disguise alcohol on your breath, aniseed balls are better than mints."

I felt myself blush. "I was sort of celebrating last night."

She picked up her bag. "It's okay. Harry does it all the time. You can always tell when he's been drinking because he reeks of aniseed. He thinks I don't notice. I'm Zosia Trzetrzelewska, by the way. Everyone calls me Sophie."

"You're Polish?"

"Well, obviously."

"My grandmother was Polish. From Lwów."

She looked a little sad. "That's in Ukraine now."

"Yes, I know."

She smiled and slung the bag over her shoulder. "Okay. So I have to lock up now. Thanks for your help today." And then we just stood there looking at each other. I didn't have a clue what to do or say next; the whole day had been so surreal that, if Harry Dean had come into the office right then leading a large black-and-white cow on a rope, I probably would have accepted it as normal. I'd heard that in America there were some pretty strange executive mind-games, aptitude tests in effect, but I had a sneaking suspicion this wasn't the case here.

"Well, all right," I said awkwardly. "I'll be going, then. See you." And I started to leave. But I stopped at the door. "Can I ask a stupid question?" It was my second stupid question of the day.

She laughed. "Of course you can. Stupid questions don't cost anything."

"What exactly is it that you *do* here?"

"Oh," she said, as if it weren't a question she was asked very often, "we're making a film about the Blitz."

I left the office in something of a daze and wandered back towards Russell Square station. The poster on the news-stand outside the station read, CATHE-DRAL BODIES MYSTERY. I bought a *Standard* to read on the train and carried it down in the lift. I was on the train before I opened it.

The front page was almost filled with a photo of the front of St Paul's. The forecourt had been closed off with blue-and-white tape looped around bollards, and in the middle was an area of cobbles marked with what looked like smudges of soot. A policeman had found them, two blackened objects with twisted, charred, sticklike limbs, just lying there, at half-past four that morning. No sign of who they were or how they had got there. There was speculation that it was a drugs-related killing. I closed the paper and looked at the other people in the carriage and wondered if it wasn't time to leave London altogether if people were going to start setting fire to other people in front of St Paul's.

3

"So you came back," Sophie said when I arrived at the office the next morning.

"I didn't know what else to do," I said, still a bit breathless after the stairs. "Do I work here or what?"

"I don't know," she said, handing me a piece of paper, "but Harry left you a list of things to do if you did turn up."

I looked at the piece of paper. It was a list of places to go, and instructions about what to do when I got there. There were also instructions about how to get there, which buses to use, which Underground stations, how much Harry expected me to pay in fares, how much petty cash Sophie was going to give me. I turned the paper over.

"Something wrong?" asked Sophie.

"I was just wondering if there were instructions on the back about how to suck eggs."

She looked puzzled. "Eggs?"

"It's a joke," I said.

Sophie thought about it, then shook her head. "No," she said doubtfully. "Sorry. Could you explain, please?"

"It's—" I looked down at her, sitting at the typewriter with her head tipped inquisitively to one side, smiling gently, and realized I had no idea what that old saying about grandmothers and eggs meant. I suddenly felt about six inches tall. Maybe less. "Well . . ."

"Perhaps I can look it up," she said, nodding.

"Yes," I said, trying not to show how relieved I felt. "Yes, perhaps you could. It's difficult to explain."

"I'm sure it is." She took an envelope from a drawer and handed it to me. "If you have any change, Harry will want it back."

"Right." At that point, my presumed employer and I had spent roughly one minute in each other's company, including the time it had taken him to walk across the office from his room and back again. "Will I actually be meeting Mr Dean again?"

She nodded. "Oh yes, I imagine so." She smiled brightly at me. "Is there a problem?"

I looked at the sheet of instructions and the envelope of money. "No," I said. "No, I don't think so."

The envelope contained a single five-pound note. I used it to buy a travelcard at Tottenham Court Road station.

Harry's itinerary turned out to be a tour of tiny photo agencies, antique shops and junk shops. At each of these places I was given a sealed package and an invoice and a hard stare from the owner. By the end of the morning I was starting to accept the hard stare as part and parcel of working for Lonesome Charley Productions.

I worked out that, if I followed Harry's directions, I would have roughly half an hour for lunch. Using Sophie's *A to Z* to re-plan the route, I thought I could extend that to fifty minutes.

When I finally made it back to the office, Sophie and Harry had gone home. There was a note in the typewriter that read, "Leave the change in the drawer and the packages in the safe. Close the safe door and spin the combination. Turn off the lights when you leave and don't forget to give the door a good tug because the lock sticks."

I glared at the note. I'd been on the Tube and on buses all day. My new route had left me with no time at all for lunch, but I found some small consolation in thinking that, if I'd followed Harry's instructions to the letter, I'd still be out there somewhere, picking up packages and receiving hard stares.

I put the change in the drawer, put the packages in the safe, and gave the door a good tug on the way out.

4

"Hello?"

"Hello, Dad."

"Yes?"

I sighed. "I just wondered how you were."

"I'm all right. Are you drunk or something?"

Eric came out of his living room and saluted me with his cigar on the way to the kitchen. I was sitting at the bottom of the stairs with the phone in my lap, staring into space.

"I got a job, Dad."

"That's nice."

"It's with a film company," I said, doing the best I could not to get annoyed. I was doing Lonesome Charley a favour by describing it as a film company, but my father would never know.

"Oh?" Then he made a monumental effort and said, "Is the money good?"

Startled by his interest, I said, "No, not really."

"Well, why did you take it, then?"

"It's better than being on the dole, isn't it?"

"I'm sure you know more about that than I do," he said smugly. He hadn't missed a day's work for any reason at all in thirty years, and he loved to remind me about it.

The traffic cone was still sitting beside the hall table. I didn't know which was more mysterious—how it had got here, or why nobody had bothered to throw it out yet. I said, "It's better than nothing, Dad. I thought you'd be pleased I was in work."

There was a pause, then he said, "Well, it's nice of you to ring, anyway."

It was always the same. I always wound up wondering why I bothered to call him. "How's Wendy?"

"She's all right, I suppose."

"Dad," I said.

"Yes?"

"How did we wind up like this?"

"Like what?"

I shook my head. "It doesn't matter, Dad. I'll talk to you again soon, okay?"

"Well, you don't *have* to."

"No. Well, okay." I hung up and sat holding the phone against my stomach.

"Daddy?" Eric asked from the door of the kitchen.

I nodded. "The one and only." I put the phone back on the hall table. "Fancy going out for a beer?"

He shook his head apologetically. "Lisa's coming round later." Lisa was his girlfriend. Eric looked at me and said, "Has the sense of delight with our new job worn off already?"

I shrugged. "What if I phone out for a Chinese? My treat."

"Lisa's allergic to monosodium glutamate."

"Lisa doesn't have to eat it." I held up a hand. "No. All right. A pizza, then." I saw the look on his face. "Oh come on, Eric. How can anybody be allergic to *pizza*?"

"It's the mozzarella," he said.

"You're kidding." It was no wonder Lisa was so thin.

"I'm glad you've got a job, Tim," Eric said. "I really am."

"That's nice," I said. "Thanks, Eric."

"Oh, don't be such a pillock." He went back into his room, returned holding an ashtray and tapped his cigar into it. "You've been wandering about like a lost soul for weeks."

I'd been wandering about like a lost soul for an appreciable part of the day, but I wasn't about to let Eric know that. "Well, I'm glad I've got a job too."

"But there's something wrong, isn't there?"

I looked at him. We'd met during Freshers' Week. He'd been lost and I'd been drunk, and that was the way our relationship had been for three years or so. There had been an endearing innocence about him in those days. I suddenly remembered him, after three bottles of Budweiser, confiding that he had never got drunk with anybody before. I also remembered him throwing up all over me shortly afterwards.

"There's nothing wrong," I told him. "Everything's fine."

"It doesn't look fine to me."

It was unusual for Eric to be quite so perceptive. I wondered if my doubts about Lonesome Charley Productions were so obvious.

"Everything's fine," I said again. This time I tried much harder to sound convincing.

5

"You forgot to turn the lights off last night," said Harry.

"Sorry," I said.

He looked at me a moment longer, then shook his head. "I left you a note. Money in the desk, packages in the safe, lights out—"

"And give the door a good tug on my way out. Yes, I remember. I said I was sorry."

He sighed and scratched his head. "Electricity costs money, you know. You probably think it just comes out of the ground for free."

"No, I don't."

"And bulbs cost money too," he went on as if he hadn't heard me. "Three bulbs went last night." He waved a hand at the dusty, cobwebbed light-fittings along the middle of the ceiling, then shook his head again. "I'll have to take it out of your pay." He turned and walked away.

"Fine," I said, figuring that I could afford a night's lighting and a couple of bulbs. "And while we're on the subject . . ." I heard Sophie give an amused snort as I followed Harry into his room.

"While we're on what subject?" he asked, settling himself carefully into the chair behind his desk.

I stopped in the doorway. "My salary."

Harry gave me an ingenuous look. "What about it?"

"Well, there wasn't anything about it in your advert and I'd like to know what I'm going to be earning."

He smiled merrily. "You came for an interview for a job without knowing what the salary was going to be?"

"You know I did. You wrote the advert."

"Well, Sophie did." He frowned in concentration. "All right. You'll be working a week in hand. Thirty pounds a day, no London Weighting, no travel allowance, no Luncheon Vouchers. I'll want itemized expenses with receipts and VAT numbers. If you claim for a lunch without giving me a receipt to go with it you'll be taxed on it; that's the Inland Revenue's fault, not mine. Your first pay will be in a month's time on the eighth and on the eighth of every subsequent month. If you need something to tide you over until next month I can sub you and I'll stop it out of your next salary. I won't pay petrol expenses or car hire or clothing. Lonesome Charley operates no pension plan or health scheme. If you want to leave I need four weeks' notice. If I fire you, I want you out of here the same day." He sat and watched me. "Any questions?"

"Do I get time off for good behaviour?"

"No, but you do get fired for talking back to me." He leaned back in his chair and clasped his hands behind his head. "Just do as you're told and everything will be lovely, Tim."

"I'm sure it will," I said, asking myself what on earth I had done.

Two

1

The very first time I met Eric, it was obvious he was someone who had—or at least had access to—a large amount of money. His clothes looked expensive, his haircut looked as if it cost him five or ten times as much as mine, he was wearing brand-new Reeboks. He looked, in other words, like someone it might be worth knowing.

We met entirely by accident. He wasn't even in the right building—had just wandered into the corridor where I was chatting to a couple of people on my course. He had a map in his hand and a bemused expression on his face, and he finally got up the nerve to ask somebody how to get to where he should have been. He asked me, and altered the course of my life.

"Do you ever tidy up upstairs?" he asked over dinner.

"Of course I do," I said, looking up from my pork chop.

He took a drink of his beer and licked foam off his lips. "It's just that I went up there yesterday and there were clothes all over the landing."

"That was my ironing."

"There's no need to be so defensive."

"I wasn't being defensive. It really *was* my ironing. I've cleared it up now."

"And you've been hanging your washing over the banisters to dry again."

I sighed and put down my knife and fork. "So?"

"So, it'll warp the wood."

"Oh, Eric, come on." I stared out of the kitchen window. Summer evening sunshine was slanting across the garden. The lawn was freshly mown, the flower beds were neatly dug, the gnarled little apple tree was covered with fruit. Jim, my next door, was wandering around with a hose, watering his elephant grass. All was right with the world.

"It's all right you saying `come on'," he said, "but Dad'll have to replace them."

"It's only a banister, Eric."

"It's only a banister if you don't have to pay for it."

"Eric, it's been a long day."

He shrugged and went back to his meal. We had always tried to have dinner together. We took it in turns to cook, and for a while we had tried to outdo each other in terms of culinary inventiveness and extravagance. Eric had come out on top because he was able to afford black truffles for a truffle omelette. I claimed a technical foul because I couldn't afford black truffles, and I couldn't eat them anyway because they smelled appalling, but Eric had just shaken his head sadly, I'd had to admit defeat, and we'd gone back to more sensible meals.

The advent of Lisa, however, had meant our dinners together were becoming more and more rare. Which meant we tended to use the occasions to argue. We had, I thought, lived together for too long. We were getting like a pair of old marrieds.

"Nice chop," he commented.

I glared at him.

"How was work?"

"Oh God." I finished my beer, went to the Beer Bin by the fridge for another tin, and came back to the table. "How does thirty pounds a day sound to you?"

He thought about it for a moment. "It sounds like indentured slavery. Are you serious?"

"That's what I was told."

Eric reached across the table and picked up the tin I'd just brought from the Bin. He popped the top and refilled his glass. He had started his university career doing Medicine, but after his first autopsy he'd moved to a course in corporate law. It was amazing. I still couldn't work out how he'd done it. I'd spent the whole three years of my course trying to convince my tutor not to throw me out into the street.

"Thirty quid a day isn't a lot," he said, tucking into his dinner again.

"No, it's not." I picked up the tin, shook it, poured about an inch of beer into my glass, and got up to go to the Bin again. "On the other hand, I am working for a Leading Independent Filmmaker."

He looked up, saw me with the new tin in my hand, and looked at his glass. "Oh. Sorry, Tim. Did I drink all your beer?"

"Not all of it, no." I opened the tin and topped up my glass.

"What about this bloke Harry?"

"I don't know." I shrugged. "He seems all right."

"He's paying you what amounts to subsistence wages. A hundred and fifty quid a week? Jesus."

"A lot of people would be glad of a hundred and fifty quid a week," I said. After graduation, Eric had gone without very much effort into a post with a little firm of international tax lawyers and an expense account that was bigger than my weekly salary. His life seemed to be characterized by such ease. He drifted from success to success, while I just drifted.

"You can't live in London on that, Tim," he told me. "It's going to cost you over a hundred pounds a month just to travel to work."

"It's better than nothing."

"Well, yes," he said, cutting another piece off his chop. "Of course it's better than nothing."

"Meaning what?"

He looked at me. "Hm?"

"Meaning what?" I picked up my knife and fork again. "Come on, Eric. 'Of course it's better than nothing.'"

Eric stared. "I'm not criticizing, Tim," he said.

"Not much you're not."

"Tim." He rubbed his face. "I told you last night, I'm really happy you've got a job. It's great. It's a start."

"Don't patronize me, Eric."

His face took on a look of injured innocence. "I wasn't." He looked me in the eye and realized he wasn't being convincing. "As God is my witness, Tim. I wasn't patronizing you. I wasn't criticizing you either. You've got a job. Great. Go to the head of the queue; three million people behind you start to applaud. Jesus, Tim, what do you want? A medal or something?"

I looked at him a moment longer, trying to decide what I wanted, then went back to my dinner.

"Okay," he said in a patient tone of voice that was unfamiliar to me. "So the money's not very good. So it's not an ideal job. Good grief, Tim, you've only been there a day."

I looked up, wondering where this patient, competent person had come from all of a sudden. All the time I'd known him, Eric had been an amiable innocent, wandering along insulated from the worst things in life by his father's money. Eric and his father had a great relationship. His father had bought this house. Eric went up to Cheshunt every Sunday to see him. It made me sick.

"Well," I said lamely. "I'll give it a few weeks."

He smiled, not entirely persuaded. "That's my boy."

Eric's father had actually got me through university without my falling into irrecoverable debt, and that was starting to make me sick as well. The house was converted into two flats, each with a bedroom, living room and study. We shared the bathroom and kitchen. The flats had their own televisions and videos, and Eric's father let us both stay there rent-free. I hadn't thought much about it before, but I was beginning to see it as the arrogance of a man with too much money. What had once been Student Heaven was beginning to look like a rich man patronizing a poor working-class lad.

In off-guard moments, this past couple of days I'd found myself resenting Eric as well as his father. I kept telling myself it was part and parcel of working for Harry Dean; the job just seemed naturally to make you pissed-off. Yet I'd begun to feel like that before I'd even heard the name "Harry Dean".

When Eric first wandered into the wrong building at the university and saw me, I was living in what my landlord described as Clapham. It was actually the western edge of Brixton, which didn't bother me at all, but my landlord thought he'd never be able to let the place if he told people it was in Brixton. The house was three floors of draughts and leaky central heating and for some reason it always smelled of boiled cabbage. I shared it with two other students and a Press Association journalist who always looked as if he couldn't quite believe where he had wound up.

Towards the end of my first term, my landlord told us that he'd decided to do the house up and give it to his son as a wedding present, so we'd all have to move. Jill and Gary, the other students—who spent most of their time in their room getting stoned, listening to David Bowie tapes or having sex—were crestfallen. The journalist, whose name I never discovered, looked like a Death Row prisoner who has learned his sentence has been commuted. I set my sights on pastures new.

After our first meeting, I'd made a point of bumping into Eric on the odd occasion, even though our respective courses should have made it highly unlikely we would ever meet. We went out for drinks together. We went to the cinema; Eric liked *Manon des Sources* and Kurosawa. I tended to go to anything starring Bruce Willis. I liked to think there was a certain amount of cultural cross-pollination taking place, funded mainly by Eric.

He'd already mentioned the house his father had bought in Oakleigh Park. The idea was that Eric would live on the ground floor and they'd get a lodger in for the upper part of the house, but so far, for one reason or another, they hadn't been able to find anyone suitable.

I remember Eric the Innocent, telling me all this over a Sol in a tapas bar off Oxford Street one night, and me saying, "Well, funny you should mention that, Eric ..." It never occurred to me that over the course of three years or so Eric and I would actually become quite good friends.

2

"No," said Harry.

"What?" I said.

He picked up my painstakingly assembled expenses sheet and waved it in my general direction. "No."

I rubbed my eyes. It was the third expenses sheet I'd presented to Harry that morning; I'd already carved off every superfluous meal, bus-ride and Underground journey I could find. I looked round his office, at the piles of videotapes and fold-ers, the mound of letters on his desk. Then I looked at him and shrugged.

"This bus journey between City Thameslink and Bank," he told me. "There was no point in that. You could have walked."

"Oh, you can't be querying that," I said, shifting uncomfortably on the paint-spattered kitchen chair Harry kept in his office for visitors. "What possible difference does it make?"

"It's not efficient."

The experience of being lectured by Harry Dean about efficiency had rapidly worn thin. I'd been with Lonesome Charley Productions for three weeks and he hadn't passed any of my expenses sheets yet. You had to pitch each one to him as if you were trying to sell him double-glazing or a particularly expensive set of encyclopaedias. I was inefficient. I was spending too much money. I was already costing the company too much. He burst out laughing at one sheet I gave him.

"Tim," he said more reasonably, seeing the look on my face. "This company is funded by a government enterprise grant, a small-business loan and the money from the television people." He waved the sheet of paper at me again. "I just don't have the cash to pay extraneous expenses. Haven't you got a travelcard?"

I did have a four-zone travelcard, as it happened. It was just that, on that particu-lar morning, I'd been going up the escalator at Moorgate and discovered that my travelcard had expired, and I only had a couple of quid on me to pay my excess fare. This had necessitated a quick detour to City Thameslink, where there were no ticket barriers and, if you were very, very lucky, sometimes no ticket inspectors either.

I had no intention of telling Harry any of this, so I just shrugged awkwardly.

This gave him the opportunity to look wise. "You should have bought a one-day travelcard," he told me.

"I was at City Thameslink at a quarter to nine," I said. "You can't buy a one-day travelcard before half-past."

"You see what I mean about inefficiency?" Harry looked sad. "You should have planned your day more carefully."

"I paid for all those journeys," I said. I had learned that it was possible to be stub-born with Harry. It just never did any good.

"Well, that's not my fault," he said, handing the sheet back to me. "Put it down to experience and try to be more careful next time, eh?"

I took the piece of paper. "I'll have an industrial tribunal on you," I told him without any force.

Threats like that just went right by Harry. He smiled. "If you want to write it out again, I'll have a look at it . . ." He gave a little shrug that I had learned to interpret as an expression of fatalism. "I told you your terms of employment when you started here."

"I know." I nodded. "No London Weighting, no Luncheon Vouchers. Sometimes not even a thankyou."

"Oh well," he said. "If we're talking about *thankyous* . . ."

"No." I shook my head. "Don't start, Harry." I was tired of having this conversation. We had it every Monday morning, and it always ended with me wandering off out of pocket. The bottom line seemed to be that, along with all the other fringe benefits most employees working for companies in London took for granted, Lonesome Charley Productions did not pay expenses. "I haven't the energy for it this morning."

This, of course, was Harry's management style. He was the classic Immovable Object. He just sat there and let you wear yourself out, and when you were too tired to argue he changed the subject and you found yourself back on the street running an errand for him.

"Well," he said, true to form. "If we're finished here I want you to pop over to Ruislip and see Mrs Lewis."

I groaned. I had nothing against Ruislip per se, but in just a couple of weeks I had learned to fear the very name of the place.

"It's on the Central Line," Harry informed me with the tones of a yogi handing down the Secret of the Universe, "so you'll have no trouble getting there." This was a bit rich coming from a man who hated travelling on the Underground.

I got up. "Any more instructions, oh Lord and Master?" I asked wearily.

"Just do your job, Tim," he said, beaming proudly at me, happy to have won his weekly head-to-head over the expenses. "Everything will be just fine."

"Can I ask a question?"

He shrugged. "You can *ask*," he said vaguely.

"It's just . . . well, I go out all day and pick up photos and bits of ciné film and tape interviews for you. I was just wondering, do you actually *use* any of it?"

His expression never changed. He just kept smiling at me. "It probably looks a bit chaotic to you right now," he said.

I nodded. I hadn't suspected Harry was capable of understatement.

"But the film is coming together all right," he finished. "Every little bit helps. Photos, interviews, bits of film. It's all coming together very well."

It was a pronouncement of such Papal confidence that I hadn't the heart to argue, so I took my expenses sheet and went back into my room.

The three dark rooms on the top floor were rented. The windows were tiny and so dirty it was necessary to have the lights on all the time. On lengthening grey evenings with the rain pouring down outside it was like being inside a submarine.

Sophie had the room by the door. While not strictly speaking a secretary, she was the only one of the three of us who could operate the IBM golfball typewriter which Harry had picked up at some bankruptcy sale and which made a sound like hamsters being methodically trodden on, so by default she fulfilled the function of Lonesome Charley's secretary.

I had been given the middle room, which comprised a table piled up with empty files and bits of scrap paper but no chair, so I spent most of my time in Sophie's room.

And Harry had the far room, with its desk and fire-damaged swivel chair and its safe, shelves of tapes and walls of photographs. It was the office of a man who was serious about what he was doing, a man with a single purpose, but somehow it still had the half-cocked look I was starting to associate with everything concerning Lonesome Charley Productions.

In the three weeks I'd been there I had begun to think that replying to the advert in *Private Eye* might not have been the smartest thing I had ever done. I'd started to think that way last week, when Sophie let slip that I had been the only person to apply for the job.

It should have been obvious to anybody with an IQ higher than an artichoke that Harry Dean was not a Leading Independent Filmmaker at all. The only part of his job description that was strictly true was the *independent* bit. If nothing else, he was certainly independent.

The *filmmaker* part of Harry's job description was untrue because he had never made a film before. He was not a director or a cameraman or a soundman; he wasn't even a voiceover artist. Harry was a man with a mission. I sometimes thought he believed the film *was* the Blitz, the definitive documentary record. I didn't know how he had acquired his obsession. I was only concerned about when the film was going to be finished.

I was probably more concerned than Harry was. After all, finishing the film would mean him having to give up his research, having to stop looking at photographs of burning buildings and the rubble left behind after they had stopped burning, having to stop reading eyewitness reports from ex-ARP wardens, ex-policemen, householders. The walls of his inner sanctum were lined with hours of scrupulously indexed audio- and videotaped interviews, as well as hundreds of books and literally thousands of letters.

Harry conceived his film as a Studs Terkel kind of thing, an oral history of the Blitz from hundreds of eyewitnesses, illustrated by film and stills never before seen in documentary footage, but mostly I thought he just liked listening to people talk about it.

He had collected Blitz footage and eyewitness accounts from all over Europe; it had turned up in cupboards in Manchester, attics in Leipzig, even a barn in Milan. How film of the Luftwaffe bombing London had managed to scatter so far was beyond me, but Harry's contacts had winkled it out wherever it was. If nothing else, the collection of material was pretty impressive, even if Harry had yet to do anything with it.

Sophie and I were sent out to pin cards on notice boards in old folks' homes and local historical societies, promising money for photos and reminiscences. We put advertisements in local papers. And then Harry would go and talk to whoever replied. He didn't do anything as gross as recording the conversations or buying the photographs himself; he sent us afterwards, to listen to interminable stories about sheltering in Tube stations, digging people out of bombed buildings, rationing, and having to put gummed-paper crosses on your windows to protect them from blast damage. Initially, it was pretty interesting, but after a while it became boring, and then it started to get brain-numbing.

"No luck?" Sophie asked when I went into the front office for my coat.

I shook my head, tore my expenses sheet in half, dropped it in the waste-paper bin, and started to rummage in the drawers of her desk for the office tape recorder.

"Oh, he's such a sod sometimes," she said. "Do you want me to have a word with him?"

I found the battered little personal tape recorder Harry had bought in an office clearance sale. "I think Harry and I are beginning to come to an accommodation," I said, closing the drawer. "I don't complain, and in return he treats me like a pillock." Thinking about it, it had taken an astonishingly short time for my respect for my employer to vanish.

"It's disgusting," Sophie said. "How can he expect to keep staff if he behaves like this?"

I was searching another drawer for blank tapes. I stopped and looked up.

She shrugged. "Before you there was Alec. I liked Alec. He was Scotch. Is it correct? 'Scotch'?"

"Scottish," I said.

"Scottish." She nodded and rolled a letter out of the IBM and laid it on the desk beside the typewriter. She looked at the wall over the desk and concentrated. "He was here eight days, and on the ninth day he didn't bother to come in. Or on the tenth day. Or the eleventh. And so on." She sighed and took a narrow buff envelope from a drawer. "And before Alec there was Sue." She picked up a felt-tip pen and started to address the envelope. Her handwriting was as flawless as her skin. "Sue had earrings."

"I have an earring," I said.

"Yes." She nodded. "I know. But Sue had them *everywhere*." She gave a little shudder. "Anyway, she was only here four days. She argued with Harry a lot."

"So do I."

"Yes." She smiled at me. "You know something, Tim? Harry never fires anybody. People just leave." She let me think about that for a moment, then said, "Where are you going?"

I finally found a couple of blank tapes. The stock was getting pretty low. "Ruislip."

"Oh dear," said Sophie.

3

"Will you have another cup of tea, dear?" Mrs Lewis asked.

"I've still got some left, thank you, Mrs Lewis," I said, indicating the inch or so of insipid milky fluid in my cup.

"Well, do let me know, won't you? Fig roll?"

I had already vowed never to touch another fig roll as long as I lived. "I'm fine, thanks, Mrs Lewis."

She sat back in her tall, high-backed chair, crossed her hands primly in her lap, and looked at me over the top of her half-lens spectacles. Mrs Lewis was in her late seventies, and the front room of her little house in Ruislip was scrupulously neat. I had been there four or five times now, and I always sat down feeling as if I should have been thoroughly buffed and polished first. I didn't know who came in to do her cleaning, but I knew I felt sorry for them.

"We really thought it was over, you know," Mrs Lewis said to the tape recorder sitting on the coffee table. "We'd had almost six weeks without raids."

I nodded. Some of the old folk I spoke to needed encouragement to tell their stories. Not Mrs Lewis.

"My friend Louisa and I—I told you about Louisa, didn't I?"

I nodded again. I'd heard so much about Louisa and her parents and her big townhouse in Pimlico and the pony out in the country that she'd had to sell that I'd started to hate her.

Mrs Lewis sat back again and composed herself. Her hair was snow-white and set in a kind of wavy helmet by tons of hairspray; her makeup was neat and unobtrusive, and her clothes subtly out of date. She was still a handsome-looking lady, and in the photographs she'd shown me it was obvious she'd been nothing short of stunning when she was young. It was just that Mrs Lewis and the truth only intersected each other at a tangent.

"Well, Louisa and I decided to go out one night," she said. "March the eighth, 1941. Louisa wanted to see Douglas Byng, who was billed to appear at the Café de Paris."

My attention started to wander. Mrs Lewis was an inexhaustible source of Blitz stories. If you looked at them objectively, it was impossible for her to have had all those adventures, but she went on and on, filling tape after tape after tape, and Harry loved her. He called her the authentic voice of the Blitz.

I knew the story of the Café de Paris bomb. I also knew that Mrs Lewis hadn't been there; the last time I'd dragged out to Ruislip she had claimed to have been somewhere else on the night of March 8, 1941. She knew the story because she'd read it in a book, and I knew she hadn't been there because I'd read the same book.

"There was a very dashing young officer there," she said. "A Major, he said. Very handsome. Danced like a dream. Oh, it was so good to try and forget the Blitz for a little while."

I stifled a sigh. All of Mrs Lewis's adventures had taken place while she was trying to forget the Blitz for a little while. She was the epitome of the Stiff Upper Lip, trying to carry on against a background of adversity while that little rotter Hitler spoiled her social life. I had the feeling that none of it had happened, that Mrs Lewis had worked as a Land Girl out in Norfolk or had gone to stay with relatives in Scotland for the duration, but by now she had convinced herself she had been in London throughout everything the Luftwaffe had thrown at it and had survived with her smile intact and a pair of nylons daringly purchased from a shady but endearing chap who bore more than a passing resemblance to the Flash Harry character George Cole played in all those St Trinians movies.

I looked at Mrs Lewis, with her thin, tight mouth and her string of pearls, mouthing bullshit and thinking she could get away with it because I was too young to know any better, and I thought of the hundred quid this was costing us, and of the expenses Harry had refused to pass that morning, and I mentally began to draft my resignation letter.

"I never want to do that again," I told Sophie, dropping the tapes on her desk. She smiled. "Where was it this time?"

"Café de Paris."

One adjunct of working for Lonesome Charley was that you gained a familiarity with a sort of *A to Z* of bombings. Café de Paris. Bank Junction. St Paul's. Surrey Docks. It had taken me only a couple of weeks to get up to speed, and now the sites of German bombing raids were almost as real to me as present-day Tube stations.

"She wasn't there," Sophie said. "I typed up the transcript of the last tape you did. She said she was somewhere else."

"I know." I took my coat off and rubbed my eyes.

"So she is lying."

"That's my analysis of the situation," I said. I hung my coat on the rack and pulled up a chair. "I'm not sure I care any more."

Sophie looked at me for a while. Then she took a sheet of paper from a drawer. "I've been thinking," she said. "What do you think about this?"

I took the piece of paper. It was Sophie's expenses sheet. I read it and handed it back. "Your handwriting is lovely."

She handed it back to me. "I included all the money you claimed as well," she said.

I looked at it again. Now I knew what to look for, I saw that Sophie had made a lot more journeys than was strictly necessary for a secretary. Her meals had been subtly expensive, as well. "He'll never pass this," I told her.

Sophie's face broke into a smile like the sun coming out from behind storm clouds. Then she handed me a wad of five-pound notes, and I suddenly couldn't remember the text of my resignation letter.

Three

1

On the day of my "interview" at Lonesome Charley, the two burned bodies on the forecourt of St Paul's had been front page news in the *Standard*. The next day, it had appeared on the front pages of all the nationals as well.

The following day, it had disappeared from the front pages of the broadsheets, and it survived on the front pages of the tabloids for only another twenty-four hours.

After that, the mystery of the burned bodies sank gently towards the sports pages in diminishing column-inches, and finally vanished. There were rumoured arrests, real arrests, but none came to anything. Drug-related? Gang-related? A bizarre crime of passion? Nobody knew. Gradually the papers lost interest, and so did I. Something else was occupying my attention.

She was thirty-one, and she had been in London for three years. She said she'd come to improve her English, but her English sounded fine to me; you had to listen hard for the little errors of pronunciation, the slight accent, that marked her out as a non-native speaker.

She had come to Harry through the friend of a friend of a friend's friend (there was also someone's cousin or second cousin involved somewhere along the line; it was too complicated for me to follow) because Harry said he could get her a work permit. It sounded unlikely to me, but I was rapidly ceasing to be surprised by Harry.

The work permit arrived, and even an extension of her visa, and Sophie had intended to move on to another job, something better-paid, but somehow she'd never got round to it.

"I seem to be stuck here," she said soberly, looking round the office. "Do you think this might be my natural habitat?"

"Christ, no," I said, possibly a little too quickly, because she gave me an odd look and then smiled.

"Do you think this is *your* natural habitat, Tim?" she asked, still smiling.

"Oh, Lord, I hope not."

"What was your plan when you went to university?" she asked.

I shrugged and sipped my coffee. We were having our eleven o'clock break: fifteen minutes for coffee and a chat. There was a percolator in the office, but it hardly ever worked properly, so one of us—usually me—had to go six flights down to the sandwich bar for coffee.

"You must have had some idea," Sophie said, picking up a fragment of her Danish pastry. "I wanted to be a drama critic."

"I'm glad to see your career is going so well," I said.

She popped the pastry in her mouth and grinned. She had the most beautiful smile I had ever seen. It was calm and all-knowing and I was breaking my back cracking jokes because I wanted to see her smile all day long.

She swallowed her bit of Danish and said, "But here is the capital city of drama." She reached for her styrofoam cup of coffee. "Here I can go to the theatre as much as I want." She took a sip. "Do you go to the theatre much?"

"Yes," I lied immediately. "But couldn't you go to the theatre as much as you wanted in Poland?"

"Ah." She shook her head. "It's not the same, Tim. Here is the land of Shake-speare. Here, I feel . . . I feel connected to a great tradition." She raised her eye-brows. "Is it correct, 'connected'?"

I nodded. She didn't often have to check her English with me, but when she did my heart soared. I felt connected too. "It's fine."

She sat back. "Anyway"—she waved her cup as if looking for the right words—"I feel this tradition every time I go to the theatre here."

"Is there no theatre tradition in Poland, then?"

"Oh, but of course!" She looked at me as if I'd accused the Pope of transvestism. "There is a great tradition of theatre in Poland. And of film, of course." She looked sad. "But you must see a play in its native language. Otherwise it's not the same, Tim. Believe me."

I was perfectly prepared to believe anything and everything she told me. I wanted to spend all my time with her, but Harry sent one or both of us out for hours on end on his little errands, and I found myself trying to remember every word, ev-ery nuance of the moments we spent together, putting together Sophie's life story, getting closer to her.

Sophie's father was dead, but her mother still lived in Zabrze, in Upper Silesia, the poisoned south of Poland. "Very polluted, Tim," she said. "Makes Los Angeles look like the Alps." She was an only child. I had a sister, and we spent one joyous af-ternoon while Harry was out discussing the difference it had made to our lives. Pri-vately, I wouldn't have wished my sister Wendy on my worst enemy, but I think Sophie missed having a sibling.

"You could have my sister," I suggested.

She shook her head. "It wouldn't be the same."

"Perhaps we could work out a time-sharing agreement or something," I said, and watched her face light up. She was probably the only thing keeping me at Lone-some Charley. Seeing her smile kept me going down the railway lines to King's Cross and on the Underground to Russell Square day after day. It made me immune to whatever the West Anglia & Great Northern Railway and London Underground could throw at me in the way of late trains, cancelled trains and mysteriously absent drivers.

The money kept me going too, I suppose, pathetic though it was. I had finished my degree thinking the world owed me a living. When I discovered it didn't, I expe-rienced a period of intense jealousy for the graduates before me to whom the world *did* appear to owe a living. In Eric and Lisa's case, it was more than a brief period of jealousy. On the other hand, what they did didn't seem to me to be work.

2

It was pouring with rain when I got off the bus in Muswell Hill. It had been dry when I left home, so I hadn't bothered to bring an umbrella, and I stood under the shelter at the bus-stop with my hands in my pockets for fifteen minutes while the rain eased off. I was already late; I didn't think a few minutes more would make much difference.

When the rain had reduced to a drizzle I walked a little way along the main road, then turned down a side street lined with big houses, the pavement planted with gently dripping trees.

Once, not all that long ago, all these houses had been inhabited by smart suburbanites who had moved out of the centre of London looking for cleaner air and a quieter life. Since then, suburbia had moved further north, had geared itself up for the great leap across the North Circular and into the southern edges of Hertfordshire, and left Muswell Hill behind.

In the wake of suburbia a lot of the houses had been bought up by landlords who split them into flats and then rented or sold them. The houses were starting to take on an air of genteel neglect, paintwork not quite as bright as it might have been, front gardens allowed to grow a little wild, windows lined with the nearly opaque none-too-clean plain net curtains I always associated with bedsit-land.

The house I was looking for was near the end of the street and didn't look too much different from all the others. Its paintwork was just as shabby and peeling, though the little garden in the front was better looked-after than those of its neighbours. I patted my coat pockets to make sure I had everything, then I walked up the path and rang the doorbell.

He was a long time coming to the door. I looked down the street. A very large black dog, soaking wet from the rain, was trotting along the pavement on the other side. I looked about but there was no sign of an owner. The dog went to the end of the street and trotted unhurriedly round the corner. I watched it go. Just before it went out of sight it paused on the corner and stood very still for a moment as if thinking hard about something. Then it shook itself all over and a shockwave of spray flew off its fur.

"Wish I knew who he belonged to," said a voice behind me, and I jumped off the step. I hadn't heard the door open.

I turned round. The man standing in the doorway looked a lot like my father: tall, seventy-ish, very thin, nearly bald. His face was tanned and he was smiling gently at me.

"Mr Pearmain?" I said, feeling foolish at being startled. "I'm Tim Ramsay." He smiled down at me, obviously uncomprehending. "Harry Dean sent me."

"Oh, of course. He said you'd be coming over."

"I'm a little late. I'm really sorry."

"Are you late?" He looked at his watch. "Well, I don't suppose that matters very much. Please, come in."

As I stepped inside he said, "I see that dog three or four times a week, you know. There's never anyone with him. He just wanders about." He closed the door. "The living room's through there, first on the right. Go on through and make yourself comfortable. Would you like a cup of tea?"

I stopped in the short dark hallway. "Don't you want to see my identification?"

"Do you have any?"

I thought about it. "Driving licence?"

"Does it have your photograph on it?"

I got the feeling that he was laughing gently at me. "No, it hasn't."

He shrugged. "Well then."

"Is everything all right, Father?" asked a voice behind me. I looked over my shoulder. A very large man in his forties was standing at the end of the hall with a tea-towel in his hand. He looked as if he had once played prop-forward for some rugby team.

"Mr Ramsay has come to pick my brains, Stephen," Pearmain said.

So much for worrying about pensioners on their own. "Tim Ramsay." Stephen and I shook hands and I came away still able to move my fingers, more or less.

"Go on through," Pearmain said. "I'll put the kettle on."

The living room was bright and airy. One wall was lined with shelves, stacked alternately with books and CDs. There was a CD midi-system in one corner with a pair of headphones plugged into it; beside it was a big, comfortable-looking armchair. Against the wall opposite the chair were a television and video, above which another set of shelves supported dozens of video cassettes. At the far end of the room was a long sofa piled with multicoloured cushions.

I walked along the bookshelves. There were paperback Forsythes and Deightons, an old leather-bound set of Dickens, books on twentieth-century history, a few Stephen Kings and Peter Straubs. The CDs surprised me. As well as Vaughan Williams's symphonies and some Bartók, Mr Pearmain appeared to possess almost every piece of music ever released by Frank Zappa.

"It's Stephen's fault, I'm afraid," he said, coming into the room with a tray of cups and seeing me reading the sleeve notes of *Ship Arriving too Late to Save a Drowning Witch*.

I looked up. "Beg pardon?"

"My taste in music," he said, putting the tray down on a coffee-table under the window. "When he was younger and a little more adventurous he bought a copy of *Uncle Meat*. I rather liked it. I think he was rather startled about that." He sat down on the edge of the armchair and began to pour the tea. "He grew out of it eventually, but I didn't. Do you take milk, Mr Ramsay?"

"No, thanks." I put the Zappa CD back on the shelf. "My father hates my taste in music."

He looked up, as if surprised to have struck a vein of honesty so soon after meeting me. "Well, I didn't like *everything* he brought home," he said amiably.

"My father didn't even bother to listen properly." I walked over to him and took the cup and saucer he was offering me.

"I hope you don't mind Stephen being here," he said. "The old chap two doors down was mugged in his home last month. Somebody turned up on his doorstep saying they were from the electricity board. Now if I know someone's coming to visit I ask Stephen to take an hour or so off work, just in case. He won't disturb us."

"It sounds very sensible. I don't mind at all. Did Harry explain everything to you the other day?"

Spooning sugar into his cup, he nodded. "A very interesting gentleman, your Mr Dean."

I smiled. Mr Pearmain didn't know the half of it.

He reached down beside the armchair and lifted an old shoebox onto his lap. "I hadn't thought about these for nearly fifty years, you know," he said, taking off the lid and laying it down at his side. "It never occurred to me that they might be worth anything."

I put my cup and saucer down on the table and took the envelope from my coat pocket. "You never know," I said. I handed him the envelope. "Four hundred pounds, as agreed."

He took the envelope, tucked it down the side of the chair without bothering to look in it, and nodded thanks. He lifted the photographs out of the box and smiled down at the top one. "I thought it was the worst time of my life," he said. He looked up at me. "Please, take your coat off, Mr Ramsay. You can take some of the cushions off the sofa and sit down here by the table."

I did as I was told. I took the mini tape recorder from my pocket. I put it on the table beside the tray, switched it on, and sat at Mr Pearmain's feet to listen.

Mr Pearmain had been Lieutenant Nigel Pearmain when he went off to Belgium with the British Expeditionary Force in 1939. He became Captain Pearmain somewhere on the long retreat to Dunkirk, for an act of conspicuous bravery which also won him the Military Cross. By the time he got off a Southend pleasure boat at Dover he couldn't stop shaking and the slightest noise made him cry uncontrollably.

Every war seems to have had a name for it, but in Mr Pearmain's day it was still shell-shock. He spent some time in hospital in Wiltshire, and then, by the infinite wisdom of the British Army, he was sent to a convalescent home in Muswell Hill and a ringside seat for the Blitz.

"One doesn't like to make too much of it, of course," he said, "but I was quite ill. I suppose someone somewhere thought they were sending me to the best place, but . . ."

Most nights, and a lot of the days, the home's position on the Hill gave it a grandstand view of the City and the East End being bombed. At first, the patients in the home sought cover every time the sirens sounded, but later they took to standing in the garden and watching the bombs fall and the fires burn.

I had a sudden vision of a dozen or so wackos in pyjamas and dressing gowns and slippers standing in a suburban garden watching a city being bombed to buggery while doctors and nurses tried to usher them back inside to safety. For some reason, I imagined them cheering every explosion, every burst of flame and smoke.

He laughed. "It probably sounds stranger than it was. We felt perfectly safe, of course, otherwise we wouldn't have been standing there." He poured himself another cup of tea. "Madness, in retrospect; the main West Coast Line from King's

Cross to Edinburgh runs about a mile from here. It's very bad form to run about in a garden a mile from a major strategic target while an air raid's going on."

Strange or not, Captain Pearmain, who had virtually had to be brought back to England in a rubber bag, actually thrived. He got better. He got better than better.

"It was as if we were military commanders of old," he told me, "overlooking the battlefield. Or gods. One poor chap started to believe he was Odin, hurling destruction down on London." He looked at the tape recorder, watched the little white lines on the tape spindles going round and round for a moment. Then he looked at me. "This isn't really relevant, is it?"

"No," I said, shaking my head. "But carry on anyway. I've got plenty of tape." I was spellbound. This was nothing like Mrs Lewis's second-hand stories; this was something entirely different.

So one poor chap thought he was hurling destruction down on London. It was narcotic. Pretty soon they were all doing it, making whistling noises as the bombs rained down, pointing at buildings and whole districts and ordering their devastation.

"Had to stop, of course," said Mr Pearmain. "There was this lad who was with me in Belgium. He started to believe he was actually causing the Blitz. He hanged himself with his pyjama cord, and then the staff began to crack down on us."

Shortly afterwards, Captain Pearmain was moved to a nursing home in the Cotswolds, and there his war effectively ended, though in 1944 he was scooped up by an offshoot of military intelligence and put to work he couldn't tell me about. No statute of limitations on the Official Secrets Act, apparently.

Still, in his time at the nursing home he took dozens of photographs, magnificent panoramic stills of London *in extremis*. He photographed the East End under a vast pall of smoke; he photographed the City around St Paul's burning at night. They were magnificent photographs, his testimony was wonderfully weird, and nobody had ever asked him about it before.

Later, after more tea and a plate of toasted sandwiches made for us by the strong but silent Stephen, Mr Pearmain took me outside to show me his garden. We pottered about for twenty minutes or so, inspecting a rockery of dwarf conifers and heathers and discussing how to save his lawn, which was neatly trimmed but nearly dead.

"I blame the cats, you know," he said without any real force, shaking his head sadly at the little expanse of brown grass. "All the cats in the neighbourhood seem to use my garden as a lavatory." He smiled at me and raised his eyebrows, but it was a mystery to me as well.

He looked at me a moment longer, then turned away, shaking his head again. "I did go into London once, you know," he said, bending down and pinching a tiny weed out of one of the flower-beds.

"Sorry?"

Now he had the weed in his hand, he seemed slightly at a loss as to what to do with it. He gazed at it, spun the stem gently between his fingers. "During the Blitz." He glanced at me, then unobtrusively flicked the weed over the fence into next door's garden. "Just the once, not long before I was discharged from the clinic."

It occurred to me that I should probably be recording this as well, but I was out of tape, so I just stood there with an attentive expression on my face.

"It was terribly sad. This must have been the beginning of May, 1941, so the Blitz was nearly over." He brushed his hands gently together and gave the garden a gentle, faraway look. "You'll promise you won't laugh if I tell you something?"

"Of course," I said.

He smiled at me. "I think I saw a ghost."

"A ghost."

"Or some poor old chap who was even battier than I was at the time. Or perhaps I was further away from recovery than everybody thought and I just imagined it."

"You saw a ghost?" I said.

Mr Pearmain laughed. "I suppose at the back of my mind I wanted to see it all close up, all the things we'd been watching from Muswell Hill. It really was very sad; you'll know about all the damage, of course."

"I'm starting to learn."

He shook his head and bent down to tug up another weed. It followed the first over the fence. I wondered what the neighbours thought of Mr Pearmain's weeding technique.

"The whole area around St Paul's was rubble, naturally," he said, "and there was damage along Fleet Street and in The Temple. I was walking up Fleet Street towards the Strand when this chap just stepped out of thin air right in front of me." He put his hands in the pockets of his cardigan and looked soberly at his dead lawn. "He looked like Dr Johnson. You know, the old paintings you see of Dr Johnson? Stout, middle-aged chap in knee-britches and white stockings and a black coat. He had silver-buckled shoes on. Well." He looked at me. "I don't know which of us was more surprised, me or him. I started to say something to him, and he did this odd little *shuffle* with his feet and just vanished into thin air again. Very odd."

I stared at him. Very odd. I thought it was a wonderful story, even if it must been a product of his shell-shocked imagination.

"Do you believe in ghosts?" he asked pleasantly.

"I'm still waiting to be convinced." But if Mr Pearmain wanted to believe he'd seen Dr Johnson's ghost on Fleet Street in 1941 that was fine by me.

"You won't mention this to Mr Dean, will you?" he asked, taking hold of my elbow and leading me gently back towards the house.

"Not if you don't want me to."

"It's just that one doesn't like to be thought of as completely batty, you know."

"I know the feeling," I said, patting his arm. "Don't worry. Your secret's safe with me."

3

"Have a good morning?" Harry asked.

"Very amusing." I gave him the shoebox and he lifted the lid and looked inside.

"These are very good," he said half to himself. "Very good." He looked up. "And the tape?"

I took the recorder and three cassettes out of my pocket and handed them over. "There's another one in the machine."

He checked his watch. "I thought you'd been gone a long time. That old lad doesn't half go on. I still need you to go out to Limehouse."

I felt my shoulders slump. "Oh come on, Harry; I haven't had anything to eat since breakfast." I looked round the office. "What have you done with Sophie?"

"She's up at Colindale."

"Up at Colindale" was Harry-speak for sitting in the British Museum's newspaper library copying out obituaries from 1940 and 1941 editions of *The Times*. "Jesus Christ, haven't you got enough of those yet?"

"You can never have enough obits." He smiled. "And now, to prove what a caring employer I am, I'm going to take you to lunch."

I was astounded. I stared at him. "You're kidding."

Harry sighed and fixed me with his mildly exasperated expression. "When the boss offers to take you out for lunch," he lectured, "the correct response is not, 'You're kidding.' The correct response is, 'Thank you very much, boss, you're too good to me.'"

I shrugged. This kind of thing happened about as often as Polish Popes. "Thank you very much, boss," I deadpanned. "You're too good to me."

Four

1

"I didn't really think this was what you had in mind," I said.

Harry grinned. "I'm paying, aren't I?" He lifted the top off his bun and started to lay chips on the burger.

"Thank you very much, boss." I said. "You're too good to me."

He tore the corner off a sachet of salt and sprinkled it over the chips. "You," he said, replacing the top of the bun, "don't know when you're well off."

"I'm such an ungrateful bastard," I said. On the other side of the window, crowds of pedestrians were crossing the bottom of the Tottenham Court Road. Young people with shaky grasps of English were standing near the steps leading down to the Tube station, handing out advertisement cards for schools teaching English as a foreign language. They probably got paid about two pence for every card they got rid of. I had taken two, on general principle. I watched the pedestrians and sipped my milkshake.

"Milk moustache," Harry said.

"What?"

He gestured at my face. "You've got a milk moustache." He lifted his burger-and-fries sandwich and bit into it.

"Thank you." I wiped the frothy milk off my top lip with a napkin. "So. Do you come here often?"

He washed his mouthful down with a swig of Coke. "Christ, no." He looked around the restaurant. "And I don't think I'll come here again." He leaned forward slightly, dabbing his fingers with a napkin. "Do you know why they call it fast food?"

I shook my head. "Not a clue."

"It's not because the food is fast. It's because people can't bear to stay in these bloody places after they've finished eating. They should call it 'fast people'."

"*They* don't seem in much of a hurry," I said, nodding at a boy and girl three tables away who seemed to be spending most of the time staring wordlessly at each other and smiling.

"Ah." Harry looked at them sadly. "Love will do that to you."

"Will it?" This was a startling piece of information from a boss whose previous communication with me had consisted almost solely of orders and complaints.

He nodded approvingly. "They don't care that the seats are just a tiny bit too uncomfortable to relax on, or that the tables are just that fraction too low to lean on comfortably. Places like this rely on throughput." He repeated the word, as if tasting it.

I looked at him. He had a bland, weatherbeaten face that couldn't properly be called handsome or ugly. His eyes were a weak, watery blue, and sometime in the past his nose had been broken and inexpertly reset. Sophie had told me he'd spent a large part of his life in the Navy, but she didn't know how he had come to be running a film production company. I should have taken advantage of his mood and asked him, but instead I said, "Are you a cynic, boss?"

He grunted. "Probably." He took another sip of his Coke. Under a battered and stained raincoat he was wearing his usual uniform of baggy black cords, a white shirt and a black cardigan, and he didn't look any more at peace with the world than he usually did. Most of the time, he seemed to view the world as something which stood between him and the completion of his film.

"Can I ask a question?"

He looked up from his burger. "No. My taking you out to lunch doesn't mean you can have a raise."

"That's not what I was going to ask. But while we're on the subject . . ."

Harry shook his head and raised a hand. "Don't bother. We can't afford it."

"Maybe if you paid my expenses . . ."

He smiled sadly and shook his head again. "Cash is very tight." He picked up a chip and popped it into his mouth. "What did you want to know?"

I sat back and folded my arms and considered making more of an issue about my salary. Then I decided it wasn't worth it. "What do you need all those obituaries for, Harry?"

He regarded me levelly for a moment. Then he nodded at my lunch. "Eat up and I'll show you."

Harry and Viren had been at university together sometime during the late 'sixties, according to Sophie. Viren had read electronics and computing and had then gone back to Warrington to run his father's carpet-cleaning business. Harry had finished his degree—he'd never told Sophie what it was in—and then gone off to sea. He'd only come out of the Navy a couple of years ago, and by that time Viren had sold off the carpet-cleaning business and established a short string of electronics shops in London and the Home Counties.

"The boss in?" Harry asked breezily as he let the door of the shop bump back on its springs.

"He's out," Roger, Viren's shop assistant, told us without much interest. In the admittedly short space of time that I'd known him, I had never seen Roger smile. He never seemed particularly enthusiastic about anything much. I wondered why Viren kept him on.

"Never mind," said Harry, walking through to the rear of the shop and opening the door to the back. "We'll look after ourselves."

Roger shrugged and went back to organizing the shelves.

"I bet he's a real asset to the business," I said, closing the door behind us.

Harry looked round. "What?"

I shook my head. "Never mind." It was the first time I'd been in the back room of the shop and I was busy looking around. Against one wall there was a huge old leather sofa, in front of which was a scar-topped coffee table covered in ashtrays and television and video remote controls. Stacked on shelving along the opposite wall were about twenty television sets and video recorders. Through an open door to a further back room I could see equipment which I presumed was the gear Viren used to transfer ciné film to video, and what I thought were two video mixing desks. The place smelled strongly of joss sticks, and underneath that, faint but unmistakable, the smell of old dope.

We had gone back to the office for a couple of minutes before coming up here, and Harry had taken something from the safe. Now he took it from a pocket of his coat and I saw it was a videotape. He put it into one of the recorders and walked over to the coffee table.

"I shouldn't be showing you this," he said, sorting through the pile of remote controls on the table. "It's bad luck to show people something that isn't finished."

"You never struck me as the superstitious type," I said.

He turned to look at me, a remote control in either hand. "We can always go back to the office," he said.

I put my hands up. "Don't mind me."

He sighed. "All right." He pointed a remote at the wall of televisions and one of them lit up with the end-titles of the afternoon showing of *Neighbours*. He pointed the other control and pressed a button and the screen filled with snow.

"This is all just working material so far," he said, sitting on one of the sofa's arm-rests. "No music, no dialogue."

I sat down on the opposite armrest. "Maybe I could play the piano or some-thing." Harry glared at me. "All right, OK. Not another word. Promise." And I looked back at the screen just as the snow cleared from a black background.

There were a few moments of blackness, then the words THE BLITZ: AN ORAL MEMOIR appeared in white. The title remained for a couple of seconds, then faded and was replaced by A FILM BY HARRY DEAN. It occurred to me to make some wisecrack about the auteur theory of filmmaking, but I decided against it.

The words faded away, and the black background lightened to grey. Then a col-umn of names began to scroll upwards from the bottom of the screen. I quite im-pressed myself by recognizing some of them, and I presumed the others were taken from the *Times* obit columns as well.

"Harry," I said after a few moments, "not all these people died in the Blitz."

His attention on the screen, Harry lifted a finger to his lips and went, "Shh."

"I remember that one. 'Burton, J.S.' He was run over by a lorry in Battersea."

Harry sighed, pointed the remote across the room, and pressed a button. The names stopped scrolling. "I told you," he said.

"Yes, I know, but—"

"I don't have to explain myself to you, Tim. I don't have to show you this at all." He was speaking in a quiet, calm voice which usually meant he was about to start shouting. "So. Do you want to watch?"

"Absolutely." I said, and for the next two and a half hours I didn't say a single word.

"Don't get comfortable," said Harry when we got back to the office. "I still need you to go over to Limehouse. Then I want you to go to Martin and Bob's for me."

I had been taking off my coat. I stopped with one arm still in its sleeve. "Why can't you go?"

"Because I pay you to do things like that, that's why. You've had a good long lunch-break and I've paid for it. Now you can go back to work."

I'd been fooled into thinking I'd witnessed a new dawn in our working relation-ship. I should have known better. "You could have told me this before we came back here," I said grumpily. "Now I've got to walk back to Oxford Street."

"You mustn't complain," he said. "You're lucky to have a job these days."

"You're taking the piss," I said incredulously.

He shook his head. "Not at all." He wagged a finger at me. "Do you know how many unemployed graduates there are?"

"No, Harry. I've forgotten since the last time you told me."

"And almost all of them have better degrees than you," he added, choosing to ignore my sarcasm in favour of delivering a straight old-fashioned insult.

"And I imagine most of them aspire to being something better than a glorified errand-boy."

"At least they can expect something better."

"And not very glorified, at that," I said. "Are we going to pay Martin today?"

Harry turned and started to make his way towards his room. "Tell him we'll pay him next week."

"I told him that last week."

"Well, tell him again. You can do that, can't you?"

"I'm getting worried he'll set Bob on me."

Harry laughed. "You should be so lucky." As he vanished into the far room, I heard him say, "And take a bus. You're costing me a fortune in taxi fares."

"I can't see how," I muttered, ramming my arm back into my coat-sleeve. "You never pay my expenses."

2

I considered taking a taxi, just to spite him, but Harry and I had never resolved our differences over my expenses sheets. Sophie and I had got into the routine of putting all my expenses together with hers and then splitting the money. Harry never appeared to notice.

Harry had a different idea of what the word "researcher" meant to the one I had. I thought it meant someone who did research. He thought it meant general dogsbody. When I'd replied to the advert, I thought I would be out collecting information, digging into documents, unearthing secrets. Instead all I did was run around all day picking things up or dropping things off. Apart from occasional gems like Mr Pearmain, I didn't consider listening to old folk telling me about the Blitz to be research. The closest I came to doing research was when I went up to the newspaper library to copy out lists of obituaries.

He was right, though, I thought disconsolately: I was lucky to have a job. One bloke from my class at university was working on a dustcart in Lambeth, and another was digging drainage ditches in the West of Ireland. I didn't have any particular prejudice against manual work, but I knew what I would rather do, given the choice and notwithstanding the little eccentricities of Harry Dean.

The sky was starting to look grey and heavy again. I turned up the collar of my coat. It started to rain as I reached Tottenham Court Road station. It had been that sort of day.

"We know it's not your fault, Tim," said Bob, "but we've got bills to pay as well."

I sat back. I'd bought a carton of Ribena on the way up Ladbroke Grove, and I sucked morosely on the straw.

"We know he sends you because he thinks we'll feel sorry for you and give you the film," Martin said.

I looked at him, then I looked at Bob. Then I sucked on my drink again. There was a tiny hole in the side of the straw and it made a little farting noise every time I tried to drink. Any hope I'd had of maintaining my dignity had evaporated.

"It's really getting beyond a joke, you know?" Bob said. She sipped her tea. "None of our other customers gets away with this."

"He's having a fucking laugh with us," said Martin. He leaned forward menacingly. "Your boss is having a fucking laugh, isn't he?"

This bad-cop-good-cop routine had happened so often in the past few weeks that I was used to it by now, although to be honest I enjoyed it more when Bob was the bad cop; all Martin did was swear and loom over me. The first time he did it I almost fled screaming into the street, but now I knew Martin's heart wasn't really in it and so I just sat there drinking my Ribena.

Martin and Bob were brother and sister, Oxford graduates whose father owned an improbable amount of Western Scotland. They'd traded a shared interest in archive film into a thriving filmfinding business without using any of Daddy's money, and the only dark cloud on their horizon had Harry Dean's name on it. Actually, it was beyond me why they'd put up with him for so long.

"We let him get away with it once and now he thinks this is how we do fucking business," Martin said.

"Is he like this with everybody?" asked Bob.

I rubbed my eyes. "This isn't fair," I said. I always said that at some point, and the time had about come. It was no more significant than Martin's threats or Bob's reasonableness. All three of us knew we were just going through the motions and it wouldn't change anything, and what pissed us off was that Harry knew it too.

"Bollocks," Martin said, and sat back on his stool.

We were in the back room of their office. There were a sofa, an armchair, and a tall stool. There were also a huge colour television, a state-of-the-art video, and a small pile of Hungarian pornographic videotapes. Bob was doing her postgraduate thesis on the explosion of pornography in post-Communist Eastern Europe, and I wondered why I hadn't had the wit to think of doing something like that. Bob joked that she had learned to fake an orgasm in four Slavic languages.

I said, "It's not my fault," because it was time to say that, too.

"He's not having the film this time," Martin said. "I've fucking had enough of this."

"I don't even want the fucking film," I said, shaking the Ribena carton to see if there was any drink left in it.

"I think he just watches it in the dark and has a wank over it," said Martin. "He's some kind of fucking Blitz pervert. How much of this fucking film has he actually made?"

"Don't swear so much," Bob chided, which was a bit like asking the Polar ice-caps not to calve so many icebergs.

I opened my mouth, about to tell them what I'd seen that afternoon at Viren's shop, but I still wasn't sure precisely *what* I'd seen. I closed my mouth, looked at Bob and Martin, and shrugged my shoulders miserably.

"Fucking brilliant," Martin said. He crossed his arms across his chest and glared at me.

"We will take him to court, you know?" Bob told me from the sofa. "And if we take him to court it'll affect you too."

"It's not much of a job anyway," I said. The trip to the printer's in Limehouse had been uneventful, and I had five hundred sheets of note-paper with Lonesome Charley's letterhead in a carrier bag to show for it. The most alarming thing about it was that both my name and Sophie's were beside Harry's on the letterhead as directors of Lonesome Charley Productions. I wondered if it was Harry's way of sharing the responsibility for his debts.

"He owes us five hundred quid," Martin said. "Five hundred fucking quid. And the fucking rent's due on this place next week."

I put my hands up. "You're preaching to the converted. I have to put my expenses in with Sophie's just to get them by him."

"You see?" Martin appealed to Bob. "He's trying to make us feel sorry for him!"

"It's true," I protested. "It's the only way I can get any expenses out of Harry."

"I do feel sorry for him," said Bob.

"Oh no!" I cried, covering my head with my arms. "Not pity! Anything but that!"

Martin and Bob exchanged glances. Martin sighed and ran a hand over his Mohawk. He shook his head and grinned ruefully at me. I grinned back, just to show him there were no hard feelings.

"How do you do that, Ramsay?" Bob asked.

"Do what?"

"Just sit there and let yourself be bullied. How do you do that?"

"It's the way I was brought up."

She shook her head wonderingly. Martin got up. "I'll get you the fucking film," he said.

"Take him to court," I said. "I don't care."

"He can have it this time," Martin said. "But tell him this is the last one. We want paying."

I nodded. "I promise."

While Martin was looking through the previous day's deliveries, Bob said, "You know Harry's taking advantage of you, don't you?"

"I'm lucky to have a job," I said.

"Oh, come on."

"It's actually true." I tossed the Ribena carton into the waste-bin. "I really am lucky to have any job at all. And I'm too tired to debate it, Bob."

"You're becoming a sheep, Ramsay."

"Baa."

She looked sad. "Don't be an idiot all your life, Ramsay. You can do better."

"Listen to Bob," Martin said, coming back with a film can. "She's right."

I took the film from Martin and put it in my pocket. Mission accomplished. I felt stupid and rather cheap. "Can I borrow one of those videos?" I asked Bob.

2

"Hello?"

"Hello, Dad."

"Yes?"

All day long I'd been thinking about Mr Pearmain and his son, who would drop his day's business at not much more than a moment's notice to make sure his father wasn't robbed by visitors. I hadn't been able to get them out of my mind. My father and I had never been that close. Even if I'd offered to look after him, he would just have been indifferent.

"What did you do in the war, Dad?"

There was a long silence. I realized that this was one of the rare occasions on which I had managed to surprise him. My father liked to give the impression that the world held very few surprises for him.

"You know what I did," he said finally. "Why do you want to know?"

"I had a chat today with this old bloke who was at Dunkirk."

Another silence. My father had spent the war helping to design weapons of mass destruction at a government establishment somewhere in Berkshire. When he came home to Nottingham after the war he went back into engineering, and he and a friend set up a little company that made precision machine-tools.

His friend, the apocalyptically gloomy Terence, had died a few years ago, and the little company was still a little company, just about hanging on and never generating a great deal of money. On the other hand, it was still in business, which was an achievement in itself these days.

"Dunkirk, eh?" he said noncommittally. "Bad do, that." He sounded suspicious, as if he expected me to change the subject all of a sudden and start asking him to send me some money.

"Did you ever go to London during the Blitz?" I asked.

There: I'd surprised him again. More silence. Perhaps the day hadn't been wasted after all.

"Don't be stupid," he said, still sounding suspicious. "Why would I want to do that?"

I felt a little ashamed; this was the closest thing my father and I had had to a proper conversation in months, and all I was doing was asking stupid questions.

The doorbell rang, and Eric came out of his room to answer it. Lisa was standing on the doorstep. She was wearing immaculately pressed jeans and a leather blouson that probably cost more than my annual salary. She and Eric hugged and kissed. When she saw me sitting on the bottom of the stairs with the phone all I got was a cooly neutral nod of recognition.

"Look, Dad, I'll have to go. Someone's just turned up."

"All right, then." He sounded vaguely relieved that the conversation was over.

"I'll give you a ring next month."

"Well, there's no need." He'd recovered some of his equilibrium, recovered that there's-no-need-to-bother-if-you-don't-want-to tone of voice I knew so well.

I hung up and put the phone back on the hall table. Eric and Lisa were still standing by the door, whispering. Lisa and I looked at each other, waiting for one of us to say hello. Lisa was one of those bone-thin girls who always look as if they need a good meal. There was something hungry and longing in her eyes, as if she could never have all the things she thought she needed. She had disliked me from the moment we first met, but it was only recently that hostilities had begun to come out into the open. This confused Eric, because he liked me and loved Lisa. Sometimes I could see him trying to decide whose side he ought to be coming down on. For the moment, it seemed he had decided to remain neutral, a sort of Switzerland in a smart suit.

"We're off to the cinema," he said. "Fancy coming with us?" Lisa looked up at him and stared disbelievingly.

"No, it's OK, Eric," I said, still looking at Lisa. "I wouldn't want to be a gooseberry." I winked meaningfully and Lisa glared at me. "Have fun."

I turned and went up the stairs towards my room. I'd managed to confuse my father and irritate Lisa, all in the space of a couple of minutes. Life didn't throw opportunities like that at me too often; I had to take my laughs where I could.

Five

1

My lunch with Harry had one immediate and entirely unexpected side-effect. The next morning, while Sophie and I were sitting in the outer office dunking croissants into our breakfast coffee, he came out of his room with a bulging beige cardboard folder under his arm.

"Since you're not too busy right now," he said to us, "I thought you might like to give me your opinion of this." And he dropped the folder on Sophie's desk and walked back through the office.

Sophie and I looked at each other. She tapped the file with a fingertip. "What is this?"

"I don't know." The file had made a considerable thud when it hit the desktop. "We had lunch together yesterday."

She raised one delicately plucked eyebrow. "Lunch?"

I nodded. "Lunch."

The other eyebrow went up. "You and Harry?"

"Me and Harry." I put on a smug grin. "And we didn't talk about you once."

She reached across the desk and punched me on the shoulder, a little more soundly than was necessary. "You and Harry had lunch and did this male bonding thing, yes?"

"Insofar as Harry is capable of male bonding," I said, rubbing my shoulder. "And he paid."

She shook her head wonderingly. "My God. The things I miss when I go to Colindale."

I picked up the folder and opened it. "Yes, we had a real boys' day out. What the hell is this?" Inside the folder was a solid wad of typescript almost three inches thick. Then I saw the title sheet and knew what it was.

"I think," said Sophie, "that Harry is letting us look at the Holy Grail."

"He showed me the film as well," I said quietly, putting the pile of paper down. Her eyes widened. "Why?"

"I asked what he wanted the obituary names for and he just took me up to Viren's and showed me."

"Oh my God!" she whispered, smiling incredulously. She pulled her chair closer to me and her shoulder brushed mine. "He's never shown *me*. What's it like?"

"I don't know."

"What?"

"I don't know." We were both speaking in scarcely audible voices now. "I don't know if it's a masterpiece or a mess."

"You must have *some* idea."

It was the closest I had ever been to her. In order to hear me better, she had turned her head so that her ear was near my mouth. She was wearing Anaïs-Anaïs and the smell was almost intoxicating. I could see the fine hairs along the curve of her ear. I had a barely resistible urge to bury my face in her hair and just inhale her.

"It's one bit of archive footage after another," I said. "And some rostrum stills. German bombers. Bombed buildings. Two and a half hours of it."

"So? I had more or less imagined it would be like that."

"But it's all just banged together. Even I can tell that." She had moved forward slightly, and the side of her left breast was pressing gently against my forearm and I was having difficulty concentrating on the conversation.

"So it is obviously a work in process."

"Progress," I said, leaning forward as unobtrusively as I could to press myself against her a little more. I was in heaven, drunk on our proximity. My voice was barely audible. "Work in progress."

She nodded. "A work in progress. So what?"

I shook my head. The whole film had just looked wrong, but I didn't know how to explain it to her. Harry had been working on it almost since he had come out of the Navy, and all he'd managed to produce was this sequence of old clips.

"I'd actually started to believe in it, you know?" I said, and regretted it instantly because she sat up and frowned at me. I sighed. "I feel let down. I thought we were actually doing something."

Sophie shook her head. "How did you get so cynical, Tim?"

"Three months of working here, I suppose," I said. We had never really argued, but we had disagreed several times, and I hated it each time. I usually broke out in a sweat as I watched myself falling in her estimation. She was almost ten years older than me, and sometimes she seemed wiser than I could ever dream of becoming, which made my lapses into peevishness even worse.

She picked up the pile of typescript and held it out. "Perhaps it seems a mess because you saw only one half of it, just the pictures. Perhaps the words help it all make sense."

I took the script of Harry's film from her. "We'll see."

The script started with the list of names from the *Times* obituary columns, and was typed on fairly new paper, so I knew Sophie had done it.

Not all the paper was new, though. A lot of it was stained and yellow with age and had been creased and crumpled at some time in the past. The typing on these sheets had been done on another machine, and was dotted with mistakes and Tipp-Ex. I wondered if Harry had been dreaming of this, all those years at sea, scribbling notes to himself and then typing them up whenever he had the chance. Dreaming of London in flames, of stick after stick of bombs raining down on the East End, of a populace stolidly refusing to back down in the face of the worst that Hitler could throw at them. Dreaming of the Spirit of the Blitz.

He'd made notes to himself. Things he needed—a soundbite about rationing, some lines of nostalgia about sheltering in the Underground. In that respect, it wasn't so much a script as a blueprint. Harry knew what the final shape of the film would be, and all he had to do was find the material and slot it in.

Unfortunately, the final shape of the film was not included in the script. Without the script, the video I'd seen yesterday had been largely meaningless. And without the final shape—which I presumed existed only in Harry's head—neither the video nor the script made a lot of sense.

Harry wouldn't let me take the script out of the office, so I scrunched myself up on one of the deep little windowsills in the middle room and read through it. Then I read it through again. I thought I could see what Harry was getting at, but when I read the script again it made even less sense than before. By the time I had had enough of it, Sophie and Harry had both gone out for lunch. I gave up, left the thing on Sophie's desk, and went to get something to eat.

Lunch usually consisted either of sandwiches and fruit juice in the office, or a pint and a pie in any one of half a dozen pubs within ten minutes' walk. This lunchtime, I started out intending to visit the sandwich bar downstairs, and just kept going.

I was walking past Chancery Lane station before I really noticed what I was doing. I'd walked all the way down through Bloomsbury and Holborn without thinking about it, and managed to cross at least two busy main roads in the process. Shit.

I walked down to Ludgate Circus. Harry had a photo of Ludgate Circus pinned up on the wall of his office. The morning of May 11, 1941, the junction crisscrossed with fire hoses, the shop on the right at the bottom of Ludgate Hill still burning, and the dome of St Paul's just visible through the smoke beyond the railway bridge.

Now the railway bridge was gone, removed by the redevelopment of the late 'eighties rather than by the Luftwaffe. The view up Ludgate Hill to the cathedral was unobstructed. It was as if the picture in Harry's office had been faked, as if it had come from a movie. The block of buildings which had once contained the Old King Lud had been demolished and rebuilt; the pub had reopened on its old site, but it didn't look the way it had in that photo. Nothing did.

It was a bright, breezy lunchtime, and Fleet Street was full of people. All the newspapers were gone now, to Docklands or other places across London. The rear of the *Telegraph* building had been completely obliterated and something huge and pale blue and glass built behind the listed facade. The *Sun* building had gone completely.

Harry would have come back from the sea at the end of the 'eighties and seen all these changes, all together, all at once. Other Londoners had endured years of demolition, building sites, scaffolding, gradually forming buildings. Harry had come home and seen it new and shining, familiar buildings gone and new ones in their place. Was that what the film was all about? Was that the shape in his head? Not the shape of London during the Blitz, but London before he came home. The shape of the London he left when he went to sea. Never underestimate the power of nostalgia.

"Well?" Harry said when I walked back into the office. "What did you think?"

"I'm not worthy," I said, as deadpan as I could. I still hadn't had any lunch.

2

"So?" said Eric.

I shook my head. "Look, I knew you were stupid, Eric . . ."

He fixed me with what he liked to think was his shrewd stare. All it did was make him look shortsighted. "So, so funny, Timothy."

I waved my hand in the air, trying to find the words. "It's . . . it's not a *film*, Eric. He's not *making* a film. It's as if he's trying to fix a place and time in his mind. He's not doing it for the television. He's doing it for himself."

Eric took a large gulp of his morning coffee. "I can't see your problem. He's still paying you, isn't he?"

"Well, *some* would call it pay, I suppose."

"You were happy enough when you got the job," he pointed out. "I seem to remember you being over the fucking moon, in fact." He thought about it. "Well, for fifteen minutes or so, anyway."

"Eric, I've only just realized." I looked at the remains of my breakfast and sighed. "He's got me on the company letterhead as a director. Can he do that?"

"It's his company. He can call you what he likes. He could put 'Timothy Ramsay, Tea Boy' on the letterhead if he wanted to."

"Does it make me liable for his debts?"

Eric sat back and looked sternly at me. "Oh, come on."

"I'm serious, Eric."

He lit a cigar, crossed his arms, and regarded me steadily. "You're in the clear, Tim. Trust me."

I shrugged.

"As a worst-case scenario, it might get a bit slippery, but there's nothing for you to worry about."

I sat bolt upright. "What do you mean, 'a bit slippery'?"

He shook his head and waved his cigar in my direction. Through the window behind him the garden was being lashed with nearly horizontal sheets of rain. "Don't worry, Tim. All right?"

"Easy for you to say." I muttered. "You don't know what he's got me doing this morning."

Eric tilted his head back and blew a stream of smoke at the ceiling. "I think," he said, "that what you need is a party."

"Where've you been?" said Harry.

"Amersham." I said, trying to wrestle out of my soaking overcoat.

"What in the name of God for?" he asked. His hair was awry and his face flushed, a usual sign that he had been on the phone with a creditor.

I finished taking off my coat. I had been soaked to the skin three times this morning and was in no mood to argue. "I've been to that old folks' home. Remember? You told me on Friday to go there this morning?"

He'd obviously forgotten, but this sort of thing didn't faze Harry for more than a fraction of a second. "What took you so long?"

"London Underground took me so long. There was a tree fell across the Metropolitan Line outside Chorleywood last night."

"So what?" Harry had a low tolerance for London Underground travel stories. As far as Harry was concerned, the Underground was something which happened to other people, on the whole.

"So nothing." I hung up my coat. I'd spent an hour waiting at Baker Street, and the first train that came in took me only as far as Wembley Park. It had taken me the whole morning to get out to the far end of the Metropolitan Line, and after that I had spent the early afternoon in the company of two octogenarian sisters who had delighted in contradicting each other on every detail of a night spent sheltering from an air raid in Piccadilly Circus station. I handed over the tapes. "The sisters Gregory: their war."

Harry turned the tapes over in his hands. "April the seventh, 1941?"

"The very same." I looked around the office. "Where's Sophie?"

"Up at that travel agent's sorting her ticket out."

"Oh, that's right, rub it in." Sophie was about to depart on Lonesome Charley's great expedition. While I fetched and carried for Harry, she was going to Poland to negotiate the purchase of some Blitz footage.

Harry looked innocently taken aback. "I can't very well send you, can I?"

"My mother's Polish," I protested. "I speak a bit of the language."

"Well, that's the difference between you and Sophie," he said. "You speak a bit of Polish, but Sophie *is* Polish. If the film was in China and the choice was between you and a Chinaman, I'd be pretty stupid to send you, wouldn't I?"

I'd learned early on that Harry loved a row, provided he won. If he thought I had the advantage he usually fired me, a process which consisted of him telling me to fuck off and never come back, and then phoning me that evening and giving me a list of things he wanted done the next day. So far I hadn't quite got up the nerve to hang up on him when he did that.

"You know, I hate working here," I said, but Harry was already heading for his room to listen to the tapes I'd made. Maybe Eric was right. Maybe I did need a party.

Six

1

We'd done all this before. It was second nature. On Saturday morning we moved all the furniture out of Eric's living room and stacked it upstairs in my living room. Then we put away anything in the kitchen that was breakable. While I hoovered, Eric did the booze run down to Tesco's on the North Circular, and by the time he got back I had the house more or less prepared for its state of siege.

"Food," he pronounced, dumping four carrier bags down on the kitchen table.

I looked inside one. There were party-size sausage rolls, mini-quiches, blocks of Cheddar and red Leicester, jars of pearl onions, bags of crisps and Twiglets. "Since when has anybody had time to eat at one of these dos?" I asked.

Eric was taking boxes out of the other bags and stuffing them haphazardly into the freezer. "This will be different," he said.

Scattered on the table were six trays of ready-made pork satay sticks with little tubs of peanut sauce. I picked one up and turned it over. "How will this be different?"

He looked into the freezer, frowned, then started to take stuff out again. "Different clientele."

This was news to me. I'd invited the few old members of my class who'd decided to stay in London. "No students?"

Having apparently cleared sufficient space in the freezer, Eric started to shove food back in. He looked like a man trying to solve a particularly difficult topological problem. "Grow up, Tim," he said without looking at me. "We're not students any more."

It was impossible to argue with that. This had always been a student house, though, with a student atmosphere. Something had changed now, and I thought I should have been bright enough to spot it.

Until his final year, Eric had always been the amiably shambolic youth who hadn't known where he was during Freshers' Week, but when his Finals came up he became withdrawn, haunted, serious. And when it was all over he seemed to revert back to being the old Eric, impossibly good-natured while I tried and failed to get a job. But there was something in the tone of his voice now which told me the old Eric was gone forever.

I put the satay sticks down on the table. "So, is this going to be a black tie do?"

He was still trying to fit all the frozen food into the freezer, staring at it as if there had to be a magical formula for it. "Don't get peevish, Tim."

"I'm not being peevish."

"Oh yes you are." He picked up a box of sausage rolls and held it up in front of his face, rotating it left and right to see how it would fit into the freezer. "You get depressed if the train is late."

"That doesn't make me peevish. That happens to a lot of people."

"See? You're being peevish again."

"No I'm not."

He rotated the box to the right, inserted it into the freezer, and stepped back to admire his handiwork. I thought if he took much longer with it the thing would start to defrost. "You want another student party," he said. "You want loud music and dancing and people groping each other in the bedrooms and someone spewing up in the front garden and the neighbours calling the police."

"Yes." I'd never seen anything wrong with any of those things. And neither had he.

"Well, those days are over." He turned and looked at me. "It's time you grew up."

"Bollocks."

He picked up a box of mini-quiches and waved them at me. "It's not, and you know it. This is real life now, not university."

I blinked at him. This was a new side of Eric. I found it slightly alarming. "I think," I said, "that I need some fresh air."

2

It was a nice day, and I walked past the expensive houses on Oakleigh Avenue without a thought in my head. At the mini-roundabout I crossed over and carried on down Netherlands Road towards Oakleigh Park station. As I passed the entrance to the station footbridge I heard a train coming from around the curve of track. I put my hand in my jacket pocket and found my travelcard, and I started to run. In the same situation on a weekday, I could be guaranteed to miss the train, but because this was the weekend I managed to get down the stairs to the platform and jump aboard before the doors closed.

During the week, the trains from Welwyn Garden City and Hertford North ran down to Moorgate, and I always changed at Finsbury Park for a connection to King's Cross. Moorgate's British Rail station closed at weekends, however, and the trains ran direct to King's Cross. Some of them missed out the stations at Haringey and Hornsey, as well, and took only ten minutes or so to reach central London. It always amazed me they couldn't do the same during the week, when it often took me over an hour to get to work. I harboured images of a super-efficient band of railwaymen who worked only at weekends.

I'd left the house wanting to go somewhere, anywhere, but as soon as I reached the platform at King's Cross I found myself wondering what the hell I was doing. I drifted down the steps to King's Cross Underground concourse, along the curving corridor, down another set of steps, through a ticket barrier, and onto a Metropolitan Line train.

I got off at Farringdon and wandered up the stairs off the platform. At the top, I put my travelcard into the ticket gate and stepped through. Thousands of people did this every weekday, but today there were only me and a family of confused-looking American tourists.

"Excuse me, sir?"

I was standing on the pavement outside the station. I looked round. The father of the American family was standing behind me. I smiled.

"Excuse me, sir, but we're trying to get to Saint Paul's Cathedral?"

I stared at him. He was in his early forties. He didn't look stupid. He looked more or less capable of reading a map. His wife was pretty. His two kids seemed intelligent and well adjusted. He'd just got on the wrong Tube platform somewhere and now he was lost in an unfamiliar city and he was starting to look worried. A temptation crept over me to do something unbelievably cruel.

"St Paul's?" I said.

He nodded enthusiastically. "Yes, sir. Saint Paul's."

"Are you a Texan?" I asked.

He looked suddenly confused. "Sir?"

I didn't think I'd been called "sir" so many times in my life. "You sound as if you're from Texas."

He shook his head. "No, sir." He put his hand out for me to shake. "James Mac-Donald. Waukesha, Wisconsin."

"My mistake." I shook his hand. "Your accents, you know . . ."

He grinned, obviously relieved to find one of those dim but harmless Brits he'd heard about back home. "I know. I have the same problem with your Yorkshire men?"

I grinned back. "Me too." I pointed down to the bottom of Cowcross Street. "Go down there and turn right. It's quite a walk, though."

He looked crestfallen. "The map says there's a Tube station at Saint Paul's."

"It's closed," I said with a straight face. "They're retiling it."

"Really?"

"I'm sorry. You can get a bus, though. Any bus that goes along that street."

"Yes?"

"Absolutely. They all go to St Paul's. Just show the driver your passes and don't worry. You don't even have to ask where they're going."

He grinned again and shook my hand one last time for luck. "Thank you very much, sir."

"Don't mention it, Mr MacDonald." I stood where I was for a few minutes, and I watched Mr MacDonald lead his family back in the direction of King's Cross and felt as if I'd committed an act of random violence. When they were out of sight I walked to the end of Cowcross Street and turned left, towards St Paul's.

I didn't go down to Ludgate Circus and up to St Paul's. I turned up Charterhouse Street and walked through Smithfield. Everything was very quiet. I wondered if the MacDonalds had got back to King's Cross yet.

At the top of Charterhouse Street I crossed over and went into the Barbican.

Even as far away as Nottingham, the Barbican had become a byword for inaccessibility. You could get lost among the concrete towers and die of starvation before you made it to the Barbican Centre for your performance of *The Four Seasons*. I'd found all the rumours exaggerated. Privately, I thought only an imbecile could get lost in the Barbican. Maybe Mr MacDonald had thought the same about the Underground.

I sat for a while at the Lakeside, watching the fountains. Then I walked on through the Barbican to Moorgate, and then down Moorgate to Bank Junction. I caught a bus.

The City is a rather eerie place at the weekend; you can walk for ages and see hardly a soul. I liked it that way.

The bus went along Cheapside, round St Paul's, and down Ludgate Hill onto Fleet Street. The steps up to St Paul's were covered with tourists. I thought of them cavorting about where the two burned bodies had been found. I looked as we went past, but I couldn't see if the stones were still marked. As far as I remembered, the stories of arrests and police leads had simply petered out. The last thing I remembered reading about it was that the bodies were still unidentified. I wondered what the chances were of killing someone like that, in such a public place, and getting away with it.

The bus dipped down Ludgate Hill. There were more tourists here, and others walking up Fleet Street, but it was only after we crossed into Westminster, outside the Law Courts, that I started to see large numbers of people.

The Strand was choked with traffic, and Trafalgar Square was full of people. I watched them from the window of the bus as we shouldered through the traffic into the proper lane, trying to remember when a visit to London was a novelty to me. We'd had school trips to the theatre and the British Museum, and they'd always seemed like special days, but it occurred to me that since I'd come down here to live I hadn't done any sightseeing. It was no more exciting than living in Nottingham, and yet for all those people having their photographs taken beside Landseer's lions it was something wonderful, the trip of a lifetime. A mystery to me.

I'd spent months listening to people telling me about the Spirit of the Blitz, and all London was to me was trains cancelled because of signal problems or "defective units", Underground lines paralysed by "passenger action", motorcycle couriers shaving moments off their journeys by sliding through amber traffic lights, and at least one taxi driver who I was convinced was determined to run me over. I couldn't celebrate London like all the old people I talked to; most of the time it was an obstacle to a happy life and I couldn't work out why I put up with it.

I got off the bus in Regent Street and walked back across Haymarket to the bottom of the Charing Cross Road. I wandered north, from bookshop to bookshop, buying here and there just for the sake of buying something.

It was stupid to get upset at what Eric had said. He thought it was important to leave all the university stuff behind and move on with his life, but I wasn't sure I was ready for that. And that made me wonder whether what I was doing at the moment was just marking time. I was just wandering around London like an idiot.

I walked back past the office on the way to Russell Square station, and as I turned the corner into Bedford Place I heard someone behind me calling my name.

"What on earth are you doing here on a Saturday?" I asked, turning round.

"I could ask the same question," Sophie said when she caught up with me. She was wearing jeans and a black denim jacket and her hair was tied back. She looked lovely.

I shrugged. "I've been checking out the bookshops on the Charing Cross Road." I held up my carrier bag as proof of this.

She grinned. "Did you buy anything good?"

"I should hope so—I can't afford to buy bad books. What about you?"

"Sorry? Oh, Harry wanted some letters typing for him." She waved a hand vaguely behind her. "I was planning to visit the British Museum anyway; I thought I might as well do them while I was here."

"I hope you're getting overtime."

"I doubt it." She smiled. "It just means there will be less to do on Monday. It didn't take me long, anyway." She slipped an arm through mine and walked along with me. "So. Where are you going now?"

"I was on my way home."

"Where is home?"

"Oakleigh Park. Up in North London. Near Muswell Hill."

She nodded. "But you don't have a London accent, is that right?"

"Yes. I'm from Nottingham, originally."

"And you are now a Londoner, yes?"

We turned the corner into Russell Square, started to walk around the south side of it towards the station. "I'm not sure *what* I am now, to be honest. When are you off to Poland?"

"Friday." She smiled. "It will be nice to see home again."

"And nice to get away from bloody Dean for a while, too."

She nodded. "That too, yes."

We had reached the corner of Russell Square and Southampton Row. I nodded up towards the station. "I'm afraid I go up this way."

She pointed down towards Holborn. "I must get the Central Line out to Stratford, and then I have a bus."

"OK, then. I'll see you on Monday."

"Yes, see you then." She gave my arm a little squeeze. "And try not to look so sad, Tim." And she walked away.

"Did I look sad?"

She looked round. "You looked *tragic*." She waved and headed towards Holborn. I could barely see her among the other pedestrians when it occurred to me that I should have invited her to the party. It also occurred to me that I hadn't asked if she'd read Harry's manuscript.

I looked about me, at the traffic, at the gardens of the Square, at the crowds of pedestrians, and I said, "Bollocks."

Seven

1

I left the house early on Monday morning because I didn't want to bump into Eric at breakfast. I'd managed to avoid him on Sunday only because he and Lisa had spent most of the day in his rooms, watching the Hungarian porno video I'd borrowed from Bob.

Lisa had read one of those sex-advice books, and had come across the advice that watching porn together might spice up their sex-life. She'd been badgering Eric about it for weeks, but Eric was an innocent abroad so far as the seamy underbelly of life was concerned. He didn't know where to go to get porn, and he was afraid that if he sent off for it by mail-order from one of the magazines on the news-agent's top shelf his address would one day wind up in police hands. So naturally he turned to me.

He had always been like that. At university it was transparently obvious to him that dope was all around him, but he was simply unable to get hold of any, so he came to me, and I was the one who had to risk getting busted.

Appearance and status had suddenly become very important to Eric, and I was shocked I hadn't seen it coming. At the party I had seen Eric's vision of a New World Order, and it was populated by well dressed, well behaved couples who did-n't seem to sweat, who planned their lives day by day and looked three or four years ahead to the time they would have a baby. It wasn't a world that included me.

The party had been polite and quiet and entirely unnerving. Eric's friends talked about skiing holidays and their last trip to the States and the possibilities of promo-tion, bitched about business contacts. They all had smooth skins and gold jewel-lery, and the men didn't seem to require a shave. Nobody groped anyone, nobody was sick in the garden, and the last guests left at half-past twelve. By that time all my friends had already gone on to another, livelier party in Bounds Green. I would have gone with them but I didn't have the energy. I was asked several times what I did for a living, and every time I said I was a researcher for a film company I saw a glazed, uninterested look appear in response. I was glad I hadn't invited Sophie, in the end. It would have been too embarrassing to watch her trying to mix with all those corporate androids. The only comfort I managed to gain from the entire eve-ning was that, if Eric's world didn't include me, it didn't include Harry and Sophie either, which I thought was oddly quaint. For all Harry's faults, at least he was still a human being.

The worst thing, the very worst thing, about the party, was looking round at one point in the evening and seeing Lisa staring at me with a maniac's smile of victory on her face, the kind of smile I imagined the mammals giving the dinosaurs just af-ter the comet struck.

This early, the train was refreshingly empty, and for a change I managed to get a seat. It was a misty morning, and the parkland around Alexandra Palace was lost under horizontal panes of drifting white as we went by.

At Finsbury Park a gang of workmen was enthusiastically digging up the surface of one of the platforms. I stood and watched them until the connection came in. There wasn't a soul in the carriage with me, and I was very daring and sat in the first-class compartment for the four-minute journey down to King's Cross.

It was still ridiculously early when the train pulled in; the real rush down the tracks from Hertfordshire and beyond was just getting into its stride. Instead of go-ing to Russell Square I stayed on the Piccadilly Line and went one stop further to Holborn, then walked through Lincoln's Inn to Chancery Lane.

About halfway down Chancery Lane there was a sandwich-bar-cum-restaurant that did early breakfasts. One of the picture-agency people had taken me there in a rare fit of generosity, expressing sorrow that I had to work for Harry Dean. Though it was still early there were a lot of taxi drivers and postmen from the post office a little further up the street tucking into their breakfasts. I ordered sausage and bacon, fried mushrooms and tomatoes, and sat reading the second section of the *Guardian*.

After breakfast I walked back up Chancery Lane and Holborn towards Bloomsbury, against the increasing flow of workers coming down from the Tube station. The early mist had turned into a light drizzle, and a few sensitive souls had opened their umbrellas against it.

It was still only twenty past eight when I got to the office. I thought I could buy a coffee from the sandwich bar and sit in the office trying to decide what to do about Eric while everything was still quiet, but when I got to the top of the stairs the office front door was wide open.

Thoughts of burglars and muggers ran through my mind. Harry had a small amount of cash in the safe, and in the past week he had splashed out on a nearly new portable television and video recorder from a bloke he'd met in a pub so he didn't have to keep going up to Viren's shop to watch tapes. I dawdled on the landing outside the door. The smart thing to do would have been to go downstairs to the sandwich bar and use their phone to call the police. The second smartest thing would have been to make as much noise as possible, stand aside, and let whoever might be left in the office flee. Of course, I did none of those things.

I got down on hands and knees, left my coffee on the landing, and crept through the door. I reached Sophie's desk and I heard someone moving about in the far room. Keeping my head down, I reached up and felt about on the desk. I remembered Sophie leaving a heavy glass paperweight on the desktop on Friday, but she must have moved it on Saturday, because I couldn't find it. I started to grope frantically around the desktop. It was the only weapon I could think of, and it wasn't there.

"Is that you?" asked a familiar voice.

I got up on my knees and looked over the desk. Harry was standing in the doorway of his office frowning at me. "What the Christ are you playing at?" he asked.

I got to my feet. "I thought we were being burgled." It was unheard-of for Harry to be in the office this early. He operated on a flexitime incomprehensible to anybody but himself, but it certainly precluded his presence in the office much before ten in the morning, more often than not with a definite aura of aniseed about him. "What are you doing here?"

"Have you had chickenpox?" he asked.

I had gone back out onto the landing to get my coffee. "What?"

There was a flustered look to him that I wasn't familiar with. "Have you had chickenpox?" he asked again with what I realized was barely contained agitation.

"Yes. I think so, anyway. My mother always said I'd had all the childhood diseases except mumps."

His lips thinned down to a fine line. "Have you had chickenpox?" he asked slowly.

"Yes. Yes. How many times do I have to tell you?"

He nodded and turned away. "All right. You're going to Poland."

I stood where I was for a moment, trying to understand what had obviously been a message in code. Then I walked through the office. "What?"

"I got a call from Sophie last night," Harry said when I reached the door of his room. "She's got chickenpox." He was sitting at his desk, sorting through bits of paper. "The whole bloody house has chickenpox." He looked up. "Oh, don't stand there looking at me like that. Call the travel agent."

2

"Hello?"

"Hello, Dad."

"Yes?"

"I'm going to Poland."

"Oh? Why?"

Lisa came out of Eric's room and gave me the same look of triumph she'd given me on the night of the party, the look that told me I was about to become extinct. I watched her go into the kitchen. I really wanted to thump her.

"I'll call you when I get back, Dad," I said.

"There's no need to bother if you don't want to," he said.

"I'll call you." I hung up.

Part Two

Mr Sierpiński at Bank Junction

Eight

1

The Tupolev's engines were very loud, and they were only a couple of yards away on the other side of the window. I pressed my forehead to the plastic and looked down. Far below, I could see fields lightly dusted with snow, and huge dark areas that must have been forests. What I couldn't see was an airport.

The plane bumped and descended another couple of hundred feet. I could see sparsely lit country roads, buildings that I presumed were farmhouses, and occasional car headlights. Still no sign of a city. I wondered if I should tell someone.

I looked down the cabin. The Friday evening flight from London to Kraków was packed, and nobody seemed the slightest bit disturbed that we had just made our third wide banking turn over what appeared to be empty countryside. By my judgement, there should have been an airport beneath us by now.

The note of the engine noise changed and we started to sink smoothly, like a neatly crowded lift. I stared, spellbound, as fields and clumps of trees rose towards us. Was this what a plane crash was like? Everyone sitting calmly while the bloody thing just ploughed serenely into the ground? There was a shudder through the body of the plane as the landing gear came down. The ground was getting closer and closer, the trees seeming to barely brush by. I opened my mouth and took a deep breath, and a row of yellow threshold lights zipped by just beneath us.

I closed my mouth and a strip of runway appeared like magic under the plane. There was a gentle bump, then a more severe one. The silhouettes of trees against sodium-lit clouds went by at high speed. I gaped, astounded. We'd not only managed to land, we'd also managed to land in a field. It was amazing.

By the time we'd taxied to a stop, it was obvious we *hadn't* landed in a field, but it was also obvious that Balice Airport wasn't up there with Heathrow and O'Hare and Narita in terms of sophistication. We taxied for a very long time, and I couldn't see any other aircraft or airport vehicles outside. There was nothing but the concrete we were rolling along, bounded by woodland. It was like going slowly down an empty motorway.

The plane was flying on to Warsaw after this stop, and when we came to a halt about a third of the passengers stayed in their seats while the rest of us wrestled our cabin baggage down from the overhead lockers and shuffled down the aisle to the exits.

Just outside the door, at the top of the steps, I stopped and took a deep breath. The air was cold and smelled faintly of the emissions of hundreds of steelworks and factories.

Poland. Land of my ancestors. I went down the steps grinning like an idiot. After all those endless bloody stories of my Gran's about the Old Country and the family's lost estates, I was finally here. I reached the bottom of the steps, put my heel in a patch of slush, and wound up flat on my back on the concrete with my flight luggage bouncing away under the aircraft.

One of the passengers who had been coming down the steps behind me retrieved my bag and came back to help me up. I couldn't help thinking that Poles had their priorities subtly wrong, but as he helped me up I said, "Thank you," in Polish.

"English?" he asked.

"Yes," I said, brushing wet dirt off my jeans and coat.

He smiled and shook his head and walked away.

Bending down to rub my knee with every other step, I followed him towards the terminal, a couple of small one-storey buildings outside of which a small crowd had gathered.

The crowd was waiting for its luggage, which was being manually unloaded from our flight, piled onto trolleys, and towed over to us by little tractors. When it reached us, it was up to us to unload it, tugging bags and suitcases out of the heap, and then filing into what I gathered was the immigration building, which was about the size of a comfortable holiday chalet.

I had been early checking in at Heathrow and my baggage had been amongst the first to go onto the plane. Therefore it was amongst the last to come off, and I was almost alone outside the building when my suitcase finally arrived.

Inside, we were herded into two queues to pass through Customs and passport control. My suitcase and shoulder bag were ignored by the uniformed Customs officer, my currency declaration and passport were stamped by the passport officer, and I stepped out into the reception area.

There were only about half a dozen people still waiting for passengers from my flight. One of them was holding a piece of cardboard with the word RAMSAY written on it in thick felt-pen.

"Hello," I said, walking towards him, tugging my suitcase along behind me on its little wheels. "I'm Tim Ramsay."

He was very tall and very thin, with a shock of badly barbered black hair and an immense bushy Wa³êsa-style moustache. He didn't appear to be in a very good mood. He looked at my suitcase. Then he looked at me.

There was a small, dumpy young woman standing beside him. She had long brown hair and sad eyes. In English, she said, "Are you Zosia's friend?"

"Yes," I replied in Polish. "My name's Tim Ramsay." I let go of my suitcase and held out my hand. The man with the sign grabbed the suitcase and started to march out of the building. The woman and I followed.

"I am Julia, and this is my husband, Witek," the woman said.

"That is pronounced with a 'V'," said the man in English, marching ahead of us and not looking back. "*Vee-tek*. And my wife's name is *Yoolia*. It is spelled with a 'J' but pronounced with a 'Y'. Understand?"

I understood him only just. His accent was almost incomprehensibly strong. "I'm not an imbecile," I joked as we passed through the glass doors and out into the night.

He snorted. "You speak Polish like an imbecile." We had reached a small dark Fiat, one of those cars that are about the size of a box of aspirin and have a hairdrier motor in the back. One of the girls on my course had had one, and she'd let me drive it a couple of times, and it had been a little sod of a car. "Speak English and let me translate, or people will think you're my idiot brother."

Only an idiot would have taken us for brothers, but he sounded too angry to argue with. "OK."

We stowed my bags and got into the car. I was crammed into the back, while Julia and Witek folded themselves into the front seats.

"Don't worry," Witek ordered me. "I am a registered interpreter and I teach English."

"OK." My Polish was awful, his English was nearly unintelligible. It had the characteristic stamp of a Lonesome Charley enterprise. I tried to struggle into a more comfortable position in the back of the car, but there was so little room I wound up with my knees up on either side of my chin.

Witek slammed the driver's door and started the engine. Then he squirmed around and looked me in the eye and said, "Did Zosia give you something for me?"

Sophie had not given me anything, but she had phoned me on Wednesday and told me what to bring. I unzipped my hand baggage, took out the bottle of Scotch, and handed it over.

Witek settled back into his seat and read the label on the bottle. "I don't know this 'Tesco'."

"It's an old Scottish family," I said.

"Ah." He nodded, took off the cap, and took a big swallow. "An old Scottish family. Good." Then he put the bottle down beside his feet, grabbed the steering wheel, and floored the accelerator, all in one movement. I suppose we must have gone from nought to sixty in about three minutes.

I'm a notoriously bad passenger. Once my father, driving us to our annual holiday at Mablethorpe, stopped our ageing Austin Maxi and ordered me out at the roadside when I complained he was driving too fast. Then he drove off and left me standing there. I was eight. He came back, but I think it had more to do with my mother's urging than anything he particularly wanted to do.

I had thought it would get better once I learned to drive, but at my first lesson my driving instructor spent the whole hour telling me exactly what damage a car could do to a person. He succeeded in getting me through my test, but he also succeeded in making me thoroughly paranoid when I got into a car, whether I was driving or not.

But I didn't say a word about the driving in the two hours or so that we drove from the airport. It was partly due to the fact that, after I'd converted the speedometer from kilometres per hour to miles per hour, I realized the little car wasn't doing much more than fifty-six and was straining to keep that up, but mainly it was because I wasn't altogether convinced that Witek was completely rational. Being dumped at the roadside in Lincolnshire during the day was one thing. Being dumped at the roadside somewhere in Upper Silesia at night was something completely different.

Having said that, the traffic was so sparse I thought we were on a slip-road for almost twenty minutes before realizing we were already on the motorway. The road was only intermittently lit. The few villages we passed through seemed deserted. My adrenalin occasionally peaked when we approached intersections, because Witek didn't bother to slow down for them. He just sailed through, as if he didn't care who lived or died in the process. If he'd been at the wheel of a more powerful car, I suppose I would have said that he drove like a maniac. As it was, it was slightly pathetic to be sitting in this howling ruin of a vehicle. And, judging by the number of times the car bounced and banged my head against the ceiling, the roads were in a shocking state.

Julia must have been used to it, because she showed no sign of alarm or tension.

"How is Zosia?" she asked in English.

"She has chickenpox."

That appeared to defeat Julia's English. "*Proszé?* Chickenpox?"

"It's, um, something children usually have." I made scratching motions. "You get little hard spots. Very itchy."

She nodded when she recognized what I was trying to describe. "*Ospa wietrzna.* But it can be very dangerous for an adult, no?"

"Sometimes, I think. But she has a very good doctor." I had no idea what kind of doctor Sophie had. "Didn't Soph—Zosia tell you?"

She shook her head. "She just said she could not come, and that you would be coming instead."

That seemed slightly perverse, since Sophie and Witek had been friends at university in Kraków and Julia was Sophie's third cousin or something. Maybe she hadn't wanted word to get back from Julia and Witek to her mother and worry her.

"And how is London?" she asked.

I shrugged. "It's all right," I said.

"There is a lot of crime there, yes?"

"No more than anywhere else."

"My cousin lives in Uttoxeter. She says they have a lot of crime in London. And bombs."

I hadn't really considered it. I went into London every day, just like everyone else, and never thought about it. Just like the people during the Blitz. Just like Mr Pearmain. "I don't suppose there's much more crime than anywhere else," I repeated. "But, yes, sometimes there are bombs." We also burn people in front of our cathedrals, I thought, but decided not to mention it.

Julia shook her head. "It must be terrible."

I said, "Well, we just sort of get on with it, you know?"

Beside her, Witek snorted and took another drink from the bottle.

I looked out of the window. Far away, beyond the trees at the side of the road, the horizon was marked with flickering smudges of orange light, the light of steelworks and blast furnaces. Even with the windows closed I could smell the pollution in the air. I managed to lean sideways a little and put my head against the window. I felt miserable and lost.

Witek didn't say a word the whole time he was driving. He managed to get through half the bottle of Scotch, though.

2

Witek and Julia lived in a solidly built but very old block of flats in Gliwice, right at the centre of Poland's polluted industrial heart. The electricity and gas meters on the landing outside their flat were labelled in Black Letter and had been made by a firm in Karlsruhe, betraying the pre-war origin of the flats.

Before the war, all of this had been Germany. Gliwice was a border town called Gleiwitz. Zabrze, just down the road, was Hindenburg. On the map I'd bought in Dillons on Torrington Place before leaving London, half the towns and cities in Western Poland had their old German names appended in brackets under the Polish names. Wrocław had been Breslau, Posen had become Poznań. After the war the whole country had just been shoved bodily westward, while the Soviet Union filled in the space left behind in the East.

It had happened a lot. Poland has been rising and submerging on the map of Europe for centuries, at the whim of whichever more powerful neighbour has decided to take the place over. My grandmother was born in Lwów, which was called Lemberg when it was part of the Austro-Hungarian Empire, then was in Poland, then was in the Soviet Union, and is now in Ukraine and is called Lviv. Szczecin, the place I was supposed to be going, had once been in Germany and called Stettin. It was on the Baltic coast, hundreds of miles from Upper Silesia, but that was typical of a Lonesome Charley operation.

The theory had been that Witek would meet me at Kraków and then accompany me to Szczecin and act as my interpreter in the negotiation. It had seemed completely reasonable to me in London when I was told I would not fly directly to Szczecin, or even to a city near Szczecin, but instead to a city hundreds of miles away. I must have needed my head examining.

"I must need my head examining," I said on the phone.

"You're the one who wanted to go," Harry said. "It's too late to come running to me now. What is that racket?"

I looked across the living room. "Cardiacs."

"What?"

"Cardiacs," I said a little louder. "Sophie told me to bring Witek some tapes." Hearing his name, Witek looked up and waved. I waved back. He was sitting against the shelf on which his tape-system sat, a speaker above each shoulder. He had a perfectly good pair of headphones but they always seemed to develop technical problems when I was on the phone. It was one of the few things I had seen make Witek smile.

"You mean that's *music*?" Harry said.

"I quite like them, actually." I'd been a fan for years, but Harry wasn't in the mood to hear that.

"What in the name of God are you playing at, Tim?"

"He's been ill," I said. "He's had pneumonia. His son won't let us see him."

"He's been ill. He's had pneumonia. His son won't let you see him. Are you pissing me about so you can have a holiday?"

"No! No." I lowered my voice. "Believe me, the sooner I'm out of here the better."

"I thought it was supposed to be the land of your ancestors." Harry sounded amused.

"No, it isn't. It used to be Germany."

"What?"

"Nothing. Look, the son's supposed to be phoning us tomorrow to let us know how the old man is."

"He's only got to negotiate for a tin of film, for Christ's sake. He's not running the London Marathon."

"Come on, Harry. He's nearly eighty. Have a heart."

"Just get that film, Tim. And don't get sentimental and give him a couple of hundred quid extra because he's old and he's had pneumonia."

"Don't worry, Harry."

"I'm not worrying, Tim."

"Oh, not much you're not."

"No, Tim. You're the one who has to worry. I've put a lot of trust in you. No film, no job. I'll have your P45 ready, just in case."

"Fine, Harry. OK."

"Just keep that in mind, Tim."

"I'm thinking of nothing else, Harry."

"All right. See you soon."

I hung up and sighed. Witek was fiddling with his headphones. All of a sudden he reached up and plugged them into the tape deck. The music vanished. Witek put the headphones on, listened a moment, then grinned and gave me the thumbs-up. I sighed again.

Despite my protestations to the contrary, it *was* getting a bit like a holiday. Witek had decided to leave me to my own devices, so I wandered about seeing the sights and taking photographs. I was actually rather hoping that Mr Sierpiński would stay sick; Witek was talking about driving all the way to Szczecin, a journey which would probably take us a couple of days in his stupid little car and would almost certainly unhinge me.

Meanwhile, I developed a routine. We had breakfast at seven, then Julia went off to work and Witek drove away to do whatever he did during the day and I sat down with a second cup of coffee and watched some television.

Around ten, I went out. Day after day, while I waited for Marcin Sierpiński to call and tell us that his father was ready to see us, I went for walks around the town. Before I'd left London, Sophie had dictated a wants list to me over the phone, mostly composed of foodstuffs but also videos, music tapes and books which she couldn't get in London, and I toured the shops trying out my inadequate Polish, ticking off each item on the list.

I rationed myself to one item a day, a book one day, a tape the next. Most of the shops I needed were on Zwycięstwa, which seemed to be the main shopping street, which was fine for me because Zwycięstwa led up to the little market square in the Old Town and a rather nice little café I'd discovered. Most days, after the exertions of shopping, I sat in the café drinking a glass of coffee and eating cakes and watching the lunchtime crowds walking past the Town Hall that stood in the centre of the square. Subconsciously—probably due to Gran's horror stories of what the Soviets did to her country—I had half expected a grey concrete wasteland, but from the window of the café I could see a mediaeval-style market square that might have been in Austria or Switzerland except for the layer of grime over everything.

As far as I could see, the whole of Poland's topsoil was sand. It was everywhere, even in Silesia, miles and miles from the sea. It crunched underfoot, it blew in stinging clouds on the wind, it picked up the soot from the steelworks. The whole town was gritty and grimy and battered and rather lovely.

After coffee I usually took a tram somewhere. I was really getting into the trams. They went everywhere and the tickets cost next to nothing. I went out to Zabrze and Bytom, two neighbouring towns with a great deal less charm than Gliwice, and rode the trams there as well. I tried to imagine what the towns had been like in the early years of the century, when they had been clean and new and German, but now they were falling into a sort of mucky decay and their new buildings were flaking Stalinist blocks. The whole area was extraordinarily run-down, but none of the people I saw from the windows of the trams seemed to notice. I wondered if the tourists in London looked at me and thought much the same thing. Sophie's mother lived in Zabrze. I kept reminding myself to ask Julia if she knew what her address was, but I never got round to it. It never occurred to me to wonder why Sophie hadn't given me the address herself and asked me to drop in.

The early cold snap fizzled out and the weather started to get balmy. I noticed a lot of people wearing big sheepskin-lined denim jackets with zip-off sleeves. I spent days looking, but I never found a shop that sold them. There were, however, a depressing number of shell-suits about.

I rode the trams and I usually smiled a lot. Land of my ancestors. Here at last. Gran would have loved it.

Witek and Julia's flat was four rooms that were miracles of space-saving. They slept on a sofa-bed in the living room while I slept on a sofa-bed in Witek's study. Witek had a cheap Czech PC, shelves of dictionaries, language books and pulp novels, and a stack of *Swamp Thing* magazines that Julia's relatives in Uttoxeter had sent him. On my first night, too nervous to sleep, I had read through the whole stack, and when I did finally manage to nod off I had a frightful nightmare.

It was a lot harder to like Witek than it was to like Poland and Poles in general. He was curt, surly, sometimes openly abusive. He was grumpy in the mornings and contemptuous of my faltering attempts to speak Polish. He kept telling me to shut up and let him do the talking, but he was never there when I needed him to do some talking. He clearly regarded me as some kind of half-wit.

"No, I don't think so," Julia said one morning when I mentioned it to her.

"He called me a cretin last night," I said.

She smiled and lit another cigarette. They both smoked like little steam engines. "No, he was joking."

"It's a joke he makes rather a lot, Julia." I buttered another slice of bread. Breakfast was a selection of cold meats, kabanos sausage, paté, sliced tomatoes, baguette, rye bread and seemingly inexhaustible supplies of coffee and tea. I'd been expecting shortages and food queues, but we ate very well.

Julia yawned and stretched. She worked long hours as a nurse at the Oncology Hospital and seemed to be tired all the time. "I will speak to him, Tymoteusz," she promised.

"Just Tim," I reminded her. Gran had always called me Tymoteusz. It may have been the Polish rendering of my name, but I thought it made me sound like a shampoo. "No, don't bother, Julia. He'll only do it more if he knows I'm irritated."

"Are you irritated?" She suddenly looked concerned, as if worried that word would get back to England that she wasn't a good hostess.

I sighed. I reached out and patted her arm. "I'm not irritated, Julia," I said. "You're really taking good care of me."

I probably didn't sound too reassuring, because from then on Witek drove me everywhere. He didn't do it willingly, and privately I thought it was a shame because I'd grown rather fond of travelling on the trams, but I kept my disappointment to myself for the sake of the annoyance it obviously caused Witek.

I don't know what sort of discussions the two of them had when I wasn't around, but something was going on, because one day at breakfast Witek said, "Today you will be a tourist, English boy."

"I seem to have been spending a lot of time being a tourist, Witek," I said, pouring myself another cup of coffee.

He looked at me as if I were only a couple of chromosomes away from being a mushroom. "We are taking good care of you."

"I never said you weren't." I looked from him to Julia and back again. "Look—"

"So," he said, stubbing his cigarette out in his ashtray and spilling ash all over the tablecloth, "today you will be a tourist."

"If you say so, Witek." Anything for a quiet life.

3

Witek had worked for a couple of years as a guide at the Wawel, Kraków's royal castle, which I thought must have done no end of good for relations between Poland and the English-speaking world. He seemed intent on recapturing those days, marching Julia and me up the cobbled street on Wawel Hill and declaiming in all directions.

"For five centuries this was the capital of Poland," he said in a loud voice, as if volume alone could compensate for his awful accent. "Almost all the kings and queens of Poland are buried here at the cathedral."

The steep street up the Hill was lined with artists, their paintings and drawings stuck to boards or leant up against the castle wall. Some of them were appalling but most of them were pretty good. I wondered if there was any money in patronizing up-and-coming Polish artists. The exchange rate was about twenty thousand złotys to the pound, and I could have bought a couple of dozen of these paintings for the cost of a longish taxi-ride in London.

At the top of the hill we passed through a gateway and out into a large open space. Witek announced that there had once been a little town here, before the Austrians cleared it for a parade ground.

We did the cathedral from top to bottom. It was a masterpiece of Gothic overkill, from the ornate coffins of Polish royalty and heroes to the golden dome of the chapel, which Witek claimed the Poles had covered with pitch during the war to hide it from the Nazis. By the time we emerged into daylight again I was stiff-legged.

Witek, on the other hand, seemed to be invigorated. He strode off towards the Renaissance-style castle, pointing in all directions and dictating random bits of information at a near-shout. He was like a man possessed. All the other tourists on the hill gave him a wide berth.

Finally we walked back down to the huge Market Square and strolled through the arcade of the Sukiennice, the immense Italianate Cloth Hall in the middle of the square. The arcade was full of little stalls, selling everything from finely made silver jewellery to religious kitsch. I bought Sophie a pair of silver earrings with little Baltic amber beads hanging from them.

It was late when we got back to Gliwice, and as we reached the top of the stairs I could hear the phone ringing inside the flat. Witek opened the door and went inside while Julia and I followed more slowly, taking off our coats and shoes. I could hear Witek talking excitedly in the living room.

I was tired. It had been a long day. I'd been on my feet for most of it, and for the rest of it I'd been tantalized by the potentially fatal hazard of being in a car that Witek was driving. I was sore, worn out and tense, and all I wanted to do was lie down and sleep for a day or so.

I put on the slippers Julia had given me and walked into the living room. Witek was just hanging up the phone. He looked at me, and he grinned like a true lunatic. And then I realized who the phone call had been from.

"Oh no," I said.

Witek grinned even wider. "Oh yes," he said.

Nine

1

"You have come a long way," said Mr Sierpiński.

"It certainly feels that way," I said.

He laughed. I felt as if I were the victim of some obscure joke. Certainly he didn't look like a man who had just been suffering pneumonia. I had some idea that medicine in Poland might be a little different than in England, but I hadn't expected a recovering pneumonic to be sitting in his living room smiling and puffing on a small cigar.

Mr Jacek Sierpiński was a small, plump, pink-faced man in his late seventies. His hair was white and fine and wispy and his blue eyes twinkled merrily from beneath shaggy white eyebrows. He had a huge moustache which would have been white too if it hadn't been stained yellow by the nicotine from his cigars. There was not the slightest sign that he had had a day's illness in his life, and I was trying not to get annoyed about the time I had wasted while he "convalesced".

His son, Marcin, was sitting on a chair by the window, watching me steadily and somewhat antagonistically. He was about my height and around Harry's age. His short curly brown hair was receding, and he had round wire-framed spectacles. He was wearing jeans and an expensive-looking black leather jacket. I had a moment of déja vu, thinking of Mr Pearmain and his son in Muswell Hill, but I knew this was different. Stephen Pearmain had been at his father's house to protect him from muggers. Marcin was here to protect his father from something quite different, and I couldn't work out what it was.

"I am really very old," said Mr Sierpiński.

"You don't look very old," I said, and to be honest he didn't look his age.

He tipped his head to one side. "Ah, but I am." His English was a little wobbly, but he had insisted we use it. Witek was sitting beside me on the sofa looking choleric; he popped in now and again with a translation when Mr Sierpiński's English failed him, but so far he'd hardly had to say a word.

Mr Sierpiński looked at his son. "Marcin," he said, "make some tea for our guests, would you?" He said it in English.

Marcin gave Witek and me another suspicious look, then he got up. "Yes, Father." He went out of the living room, and I heard a measured clatter of pots and pans in the kitchen, and water running from the tap.

"He is a good boy," Mr Sierpiński said. "But he is very ... um ... protect ...?"

"Protective." I said before Witek could jump in. I looked at the door to the kitchen. "Over-protective."

He nodded and grinned. "Over-protective. Yes, Mr Ramsay, Marcin is over-protective. He thinks I am so old that I have become a child again."

I wondered how much longer I would have to listen to old men telling me about their relationship to their sons. I wasn't in the best of spirits. I had a cracking headache, and my back hurt.

On the eve of our departure from Gliwice, Witek's car had suffered a catastrophic breakdown. I had spent hours sitting at the kitchen window watching him working on it down in the courtyard. I'm afraid I giggled when he started to hit the engine with a spanner.

It turned out that it wasn't so funny, though. I suggested that we fly up to Szczecin, but Witek had a mortal fear of flying, so we had to take the train from Kraków. It was a ten-hour train journey from Kraków to Szczecin, and even when we arrived we still had a fifteen-kilometre bus ride to the town where Mr Sierpiński lived.

The whole thing, yet again, bore the typical imprint of a Lonesome Charley operation. The address Harry had given me said Szczecin, but Mr Sierpiński didn't live in Szczecin. He lived on the outskirts of a rather attractive little town called Stargard Szczeciński, and by the time we arrived I was tired and annoyed and more than a little fed up of watching the Pomeranian countryside going by outside the windows. I had also been terrified that we'd get there and find Mr Sierpiński had had some kind of relapse. Witek said there was only one hotel in town, and I dreaded having to go back to Gliwice on the train with him without at least seeing the old man.

"I have been ill," he said.

"I never doubted that you had," I said.

He lowered his voice. "But it was not pneumonia. It was a bad cold."

"A bad cold can be very distressing," I said.

"You have come a long way," he said again. "I am sorry you had to wait, but Marcin did not tell me you were in Poland until Monday."

So Marcin had been putting us off for over a week before he even told his father I was here. He and I were going to have to have a quiet word. I said, "I don't want to do anything which might endanger your health, Mr Sierpiński."

"Endanger!" He gave a great theatrical shrug. "How can sitting in my own home and talking endanger my health?"

Witek got up and went to the window. Mr Sierpiński lived fourteen floors up in a huge Stalinist monolith faced with windows and balconies. From the window you could see the walled Old Town. Witek leaned on the windowsill and sighed.

"Marcin does not think I should be selling my film," said Mr Sierpiński.

I shrugged. "I can't force you to, Mr Sierpiński."

"I am very old," he told me for the second time. This time I didn't argue. He said, "There are some things I want." He gestured around the living room, at the rugs on the walls, the glass-fronted bookcases. "This is a nice flat, and Marcin helps me as much as he can, but I have not very much money. When I heard of Mr Dean's offer, I could not refuse."

"You can still refuse," I said for the sake of fairness.

He shook his head. "What use is it to me now?" He stubbed his cigar out in the ashtray on the table beside him, got up, and went over to one of the bookcases. He opened a cupboard and took out a film tin. I had seen too many of those since my interview for Lonesome Charley, but he held it in both hands and smiled at it as if it were the only one in the world. He looked at me. "I have a manuscript of my reminiscence, also."

I nodded. "I know. That was to be part of the package."

He frowned. "*Proszé?*"

"*Pakunek,*" Witek said without turning from the window. "Package."

Mr Sierpiński gave me a disappointed look. "Not a *pakunek*, Mr Ramsay. Not a package. Separate."

"I'm afraid I can't do that, Mr Sierpiński. You agreed with Mr Dean that you'd sell them together."

He shook his head, and my heart sank. "Your Mr Dean was not very precise about the details of the transaction."

That was hardly a surprise. "He told me you had an agreement."

He shook his head again. "No agreement. An *arrangement*. I did not sign a contract."

A surprising number of the old folk I had dealt with were quite happy to hand over their photographs and films and memories without a penny changing hands; quite often I found myself having to force them to take money. On the other hand, some of them—like Mrs Lewis—were determined to get as much as they could out of Lonesome Charley. Usually you could bargain with them until they realized no more money was going to be forthcoming, but I had a feeling this was not one of those times.

"All right," I said, on the basis that it was better to be shouted at by Harry for spending too much money than fired for not bringing anything back at all.

"A thousand pounds," he said.

"Not a chance," I said, sitting back surprised. We were only paying eight hundred for the film. "Two hundred."

"Seven hundred."

Witek turned and looked from me to Mr Sierpiński and back. He shook his head and pulled a face.

"Three hundred and fifty," I said.

Marcin came back into the living room with a tray of tea-glasses and little plates of cakes. He looked confused for a moment, then his face set in a sour expression.

"Six hundred," Mr Sierpiński said without moving from in front of the bookcase. He had never stopped smiling.

"Four."

Marcin heaved a world-breaking sigh and put the tea things on the table. "Father," he said.

Mr Sierpiński held up a hand and said to me, "Five hundred and fifty."

"Five."

He lifted the hand into the air and announced, "*Koniec!*"

"Finish?" I said, confused by the abruptness of it.

He nodded. "All finish. Good." He walked over and handed me the film tin. He shook my hand. "Now we will have tea and cakes, and I will tell you my story for the voice which Mr Dean wants."

I looked at the film. "All right." I wondered what I had done, whether the whole business with the "pneumonia" had been manufactured to soften me up for the negotiations. Witek was staring at me, and I wondered if he was getting a cut from the Sierpiński's as well as from Harry. Then I realized I didn't care. I could go home now. I smiled at Mr Sierpiński. "All right."

2

Two days before I was due to leave, British Airways and the Polish state airline LOT had a difference of opinion involving routes and schedules which resulted in Britain banning LOT flights and the Poles banning BA flights into each other's country.

Witek informed me of this with great relish. "Bastard English," he announced. "They do not frighten us."

"Witold," Julia said, "he does not want to hear you speak like this."

"Bastard English think they are so big and we are so small," Witek said, waving his glass so that vodka spilled over the side. "They think we are frightened of them, but we are not."

"Witek still remembers the visa which the British Embassy refused to give him," Julia explained without looking up from her book. "In 1985." Witek glared at her but she just went on reading.

I stared at the television in the corner. The newsreader had gone on to another item, something about a massive shunt on a motorway near Wrocław. I had become used to car-crash stories. After almost a month in Poland and nearly two weeks of being driven about by Witek, I was astounded that Poles managed to survive more than a couple of months after passing their tests.

"All those years while the bastard Communists were in power," Witek muttered loudly as he topped up his glass. "All those years and all the British could say was, 'Poland must be free!' And now Poland is free what do they say? They say 'Those bastard Poles are trying to steal our jobs! We must keep them out of our country! No more help for those filthy bastard Poles!'"

"Witold," Julia tutted.

He turned from the cupboard and glared at me. "Is it not true, English boy?" He walked over and leaned above me in the armchair. His English actually improved when he was drunk; when sober he tended to be sullen and withdrawn. It was all I could do to get a grunt out of him some mornings. "So," he said, "is it true? That Yowta was not a mistake? That you hate Poles?"

"Excuse me?" I asked. "'Yowta'?"

"Yes!" He waved his glass again, showering me with vodka. "Yowta! Yowta! Stalin! Churchill! Roosevelt! *Yowta!*"

Oh Christ, he meant Yalta, where Churchill and Roosevelt had given Poland to Stalin. I still had no idea whether the Poles had forgiven the Allies for that. Personally, I wouldn't have if I'd been in their place, but I didn't think that would be good enough for Witek tonight.

I looked up at him. "Witek," I said, "how in Christ's name am I going to get home?"

3

"Thirty-two hours," Witek told me triumphantly as he stood on the platform and I leaned out of the carriage window. "Kraków, Warsaw, Germany, Holland, home, eh?" And he laughed.

"Very funny, Witek," I said.

He looked suddenly concerned. "You do not want to go home, English boy? Perhaps you would like stay with Witek and Julia?"

"Not even as a joke, Witek."

He laughed. Witek had decided that his responsibility to me ended right here in Kraków station. Or, to put it another way, he couldn't be bothered to come with me to Warsaw. The train gave a jerk which almost threw me off my feet, then started to pull out of the station. Witek began to jog along the platform, keeping pace with my window. "You post our letters, English boy!"

Julia had given me a two-inch-thick stack of post for relatives in England, as well as a huge sack of parcels for various people in London. "I won't forget, Witek," I promised.

The train started to gather speed. Witek was in no condition to keep up, and he gradually fell behind. I waved to him for a while, just for appearances' sake, then I went back to my compartment. I felt like crying.

I'd barely sat down to contemplate the horrific prospect of the journey ahead of me when the train started to slow again, then stopped. We were only half a mile or so out of the station. I got a book out of my bag and tried to read, but after about ten minutes I put it down, got up, and slid the compartment's window down.

We had stopped in a complex of sidings and junctions overlooked by some worn-out-looking blocks of flats. Leaning out of the window and looking along the train, I could see a little group of figures clustered on the gravel beside the engine. Brilliant. I had only half an hour's grace between getting into Warszawa Centralna station and the Moscow-Paris Express leaving Warszawa Gdańska. Witek had told me there would be no problem getting a taxi to take me across town to catch the express, but it would still be nice to have the whole half-hour, just in case.

I was about to go back and sit down when the train gave a jerk and started to move again. The little group of figures started to draw slowly towards me. I saw that some of them were wearing uniforms. They seemed to be standing around something which lay between the tracks parallelling the ones our train was running on.

Closer still, I suddenly realized that some of the uniforms were police uniforms. As my carriage passed the group, we slowed down again, just for a moment. The policemen, along with a number of men in railway uniforms and several others in suits or casual clothes, were standing in a circle. One of the plainclothes men, wearing an ill-fitting suit, turned and looked up at me as I went by. He was short and stocky and white-haired, and as he turned he opened a gap in the circle and I saw that they were all standing around a body.

The body was covered in blood. It was wearing shorts and a short-sleeved shirt. Its feet, in ankle-socks and sneakers, were tipped at peculiar angles, and where its head and left shoulder should have been there was just a ruined pulverized mess that looked like raw mince.

The white-haired man and I looked at each other. He and the body and the policemen slid away behind me. My stomach forward-rolled, and I was sick down the side of the train.

I hung there for some time, while the policemen vanished into the distance the accelerating train was putting between us. I waited until I was reasonably sure I wasn't going to be sick in the compartment, then I flopped down on my seat.

I left the window open all the way to Warsaw, just in case.

4

I got off the train in Warsaw still thinking about the body I'd seen in Kraków, remembering the mass of raw meat where its head and shoulder should have been. I had to ask the taxi driver who took me to Warszawa Gdańksa to wind all his windows down.

By the time I got to the express that would take me to The Hook, I was feeling miserable and exhausted. I found my carriage and surrendered my ticket to the attendant, and when he led me to my compartment I found it was already occupied, and my spirits sank.

My compartment-mates were three huge crimson-faced men from the mountains in the south of Poland. They talked incessantly but their dialect entirely defeated my Polish. Fifteen minutes out of Warsaw they produced the first bottle of vodka, and I suspect they spent the rest of their journey dividing their time equally between getting pissed and laughing at me.

PKP, the Polish railways, run trains in conditions which would make British Rail cry into its cocoa and mutter about the wrong kind of snow, but it was still the longest train journey I have ever endured. It was the longest journey of *any* kind I have ever endured. I had already witnessed what was either the aftermath of a terrible accident or some awful murder, and now I found myself travelling with three dangerous-looking mountain-men who found me funny.

One of the *Górale* told me that he and his friends were travelling to Amsterdam to work in the flower markets. At least that was what it sounded like. At any rate, he kept repeating the name "Amsterdam" and laughing, and that was enough to make my spirits sink even further; I'd hoped they were going to get off in Poznań, or before the border at any rate. I stuck one of the tapes I had made in Stargard Szczeciński into my Walkman, put the headphones on, and tried to ignore my fellow travellers.

Mr Jacek Sierpiński had had a long and mostly uneventful life, but a brief and very busy war. In 1937, aged eighteen, he became an apprentice engineer at the Bayerische Motor Werke in Nuremberg. During an extended and rambling conversation, aided occasionally by Witek when his English faltered, Mr Sierpiński told me he had once seen Adolf Hitler at a Nazi rally.

Bavaria had become unnerving enough for a young Pole by then anyway, but that one sight of Hitler in action was the last straw for Mr Sierpiński. He had no family back in Poland, no friends to speak of, nothing to lose.

On the day the Germans invaded Poland, Mr Sierpiński was heading in the other direction, crossing the border by train into Holland. The irony was not lost on me in my present situation.

At the border, a little group of neo-Nazis was standing on the German side looking despondent and stupid in the rain. They started to shout at us as we went by. The three mountain-men, in their too-tight suits and their loud ties, hung out of our compartment's window and shouted back at them, and the skinheads scattered. I was actually rather impressed by that. The skinheads vanished behind us and we sailed into Frankfurt an der Oder.

At Frankfurt we sat for about an hour while Customs and passport formalities were gone through. I had been vaguely worried about the border because of Mr Sierpiński's film. I could imagine situations in which the Customs officers might impound the film, in which case Harry would suffer a meltdown.

In the event, however, my three friends worked their magic again. The German Customs man took one look at them, stamped our passports in record time, and made himself scarce.

A few days after crossing into Holland, Mr Sierpiński was standing on the quayside at Dover with his suitcase and not a word of English.

"I did work here and there," he said. I could hear one of us—Witek, probably—noisily stirring his tea. "A little this, a little that. I learned English in the night. I tried to join the RAF, but I failed the medical examination. A problem with the inside of my ear." I remembered him putting his hand up by his temple and wiggling his fingers very quickly.

"Vertigo," Witek said. He pronounced it "wertigo", and hearing it again made me smile.

I heard myself say, "How did you come to have film of the Blitz?"

"Were you not told?" Mr Sierpiński said. I could see again the look of surprise on his face, and the look of pride when he explained: "I am a filmmaker."

After Berlin, the Three Musketeers decided it was time to bed down for the night. The beds were bunks that hinged down from the front and back walls of the compartment and came complete with sheets and blankets and pillows. One of the top ones was selected for me. This put my head about three-quarters of an inch from a small box-like device which had something to do with the compartment's air conditioning or lighting. Whatever, it spent the whole night making a loud buzzing noise. There was another little buzzing box attached to the compartment wall near my feet, so that my sleep could be disturbed no matter which direction I chose to lie in. Around one in the morning I got used to the buzzing. And then my travelling companions started to snore. Somewhere around the border with Holland the heating in the compartment failed and the temperature plummeted.

Mr Sierpiński loved home movies. The only thing he brought with him from Germany, apart from his clothes and some odds and ends of jewellery to sell, was a ciné camera.

"I left many cans of film in Nuremberg when I departed," he said. He had been looking out of the window when he said that. "I wanted to bring them with me, but I simply could not carry them all."

"Did you bring any of them?" I asked. I'd been thinking about the film he might have taken of Hitler, about what that could have been worth today.

He shook his head sadly. "All gone. All gone."

"Father." Marcin's voice. He said to me, "You are making him very tired."

"I am all right, Marcin."

"No, you are not, Father." Marcin's voice was hard, insistent, pissed-off.

My voice said, "But we haven't got to the Blitz yet."

There was a rustle on the tape, and I had to rewind it and play it a couple of times before I identified it. Mr Sierpiński passing the envelope to me.

"All here," he said. "All here."

By the time we reached Amersvoordt and the *Górale* got off for their connection to Amsterdam, I was red-eyed and twitchy and the back of my throat was tickling. They shook hands with me and left the train sniggering. I was finally able to stretch out and get some sleep, but less than an hour later we arrived at The Hook and I had to get off.

The boat was full of British fun-seekers returning from a weekend in Amsterdam. Most of them were so drunk that I started to look nostalgically on the mountain-men. The North Sea was a little frisky that day and I belatedly discovered that I was prone to seasickness.

Seven hours of misery brought me to Harwich and the moment I had dreaded the whole journey. I just knew that my luggage would be searched and the film confiscated. In the event the Customs men only looked at me as I walked through to the railway platform and the waiting express for London.

Witek's promised thirty-two hours ended in the huge, surreally echoing spaces of Liverpool Street station. I used a trolley to wheel my luggage down the platform, not because it was particularly heavy but because I needed something to lean on.

I walked the trolley as far as a telephone and called a cab.

5

The house was cold, there was no food in the kitchen, and there were eighteen messages on the answering machine from Harry telling me to call him when I got home. I ignored all these things and collapsed on the living room couch in front of a repeat of *Lovejoy*. I didn't even bother to unpack.

Ian McShane was just doing one of his laddish bits-to-camera when the phone rang. I had to go downstairs to answer it. I'd automatically turned off the answering machine as I came in, and Eric still wasn't back from wherever he and Lisa had gone tonight.

"Tim?" said Harry. "You're back."

"Oh shit," I said.

"Have you got it?" he said.

I thought about what I had just been through. The body, the mountain-men, the long, long journey, the seasickness. I said, "Fuck off," and hung up. Then I unplugged the phone.

The hammering on my door woke me slowly. I incorporated it into a dream in which Witek and the mountain men were beating neo-Nazis to death with huge Polish sausages. I was enjoying it so much that I left it only reluctantly. Going to the door I fell over one of my bags and went full-length on the floor.

"Visitor for you," Eric said when I'd got up and opened the door. Because he had the ground floor he had door-answering duty, which was fine because usually the only visitor we had was Lisa. It annoyed him when I had visitors. He looked furious.

"Thanks, Eric," I said numbly. Harry edged into the doorway and my heart sank. "Hi, Harry."

"I was almost mugged tonight," he told me, barging past into the room. He had the flushed, uncombed look which usually meant he'd been on the Tube.

"You could have saved yourself a journey and waited till tomorrow," I told him, closing the door. I looked at the clock-radio by my bed and sighed. "All right, so it *is* tomorrow. You could still have saved yourself a journey."

"Did you get it?" he asked, wandering along my bookshelves with his head tipped to one side to read the titles.

"You and I have got to get some things straight—*oi!*"

He had unzipped one of my bags and was rooting around inside. "Is it in here?"

"No." I stepped over and grabbed the bag away from him. "No it's not."

He picked up another bag and started going through it. "In here?"

I grabbed that one away from him too and hugged both bags awkwardly to my chest. "This isn't fair, Harry. Get out of my bedroom."

"Your phone was engaged."

"I unplugged it."

He went back to the bookshelves. "And that's another thing. You mustn't ever tell me to fuck off, because I'll knock a week's pay off your salary."

I sat down on the bed and dropped the bags around my feet. "Do you want a cup of tea?"

"No." He turned to face me. "Did you get it?"

"Yes, I got it."

"Was it expensive?"

"I've still got a couple of hundred quid of the money you gave me, if that's what you mean."

He smiled. Now he was getting what he wanted he was perfectly patient and reasonable. "We can sort that out tomorrow. Now, can I have it, please?"

I got up and lifted my case onto the bed. Inside, nestled among badly laundered shirts and jeans, was the film can. I handed it to Harry and he smiled.

"The manuscript too?"

"All here." I took the fat heavy A4 manila envelope from the case and handed him that as well.

He reached into his pocket, took out a Tesco's carrier bag, and put the envelope and film tin in it. "What condition's it in?"

"I only glanced at the manuscript. It's a bit yellow. I don't know about the film. Do you want to take Sophie's food with you?"

He shook his head. "You bring it in tomorrow." He started to move towards the door. "Oh, she's much better now, by the way. She came back to work last Wednesday."

"That's lovely." I watched him leave. Dead bodies, mountain-men, wimpish neo-Nazis. I'd carried that can of film halfway across Europe, and Harry had never even said thank you. I wondered what he planned to do if he was mugged while he was carrying the film about. And then I wondered how in hell he planned to get home now the Underground had stopped running for the night.

Ten

1

Autumn had arrived in the month or so I'd been away, and all the leaves had gone from the trees outside the office. They had been pretty poor trees even with their leaves, but now they just looked stupid growing out of the pavement outside the building.

"You're back," Sophie said, looking up from some paperwork that looked suspiciously like a final demand from the Electricity Board.

I glanced at the card on the door. It was a little more dog-eared and grubby than I remembered it. When questioned about the choice of name for his company, Harry would tell anyone who cared to listen that Lonesome Charley Reynolds had been General Custer's favourite scout. I had no idea what the relevance of this was.

"How's life at the Little Bighorn?" I asked, looking around the office. I hadn't been gone all that long, but I'd almost forgotten how shabby Lonesome Charley's premises were.

Sophie shrugged. "He's been a sod." She got up and came round the desk to give me a peck on the cheek. She smelled of cinnamon. I hadn't seen her since that Saturday afternoon outside the office, and I'd been worrying that the chickenpox might have scarred her, but there wasn't a mark on the perfect skin of her face. "How was home?"

"Home was all right," I said, putting my rucksack down on the desk and starting to unlace the top. "Your mate Witek is a bloody psychopath, though."

She laughed. "He's not so bad."

"A true original, our Witek." I put my hand into the rucksack and took out a poppy-seed cake and she gave a little squeal of delight. There followed a rye-bread loaf of the kind she claimed to be unable to find in England, a little plastic bottle of *barszcz* "starter" for making beetroot soup, dried wild mushrooms threaded on a string, six large Polish sausages of various types wrapped in silver foil which would almost certainly have got me taken aside for questioning if my bag had ever gone through an airport X-ray machine. By the time my rucksack was empty, the top of the desk resembled the counter of a small Polish delicatessen.

She unwrapped and sniffed everything, smiling. She had the most beautiful smile I had ever seen. I'd been planning to save the earrings for later, but I took them from my pocket and handed them over. She looked at them for a moment, and I swear I thought I saw her eyes grow wet. She flung her arms around me, gave me an earth-shattering hug and kissed me on both cheeks. "I will marry you, Tim," she said solemnly.

"God but you're easily bought," I said. I sat down in the visitor chair and sneezed.

"Bless you," she said.

"Thank you. Is he in yet?"

She shook her head. "He telephoned about twenty minutes ago. He won't be in at all today; he says he has to see Viren."

Fine. I looked at my watch. "Lunch?"

We ate at the pizza restaurant on New Oxford Street. We shared a medium deep-pan covered in all kinds of meat, and watched the pedestrians go by outside. She quizzed me at great length about "things at home". I didn't mention the body in Kraków.

"Witek had a very difficult time under Martial Law," she said between mouthfuls of pizza. "He was a Solidarity organizer, and he was arrested and imprisoned for eight months." She tipped her head to one side and looked out of the window. "I don't think that was so bad for him, you know? All his friends were there. They were heroes of a sort, I think." She looked back to me, her pale, crystal-blue eyes sad. "No, it was afterwards, when the Communists fell." She shovelled some more salad out of her bowl. "When it all fell to pieces and we started to see Wałęsa as a power-hungry oaf and we had government after government. All the things Witek believed in . . ." she made a small, upward-twisting motion with her fork. ". . . gone." She gave a little sad smile and I wanted to hug her.

"He drank the bottle of Scotch I took for him," I said instead. "On the first night." I could hear myself whining but I couldn't stop myself. "On the second night he drank the bottle of brandy I took for Julia. Then he started shouting about the bastard English."

"He is very confused."

"He'd be a lot less bloody confused if he didn't drink so much."

She blinked mildly at me. "You are a very intolerant man, you know, Tim," she said without any force.

I sat back. "Oh, Sophie, I'm really sorry."

"I think we are all very confused now."

I couldn't be entirely sure who she was referring to. "I didn't mean to go on like that."

She smiled and nodded as if she actually understood *everything*; it was an extraordinary talent she had. "I think you just need a little more perspective, Tim," she said.

Perspective. OK. "Fancy a drink?"

Roger looked up as I walked in. "He's not to be disturbed," he said, nodding at the door to the back room.

"Come on, Roger, it's only me."

"He's busy," Roger insisted sadly, coming round the counter and walking up to me. "He says he's not to be disturbed."

I looked at the door. "Has he got Harry in there? Or is that classified information?"

Roger seemed to be struggling with this question when the door opened and Viren popped his head out. "Harry says go back to the office and do some work," he told me.

"I haven't got any work to do," I said.

From somewhere behind Viren, in the darkened depths of the back room, I heard Harry say, "Well *make* some bloody work to do then."

"Ah, the Lord and Master speaks," I said. "Hail, Lord and Master."

"Has he been drinking?" Harry muttered.

"He wants to know if you've been drinking," Viren said.

"I know—I heard him. No, I haven't been drinking because Sophie wouldn't come to the pub with me and anyway neither of us has very much money."

"You still have a couple of hundred quid of the money I gave you to go to Poland with," Harry called.

"I put that in the safe."

"Good. Now bugger off and let me work."

Viren's head withdrew and the door closed again.

I sighed. "Welcome home, Timothy," I said to Roger. I blew my nose.

"Yeah," Roger said. "Welcome home. You getting a cold?"

Back in the office and lost for anything to do, I went into the furthest room and sat down in Harry's worn leather swivel chair. The chair's swivel had rusted, and it took a large effort to get it to move more than an inch in either direction, but you had to be careful when you sat in it because one wrong move would tilt it backwards to the horizontal. The first time I used it I had been left flat on my back kicking my legs helplessly in the air, much to Sophie's amusement.

Harry's office had been done out in a style I called Early Chaos, a seemingly intractable mess out of which islands of stability had condensed, stacks of files and piles of videotapes rising out of the general rubbish on the floor. He had once asked Sophie to tidy it up and she had taken one look at it and told him to fuck off. I gazed around the office and wondered if he'd knocked a week's salary off her pay.

I sat back gingerly, clasped my hands across my stomach, and looked at the photos on the walls. If nothing else, I supposed I had picked up a working familiarity with the violence visited on London by the Luftwaffe. Here was a picture of a huge hole in the road, choked with rubble and beams, the Royal Exchange and the Bank of England in the background: Bank Junction, January 12 1941, the morning after a bomb collapsed the roof of the Tube station concourse under the road. Over a hundred dead, most of them blown off the platform and under an oncoming train by the blast. Here was St Clement Danes on fire, its tower burning like a huge chimney, the night of May 10, 1941. The wreckage in the Café de Paris the morning after a fifty-kilo bomb went through the Rialto Cinema above and exploded next to the bandstand. Thirty-four people dead, including Snakehips Johnson, the bandleader. March 9, 1941. Mrs Lewis was lucky she hadn't been there.

I sighed and started to poke around in the pile of correspondence which always seemed to be sitting on Harry's desk. Through the open door I could hear the IBM chattering and squealing as Sophie started to translate the manuscript I had brought back from Poland. Her typing was so fluent that she might have been typing up one of Harry's letters rather than translating.

Looking through the mail, I started to sort the bills and letters into two separate piles. The earliest bills looked dangerously old. All the envelopes had been opened, and the bills taken out and then stuffed back none too neatly. I pulled one out and read it. Then I pulled another one out.

"Sophie?" I called.

The noise of the IBM stopped. "Did you shout, Tim?"

I got up and walked to the door. Looking through the middle room of the office I could see her sitting at the typewriter. "I've just found two demands from that agency in Bermondsey," I said, holding up the bills.

She shrugged. "For what?"

"Fifteen photographs," I said, reading from the first bill. "No identification, just catalogue numbers. SW2143, SD9847 . . ."

"Oh, Christ." She got up and came through the office. "That's the Holborn Circus stuff. Didn't he pay that? How old is it?"

"About a month."

Sophie grabbed the letters from me and read them. She shook her head. "We'll all be in prison before he's finished."

"There's a stack of them about an inch thick on his desk." I wasn't sure why I was even bothering to be surprised.

She pushed past me and started to leaf through the bills, tutting and muttering to herself. "This has got beyond the joke, Tim. We have to get him to sort these out."

"Good luck."

Her jaw set. "No," she said firmly. "You will have to tell him."

"Why me?"

The phone on the desk started to beep. "Because you are a man."

"Oh, now wait a minute, Sophie . . ."

She shook her head. "He won't listen to me. You must do it."

"That's not—look, is one of us going to answer this thing?"

Sophie smiled and picked up the receiver. "Lonesome Charley Pro—oh, hello." She listened for a moment and I watched frown lines dig down between her eyebrows. "Why?" She looked at me. I was blowing my nose; I was starting to feel bunged-up and shitty. "Well, he's here; do you want to speak to him?" Pause. "Well, what are we supposed to do? Hello? Hello?" She took the receiver from her ear, looked at it for a moment, then hung up.

"What was all that about?" I asked.

She sat down in the swivel chair and looked around the office. "That was Harry," she said. "He won't be back for a few days. He's going to Poland."

"He's what?"

"He says he's going to Poland today."

I thought of my train journey. "*How?*"

She shook her head. "He says you're in charge."

"Good grief." I was still trying to get my head around the concept of Harry Dean leaving the country of his own volition. It was amazing. Harry hated going much further out of central London than Swiss Cottage.

"He says I'm to do whatever you tell me," she said, looking up at me.

As it started to sink in, I felt a smile pull at the corners of my mouth. I felt it become a wide grin. I always suspected I might be power-mad.

2

I was tempted to start the next day late, mostly because I was still worn out after the train journey and my cold was getting worse, and partly because it was one of the privileges of being the boss. But I was determined to use my time in charge to try and sort out the financial mess Harry had got the company into.

Sophie must have had the same idea, because when I arrived at the office at five to nine she was already there.

"The percolator's broken again," she said.

"The percolator is expendable," I said, hanging my jacket on the coat rack. I thought it was a suitably tough boss-like thing to say.

"So I bought you one from the sandwich shop," she said, reaching into a paper bag on her desk and bringing out a big styrofoam cup.

"I wonder if Harry would mind if I gave you a raise while he's away," I said, taking the lid off the cup. The coffee was still steaming hot; when I bought coffee from the sandwich bar it was always lukewarm by the time I got it to the top of the stairs.

Sophie smiled. "I think you're going to be spending enough of Harry's money without giving me a raise. I got you a Danish, too."

"When all this is over, will you come and be my secretary?"

"You couldn't afford me. Shall we do some work?"

"Love to."

"And I'm not a secretary. I'm a researcher for a Leading Independent Filmmaker."

"Will you come and be my researcher then?"

"You still couldn't afford me."

Over coffee and pastries we sorted through the mess on Harry's desk. As we dug down towards the desktop my heart began to sink. Things were a lot worse than I had thought; I kept expecting to open an envelope and find a writ or a county court order inside. Over the months with Lonesome Charley I had managed to forget that not everyone had Martin and Bob's sense of humour.

"I can't believe this," Sophie said, putting another invoice on the "urgent" pile. "How does he keep getting away with it?"

"Animal magnetism?" I looked gloomily at the piles of bills and invoices. One was for stuff that couldn't wait, one was for stuff that could wait a little while if copious apologies were offered, and one was for stuff that could wait until Harry got back. "We'll have to take all of this over from now on, you realize."

"That's probably what he wants."

I was pretty sure that was exactly what Harry wanted, but we went on anyway. The "urgent" pile grew so tall I called a halt and we went out for a pub lunch.

In the afternoon, while Sophie worked on the translation, I went through the urgent bills again, subdividing them into simply urgent and extremely urgent. The simply urgent ones could wait until tomorrow.

We split the extremely urgent bills between us and, armed with *A to Z*s and the company chequebooks, we went out to make some people happy.

3

"That was a very bad day," Sophie said the next morning, stirring hot water into a mug of Lem-Sip. The percolator appeared to be, finally, unrepairable, and she'd brought in an electric kettle so we didn't have to keep going downstairs for coffee. "Harry should be ashamed of himself."

I sneezed. "Why the hell has he gone to Poland?"

She handed me the mug. "I have no idea, but it's a good thing he did, otherwise all those bills would still be unpaid."

"Mm." I took a sip of the drink. "How are the accounts?"

"We should be OK," she said, checking her filofax. "The grants are due in tomorrow. Drink that while it's hot, or it won't do you any good. How was your afternoon?"

I took a big gulp of Lem-Sip. It scalded the back of my throat. "There are a lot of people out there who do not think very highly of Harry Dean," I managed to say.

Sophie picked up the not-so-urgent bills and leafed through them. "There is at least one person in here who feels the same way," she said. "Same thing today?"

I nodded. And later I was going to have to telephone all the creditors outside London and promise them that cheques were on the way. I was really looking forward to that.

"You look awful."

"Thank you." I blew my nose.

A gust of wind pattered rain on the window. "You shouldn't go out today."

I shook my head. "I want to enjoy my time as boss as much as I can." I'd already spent twenty minutes at Oakleigh Park station in the rain waiting for the train this morning. If there was damage to be done, it was done. "Did you get Danishes this morning?"

She reached into the bag beside her chair. "Bagels."

I was actually starting to get into this. Considering I'd never done anything like it before, it all seemed pretty straightforward. How much harder could it be to run ICI or General Motors? Of course, I hadn't advanced the progress of the film by any significant amount, unless you counted keeping Harry out of court as advancing the progress of the film.

There weren't as many not-so-urgent bills as there had been urgent ones. We spent fifteen minutes with the *A to Z*, divided the bills so we would be working towards each other from opposite ends of the city, and went our separate ways at Russell Square Tube station.

It worked. There really was nothing to it. At one o'clock I was standing outside the Virgin Megastore at Marble Arch, and five minutes later Sophie came out of the Tube station.

"You look pleased with yourself," she said.

"I can't understand why people make business out to be so complicated," I said. "All it takes is a little planning and common sense."

She gave me a hug, and my heart leapt. "You're lucky," she said. "I'm not a typical Pole. Poles have a sort of abstract view of time; if I was a typical Pole you'd still have been waiting for me at three."

I returned the hug. "Well, thank God you're not a typical Pole, then."

She moved away and blinked up at me. "Is the boss going to buy me lunch?"

I elected to do something impulsive, and kissed her on the end of the nose. "The boss is going to buy you lunch. What's more, the boss is going to pay for it from the piss-poor salary *his* boss pays *him*."

Over lunch at the Strand Palace we compared notes. All the most pressing bills had been paid, and the bulk of the less pressing creditors had been mollified.

"I'd call that a good morning's work," I said over coffee.

"Of course, it's only taken us two days," said Sophie.

"Ah." I waved my pen at her filofax. "But that's because there was so much to do. From now on, we can do it all by post."

She made a sour face. "I hate grovelling to people." She raised her eyebrows. "Was it correct, 'grovelling'?"

I nodded. "'Grovelling' about covers it, yes."

We had both done more than our fair share of "grovelling" that morning, first to the people who had to be paid, then to the people we could get away with just promising payment to, and by and large it had worked, though I'd had a couple of itchy moments with Ron Booth, the rostrum cameraman Harry had put on a retainer in order to have him available at a moment's notice.

Ron had been twiddling his thumbs for weeks, turning down other offers of work, waiting for Harry to make use of him, and he was starting to get anxious. He calmed down when I told him there would be no rostrum work for the next fortnight and he could take whatever offers came his way until then. I slipped him fifty quid to keep him interested.

"I think we work very well together," Sophie said. "What do you think?"

I lifted my coffee cup in a toast. "Harry doesn't deserve us."

Eleven

1

On Thursday, to celebrate our success in rescuing Harry from debtors' prison, I declared a half-day's holiday and invited Sophie for a walk round Highgate Cemetery.

"You romantic bastard," she said.

It started to drizzle as we reached the Cemetery gates. She slipped her arm through mine and we walked along under her hideous paisley-pattern golf umbrella.

"Are you sure you'll be all right in this rain?" she asked.

"I'll live," I told her.

"I don't want your cold to get any worse."

My nose was bunged up, my eyes felt gritty, and my sinusitis had reached the point where I felt as if I had a little pebble under each cheekbone. If I'd had any sense I wouldn't have been there at all. "I don't think it *could* get too much worse," I said. "Come on—I've got something to show you."

I'd been there before, so I knew about the Polish graves near the entrance to the cemetery, but for Sophie it was a complete surprise, and we wandered about with her reading out loud the words on the polished black tombstones and softly calling out names that ended in "-ski", "-ska" or unlikely combinations of the letters "c", "z" and "s".

"I never understood why there were so many Poles here," I said when we were walking along one of the paths between wet, overgrown bushes.

"They couldn't be buried at home," she said.

"Why not?"

She gave me a long-suffering look. "Oh, really, Tim."

I shrugged. "I'll take your word for it."

"They didn't truly have anything to do with Poland, anyway."

"What?"

"Expatriates never dream of their own country," she said, looking from left to right. "They always dream of the country they remember, and they never remember the truth."

"Did somebody say that?"

She laughed. "The old boys and girls, they dream of Poland before the war, not *my* Poland. They want things back the way they were. Your grandmother was the same, I'll bet."

It was true, as it happened. Gran used to bore me rigid with stories of her childhood in Lwów, before Stalin uprooted the ethnic Polish population of the Ukraine and shipped them west to Silesia. "We had estates, before the war. Servants, horses, a big house. Gran never stopped talking about it."

"Exactly," said Sophie. "The riot police used to put dye in the water they used for the water-cannons, you know, so they could identify demonstrators later. It took days to come off your skin. A friend of mine and I were soaked in Gdańsk in 1985; we were younger than you are, just went to the demonstration for fun. We didn't dare come out of her flat for a fortnight. We scrubbed ourselves raw trying to get the dye off. We had to burn our clothes." She jerked a thumb behind us. "And those old folks were dreaming of galloping through the forests and across the fields like something out of a Sienkiewicz novel." She shook her head sadly. "You have no idea, Tim."

It struck me as a very cruel thing to say about people who had been exiled, through no fault of their own, from their homes, and had been unable to go back, even in death. My grandmother and my mother and my Uncle Peter had been exiled. So what if they had dreamed of an idealized Poland? Where was the harm in that?

"I lived through Communism, Tim," she said as if reading my mind. "I didn't have any choice."

"Neither did they," I said. "And you're here now, aren't you, rather than in Poland." I regretted it instantly. I'd never been quite so critical of her before, and I expected a sober, sad lecture on the vagaries of life. But instead her arm tightened around mine and she moved closer to me, as if she were suddenly feeling the cold.

We stopped at Marx's grave. It was the thing I'd meant to show her in the first place. I had a vague idea she might feel like dancing on it, but all she did was nod.

"He always expected the revolution to happen in Germany," I said, staring at the oddly proportioned bust on top of the tomb. "Must have given him the shock of his life when it happened in Russia instead."

She nudged me. "Idiot. He was dead by then."

"Oh."

"Anyway," she said, turning and walking away, "we can't be sure he's really under there, can we?"

We walked back through the Village and down past Highgate station towards Muswell Hill. The drizzle had stopped and the sun was trying to come through and, emboldened by the improvement in the weather, I offered to cook dinner. I regretted it as I said it because I suddenly remembered neither Eric nor myself had bothered to do the shopping recently and there was hardly any food in the house. Sophie decided to be perverse and not make a polite excuse.

"I love these places," she said.

"Pardon?" I was trying to keep the trolley moving in a straight line while the trolley was trying to go off at a tangent and mow down every pensioner in its path.

"Supermarkets." She waved a hand at the shelves on either side of us. "I love them."

"Mm. What do you fancy for dinner?"

"Oh, I don't know." She smiled at the shelves. I couldn't help noticing it was the same wonderful smile she used on me, on everyone. "What were you planning?"

I managed to crab the trolley into the fresh meat section. "I hadn't really thought about it."

Sophie came to an abrupt stop. When I tried to do the same the trolley wanted to go on to places unknown. "You invited me to dinner and you hadn't really thought about what to cook me?"

I got the trolley to stop and said, "Um."

She gave me a strongly disapproving look. "You're unbelievable, Tim," she said, and set off again.

"I know," I muttered, giving the trolley a shove to get it going. "I surprise myself sometimes."

She marched down the aisle, grabbing trays of meat and slinging them into the cart as I tried to keep up. I wasn't sure I could afford what she was buying, but it was hypnotic just watching her. She went through Tesco's like a small blonde cyclone, urgently beckoning me to follow and hurling produce into the trolley without bothering to check if it was behind her or not.

"If you haven't really thought about it," she said, "then I will cook for you."

"Fine," I said, intoxicated.

"Imbecile," she said. "Where is the sauerkraut?"

2

We finished one bottle of wine while whatever she was cooking was cooking.

"If you're going to invite a girl to dinner, you should at least have some idea of what you're going to cook," she said.

"I never expected you to say yes," I said.

"So why did you ask me?"

I shrugged.

Sophie shook her head. "Is it correct, 'bewilder'?"

"It's correct."

"You bewilder me, Tim."

"It's a gift."

Sophie pointed a finger at me. "It's a curse, Tim. It's not, what do you say, 'boyish charm'?"

"I'd always rationalized it that way," I said, a little disappointed.

She got up, went over to the cooker, and lifted the lid on Eric's largest cooking pot. The smell of cooking meat and sauerkraut filled the kitchen.

"It's not boyish charm," she said. "It's just an excuse to be disorganized. Harry does it too. He thinks it makes him charming."

"Well, maybe he's never tried it on me."

She snorted and said, "'Boyish charm'," again and poked a wooden spoon into the cooking pot.

Her cooking style was extraordinary. In order to produce one pot of food, she had managed to utilize every knife, fork, pot, pan and jug that we possessed; the kitchen looked as if a chef had come in and had a massive nervous breakdown. The sink was overflowing with dirty cutlery and plates, every surface was covered with torn clingfilm and polystyrene trays, and there were bits of sauerkraut everywhere. I thought she was being a little unfair calling Harry disorganized.

"Harry likes you, you know," she said, putting the lid back on the pot.

I stared. This was information worth doing the washing up for. "Not enough to pay my expenses," I said.

She came back and sat down opposite me. The table was littered with glasses and bits of husk from the pumpkin seeds she had bought at Tesco's and had been chewing all evening.

"Where is this Eric?" she asked.

"He's staying with his girlfriend tonight."

"Ah." She looked downcast. "But I wanted to meet your famous flatmate." She picked up the bottle of wine, looked at it, and put it back down. "This is empty."

"No problem." I took another bottle from the carrier bag on the floor, pulled the cork, and poured us each a glass. "I think Eric's about to get married."

"Mm?" She looked fascinated. "How do you know this?"

I shrugged. "I don't know. They've just started to look as if they're going to get married."

"Really?" She leaned forwards across the table, the stem of her wineglass clutched in her fist. "Is there a special look that English people get when they're going to get married?"

"No. Yes. Well," I shook my head. "I don't know. I've just got a feeling."

She sighed. "You will have to move."

"What?"

"When they get married. Eric won't want you here then, will he?"

I was fairly certain he didn't want me here now. "I suppose so. I hadn't really thought about it."

"Do you really think about anything, Tim?"

I took a sip of wine. "I think a lot about how Harry's screwing me."

She shook her head. "No, I don't mean that. You seem to just improvise. I've watched you: you don't make plans. You just let things happen to you and then you deal with them."

I hadn't noticed. "Is that a bad thing, necessarily?"

"I don't know. Don't you make plans?"

I thought about it, then I shook my head.

"Don't you think it's a way of evading responsibilities?"

"No."

"I mean"—she waved her glass at me—"you haven't thought about whether you will have to move when Eric gets married. You could plan for that now, but you haven't thought about it. You'll deal with it when it happens, not before."

"I don't see any point in worrying about it before it's happened, Sophie." I took another sip of wine. "I'm not even sure it's *going* to happen. Like I said, it's just a feeling." I looked out of the window. It was dark outside, and all I could see was my reflection in the glass. "However, I'm starting to feel edgy about it now."

Sophie reached out and touched my arm. "I don't think you're a bad man, Tim. I think you're just very young. You haven't had to face a lot of things or to plan your life yet."

I looked at her. I'd never before met anyone who was so openly, honestly and confusingly critical of me. I said, "I love you."

She nodded, completely unsurprised. "As a friend."

"No. I really love you."

"Ah." She looked at her glass. "You want to have sex with me."

I shook my head, desperately aware that I was making an immense fool of myself but unable to stop. "No, Sophie. I love you. I want to marry you, set up home with you. I want to be with you. Everything."

She smiled sadly at me. "I don't believe you."

I just sat staring at her. I could have expected her to laugh at me, to slap my face and storm out, even in my wildest dreams to throw herself at my feet and pledge her undying allegiance to my body, such as it was. The last thing I expected was that she wouldn't believe me.

She drained her glass and got up. "Come on, Tim," she said. "Let's eat."

The meal she had cooked for me was called *bigos*. I can't remember what it tasted like.

Twelve

1

I'd hoped Harry would phone on Friday morning, but the only things that happened on Friday morning were me waking up with a dreadful headache and a tickly cough and Viren coming into the office with a videotape. I sat him down in Harry's room and opened the office Scotch.

"You look terrible, old son," he said.

"Thank you, Viren."

"You know there's a lot of flu going about?"

I mopped my nose with my hankie. "Have you any idea why he's in Poland?" I asked.

Viren sipped his whisky and shook his head. "Not a clue. Sorry."

"Didn't he say *anything* to you?"

"He was watching that film you brought him." Harry used Viren's film-transferring gear as an unofficial screening-room for the bits of ciné film our searches turned up. "Then he just got up and started phoning travel agents. Then he phoned you. Then he left." He took the video out of his jacket pocket and put it on the desk. "I put it onto tape. Harry said I could hang onto the film a while longer. Tell him there aren't any splices."

"Fine." I picked up the tape. "No problem."

After Viren had gone I put the tape he'd brought into Harry's video machine, switched on Harry's television, sat in Harry's chair, poured myself another glass of Harry's whisky on medicinal grounds, and put my feet up on Harry's desk. Sod Harry. From the front office I could hear the sound of the IBM.

Sophie and I had finished our meal the night before and I had called a taxi to take her home. We had parted with a slightly strained formality but she had given me a strong, solid hug before going out to the cab.

I'd been dreading coming in this morning, but Sophie was behaving as if nothing had happened. I'd arrived to find her at her desk, with coffee and a Danish ready for me. I felt young and ill and irrecoverably stupid.

The screen filled with a familiar scene. A huge hole in the middle of the road choked with rubble and girders, policemen and ARP workers swarming all over the place. Bank Junction, the morning of January 12, 1941. The camera panned across the façade of the Royal Exchange, with a huge DIG FOR VICTORY banner stretched across the middle six columns, then back to focus on the crater.

The scene changed. Bank Junction again, but this time before the bomb. Cars and open-topped buses with curving stairs leading to the top deck went past the Bank of England and up Threadneedle Street and Cornhill. He must have been standing on the corner of Princes Street and Poultry when he was filming this. City gents crossed the screen: pinstripes and wing collars, bowlers and rolled umbrellas.

I thought people actually *looked* different in those days. Not just a question of dress but actual physical differences. I'd watched dozens of bits of documentary film from the early 'forties, and the people never actually looked quite real.

Another cut. Back to January 12. Nobody seemed to know what to do: they were just walking around the crater. Some men in overalls were moving smaller bits of rubble and shattered roadway. A little crane was standing idle at the edge of the shot. Mr Sierpiński was standing on the corner of Poultry and Princes Street again. I was mildly surprised that no one was moving to stop him filming; the more explicit photos of the disaster had been suppressed at the time, the death toll revised downward, in order not to damage morale. That had happened a lot.

Bank Junction before the bomb again. There was a chaotic traffic jam of buses, cars and horse-drawn wagons in the middle of the crossing. Men on bicycles weaved through the traffic.

Mr Sierpiński crossed the bottom of Poultry, moving between the vehicles. He walked over Victoria Street and then on towards the Mansion House. His camerawork was pretty good, hardly jerky at all, though the film quality was streaked and grainy. Viren's transfer to tape was extremely good. He'd managed to match the camera's film speed exactly so the people weren't stiff-legging around too quickly. It was a shame Harry never paid him; he went up to the shop with the intention of handing over the cash, but all the two of them ever did was retire into the back room to watch old newsreels and smoke dope.

January 12 again. Or maybe it was the 13th now; the weather had changed, a drizzle was coming down. More than a drizzle—the façade of the Bank of England was dripping. The viewpoint crossed the road again, just like in the previous shot, then walked down Cornhill and onto Bishopsgate.

Another cut to the pre-bomb junction. Mr Sierpiński carried the camera across Princes Street and walked a little way along Threadneedle Street. The camera stopped moving and a newspaper came into shot from below. It stayed in shot for a moment, then moved away again.

I picked up the remote control and wound the tape back. I ran it forwards until the paper appeared, then paused it. The paper was a copy of *The Times* dated February 2, 1941. I wound the tape back and ran it again. Bank Crossing hadn't looked like that on February 2. On February 2 there had been a bloody huge hole in the road.

I took my feet down off the desk and sat forward. Viren had said there were no splices on the film. This was the film as it had been shot. Bomb damage, no bomb damage, bomb damage, no bomb damage. No splices, no editing. In chronological order . . .

"Tim?"

I looked up. Sophie was standing in the doorway, holding a sheaf of typewritten pages, and I knew it was the translation of Mr Sierpiński's manuscript. I said, "It's—" and the phone rang.

"There's something wrong with that bloke Witek," Harry said. He handed Sophie a carrier bag. "Are you sure it's legal to bring that stuff through Customs?"

She looked inside the bag. "It's only kabanos and stuff, Harry. It's cooked meat. Don't worry about it."

"How on earth did you get there?" I asked.

"Lufthansa to Frankfurt, LOT to Warsaw, train to Szczecin," he said with a matter-of-factness I didn't usually connect with Harry and travel. "Get out of my chair."

I got up and walked around the desk. "You went to see Mr Sierpiński, didn't you?"

He was rummaging in his duffel coat, patting the pockets. "I think I left my passport in the taxi," he said, which was more in character. "Yes, I went to see the old boy. Do you know what he told me?"

"He told you that I wouldn't have bought the film if he'd let me see it first."

Harry smiled at me as if I were a dim student who had just learned a new lesson. "He says he visited the site of the Bank Junction bomb on eight separate occasions after January 12, and on four of them the bomb hadn't fallen yet." He went and sat behind his desk and grinned at us. "What does that tell us?"

"I don't know," I said.

"I do," said Sophie, who had read the manuscript.

Harry sent Sophie to the bank to put the original of the manuscript into a deposit box, and me to Prontoprint to run off half a dozen copies of the translation. He went up the Tottenham Court Road himself to get the film back from Viren and have a couple of copies made of the video.

When I got back the office was empty. It was half-past five. I took one of the photocopies for myself, put the rest in the safe, and went home.

2

I made myself a large hot lemon and whisky, filled a hot-water bottle, and took myself to bed with the manuscript, dropping each page on the floor after I'd read it.

After the war, unlike the Government in Exile, Mr Sierpiński didn't remain in England—didn't stay far away and dream of a long-ago, unreal Poland. He went home, which was actually a pretty brave thing to do in those early days of Poland's Communist occupation. He outlived Stalin and Kruschev, Brezhnev and Andropov, Chernenko and the Cold War and the Soviet Union. He had learned a great Secret in London, according to his manuscript. The past, as someone once said, is a foreign country. And just as with a foreign country, Mr Sierpiński said, under the right circumstances you can go there.

He went to Bank Junction eight times between January and March 1941, and four times he found the place unmarked, as if the bomb had never fallen. Three times he seemed to have arrived the morning after the bomb.

At first he thought he was going crazy, but as he visited and revisited the disaster he started to formulate a theory.

He had an interesting view of time, did Mr Sierpiński. He saw spacetime as an infinite strip of ciné film, which stayed still as the lens—the present—moved along it.

He believed that under certain circumstances—certain violent circumstances—the lens was somehow induced to strip a layer off the film, curl it up like a wood-shaving, and carry it along with it. Each curl represented a violent event, carried along with the present, repeating over and over again but separate from the main body of the film strip.

Mr Sierpiński likened it to villages on a road. You drive past a village and it's behind you, but that doesn't mean the village has ceased to exist. You can always drive back down the road and the village will still be there, the houses unchanged. That was the past as Mr Sierpiński conceived it. Little villages. Little villages created by acts of extraordinary violence.

I was starting to see how I'd been set up in Poland, and why. If Mr Sierpiński had told me all this in Stargard Szczeciński I would just have turned round and come home, and if I hadn't been kept waiting for so long I would probably have asked to see the film before buying it. There had been no "pneumonia", just a ploy to get me to buy the film sight-unseen. He'd been afraid I wouldn't buy it otherwise, and he'd been right.

I made another hot toddy and returned to the manuscript. I switched on the clock-radio beside the bed. There was a jazz show on GLR; I turned it down low for background and read on.

Mr Sierpiński found other villages. On March 3, 1941, he found one at Moorgate: the night of December 29, 1940, when the Tube station had been completely gutted and the buildings surrounding it devastated.

The villages were everywhere; he stumbled over them without even wanting to. On an evening in August 1941 he found himself watching fire-brigade teams attending the bomb which had blown out part of the front of the Old Bailey at midnight on May 10.

I dropped page after page on the floor; there was a pile half an inch deep and almost a yard across by the bed now. With every one that floated down to the floor I became more and more miserable. I had spent a huge amount of Harry's money on some sophisticated con-trick, on a faked-up bit of film and the manuscript to a bad science-fiction novel that Mr Sierpiński had written to fool money out of naïve Englishmen. I'd been made an idiot of, but I kept reading anyway.

It wasn't really time travel, Mr Sierpiński argued. Rather, the villages were areas in which specific events happened over and over again, independent of outside time, which continued as normal. He went back and filmed all the ones he could find. He wrote that he usually started with a copy of that day's *Times* in front of the camera to establish the day's date, and then went on to film the event. Sometimes he went back time after time to film the same event.

He made absolutely no attempt to keep his discovery secret. He told everyone. His landlady, his friends, policemen. He wrote to *The Times*, to the Prime Minister. Not a soul believed him, but he made enough of a nuisance of himself to be arrested and interned at a prison in Nottinghamshire, where he stayed until the war was over. His films were impounded, and all but one vanished during their time in storage.

It was almost two in the morning when I dropped the final page over the side of the bed and lay back against the pillows. I'd had four or five hefty toddies, and that and the cold made me feel drifty and not-quite-there. The jazz show had long since finished, and the World Service programme which had replaced it sounded as if it was coming through from a distant star.

When I woke up the next morning the radio was playing light rock music and chat and I felt as if I had been soundly beaten.

It got worse. By Monday my muscles ached and my joints hurt and I was wandering around the house as if I were a thousand years old.

"It's flu," I told Harry over the phone.

"You looked a bit peaky on Friday," he agreed. "How many copies of that translation did you do?"

"Six, just like you told me."

"There's only five here."

"I brought one home to read. I was curious, is that all right?"

"Oh yes, fine. Fine."

"What are you going to do about it?"

"I haven't decided just yet," he said. "But I'll think of something. Don't worry."

"I'm really sorry, Harry."

"What about?"

"This whole sodding mess. The film, the manuscript. The old bastard ripped me off. I should have asked to see the film first. You've already *got* footage of Bank Junction."

There was a short pause and then Harry said, "I suppose so."

"Look, you can take the money out of my salary. I'll pay you back twenty pounds a week." I couldn't stop. On Friday night, delirious with flu and pissed out of my mind on hot toddies, I had drifted between believing everything in the manuscript and dreadful embarrassment at being conned by my mother's countrymen. This morning, I was sure I'd made a terrible mistake. Lonesome Charley didn't have the money to waste on con-men.

"Don't worry about it," Harry said.

"Thirty pounds a week," I said. "I'll do everything you tell me and I won't talk back. I promise."

"I told you, don't worry," Harry assured me. "Just get better. Keep warm and drink plenty of fluids. I'll see you later. We'll talk about it then."

"OK. Right."

3

It was Thursday before I felt well enough to go in to the office. I was the first one there. I sorted through the post, made a mug of tea and took a couple of aspirins.

That took me up to eleven o'clock. I got up and paced from window to window. Outside, snow was starting to drift down out of a yellow-grey sky. I went back to my desk and read the *Independent*. At twelve I rang Harry's home number and got no answer. I rang Sophie and got her answering machine. I rang Viren's shop, only to be told by Roger that Viren was in bed with the flu.

At one, I got a bus down to Holborn and had lunch in the Burger King by Chancery Lane station. Then I got a bus back up to the Tottenham Court Road and did a tour of all the record stores on Oxford Street.

It was almost four by the time I got back to the office. My feet hurt. There was still nobody there. I sat about twiddling my thumbs for another twenty minutes, then I went home.

Friday was more of the same. I phoned Harry and Sophie again and got no answer. I dug the script of the film out of its filing cabinet and spent the morning reading through it, mentally cutting in rostrum shots and ciné footage. I made some notes but my heart wasn't in it.

At lunchtime I walked along to Marble Arch and caught a bus up to St John's Wood.

Harry lived in one of the huge pre-war blocks of flats on Wellington Road, just beyond Lord's. I pressed his entryphone button but there was no answer. Two Arab women, covered from head to ground in black cloth, came out of the front doors as I was pressing the button again, and I nipped inside before the doors had time to swing shut.

The foyer was carpeted in green and gold; a marble staircase with a brass banister doglegged up to higher floors. I took the steps two at a time.

Harry lived on the sixth floor. I leaned on his doorbell, to no avail. I started to hammer on the door, but only succeeded in bringing Harry's neighbour, an Iranian property developer, out of his flat down the hall.

"It's only me, Mr Pahlavi," I said.

He peered myopically at me. "You were here before, yes?"

"That's right. I brought Mr Dean some files one evening." Files which Harry had told me were urgent but which he promptly lost. He found them a week later under his sofa.

Mr Pahlavi came along the hall towards me. He was in his fifties and starting to go to fat, but he was immaculately barbered, manicured and tailored. He was always smiling, as if the world were a continual delight to him.

"Tim," he said. "Yes. That's you. Tim."

We shook hands. I said, "Have you seen Harry recently, Mr Pahlavi?"

He thought about it for a moment, then shrugged and shook his head. "Is there a problem?"

"No, I don't think so." I looked at the door. "It's just that he hasn't been in the office for a few days."

"Perhaps he has taken a business trip?"

"He never mentioned anything," I said. Of course, he hadn't mentioned his trip to Poland until he was already on his way. "Do you remember when you saw him last?"

He looked up at the ceiling, as if he'd jotted a memo to himself there. "Tuesday. I saw him on Tuesday."

"You're sure?"

"Yes. It was the day I came back from Paris; we passed each other downstairs, me coming in, him going out." He looked thoughtful. "Do you know, perhaps he *has* gone on a business trip."

"Why?"

"He had his suitcase with him."

"Suitcase."

"Yes. I made a joke with him; me coming home with my suitcase, him leaving with his. I'm so sorry. I really should have remembered right away, but I have been so busy this week."

"That's all right. Really. Could you do me a favour?"

"But of course."

"If you see Harry before I do, could you get him to phone me? Doesn't matter what time it is. I really should speak to him soon."

He nodded enthusiastically. "Absolutely. No problem. Now, will you have some tea with me?"

I thought about it, but I shook my head. "It's very kind of you, Mr Pahlavi, but I have someone else to see. Maybe another time."

I went back downstairs and pushed open the door. Outside was a bright, cool, breezy autumn day. I stood on the pavement watching the traffic heading up towards Swiss Cottage, wondering where the hell Harry had been going on Tuesday with his suitcase. I flagged down a taxi. If Harry wasn't here, he couldn't very well complain about me using the petty cash.

"No," Roger said.

"Come on, Rog, it's really important."

He shook his head. "I'm not to give his address or phone number to anybody."

"Yes, but that's just in case the VAT inspectors come round. This is me, Roger. Tim. Remember me? Cheerful dogsbody and general factotum to Lonesome Charley Productions?"

We were standing in the middle of the shop arguing in loud voices. Three customers were wandering about looking at the equipment as if nothing out of the ordinary was going on. Maybe this was a normal occurrence in Viren's shop.

Roger started to look even more unhappy than usual. I was driving him slowly and steadily into a corner. "But he told me never to give his address or phone number to anybody," he said with an edge of desperation in his voice. "He'll have me back on the dole if I give you them."

"Harry's gone missing," I pressed. "I need to know if he told Viren where he was going."

"Viren's got flu, Tim," he told me for the third or fourth time. "He's in bed."

"I just need to talk to him for five minutes. Five minutes, that's all."

"You've had flu," he said. "Did you want people phoning you all the time when you had flu?"

I shrugged. "I wouldn't have minded," I said. "Much."

"Well, Viren *will* mind. He'll be really rude to you, then he'll fire me."

"When's he due back?"

"Not for another week, at least."

His face had set in a look of determination I hadn't seen before. I hadn't suspected that Roger was capable of such stubbornness. "Have you seen Harry recently, then?"

He relaxed, obviously pleased I wasn't needling him any more. "He was in on Tuesday."

"Tuesday."

"Yeah. Tuesday. About eleven."

"Did he talk to Viren?"

The mention of his boss's name made Roger defensive again. "Of course he talked to Viren. He didn't come here to talk to me, did he?"

"Did he have anything with him?"

Roger gave me a suspicious look, as if he thought it was a trick question. "Like what?" he asked carefully.

"Roger," I said, trying very hard not to get irritated, "was Harry carrying anything?"

He watched the customers fiddling with the stock while he thought. "Yeah," he said finally. "He had a suitcase."

Back at the office, I sat and stared at the phone wondering exactly how long I should wait before I started to panic. If Harry had done a runner for some reason, I should probably be trying to deal with it right now. On the other hand, if he'd simply buggered off on another spur-of-the-moment excursion I should just sit tight and keep things ticking over until he decided to come back. For all I knew, Harry's trip to Poland had given him the wanderlust. I didn't know what to do, so in lieu of doing something I locked up early and went home.

I tried Sophie's number again when I got there, but there was no reply. I made myself an omelette and a mug of tea and sat in the kitchen eating and reading a months-old issue of *Viz*. The house was very quiet without Eric and Lisa, but I knew they weren't going to put up with me for much longer. Eric and I hardly spoke to each other any more and Lisa and I only interacted by being rude to each other, which was a pity because I could really have used some advice.

I left my plate and the frying pan in the sink and went into the hall. I took the phone off the hall table and sat down at the bottom of the stairs with it in my lap. I pressed the redial button.

Five o'clock came and went. I made myself another mug of tea and returned to the phone and the redial button. I timed myself. I pushed the button every fifteen minutes, let the phone at the other end ring until the answering machine cut in, hung up, and every hour on the hour I made myself some more tea. It was sort of refreshing not to have to think about anything but tea and the telephone.

Eric came home at five past seven. He looked at me for about a minute, and for a fraction of a second I thought he was going to say something, even if only to complain about me hogging the phone, but he just shook his head and went into his room. I checked my watch and pressed the redial again, and this time someone picked Sophie's phone up.

"Hello?"

I was so surprised I was almost struck speechless. "Um . . ."

"Hello? Who is it?"

"Er . . . is Sophie there?"

"Who is that?"

"My name's Tim Ramsay. I work with Sophie."

"Oh, right." She laughed. "You're the one that loves her, right?"

I hung up.

Eric came out of his room, pushed past me, and went wordlessly up the stairs to the bathroom. I stared at the front door. The top half was an abstract design in stained glass, leaded in just like a church window. One of the smallest pieces was cracked. I'd never noticed it before. I heard the toilet flush upstairs. I pressed the redial again. The phone at the other end rang once before it was picked up.

"I can't believe she told you," I said.

"You poor soul," she said. "Is life more complicated than you expected?"

"Did you have a good giggle about it?"

"Actually, she was up half the night in tears."

I looked at the phone, the cracked piece of glass in the door. Eric came back downstairs, went into his room, closed the door.

"Is she there?" I asked.

There was silence on the other end. Then she said, "My name's Joanne."

"Is Sophie there, Joanne?"

"I haven't seen her since Tuesday."

I took a deep breath. "Did she have a suitcase or something the last time you saw her, Joanne?"

Silence.

"Do you know where she's gone?" I asked.

"She didn't say," said Joanne.

"And you're not worried about her?"

"Sophie's old enough to take care of herself."

"Did she tell you where she was going?"

Silence.

"Thank you, Joanne." I hung up.

On Monday I called the police and reported Harry and Sophie missing.

Thirteen

1

I thought the trees outside the office were dying. They'd looked scrawny and dirty and ridiculous without their leaves when I came back from Poland, but now they actually looked terminally ill. I stood on the pavement outside the sandwich bar and looked at them, wondering if I should call the council and then wondering why I thought it mattered.

A cold wind blasted across Bloomsbury, shaking the bare branches. I shivered, turned away, and opened the front door.

Harry and Sophie had been gone for a week and it was the first time I'd been back to the office since reporting them missing. The place hadn't tidied itself up in my absence. As I went through to Harry's room I kicked a folder off the floor and bits of paper went everywhere.

There had been a little pile of mail stacked neatly at the bottom of the stairs, collected by the tenant of the ground-floor offices. I sat in Harry's chair and sorted through it. Bills, invoices, junk mail, more bills. I dropped it on the desk and put my face in my hands.

"Mr Ramsay?"

I looked up. Standing in the doorway was a man in his seventies or eighties, wearing one of those cheap translucent grey plastic raincoats you can fold up and put in your pocket. He had coped with baldness by combing long strands of hair from one side of his head to the other, but the wind had undone all that and now what remained of his hair hung mournfully from just above his right ear and draped over his shoulder.

"Mortimer," he said. "We spoke on the telephone."

"Oh. Right." I got up and went round the desk to shake hands with him. His hand was limp and damp, and there was a powerful aura of aniseed about him. "You're Harry's accountant," I said.

He lowered his eyes in bashful acknowledgement. "And also his legal adviser." There were little white bits of scurf in his eyelashes, and I noticed that his morning shave had missed his throat.

"Right. Would you like a cup of coffee?"

"Wouldn't have anything stronger would you, old chap?" he asked hopefully, sweeping his hair back over his bare scalp.

I went back behind the desk and took the office Scotch from its drawer. I poured him a glass and went back into the front office for one of the tins of Coke Sophie kept in her desk. When I got back, Mortimer had already finished his whisky and was pouring himself another.

"You said you'd heard from Harry," I said, sitting down.

"Well, not in so many words." He emptied his glass in one swallow and blinked at me. The whites of his eyes were the colour of old piano keys. Under the raincoat he was wearing a greasy blue pinstripe suit so creased he appeared to have slept in it, and under that a threadbare blue jumper tucked into his trousers. He looked the way I always imagined Francis Bacon's Soho drinking buddies looking. Considering the state of Harry's business affairs, I had been astounded to discover he had an accountant, but I should have known that it would be a Lonesome Charley-style accountant.

I sighed and opened my Coke. "If you're worried about your job, Mr Mortimer, I'm sorry but I don't think we can afford your services any longer."

He smiled and shook his head. "Have a proposal for you, actually, old boy." He started to pat his pockets.

"Beg pardon?"

"A proposal." He gave a little wheezy cough while still patting his pockets. "Something to your advantage."

"Have you lost something?" I said.

Mortimer shook his head. "No. Had it somewhere when I came out. Know I did. Ah." He reached into an inside pocket of his jacket and took out a crumpled folded envelope. "Here we are." He unfolded the envelope, opened the flap, and took out a couple of sheets of paper. "Yes. Here we are." He smoothed the papers flat on the desk, then he sat back and looked at me.

We sat looking at each other for quite a while. "What?" I said. "Oh. Right. Sorry." I poured him another drink; I'd got the impression he was quite capable of doing that on his own.

Mortimer took his glass, and this time he drank only half in one go. He put the glass back on the desk and said, "Ever run your own business?"

"Not unless you count keeping this place running when Harry buggered off to Poland," I said.

He nodded, took from his pocket a tobacco tin so old all the enamel had worn off, and started to roll himself a cigarette. "Enjoy it, did you?"

"Not conspicuously, no. What's going on? Are we in some kind of trouble?"

"Trouble? Oh my, no." He was spilling more tobacco than he was getting into his cigarette paper. He lifted it to his lips, wet the edge with his tongue, and rolled it shut. "No, no trouble."

I shook my head. "Look, Mr Mortimer, I'm sorry but I'm completely lost."

His cigarette was as thick as a pencil lead in the middle and about as fat as my little finger at each end. He put it in his mouth and lit it. Bits of burning tobacco snowed down into his lap. He ignored them. "You're to carry on running Lonesome Charley Productions."

I stared.

He nodded at the papers on the desk. "You're now sole director of Lonesome Charley Productions. Sole owner." He looked about him. "Sole employee." All of a sudden, he grinned at me.

"No," I said, appalled. "*No.*"

"All legal and above board. All signed and witnessed."

"I don't want it."

Mortimer shrugged. "Sorry, old lad. No choice in the matter, really."

I groaned and closed my eyes. When I opened them again Mortimer was pouring himself another drink. "I don't want it," I said again.

"Well, the simple fact is, you've got it. Yours to do with as you wish. Could even just roll the company up."

"All right. Fine. I'll do that, then."

"Of course, you'd be responsible for all the debts if you did that. Can you cover them?"

"No, of course I can't." Oh God. Without the company there would be no grants, no television money. I couldn't *begin* to pay off the creditors. The television people would want their investment back. "Was all this Harry's idea?"

Mortimer nodded.

"Jesus." Harry must have really hated me. "Mr Mortimer, I *can't.*"

"You said you did before."

"That was different."

"Oh? How?"

"Well, before, Harry had just gone away for a while. This . . ." I looked around the office and felt the walls starting to close in on me. "This is like a curse from beyond the grave."

Mortimer started to laugh, and the laugh became an alarming wheezing cough. He took out a filthy hankie and mopped his mouth. "Curse from beyond the grave," he said finally. "Terribly good."

"Do you know where he is?"

He shook his head.

"When did he do all this?"

"He came to see me on the 16th."

The 16th was the infamous Tuesday, the last day anyone had seen Harry or Sophie. It was starting to look as if the 16th had been a busy day for Harry.

I slumped back in the chair. "Why did he do it, Mr Mortimer?"

"Thought you were the best man for the job, clearly." He stood up. "Well, thanks for the drink, old chap. Must be off; more people to see." He held out his hand, and I stood up and shook it. He took a grubby card from his pocket and handed it to me. "Always about if you need me. Give me a ring."

I looked at the card. On it in smeary printing was the word, "Mortimer" and a phone number. I had a feeling it was probably the number of a pub.

After he'd gone, I sat staring around the office, at the mess of files, the photos on the walls, the scorch-topped safe that Harry had bought in a fire-damage sale.

"Oh God," I said finally.

2

"It's like a will," Eric said. "It's as if he died and left everything to you."

I stared at the sheets of paper on Eric's desk. "Don't I have to agree to it or something?"

Eric shook his head.

"Surely I had to have signed something?"

He shook his head again.

My shoulders slumped. "Isn't there *anything* I can do about it?"

He sighed and leaned back in his typing chair. The screen-saver program of his PC was drawing tiny little multicoloured spirals all over the screen, erasing them, and starting again. Some sheets of paper hung out of the laser printer on the desk beside the computer. I'd interrupted him in the middle of important corporate-clone business and he wasn't feeling inclined to be too patient with me.

"You could challenge it in court," he said.

"Which would cost money."

"It usually does, yes." He leaned forwards and took the sheets of paper out of the printer. He tapped their bottom edges on the desk to line them up, and laid them in a folder. "And courts are more used to people coming before them wanting something, not the other way round."

I watched the spirals uncurl and vanish, uncurl and vanish. It was rather soothing. Unfortunately, it wasn't nearly soothing enough.

"And then there's the question of your directorship," he said.

I looked up. "Harry just put that on the letterhead. You said he could do that."

"I also said it might get a bit slippery."

"Oh, thanks a fucking lot, Eric."

His mouth set in a line which told me I had just about exhausted his limited supply of tolerance.

"Sorry." I rubbed my eyes. "What about legal aid?"

"You probably don't qualify now. Look," he said, and I could see him summoning up what was left of his goodwill, "the only way out of this is to declare yourself bankrupt."

"But I'm not," I protested weakly.

"Precisely." He crossed his arms and regarded me with somewhat less than Christian charity. "Why don't you just go ahead and make the film?"

"*What?*"

He shrugged. "Harry gave you the company. Why don't you go ahead with it?"

"Don't be so stupid, Eric. I don't know the first thing about making a film. I'm just a researcher."

"So learn."

"So learn. Fine. You make it all sound so fucking easy."

"Isn't it?" He tipped his head to one side and looked at me. This was the first proper conversation we'd had in weeks, probably the first proper conversation since the party. I tried to think back to when it had all gone wrong. I seemed to remember everything being OK on the morning of the party, but afterwards our relationship had somehow swung into a different shape, and I couldn't work out how it had happened.

"Eric," I said.

"What?" He was looking at me the way a parent looks at an untidy child. Eric had Grown Up and I had been left behind, and here was the proof. His life was all on-line and perfect, and mine was a mess.

I shook my head. "Nothing."

"So can I get on with my work now?"

"Yes, Eric, you can get on with your work now." I stood up. "Far be it from me to interrupt your work."

"I didn't have to give you my advice," he reminded me.

"Send me the bill," I said and closed the door behind me, probably a little too energetically.

Outside, I stood in the hallway with my hands in my pockets and stared at the traffic cone, and I suddenly remembered that it was me who had picked it up at some roadworks near Oakleigh Park station and brought it home on my head, the night before my interview at Lonesome Charley. It was amazing. How do you forget something like walking through North London with a traffic cone on your head? I sighed and picked it up. It was about time it went into the wheely-bin outside.

As I opened the front door the phone started to ring. I stood in the doorway for a moment, but Eric didn't seem to be making any move to answer it. I closed the door, put down the cone, and picked up the receiver.

"I'll thank you not to terrorize my staff," said a croaky, bunged-up voice.

"Viren?"

"You really upset Roger, you know. He's not the quickest of lads, but he's got a good heart."

I carried the phone over to the stairs and sat down. "How are you?"

"I've been better. What's happened to Harry?"

"I was hoping you could tell me."

He sniffed. "No idea, old son. He never said a thing to me." There was a titanic sneeze on the other end of the line.

"Bless you."

"Thanks," he said thickly. "God, it just doesn't want to go away. I thought I'd be feeling better by now."

"I know; I was the same. Look, did you see Harry after he got back from Poland?"

"Sure. He came up to get that can of film you brought back."

Eric's door opened and he poked his head round, looked at me for a second, then went back inside. I said, "Roger told me he came to see you on the Tuesday after he got back."

"Yeah. 'Scuse me a second." I heard a thump as the phone at the other end was put down, then Viren blowing his nose. He picked up the phone again. "Sorry about that."

"Don't worry about it."

"Right. The Tuesday after he got back. He came into the shop about half-past one. Had a suitcase with him."

Busy Tuesday. Harry and his suitcase. "Didn't you ask him why he had a suitcase?"

"None of my business."

"Oh, *Viren*."

"Well, it's not, is it," he said defensively. "If Harry wants to sod off on holiday that's his affair, not mine."

"Holiday?" I sat up. "Did he say he was going on holiday?"

"Not in so many words, no."

I slumped back against the stairs again. "So what did he say?"

Viren sneezed again. "Christ," he muttered. "I'll have to get the phone disinfected."

"Come on, Viren. Please. I need to know. He's left the bloody business to me."

"He's *what*?"

"He did some sort of legal thing and now I own Lonesome Charley."

There was a stunned silence at the other end, whether because Harry had done something as final as willing the company away or because it had been willed to Tim the Office Boy, I couldn't tell.

"He said you'd be looking after things while he was away," Viren said finally. "He never said anything about it being permanent. Was he in some kind of trouble?"

I felt as if I were going around in a tight little circle. "I don't know, Viren. That's what I'm trying to find out. The business is in pretty good shape financially, I think," I lied.

"I'll get my accountant to call you first thing in the morning. He'll give the books the once-over."

"Viren, I can't—"

"It's OK. He owes me a favour. Won't cost you a thing."

I thought about it. It couldn't hurt to find out exactly what kind of financial mess I'd inherited. "Hey, it's not this Mortimer bloke, is it?"

"Harry used Mortimer? I didn't know."

"Is that bad? Should I worry about that?"

"Probably not." He thought about it. "Probably not, no. I'll get Ken to call you tomorrow."

"OK. Thanks. But you still haven't told me why Harry came to see you."

"Oh, yeah. He wanted a camcorder."

"A what?"

Another bout of sniffles, the sound of Viren mopping his nose with his hankie. "He wanted a camcorder. He thought I'd do him a discount."

That at least had the stamp of authenticity. "Did he say what he wanted it for?"

"Nope. Just said he wanted a camcorder and maybe I could knock a few quid off for old times' sake. Hello? Are you still there?"

"Yes. Sorry, Viren. I was thinking. Did you sell him one?"

"Of course I sold him one. Seven hundred quid's worth of crafty Jap technology and about a dozen cassettes. Paid me in cash."

Busy Tuesday. Harry with his suitcase and enough money to shell out seven hundred pounds in cash. "Anything else?"

"No. We had a chat about the weather, he looked at his watch and said he had to be off. That was the last I saw of him."

"You know Sophie's gone as well?"

"Yeah, I heard. Only ever met her a couple of times. Pretty girl."

"Mm. OK. Thanks for calling, Viren. I appreciate it."

"It's OK. I'll apologize to Roger for you, shall I?"

I smiled. "No, it's OK. I'll come up to the shop and do it myself."

There was a pause. "There's just one thing I'd like to ask, Tim," he said tentatively.

I'd been waiting for this. "How much do we owe you, Viren?" Harry had never, to my knowledge, paid Viren for the use of his transfer gear and his editing suite.

"Well, nothing." He sounded almost embarrassed. "Harry paid me the last time I saw him."

I felt my heart skip a beat. "How much?"

"Couple of grand. In cash."

"Jesus Christ." That sounded final. Harry wandering around London with his suitcase and enough cash to pay Viren almost three thousand pounds. Maybe the suitcase was just to carry it about in. "Didn't that make you the *tiniest* bit suspicious?" I asked.

He snorted. "He just said he thought it was time to settle up. Didn't bother to apologize for running up the bill in the first place, though." He coughed. "No, I was just wondering if you'd be carrying on with the film, that's all,"

The sixty-four-thousand dollar question. "I don't know yet, Viren. I really don't."

"Only, if you still want to use my gear, I'd appreciate it if you'd pay up front."

"Your confidence fills me with pride, Viren. I'll let you know. And thanks."

"Any time."

After we'd hung up I sat on the stairs thinking about Harry. I wondered if he'd paid any of his other debts on Busy Tuesday as well. I wondered where he'd got all that cash from all of a sudden. Maybe he'd saved it all by not paying my expenses

Eric's door opened again. He looked at me. "I forgot something," he said.

"Will I hate it?"

"It's just that if Harry reappears and wants the company back the two of you will probably have to go to court to get his will declared null and void."

Lovely. "Thanks for that, Eric."

"Any time," he said cheerfully, and went back into his room.

3

The next morning I sat down at Harry's desk and opened the folder that contained his script for the film. I stared at the top sheet with its list of names from the obit columns and wondered what he'd been playing at. The pile of notes in front of me were more like doodles than a real script. The tape he'd shown me had been the same. It had the half-finished look of something done by a man whose heart wasn't really in it, or a man who didn't quite know how to do it.

I pulled one of the desk drawers open and a pile of papers, suddenly not compressed any longer, bulged over the top and spilled on the floor. I swore and bent over to pick them up and somebody knocked on the door in the outer office.

"It's open!" I shouted, getting up and walking through the office, knocking file boxes and folders aside with my foot.

The door opened and an immaculately suited Japanese man looked in. "Tim Ramsay?"

"Yes?"

He looked at the handwritten sign on the door, then looked at me again. "I'm Ken." He dipped a hand into his waistcoat pocket and handed me a card. The card said, "Kenji Numata. Morse, Chandler & Numata, Accountants."

I looked at him and blinked. "You're Viren's accountant?"

He nodded. "He asked me to phone you, but I had a client to see on Goodge Street so I thought I'd come over while I was in the area." He had a broad Mancunian accent, much broader than my Midlands one.

"Oh," I said. "Right."

He looked at the doorway. "Perhaps I could . . .?"

"Sure. I'm sorry," I said, coming out of my daze. "Come on in, please."

Numata stepped into the office and looked about him. "Who does your interior design?"

"Entropy," I said miserably, aware of how pathetic the place looked.

He laughed. "Viren asked me to take a look at your books."

"Yes. Thanks for coming."

He looked at his watch. "I haven't got too long, though, so if you'd just show me to them I'll get on with it."

"You want to do them now?"

He smiled brightly at me. "I may as well, since I'm here."

I must have looked a complete idiot. "Right. OK. Sorry. I'm having a bad day." I waved a hand at Sophie's desk. "Try and clear yourself a space and I'll go and get them."

He nodded pleasantly and sat himself down and opened his briefcase. I went into Harry's room and took the company books out of the safe. By the time I got back with them Numata had piled most of the rubbish on the desk to one side and had arranged a little laptop, a pad and a pencil in front of him.

I handed over the books and said, "Is there anything else I can get you, Mr Numata?"

"Ken," he said, opening one of the books and looking at it. "A cup of coffee wouldn't go amiss." He smiled up at me.

"OK." I looked across at the dead coffee-maker on its table in the corner of the room. "I'll have to go downstairs for it. I was going to have a bite to eat; can I get you a Danish or something as well?"

He put the open book on the desk and bent over it. He shook his head. "No, coffee's fine. Black, no sugar, please."

I left him there and went down to Antonio's. I had to spend five minutes detailing for Antonio what I knew about Harry and Sophie's disappearance before he made me two coffees and let me have a croissant.

"He'll be back," he said as I left. "Good man, Mr Dean."

"I'm still trying to convince myself of that, Antonio," I said, "but thanks for the thought."

Back upstairs, Ken was reading through the accounts and tapping figures into his laptop. I put his coffee on the desk.

"Thanks," he said. "You had a call." He consulted his notepad. "Do you know a Mr Pahlavi?"

"Harry's neighbour. What did he want?"

"He says the police are at his flat and could you call him?" He looked up at me. "Mean anything to you?"

I shook my head. "God only knows. Thanks." I pulled up one of the upright chairs, sat down beside him and picked up the phone and dialled Mr Pahlavi's number.

He answered at the second ring. "Timothy? There are police in my flat."

"Oh." I couldn't work out why he thought it had anything to do with me. "Why?"

"They say they want my key to Mr Dean's flat."

I thought about that. "You've got a key to Harry's flat?"

"Yes. I feed his fish when he is away."

"Oh."

"He is very fond of his fish."

"Yes, I'm sure he is." All I could think of was how I could have searched Harry's flat days ago if I'd known about the key. "All right. Don't do anything until I get there. Tell the police I'm coming and don't let them into the flat until I arrive. OK?"

There was a moment's silence. "They seem very eager to get their work done," he said dubiously.

"I don't doubt it. I'm on my way. Tell them to be patient."

"Do you think that will work?"

"I'm sure it will. I won't be long." I hung up.

Ken, who had been working while I spoke to Mr Pahlavi, looked across at me. "Trouble?"

"I'm not sure. Look, I'll have to go out for a while. Will you be OK here on your own?"

He nodded. "I expect so."

I went back into Harry's room and got my coat from the back of the chair. "I don't know how long I'll be," I said, coming back into the front room. "If I'm not back when you've finished, just let yourself out. Give the door a good tug when you close it—the lock's a bit stiff."

He smiled. "No problem."

I looked down at the open account book. "How does it look so far?"

Ken looked at the book and his face became sad. "I think you need a new accountant."

Shit. That was all I needed. "Are you for hire?"

He gave the office a long analytical look, then he smiled and shook his head as if he'd just heard a mildly bad joke. "I'll leave my card. Give me a ring sometime this week and we can talk about it."

I opened one of the desk's drawers and took out the petty cash box. I took out fifteen quid to cover the cab fare to St John's Wood and back. God, I was getting to be a real wimp. Harry would have had a fit. I put the box back in the drawer. "OK. Just don't forget—"

"Give the door a good tug. Yes." He grinned at me. "Go on, I'll be OK."

I took the steps two at a time, going down.

4

At the front door of Harry's apartment building I pressed Mr Pahlavi's button on the entryphone. There was an electric crackle and the speaker grille made an incomprehensible sound.

"It's me, Mr Pahlavi," I said, leaning close to the grille.

It made another noise and the front door buzzed. I pulled it open and went inside.

On Harry's floor Mr Pahlavi was waiting miserably in the corridor with two detectives who didn't look much older than me but were considerably better-dressed. I knew one of them, a Detective Sergeant Page, because I'd given him my statement after I reported Harry and Sophie missing.

"Mr Ramsay," he said. "So nice of you to join us."

"You're a little late, aren't you, Sergeant?" I asked. "I'd have thought this would have been one of the first places you'd have looked."

The other detective said, "We've got other things to do as well, you know,"

Page grinned. "Mr Ramsay, this is Detective Sergeant Little. He doesn't have my sense of humour."

"I'm immune to bad-cop-good-cop," I warned him.

"Oh, I'm serious," he said, looking innocently taken aback. "He really doesn't have my sense of humour. Do you, Joe?"

Sergeant Little regarded me levelly and shook his head.

"Well." Sergeant Page rubbed his hands together. "Now we all know each other, could we go in, please?"

We all looked at Mr Pahlavi. He looked sad and embarrassed. He put a hand into his trouser pocket and took out a key. He handed it to Sergeant Little, who turned and unlocked the door to Harry's flat.

Page went first, then Little. Mr Pahlavi and I followed together. The door opened onto a short hallway, with a coat rack on one wall and a big wooden-framed mirror facing it on the other. The floor was of polished wood-block, and about half-way along there was a brightly coloured rug. At the far end of the hall was an arch-way. I walked down to it and stopped, amazed. I had half-expected Harry's flat to be as filthy and untidy as the office, but it was neat and clean, and it was *huge*.

The archway opened into a big bright living room with ceiling-high windows along the wall facing me. To my right, an immense sofa sat against the wall beneath a set of wooden cabinets. To my left the whole wall was bookcased, floor to ceiling. On the fifth shelf up from the floor were a big colour television and a video.

I stepped forward through the arch. The floor was in the same wood-block as the hall, and there were a couple more rugs. Beside me on an oak table was a complex-looking hi-fi. On the other side of the arch was a doorway, through which I could see the white and stainless-steel surfaces of Harry's kitchen.

"We don't appreciate being kept waiting, sir," said Sergeant Little as he walked along the bookshelves reading titles.

"I thought it was best to be here," I said. "In lieu of Mr Dean's solicitor."

Page grinned and said, "Old Mortimer, you mean?"

Little snorted. "We'd have to search this place at two in the morning to have any chance of getting him here."

"I've seen him up and about at ten o'clock," I said.

"That old bugger hasn't seen daylight in years," Little said.

"As God is my witness," I said.

Little shook his head, unconvinced.

The detectives continued to root about in cupboards and drawers. I wasn't sure what they expected to find, but I thought it must be part of the procedure in a missing-persons case. Perhaps they'd expected to open the door and find Harry sprawled on the carpet with a dagger in his back.

"The Residents' Committee will complain about this," Mr Pahlavi confided in a quiet voice. "Police searching a resident's flat. Implications of criminality."

"The Residents' Committee don't scare me," I said.

"You have never met them," he said. "Otherwise you would not say that."

By this time we were sitting side by side on Harry's huge settee. Six or seven people could have sprawled comfortably on it, but Mr Pahlavi and I were sitting knee-to-knee at one end watching the two policemen.

Next to the hi-fi was the enormous aquarium that Mr Pahlavi came in to look after, full of gorgeous tropical fish, scraps of startling colour drifting and darting through the water. They were the last thing I would have expected to see in Harry's flat.

I got up and wandered over to the aquarium and bent down to look through the glass. The fish were really exquisite. They must have cost a fortune.

"And Mr Dean said nothing to either of you about where he was going or when he might be back?" Page asked.

Mr Pahlavi and I shook heads in unison.

"You're sure it's not just an unscheduled business trip?"

"He would have told me," I said.

"Would he?"

"Yes, he would."

Detective Sergeant Page sighed and ran a hand through his blond hair. "Did he seem disturbed at all in the days leading up to his disappearance?"

"I've already been asked all this," I said. "You're the one who asked me."

He shrugged.

I rubbed my eyes. "I had flu. I didn't see him in the days leading up to his disappearance. He sounded fine the last time I spoke to him on the phone. Better than I sounded, probably."

"Business worries?"

I thought of Ken Numata back at the office trying to make sense of the accounts, and decided it might be best not to mention it until I was sure what the situation was. "He was a bit slow paying his bills," I said, aware of the understatement, "but nothing serious."

"That you know of."

"That I know of, yes. Look, what are you questioning me for?"

Page grinned. "You're the one who insisted on coming here."

I went back to the settee and sat down. "Have you any idea what's going on?"

Page shook his head. "We're no further forward than we were when you reported Mr Dean missing."

"What about Sophie?"

"Same thing."

I put my hand down the side of the cushion I was sitting on and my fingers brushed something small and hard and round. "You'd let me know if you'd found anything, though?"

"Certainly."

I closed my hand around the hard object, drew it slowly out from between the cushions, and put it in my pocket without looking at it.

Little came out of the bedroom, looked at Page, and shrugged. Page had found a folder of business correspondence in a cupboard and had tucked it under his armpit so he could stand with both hands in his pockets. He looked at us. "Well, I don't think we have to bother you gentlemen any more today."

Mr Pahlavi and I stood up.

"If we need to come back, we'll call you, Mr Ramsay."

"I'd appreciate it," I said, shaking hands with him.

When the policemen were gone, Mr Pahlavi and I stood in the corridor feeling awkward.

"I wish you'd told me you had a key," I said finally.

He looked abashed. "I know. Is it important?"

I looked at him and suddenly felt ashamed for being upset with him. All he'd done was look after Harry's fish and kept strangers out of his flat. "I don't know." I rubbed my eyes. "Probably not."

"I'm sorry."

I shook my head. "There's nothing to be sorry about, Mr Pahlavi. I don't know what I was getting so annoyed about. I apologize."

Having said sorry to each other, we stood for another minute or so, chatting. A very tall woman came out of one of the flats down the corridor. We moved apart so she could pass, and when she was gone we stepped forward so we were standing side by side again.

"Will you want the key now?" he asked.

It occurred to me that I could quite happily live here, but I shook my head. "No, you keep it. I can't promise to get here every day to feed the fish."

"So," he said, "should I carry on the way I have been until Mr Dean comes back?"

"Well," I said, "I think we have to wait seven years before he's declared legally dead." Mr Pahlavi suddenly looked alarmed, and I gave him what I hoped was a re-assuring smile. "I'm sure we won't have to wait that long. I'll call you."

He shook his head. "I don't know Mr Dean very well. Perhaps this is a family matter?"

"Yes," I said. "Let's hope that's all it is."

It was half-past three before I got back to the office, and Ken had gone. He had left the books piled neatly on Sophie's desk, and on top of them he'd left a note in brisk, neat handwriting. "You can stop panicking for the moment," he'd written, "but you do need help. Call me. KN." His business card was on the desk beside the IBM.

I put the note back on top of the account books and wandered through the office. So Harry had no business worries that I could discover, and his flat was not the flat of a pauper. Then why had he gone, with his suitcase and his camcorder and his wads of money?

I sat down in the chair behind his desk and took out the little object I'd found down the side of his sofa. I looked at it for a long time. I put it on the desk in front of me and looked at it some more.

"Oh, you *cunt*, Harry," I said finally.

Part Three

Mr Ramsay in Nottingham

Fourteen

1

Some of the trains from London stop at Beeston, but this wasn't one of them. The train just sailed serenely through the station and put another half-hour on my journey. I watched the station pass and wasn't entirely surprised. I was getting used to this kind of thing happening to me.

It was half-past six. Rain drummed on the side of the train as we pulled into Nottingham. Floodlit high on its crag, the castle was jewelled by the driving rain. We bumped over a set of points. I closed my book and watched the railway sidings close in on us. I was working my way through the *Sharpe* novels but I hadn't read more than half a dozen lines of this one during the whole journey.

As we jogged closer to Nottingham station I gathered the remains of my sandwich and coffee together and put them in the bin behind my seat. Across from me, the large gentleman who had got on at Leicester was snoring serenely, his copy of the *Daily Mirror* open on the table between us. There was something about the microscopic knot of his tie that reminded me of the *Górale* I'd shared my compartment with across Northern Europe. I'd already decided that no rail journey could ever be quite as bad as that, and beside the mountain-men the little group of drunken passengers at the front of the carriage, their empty Tennant's tins piled in a haphazard pyramid on their table, had faded into insignificance, no matter how loudly they sang and shouted.

Nottingham station looked much as I remembered it. Outside, solid sheets of rain were blowing along the road and breaking on the traffic. People ran along the pavement, heads down, bent against the wind. I had planned to walk up through the Market Square and get a bus home, but the weather put a stop to that. I walked out to the taxi rank and got a cab instead.

Harry and Sophie had been gone for three weeks and the police still had no idea where they were. I didn't know how long these things took. Hundreds of people went missing every year in London alone. Some of them stayed missing permanently; no one ever found out where they'd gone or what had happened to them. The police were looking into Harry's business affairs; it was always possible he was on the run from creditors I knew nothing about, someone who hadn't appeared in the company books.

I still had no idea what I was going to do with the company. After weeks going in to the office and sitting staring at the walls I'd decided to shut up shop for a while. I'd had enough of Harry bloody Dean making my life a misery.

The taxi reached Canning Circus and dipped down Derby Road Hill towards Lenton through the wind and rain. We went past the Queen's Medical Centre and swept around the roundabout opposite the North Entrance of the university. We drove along the edge of the campus, down to the Priory roundabout, and turned towards Beeston.

"Bit of a damp one tonight," the driver said.

"Mm," I said, looking out of the window.

"Come far, have you?"

"Far enough."

He grunted. "Me too. I'll be getting off home soon myself."

"Yes," I said, and that effectively killed the conversation. We drove down Beeston High Street, scoured clean by the rain, and into the back streets. We pulled up outside my house and I paid the driver and stepped out into the rain. I never heard him pull away. I was already soaked to the skin by then.

I ran up the path, my bag banging against my side, got my key into the lock, opened the door, and stepped inside. I had closed the door before it occurred to me that the whole house was in darkness.

I switched on the light and looked around the kitchen. Everything was neat and tidy. Clean plates and a mug on the draining board, last night's evening paper on the kitchen table.

"Dad?" I called, dropping my bag beside the table and opening the kitchen door. "Dad?" I called into the hall.

He wasn't there. I took my coat off and hung it in the hall and then went through the house, switching on lights as I went. The whole place was spotless; my father hoovered every other day. He kept the house like an operating theatre. It had driven me to distraction. In my room the dusting had been done and the bed was made up. I resisted an immediate urge to untidy it.

I used the toilet, washed my hands and face, got a towel out of the airing cupboard, and went back downstairs drying my rain-wet hair. I went into the living room and switched on the television. My father's pipes were all in their rack on the fireplace. Back in the kitchen, I switched the kettle on, sat at the table and flipped through the paper as I towelled my hair. The top story was about students being beaten up by a gang of local lads.

There was always something depressing about going home. It never changed, no matter how long I was away; my father made sure of that. He hated change. Everything had to be in its proper place. My problem was that it was my father who always had to decide what the proper place was. Nottingham never changed, our house never changed, my father never changed.

I closed the paper and looked at the front page. I thought it was pathetic: I couldn't stand being in London any more, I only had one other place to go, and it was the place I had spent most of my life trying to get away from.

I stood up and went into the hall again, the towel draped round my neck. I stared at the little pile of mail at the foot of the front door. I think I looked at it for a couple of minutes before I picked it up.

There were a couple of bits of junk mail, a bank statement, and a letter post-marked Ripon that must have come from my Uncle Jim. In the kitchen, I heard the kettle boil and switch itself off. I put the letters on the table, poured hot water into a mug and dropped a tea bag into it. My father always collected the post before he left in the morning. He left it on the hall table to read when he got home. If he got home before Wendy or me, he usually read our post as well. It was as if, because the post was being delivered to his house, all the mail was his, whether it was addressed to him or not.

Outside, the rain was coming down even harder. I fished the tea bag out of the mug, spooned sugar in, and sat at the table stirring my tea. After a while I reached into my pocket and took out the little amber-and-silver earring I had found down the side of Harry's sofa.

I put it down on the table beside my mug, put my chin on my hand and looked down at it. I remembered the day Witek had driven Julia and me on his loud and aggressive day out in Kraków. I remembered buying the earring and its twin, but I couldn't remember how much I'd paid for them.

Irrationally, it hadn't even occurred to me Harry and Sophie might have gone missing together. I'd somehow thought of Harry going off in one direction and Sophie in another. Even after I found the earring I still found it hard to believe they had run off with each other. After the first flush of anger, I found myself inventing excuses for the earring being down the side of Harry's sofa. Maybe he'd invited Sophie round for a drink. Maybe he had something he had to discuss with her. Maybe she'd been advising him about how to keep his fish . . . Sure.

The day after the police searched Harry's flat, I'd gone back to an increasingly harried-looking Mr Pahlavi, and he told me he had seen Sophie entering and leaving Harry's place at odd hours of the day and night. A few days later the police rang with the news that they'd found receipts at Harry's flat for meals and presents which I had to presume he had bought her. I was speaking to Detective Sergeant Page so often we were on first-name terms.

One day, Page brought a photo around to the office. They'd found it in one of the drawers in Harry's flat, and he wondered if I recognized the person with Harry in it.

The two of them were at a party, Sophie in a long flowing black evening dress with her hair artfully piled up on top of her head, Harry almost unrecognizable in a tuxedo, wing collar and black bow-tie. I felt my heart sink so far I imagined I heard it thud to the lino under my chair.

"It's Sophie," I said.

"Really?" Page said, taking the photo from me and looking closely at it. "I didn't recognize her."

I nodded numbly. "It's Sophie, Detective Sergeant."

He must have caught something in my voice, because he suddenly sounded concerned. "Are you all right?"

"Oh, fine. Lovely." I hadn't thought I could feel more miserable, but Colin Page had managed to shove me down to new depths.

He looked around the sad wreckage that was Lonesome Charley Productions. "You didn't know?"

I shook my head.

Page watched me for what felt like a long time, and I watched him back. I watched him sizing me up as a murderous jilted lover. He was thinking really hard; he was about my age, and I knew the capture of a murderer would do his career no harm at all. A crime of passion, a lovers' triangle. It would make all the papers. I could actually see it going through his mind.

Then he shook his head slightly, as if to physically dislodge the thought. He'd already checked up on me as a matter of course when he'd been checking Harry's other known associates. He didn't believe I was a killer any more than I thought he was one.

"So what will you do now?" he asked.

"I don't know." He was aware that Harry had willed the company to me, of course; he was also aware that Lonesome Charley wasn't worth killing anybody for. "I suppose I'll keep things going until I can work out what to do."

He looked around the office. "Good luck," he said, without any particular enthusiasm.

Over the hammering of the rain, I heard the gate to our path open and close. Someone ran down to the door and knocked.

I got up and opened the door. Outside, a coat held over her head and shoulders, was our neighbour, Mrs Murray.

"Oh, it's you, Tim," she said. "I saw the lights on."

"I just got back, Mrs Murray," I said. "Dad's not in yet."

She looked up at me from under her coat. She was in her early sixties and she'd lived next door to us as long as I'd been alive. She'd lost her husband, the large, jolly and seemingly indestructible Keith, the year before, at about the same time as I had been making a mess of my Finals. Keith and my father had been the last living husbands in our street. Over the years, the other menfolk had all, one by one, succumbed, leaving their wives to carry on alone. My sister Wendy used to call the street Widow's Row.

There was a strange look on Mrs Murray's face, a look at once surprised and comprehending. "Tim," she said. "I'm so sorry. I thought somebody must have called you."

I thought that I had known something was wrong all along. Half-past seven and nobody home, the post still on the doormat under the letterbox; these were earth-shattering anomalies in our house, and I'd been away for so long that my conscious mind had ignored them. A line of gooseflesh prickled across my shoulders. "About what, Mrs Murray?"

2

He was in a bed at the end of the ward. He was wearing his blue-and-white-striped pyjamas, the jacket half-open to show the heart-monitor sensors stuck to his bony hairless chest. His eyes were closed, and for a moment I just stood looking at him. The sparse strands of his hair were neatly brushed. There was a healthy flush on his cheeks. He looked calm and comfortable. He didn't look remotely unwell.

"Dad?"

He opened his eyes and looked at me. "Oh, you're here, are you?"

I pulled up a chair and sat beside the bed. It was so tall I had to look up at him; the top end of the bed had been elevated, so that he lay back on it like a Viking chieftain.

"Well," I said awkwardly, "what've you been up to, then?"

He waved a hand dismissively. There was a cannula in the back, held in place by an X of bloodstained tape. "Just a bit of a twinge, that's all. I'm all right."

The registrar had told me that it had been more than "a bit of a twinge", but I didn't argue. "Why didn't anybody get in touch with me?"

He shrugged. "What could you have done?"

"I could have been here earlier." I looked down the length of the quiet cardiac ward. "I only came up here tonight on spec. You've been here two days, Dad. You should have got somebody to call me."

"Wendy's been looking after me. I didn't want to bother anybody."

I shook my head wonderingly. "You daft old sod. You do it to get attention, don't you?"

He looked at me. His eyes were a watery hazel. "What?"

"All this 'I don't want to bother anybody' bullshit. You want to bother *everybody*."

He shrugged again. "If you say so." He put his head back on the pillow and closed his eyes again.

"Oh, bloody hell, Dad." There were machines on both sides of the bedhead, ticking and flashing little red and green lights. A screen on the ECG machine showed a regularly jagged line beneath a blinking dot and a set of numbers showing his pulse-rate. I looked about me again. I would have been more concerned than I was, but he was so bloody infuriating it was hard to be apprehensive.

"I'm sorry I haven't rung," I said. "Things got a bit busy after I got back from Poland."

"I've always told you not to bother if you don't want to," he said without opening his eyes.

"I don't know why we don't simply burn you at the stake and have done with it," I snapped, and instantly regretted it. He just lay there, not happy, not sad, not irritated. He made me want to shake him. "They've got you connected up to enough machines, anyway," I tried tentatively.

"I suppose so."

It was ridiculous. We'd never managed to have a proper conversation with each other when he was well. How was I supposed to try now?

"How's Wendy?"

He opened his eyes and looked over at his watch on the bedside table. "She'll be here to see me soon," he said. "She's been every night. And every afternoon."

I sighed. "Don't start that again, Dad." He delighted in playing us off against each other: Wendy loves me more than you do; Tim cares more for me than you do. It was so much a part of my childhood that I'd almost stopped noticing when he did it. I'd been eighteen or nineteen before I realized he was actually afraid of Wendy and I uniting against him, but all he'd succeeded in doing by then was to let us drift away from him.

He settled against the pillow and clasped his hands loosely across his stomach.

"The doctors say you're doing all right," I said.

He nodded. "Gillian found me."

"I know, she told me. She's been taking care of the house." Gillian was Mrs Murray. She'd told me a tearful horror story of coming to visit my father and finding him sprawled on the kitchen floor with food all over him after he'd fallen from his seat at the table and pulled his tea over himself. A frantic 999, breathless rush in the ambulance, lights flashing and two-tone howling. Mrs Murray had a gift for drama, but the registrar had said my father would have died if she hadn't found him when she did.

"You smoke too much," I said. He turned his head and looked at me, and his lips made a little moue of annoyance. I held up my hands. "Yes, all right, I know. Too late now. I know." I got up. "Look, I'm going to try and find a cup of coffee."

He nodded down the ward. "There's a machine by the stairs."

"All right. Do you want anything?"

He shook his head. I thought about Mr Pearmain and Mr Sierpiński and their sons. Everybody else had a normal father; why didn't I?

I walked back down the ward, past the other critically damaged patients. Most of them looked in worse shape than my father did, I thought, and I instantly felt ashamed for thinking it.

Wendy was outside in the waiting area, talking to the young Sri Lankan registrar I'd spoken with earlier. She saw me come out of the ward and her lips thinned down to a narrow hostile line. I went over.

"Hi, Wend."

"So you finally decided to turn up, did you?" she said.

"Nice to see you, too, Wend." I looked around. Andy, Wendy's husband, was sitting beside one of the plant displays arranged around the edge of the room. I waved hello and he waved back. "How are you, Wend?" I asked.

"Oh, don't be so bloody stupid, Tim." She was virtually shaking with rage, and the registrar decided to make a silent tactical withdrawal. He nodded to me and went off towards the landing.

"Why didn't you call me?" I said.

Wendy snorted. "What would you have done? Dropped your big important job and come rushing up here to nurse him?"

"Of course I would." I saw no point in telling her my job was neither big nor important. Or a job any longer, for that matter.

She snorted again. "Of course, you always had time for him, didn't you," she sneered. Wendy loved sarcasm. The sad thing was, she had never been very good at it. "That's why you went off at the first opportunity and left me to look after him."

"I went to *university*, Wend," I said half-heartedly. "Give me a break. You make it sound like I ran away to join the circus."

Her nostrils flared and she marched away to the darkened window across the room.

At the age of fifteen, my sister had been a plump, shy, calm girl with freckles and a fondness for the milder forms of jazz-rock. Something had happened to her, though, something so gradual that I didn't notice it until I looked at her one day and discovered she had become a thin, angry, disillusioned woman.

I knew that a large part of her anger towards me was due to the fact that I had got out of Nottingham while she hadn't. And she knew I knew, and that just made her angrier. She'd appointed herself as my father's minder to cover her failure to escape, and made herself a martyr in the process. Now she was no longer the girl whose dreams hadn't come true; now she was looking after a father who didn't appreciate her, while her bastard brother lived it up in London. If only she knew.

She wasn't a bad person, particularly, it was just that life had dealt her a particularly safe and unexciting hand, by her standards. She'd married well—Andy was a computer software expert with a little firm in town, and a nice enough bloke, if a little inclined to let Wendy rampage all over him. They had a nice house in The Park and a little boy and girl who were models of good adjustment. I couldn't remember quite how old they were. James was about four, Laura would be six now, I thought. I wondered if I'd remembered to send cards for their last birthdays. Wendy's life looked pretty uncomplicated and satisfactory from the outside; it was just that she'd always wanted more. She hated Nottingham with a passion, but she'd never quite got up the momentum to leave, and she hated me because I had. I was tempted to ask her to swap places for a while, see what life was really like when it got complicated and interesting.

She turned from the window and walked back to me. "How is he?"

"He's awake. I think he's waiting for you."

She shook her head. "He's been a real old bastard about this."

"He's had a heart attack, Wend," I said. "I think he's got a right to be a real old bastard, don't you?"

She looked at me coldly. "Don't tell me how to feel about him, Tim." She turned on her heel and strode off through the door and into the ward.

I went over and sat beside Andy. We shook hands. "How is he?" he asked.

"They say it was touch and go for a while," I said.

He reached out and took hold of one of the leaves of the plant display between his thumb and forefinger. "Is he going to be all right?"

"He's going to have to take it easy for a while. Probably for the rest of his life. But the doctor I spoke to seems to think he'll pull through."

Andy shook his head. He looked tired. "This kind of thing shakes you up, doesn't it?"

"The little machines still working you hard?"

He smiled weakly. "No rest for the wicked."

I sat back against one of the plant tubs. "The kids?"

"James has a girlfriend."

"The dirty little bugger."

He laughed. "She's eight. He says he's her toyboy." He looked at the door to the ward. "Are you staying at home?"

"Yeah. I only came up on the spur of the moment. Nobody bothered to let me know the old man was ill."

Andy nodded. "I told Wendy to call you, but you know what she's like. She's got to have a monopoly on your Dad. It gives her more to complain about."

I smiled. "Yeah, I know." Despite everything, Andy was very much in love with my sister, and I admired him for that. I knew she loved him too, even if he did represent the safe life she despised. I wished she would just wake up and be satisfied with her life instead of regretting lost opportunities.

"Have you eaten yet?" he asked.

"I had a sandwich on the train."

"Well look, come back with us and have dinner, eh? The kids would love to see you."

I looked at him, alarmed. "Will I have to read them bedtime stories?"

"It's very good of you to ring, Tim," Page said, "but you really didn't have to, you know,"

"I just didn't want you to think I'd run off, too," I said.

"Well . . ." he said.

I looked through the living-room door. The clock on the mantelpiece said half-past two. "Did I get you up?"

"No. I had to get up to answer the pager." He sounded sort of fuzzy and half-awake.

He had given me his pager number when he'd brought me the photo of Harry and Sophie, and he'd told me I could page him any time, day or night. I'd decided to see if it was true.

"Listen," I said. "Listen. I came up here on the spur of the moment, and I've found out my Dad's in hospital, so I might be here another few days. OK?"

"Hm? Oh. Yes, fine. Fine. Nothing serious, I hope?"

"What?"

"Your father. Nothing serious?"

"Oh. Right. Well, he's had a heart attack, but the doctors think he'll be all right."

"Are you drunk?"

"Marginally." Dinner with Wendy and Andy hadn't been the monstrous trial I'd half-expected. Wendy had been quiet and subdued after her visit to the hospital, and Andy had discovered a rather nice single malt which he'd insisted on sharing with me. I felt warm and relaxed and drifty. "I didn't want you to think I'd disappeared as well."

"I know. You said." Page was starting to wake up, and he was beginning to sound correspondingly annoyed. "Was there anything else?"

I thought about it. "No, I don't think so."

"All right. Well, I'll call you if we hear anything."

"Thank you."

"And Tim?"

"Yes?"

"Don't call me at this time of night again unless it's about something important, eh?"

"Absolutely."

"Good night, then."

"Night, Colin."

We hung up. I sat on the telephone seat grinning like an idiot and folded the slip of paper I'd written his pager number on and put it back in my wallet. I got up and went into the living room and lay down on the settee, just for a moment, and when I opened my eyes again it was half-past ten in the morning.

Fifteen

1

Suitably bolstered with paracetamol, I took my hangover for a long walk after breakfast. At the front gate I stopped and looked up and down the street. Nothing had changed; it was the same scene that I had looked at every morning on my way to school. The doors were the same colours they had always been; the plants and shrubs in the front gardens appeared to have neither thrived nor died for over a decade. It was as if the whole street had been flash-frozen for my benefit when I was nine or ten and nobody had ever bothered to thaw it out.

Before I set off, I walked round to the garage and opened the doors. Inside was the same green Ford Fiesta my father had bought in 1986. Wendy had dubbed it the Brianmobile.

I went inside, unlocked the driver's door, and sat down behind the wheel. It had been a while since I'd driven anywhere, and there was a short drive I would have to make while I was here, whether I wanted to or not.

But not right now. I locked up the Brianmobile, locked the garage, and wandered away up the street without a thought in my head.

It was good not to think. I felt relaxed, unburdened. My father had had a hell of a scare, but he was being looked after and he was on the mend. Lonesome Charley and all its problems were a long way away. Harry and Sophie . . . Harry and Sophie were just *gone*, and it was about time I accepted it. I had spent the last two or three weeks wandering about in a kind of daze, going back over the past few months in my mind, reexamining every word and look that had passed between Harry and Sophie during the time I'd known them. I couldn't understand how I hadn't noticed. There had to have been signs. Was I a bad observer, or just plain stupid? In the end, I'd found I wasn't sleeping.

I put some distance between myself and the house. I walked up through Beeston, across the road at the roundabout, and on through the university campus.

Plenty of students about. I remembered when I'd walked through here as a kid, and all the students looked really grown-up, part of some special, secret grown-up world. Now they looked kind of young, untroubled. Unhurt. As a youngster, I'd felt I was trespassing on hallowed ground coming up here, as if it was a great adventure; and the thing I'd wanted most in the world was to be a student and be part of that grown-up world. I felt sad, remembering that. Being a student had been OK, but it hadn't been what I'd expected, and neither was being a grown-up. Eric wanted me to grow up, and so far being grown-up seemed to involve being lied to and fucked over, and he could keep it.

The path up from the South Entrance was a long hill with a big open grassy space on one side and a tall fence and trees on the other. This side of the campus was all like that: trees and grass scattered with residences and faculty buildings. As I crested the hill and walked past the library I could see the other side, the more modern side that everyone called Science City, and the Architects' Tower rising from it.

At the North Entrance, traffic roared between the campus on one side of the road and the hospital on the other. I stood for a minute or so looking at the huge hospital building, trying to remember which floor my father was on. I tried to arrange last night in my head, but it all seemed like such a jumble now. I could hardly remember the hopelessness which had made me come here in the first place.

Just over a month ago, I had been riding trams around Upper Silesia. Sophie had had chickenpox, Harry was warning me not to come home without Mr Sierpiński's film, and everything was right with the world. Now Harry and Sophie were gone,

Mr Sierpiński's film was a howling fake, and I was back in the town I'd tried so hard to escape. Shit. I crossed the road.

"He's had a comfortable night," said the staff nurse. Her name tag said HELEN PEACOCK and her shift was about to end; she had her overcoat over one arm and a shoulder-bag dangled by its strap from her hand. "Mr Rodgers is really pleased with him."

Mr Rodgers was the consultant, who I had yet to see in the flesh. "He's not being too difficult, is he?" I asked.

She put her bag on the floor by her feet and put her coat on. "He's been an angel."

"Are we talking about the same Brian Ramsay?"

Staff Nurse Peacock smiled and picked up her bag again. "Believe me, he's been no trouble at all, but he's having a bit of a nap at the moment."

"Oh." I looked through the doors of the cardiac unit; I could see the foot of my father's bed down at the end, but I couldn't see him. "OK. I'll come back a bit later, then."

She nodded and slung the bag over her shoulder. "Rest is really the best thing for him right now, Mr Ramsay."

"Just don't take any lip from him, OK?"

"I told you: he's been an absolute angel. I don't know why you think he's not."

"I have a lot of experience. Trust me."

She chuckled. "All right, I'll trust you. But right now I need a cup of tea and a lie down. I'm back on this evening."

"Do you have far to go?"

She shook her head. "Hucknall."

Which was all the way out on the other side of the city. "Bit of a journey."

"It's not so bad in the car. Can I give you a lift somewhere?"

"No, it's OK. I'm going up into town. I need the walk."

She smiled again. "All right. Well, enjoy your walk. And don't worry. Your Dad's going to be all right."

We took the lift down to the lobby together, said our goodbyes, and she went off to her car while I walked out through the entrance to the hospital and headed up Derby Road Hill towards the centre of Nottingham.

The phone rang for a long time before I could manage to get up and stumble into the hall. I collapsed into the telephone seat, picked up the receiver, and mumbled something.

"Gotcha!" announced a voice at the other end.

"Very funny," I said.

"I just thought I'd let you know how it feels," said Page.

I rubbed my eyes. There was a spike of pain right through my head. My watch said quarter-past two; I'd been asleep on the settee for three hours. "I can't believe you stayed up this late just to get me back for phoning you last night."

"I thought you deserved it." He sounded absurdly bright and triumphant, and I knew he'd been planning this all day.

"We're not going to get into some weird sort of tit-for-tat situation, are we, Colin?"

He chuckled. "Well, that depends."

"Only it doesn't matter how late *I* stay up, but *you've* got to go to work in the morning."

Page guffawed. "That sounds like fighting talk."

I frowned as another stab of pain went through my head. It felt as if somebody had hammered a nine-inch nail between my eyes. "Are you pissed or something, Page?"

"You're one to talk."

"OK, so I've had a few drinks. Arrest me."

"You actually sound terrible."

"Thanks."

"Do you know somebody called Delahunty?"

"Which one?"

"Jesus, don't tell me there's more of them."

Page really must have wanted to punish me for phoning him so late the night before. "Is this conversation going anywhere, Detective Sergeant?"

"I went up to your office today and this big bald bird was lurking about on the landing outside."

"She's a friend. As I'm sure she told you."

"Interesting friends you have," he said appreciatively.

"I forgot to tell her I was going away." Maybe I ought to ring Martin and Bob and let them know what was going on. *Hang* on . . . "What were *you* doing lurking about outside the office?"

"Joe and I thought we should have a look round." Joe was Detective Sergeant Little, of total-lack-of-humour fame. "We got the key from your landlord. Was that all right?"

"Well, thanks for letting me know, Colin." I was more annoyed than I thought appropriate at the thought of strangers wandering around the office. "Is this some secret-police thing that got started while I was away or something?"

"We had a warrant."

"Oh, well *that's* all right then."

He didn't sound in the least bit abashed. "Don't you ever lock that safe?"

"There's bugger all worth stealing in it, Colin. You'd be better off nicking the safe and leaving the contents behind. Did you find anything useful, or is this just in the way of being a bit of crime-prevention advice?"

He laughed. "We didn't find anything useful."

"I hope you tidied up after you'd finished."

"You have to be kidding," he said, and hung up.

"Ha," I said to nobody in particular, "bloody ha." I put the phone down, got up, and wobbled into the living room.

I had a hell of a job of cleaning ahead of me when my father came out of hospital. I'd hit the house like a virus to which it had no immunity. It had taken me only a couple of days to completely untidy it. The kitchen sink was full of unwashed plates, my bedroom was strewn with dirty clothes, and the bathroom floor was covered with wet towels. But the living room was at the epicentre of all the mess. The remains of my breakfast and my dinner sat on two separate trays on the floor; I had pulled one of the armchairs round in front of the telly and shoved the coffee table in front of it to put my feet on. There were cushions in corners my father had never intended them for. I stood in the doorway and looked at the mess, and it occurred to me that I might be letting my life go the same way. It occurred to me for maybe a fraction of a second.

I wandered over, flopped down on the settee, and picked up the bottle of Bell's that I'd bought from the off-licence at the top of the road when I'd got back from town earlier in the evening. I'd managed to drink about a quarter of it before I fell asleep. I poured myself another and sat staring at the wall with the glass cradled in my lap. I wondered if I should have this last drink and go to bed, or have this last drink then make myself a mug of coffee and just write the night off as a bad job and stay up. I sipped my drink. Decisions, decisions . . .

The phone rang.

I looked at the door. Because it was in the hall, the phone's ring was amplified by the stairwell. I thought I should have put a cushion over it, or just unplugged it. Now I had to get up again. Didn't anybody sleep any more?

I carried my drink into the hall, dropped onto the telephone seat, and picked up the phone. "Not funny any more, Colin," I said.

"Mr Ramsay?" said a girl's voice. I must have been struck speechless, because she said, "Mr Ramsay? Hello?"

I looked at the phone. "Hello?"

"Oh, hello. It's Staff Nurse Peacock at the Queen's Medical Centre."

I sat up a little straighter. "Helen," I said.

There was the briefest of pauses. Then she said, "That's right. I'm afraid your father's taken a turn for the worse."

I took a deep breath. All of a sudden I realized I had actually been expecting this call, ever since I had arrived in Beeston and discovered my father was ill. "How much worse?"

She must have done this before, but she still seemed to take a long time before she answered. "Can you come over?" she asked.

2

I'd got the garage doors open before I realized I was being stupid. I'd had far too much to drink, even if the QMC was only a five-minute drive away. I locked the garage, went back inside, dragged the Yellow Pages out of the cupboard under the telephone table, and turned to the mini-cab entries.

I picked a taxi firm at random and dialled their number. The phone rang for a long time before anyone picked it up.

"Can I help you?" a bored female voice asked.

"Yes, I need a cab. It's—"

"There is a thirty-minute waiting time, caller," she told me with all the human warmth of an answering machine.

"Sorry?"

I heard her tut-tut gently. "There is a thirty-minute waiting time, caller," she repeated with the same inflection.

"OK. Sorry." I hung up. I tried the next number and got the same information, in a voice so similar to the first telephonist that I thought I'd pressed the redial button on the phone by mistake. I hung up again. This was stupid. I looked at my watch. The nightclubs in town would just about be closing now. Hundreds of drunken, sweaty people would be getting into taxis and demanding to be taken to Broxtowe, Arnold, Hyson Green, the Meadows, all points of the compass. I'd be here all night waiting. I grabbed my coat.

The only thing that broke the silence was the voice of a singing drunk. I couldn't tell where he was, but he sounded miles and miles away, and though I couldn't hear the words the tune sounded like "Come into the Garden, Maud".

I ran up the High Street, not drunk any more. A couple of cars went past me, but apart from them I didn't see any evidence of another living soul in Beeston. The whole place was deserted.

At the roundabout I went across the road at full run without bothering to check if any traffic was coming and ran on down through the South Entrance of the campus.

There must have been some sort of event or something on at the university tonight, some party or other, because there were a couple of little groups of students wandering about. Some of them shouted good-naturedly at me as I ran past them up the hill, my moonlit shadow running ahead of me.

At the top of the hill the path cut across the top of the campus, past the library, and then made a couple of huge curves before it came back to the North Entrance. There was a more direct route to the hospital off to the right, through the courtyard of the Trent Building, along the front of the Portland Building, and then through Science City. I set out across the grass and was suddenly flying through the air, arms and legs flailing in all directions. I hit the ground so hard it knocked the wind out of me, and I lay gasping, aware of several people standing around me.

"Fucking student cunt," said somebody.

"You little *twat*," said somebody else.

I opened my eyes and looked up. Five skinheads were standing over me wearing denims and extraordinary Doc Martenss that seemed to lace all the way up to their knees.

"Get up, cunt," said one of the skinheads. He leaned down, grabbed the front of my coat, and hauled me to my feet. Then he punched me in the stomach and I fell onto the grass again, retching and trying to get my breath.

"I said get *up!*" he shouted, and he lifted me up again and punched me again and let me fall to the ground again.

"Fucking clever bastard," said another of the skinheads, swinging his leg back, and I was suddenly folded around the toecap of one of his Docs, panting in agony. He pulled his boot away from me, swung his leg forward again, and it was as if something had exploded inside my head. I felt my head snap back like a football and I realized then that they meant to kill me.

I barely felt myself pulled upright again. The whole side of my head was on fire; I thought the bastard must have kicked my ear clean off. The hands let me go and I wobbled but managed to stay up. The skinheads were standing around me in a tight little circle; the smell of beer on their breath was almost enough to knock me over again. I looked quickly about but I couldn't see anybody. Never a student around when you need one . . . I put my hand to the side of my head and it came away slippery and wet with blood.

One of the skinheads pushed me hard in the chest. "You *clever* then?" he shouted.

"Must be fucking clever," said a voice behind me, and I felt an explosion of agony in the small of my back.

There was only one way out of this. I said, "I'm not a student. I'm from Beeston."

"*Fuck* off," said someone else, and punched me in the side. I staggered but didn't go down.

"It's true," I gasped. "I've lived in Beeston all my life." I looked at the skinheads in front of me, desperately looking from face to face for some sign I was going to get out of this with my life. The one directly in front of me looked familiar. I was so surprised by this that for a moment I wasn't terrified any more.

"Cunt!" yelled the one behind me and this time his kidney-punch drove me to my knees.

Someone grabbed my hair and hauled my head up and looked into my face, grinning. I knew that grin from somewhere . . . He cleared his throat and spat a huge beery gob into my face, then he used my hair to lift me back to my feet. There had always been some friction between the local boys and the students—it was probably the same in every university town—but I couldn't remember anybody actually being *killed* before. I could barely stand upright. My head felt huge and almost too heavy to hold up.

"Twat!" somebody on my left shouted in my ear, and I flinched away, but no pain arrived from that direction. Instead the person on my right punched me in the side of the face and I dropped to my knees again. There was a huge roaring in my head, like the sound of a waterfall. I looked up at the skinhead in front of me and his face suddenly clicked into place. The last time I'd seen him he'd been a heavy-metal fan with hair down to the small of his back. His name was John Bowman and I'd been at school with him. My heart soared.

"Johnny," I gasped. "Johnny, it's me. Tim. Tim Ramsay. Remember?" I could taste salt; something in my mouth was bleeding. "Tim Ramsay. Remember?"

He looked at me and tipped his head to one side, and I remembered belatedly that Johnny Bowman had not been over-blessed with brains. He was a simple organism geared to drink, sex and violence, preferably all at once. He'd always been like that. The little kids at school had been terrified of him. Some of the big kids, too.

Johnny grinned. And very, very slowly, he shook his head.

"Listen," I said desperately. My lips were starting to swell up. I'd never hurt so much before. "Listen, look, my Dad's sick; I've got to get to the hospital."

Johnny Bowman looked at me and smiled. He looked almost kind. "Well," he said, "let's help you get there, then."

I'd thought I hurt so much I wouldn't feel them kicking me any more. I was wrong.

My chest and arms were in agony. Heart attack, I thought. I'm having my very own heart attack right here. I was freezing. My legs and hands seemed far, far away.

I tried to open my eyes and only my left eyelid went up; the other one felt the size of a tennis ball. I could barely move my head to look around.

The skinheads were gone, which was good news. There wasn't a soul about. The bad news was that I was tied to one of the trees on the hill leading up to the Trent Building. My arms were stretched behind me around the tree and the wrists tied on the other side. That was where the pain in my chest and arms was coming from, apart from the pains Johnny Bowman and his mates had put there; my arms were just barely long enough to reach back round the tree.

There was a pair of trousers lying on the grass at my feet, and a shirt and a coat just beyond them. I peered stupidly down at them, one-eyed, for a long time before I realized it was my shirt and trousers and coat and that I was so cold because the skinheads had stripped me naked.

"Help," I said, but my lips were so swollen all that came out was a loud mumble.

I heard someone laughing behind me and for a moment I thought Johnny and his boys had come back, but it was a girl's voice, high and clear in the cold air, and with it a boy's voice. They were chatting and laughing as they walked back to their Hall of Residence or wherever the hell they were going.

"Help!" I tried again. It was worse than the first time, just a kind of strangled mushy noise.

It must have worked, though, because I heard their footsteps on the grass getting louder and louder, and all of a sudden they moved round in front of me.

I have no idea how I must have looked, but under the circumstances they took it pretty well. In fact, they looked at me as if they saw naked men beaten up and tied to trees every day.

The girl stepped forward and stood swaying in front of me. She was wearing one of those floaty hippy-style dresses with a long silky scarf around her neck. There were half a dozen long narrow plaits in her hair with beads on the ends. She frowned mightily and said, "Are you all right?"

Oh Jesus, I thought. I said, "Help."

"What?" she said, leaning forward slightly. "Didn't catch that."

Her boyfriend stood at her shoulder. He was as pissed as she was, barely able to stand upright if he wasn't moving. "Are you all right?" he asked, very slowly and in a very loud voice, as if talking to a foreigner.

"Get help," I said. I wanted to say please as well, but my lips were so swollen I couldn't get the word out. I thought my jaw was probably broken.

The boy looked down. "Look, Jo!" he said, pointing. "He's pleased to see you!"

Jo and I looked down at the same time, and saw that, despite the state I was in, my body, naked in the presence of a pretty girl, had decided I should have an erection, just to make my misery complete.

"Shit," I said, and the word barely made it past my lips.

Jo was fascinated. "He does seem pleased to see me, doesn't he, Rob?" she said seriously. Then I watched horrified as she reached out, grabbed my willy, and very solemnly shook it, as if she were shaking hands. "And I'm *very* pleased to see you, too," she said.

Oh God. I closed my eye. Three years since anybody but me had touched me there . . .

Jo and Rob were laughing. They were laughing in very loud voices, but their voices were fading away. I opened my eye. They were walking away, laughing and singing. Jo jumped up, flung her arms round Rob's neck, and gave him a big kiss on the side of the head. Then she whooped and ran off into the darkness. Rob gave a bellowing cry and set off after her, and moments later they were gone. I felt a hot tear dribble out of the corner of my left eye.

"Help?" I said.

I woke up in a blaze of white light and heat. I opened my one eye and had to close it again before I was blinded; purple afterimages danced through my head. I opened the eye again, just a crack, and an angel leaned over me.

"What's your name, love?" asked the angel.

"*Mphmph*," I said.

"You're going to be all right," she said. She was lovely; more beautiful than Sophie. Ethereal. "What's your name, love?"

She started to move away, but I reached out and grabbed the front of her uniform. There was a startled look on her face when she turned back to me; I don't think she'd thought I'd be able to move so fast. She tried to pull away, but all she did was pull me halfway up to a sitting position.

I gritted my teeth and tried to concentrate and I said, very carefully, "If you touch my willy, I'll kill you."

Then I let go and fell back, and kept falling.

Several floors above me, the doctors and nurses who had spent almost an hour trying to save my father's life stepped away from his bed. One of them noted down the time.

Sixteen

1

The Limes was near Pleasley, just the other side of Mansfield. It was a half-hour drive normally, but I hadn't driven for a long while, and every time I changed gear I felt a jab of pain from my cracked rib, so I took it easy and resisted the urge to see how nippy the Brianmobile was.

I was still quite a long way from being healed. I looked like the world's most inept boxer, with my cauliflower ear and the strip of tape across the broken bridge of my swollen nose, but at least I was mobile again, and could more or less bend over without going into spasms of agony. My swollen lips had gone down, and the mosaic of bruises everywhere else was fading down from the fantastic colours they had at one stage assumed. Amazingly, considering the kicking I'd received, none of my teeth were broken. If I wasn't well yet, then it wouldn't be too long.

Still not able to stand up for any length of time, I had attended the funeral in a wheelchair, wheeled myself down the aisle of the crematorium to the silent astonishment of my father's relatives and employees, humming the theme to *Ironside* very, very quietly to myself.

It was impossible to take it seriously. My father had died and, rushing to his side—possibly to tell him at the last moment that I loved him, who knows what I might have done?—I had been beaten senseless, stripped naked, and tied to a tree. It was little details like that which seemed to characterize my life these days.

My father had left a sheet of instructions in the locked drawer of his bureau about what to do when he died, which was typical. The instructions included the choice of hymns he wanted at his funeral. The first one was *Jerusalem*, which had been his school song. I had never heard of the second one, and neither had anyone else, apart from the vicar. The crematorium boomed with the sound of the vicar's loud singing and the out-of-tune mumblings and stumblings of thirty-odd other voices trying vainly to follow his lead. I succumbed to a fit of hysterical giggles and had to be wheeled out by Andy.

Afterwards we all went back to the house for the lunch. Wendy, determined to be perceived as having looked after my father in death as in life, had brought in the catering firm who did Andy's company's corporate lunches, and the entire ground floor was a cornucopia of cold roast chicken drumsticks, vol-au-vents, five or six different dips, and hundreds of little triangular sandwiches with the crusts cut off. There was chilled Chablis for those who wanted it, and I had rather too much on top of my painkillers and had to be wheeled out into the open air again by Andy, this time into the garden, laughing and crying at the top of my voice.

The cold air sobered me up a bit, and I sat in my chair, muffled up in overcoat and scarf, and watched through the living-room window as the guests milled about amongst the food and the drink.

"Well," I said finally. "What do you think? On a scale of one to ten?"

"I'd take points off for you laughing in the middle of the service," Andy said. He'd taken one of the little folding lawn chairs out of the shed and was sitting beside me with a glass of wine in his hand.

"Think he did it deliberately?"

"That second song?" He grunted. "I wouldn't put it past him. He could be an awkward bugger, your Dad."

"Yes," I said, as though it had only just occurred to me. "Yes, he could."

He gestured towards the house with his glass. "You're going to catch hell from Wendy when they're all gone."

I turned up the collar of my coat and sank my head down into it. "I can handle Wendy," I said, none too convincingly.

Andy sighed and shook his head. "Look at her. She's treating this like a business do." He sipped some wine and shook his head again as if wondering what kind of family he'd married into.

"Andy," I said.

"Hm?"

"Thanks."

He looked round at me. "What for?"

Bless him; he was such an uncomplicated soul. "For everything."

He patted me on the shoulder.

We sat there in silence for quite a long time, watching the guests circulating inside. It was a bit like watching tropical fish in an aquarium. Periodically Wendy would come up to the window and glare at me, then glare at Andy for still being outside with me, then turn and circulate back into the crowd.

"What're you going to do now?" Andy asked finally.

I sighed. "It's a council house; we have to give the keys back to the council, turn in the rent book."

"Couldn't you take it over?"

Andy came from a long line of owner-occupiers; he couldn't understand why anyone would rent when they could buy. "It doesn't work like that, Andy."

"What about all the stuff inside?"

I looked at the house, recalling all the times I'd had there and surprising myself by remembering more good times than bad. It was amazing how unfamiliar it already looked, as if it already belonged to somebody else. "I've still got some stuff here," I said. "I'll get that moved out. I suppose you and Wendy can have the rest. I haven't got any room for it."

"Neither have we."

"So sell it."

He looked appalled. "There's some good furniture in there."

"So sell yours and put Dad's in its place, I don't know and I don't care. He's dead." I felt a lump forming in my throat. "He never really liked me anyway."

"Oh, come on." He twisted in the chair so he was facing me. "You don't mean that."

Shit. I was going to cry. I nodded, not trusting myself to speak.

Andy's family were almost incestuously close. He was like Mr Pearmain's son, and Marcin Sierpiński; he'd take a day off work to help his father, and his father would be grateful. Mine wouldn't have cared. Mine would rather I stayed away than bother myself with his problems. Year after year, we'd drifted away from each other like two men on separate ice floes, until in the end we had only Wendy's incandescent temper in common, focused equally on both of us.

"He was an appalling old sod," I said in a strangled voice, tears running down my face. "You can have the fucking furniture."

I could have driven out to Broxtowe, joined the M1, and come off at the next exit but one, but instead I drove up through town, along the edge of Hyson Green and on through Arnold, past the Home Brewery in Daybrook. I couldn't remember much about Mansfield's road system so I made a wide loop of the town centre rather than get lost.

A series of long escarpments runs off eastwards from the Pennines like ripples, aligned north and south. Lincoln stands on one of them, the Lincolnshire Wolds are another. The Limes is on the same one as Hardwick Hall and Bolsover. It looks out over a great wide shallow valley, in the floor of which the M1 winds like a river. On a clear day, from the crest of the scarp, you can almost see Chesterfield.

A couple of hundred years ago The Limes belonged to some rich family. We'd done them in school, but now I couldn't remember if they were in cotton or mining. I could remember that the family had gone spectacularly bust and the house had fallen into ruin along with them. It had been rescued just before the last war by some wealthy eccentric, who had completely restored it and abruptly dropped dead before the job was quite finished.

By some circuitous route the property passed into the hands of a dispossessed Polish nobleman, who enjoyed the pre-M1 view for only a couple of years before he too died, leaving it to his wife, the Countess Lomnicka. The Countess Lomnicka died in 1956, and in her will she had endowed The Limes as a nursing home for Polish gentlefolk, God bless her.

I parked the car at the side of the big gravel semi-circle in front of the house, locked it, and walked up the steps to the front door. My leg was still a little stiff and I still walked with a stick, but I don't suppose I looked any worse than anyone else who has just come off worst in a serious beating.

"Your sister telephoned us about your father," the matron said when she met me in the marble-floored hallway.

I was surprised Wendy had taken the trouble, but I nodded anyway as if I knew what the matron was talking about.

"How is she?" I asked.

The matron shook her head, which was about what I had expected.

I was shown up to the third floor. It was like being back in Poland. All the staff were of Polish extraction, and nobody seemed to be speaking English. There was a noticeboard on each floor, and they were all in Polish too. Passing one of the television rooms I saw residents watching Polish telly on Polsat. Copies of *Gazeta Wyborcza* and *Dziennik Polski* were arranged neatly on a table in the middle of the room. The Count and Countess Lomnicki had died dispossessed, but they had not died poor. The trust set up by the Countess was more than sufficient to run the house and import unlikely amounts of Polish food, as well as, to cook it, a chef who had worked at the Hotel Bristol in Warsaw before the war. Old Antek was in his nineties and he was still a legend among the Polish community for his mastery of the cuisine.

Elderly gentlemen and ladies passed us in the corridors, as dispossessed as the house's founders but still with an unbending Middle European dignity. These were people who dreamed of faraway lost estates as fervently as my grandmother had. Some of the men were all dressed up in ageing baggy suits with medals on the breast pockets which might have been pinned there by Sikorski himself. Some of them probably knew the people whose graves Sophie and I had looked at in Highgate Cemetery. How had Sophie put it? Dreaming of riding across Poland like characters in a Sienkiewicz novel? I couldn't remember, and suddenly it seemed very important that I should.

For most of the residents, The Limes was less an old folks' home than an hotel, a spa from their long-ago childhoods in a country which had long since ceased to exist. They had never mastered the English language, or mastered the idea of living in exile. The Limes was the closest any of them would get to going home to die. It was probably closer than that; home was no longer home. It had been changed by the war and fifty-odd years as a Soviet satellite. The Limes was like going back to the home they remembered.

At a door along the corridor on the third floor, the matron paused. "She has good days and bad days," she warned. "She may not know you."

"That's all right," I said.

The matron nodded and opened the door. I took a deep breath and stepped inside.

The room was bright and airy. The windows looked out across steep lawns and manicured woods, and beyond them the faraway flash of sunlight on car windscreens on the motorway.

There was a neatly made bed, and some cupboards, and a faint smell of urine and disinfectant. A frail, beautiful, white-haired woman was sitting in a wicker chair at one of the windows.

I said, "Mama?" and she looked round, and her eyes lit up.

"Tatus!" she said.

It was a bad day. She thought I was my grandfather again.

There was a long-ago happy time buried somewhere deep back in my memory, a time before Wendy was constantly angry, a time before my father hadn't wanted people to bother themselves with his problems, and somewhere at the end of that period was my mother's absentmindedness.

It started as a family joke. Mama would forget where she'd put things. My father would make little cracks about her forgetting her head if it wasn't screwed on. She forgot the names of things and it just made her more endearing, a little eccentric. She once forgot the word "chair" and just waved vaguely and said, "You know, that thing you sit on." It was a game. Wendy and I took turns trying to guess what it was she was talking about.

But after a while it wasn't so funny. She took to cooking at odd hours of the day and night. I would come home from school to find her in floury confusion in the kitchen, unable to remember what she was trying to cook, and Wendy, whose school broke up an hour before mine, sitting in the living room crying her eyes out because she couldn't understand why her mummy was shouting and flinging eggs and raisins about.

My grandmother was in her nineties by then, but she knew what was happening, and she knew my father would be quite unable to cope with what was coming. With what turned out to be almost her last breath, she called The Limes and asked them if there was a place for her daughter.

By that time my mother was leaving the house wearing a dressing gown and wandering for miles before she realized she didn't know where she was. Often she'd be brought back by kind motorists, her bare feet leaving bloody prints on the kitchen lino.

Finally she was gone to the big house on the hill, and sometimes Dad and Wendy and I visited her. As Wendy and I got older, the family visits grew fewer and fewer, and then it was left to my sister and I to go alone, as if my father had decided my mother was dead. Maybe he had decided long before then.

I sat down on the end of the bed, and she spoke excitedly to me in Polish too rapid for me to follow. I picked out the words for "horse" and "snow", but I had no idea what she was talking about.

For the past couple of years, on and off, my mother had thought I was her father, despite the fact that, as far as I could tell from old photos, I looked nothing like him.

She herself couldn't have a very clear memory of him, because she had been only four or five when he was killed in the first few hours of the war, mown down by General von Reichenau's Tenth Army as it swept across central Poland.

Every time I visited she would sit and babble quite happily along in Polish for hours at a time. The matron said it didn't really matter any more *who* my mother thought I was; she was happy, and that was what counted. So I sat and listened, and nodded in what seemed to be the right places.

She didn't actually look ill. She never had, even in the worst moments of distress, and that somehow made it seem worse. She was bright-eyed and lively, and she held my hand with a strong grip while she talked.

She talked for a long time; the clouds parted and a bar of cold winter sunlight fell on the floor and the bed and began to swing imperceptibly up my legs.

Finally, she fell silent for a moment and I said, "Mama, Dad's dead."

She looked at me as if, along with everything else in her life, she had forgotten how to speak English. She smiled ever so faintly.

"He had a heart attack a couple of weeks ago," I went on. "He went into hospital and everyone thought he was doing all right, but, well, the first attack had weakened his heart more than anybody realized, and he had another one, and one after that, and the doctors couldn't do anything." I looked into her eyes and wondered if anything was getting through. Her face was as untroubled as a child's. "I should have let you know before, I know, but I've been in hospital too. I'm sorry."

She smiled, then started to speak in Polish. I heard the word for "horse" again.

I walked back downstairs, returning the nods and the occasional "*Dzień dobry*" from the residents I passed. I thought I ought to say goodbye to the matron, and I wandered around the ground floor with my hands in my pockets, poking my head into the communal rooms, looking for her.

At the far end of the west wing, I looked into one little room and saw a wallful of photographs.

I went in. There were dozens of photos on the walls, all carefully mounted and labelled in Polish, but I didn't need to look at the labels. Here was St Paul's drifting in an ocean of smoke. Here was the wreckage on the dance floor of the Café De Paris. Here was the crater in the middle of Bank Junction. Jesus, I was never going to be rid of them. Scenes from the Blitz were going to follow me for the rest of my life.

"Mr Ramsay?"

I turned. The matron was standing in the doorway. "I was going to say goodbye before I left," I said.

She stepped into the room and looked at the photos. "They belong to one of our residents," she said. "He took them during the war. Some of them are very good, don't you think?"

Some of them were classics, but I doubted if the old gentleman had taken them. Harry had a stack of Bank Junction photos six inches high, and the one here looked as if it came from that set.

"Yes," I said. "They're very good indeed."

The matron smiled. "I saw you drive up. Your car looks well loaded."

"It's just some of my stuff; we had to clear out the house when my father died. I'm going back to London today."

"I thought so."

"I'll try to come up when I can," I said, aware of the thousands of sons and daughters who must have said that to nursing-home matrons and then never returned. "I promise."

We left the room and walked along the corridor. "It's nice here," I said.

The matron nodded. "We do the best we can. It's a shame we can't take more residents."

"I'd have thought your clientele would be declining."

She shook her head. "You'd be surprised. For every one who dies there seem to be two more. My father was a Polish airman, but even I am surprised at how many expatriate Poles there are in this country."

We reached the front door and shook hands and I went out to the car and drove away.

I'd planned to do the trip down the M1 all in one go, but coming up to the M25 intersection just outside London my side started to hurt. I drove on a few more miles to the service station at Scratchwood and stopped for an hour to take a painkiller and have a cup of tea.

The house was empty when I finally got home. I looked at the pile of stuff in the back of the car and decided to leave it until tomorrow. I made myself another cup of tea, took it upstairs, lay down on the bed, and fell asleep before I'd had more than a couple of sips.

2

"Hello?"

"Tim?"

"Good grief."

"It's nice to hear your voice too," said Wendy.

I was amazed. Wendy had never phoned me before. I hadn't even known she had my number. "Well. Hi, Wend. How are you?"

"We have to decide what to do with the company," she told me.

"Oh." I rubbed my eyes. "Christ. I don't know, Wendy. Can't it wait?"

"We've got to decide, Tim," she pressed. "It was in Dad's will."

"Yes, I know." The reading of my father's will had taken place in his solicitor's city-centre office. We could hear the jukebox of the pub next door through the wall, which rather spoiled the occasion. When we got to the bit where he left Wendy and me equal control of the company, I imagined him smiling at the thought of the arguments it would cause.

"Well?"

"Oh, Wendy, I've already got one company to worry about. And I don't know what I'm going to do with *that*."

"Well I'm not interested in it." She sounded somehow diminished, smaller. "I just want to know what to do."

I looked down at the toes of my slippers. "We could sell it."

There was a silence at the other end of the phone. My father had built the company up from nothing. He had a dozen or so employees, and two or three of them had been there for at least twenty years. It had been one of the few constants in my life while I was growing up.

"'Sell it'," Wendy said.

"Why not?" I took a deep breath and looked at the stained glass in the front door. "You're not interested, and I've already got more companies than I know what to do with." There was more silence. "It's only a company, Wendy."

"No, it's not, and you know it."

"Yes. Yes, I know." I wasn't ready for this. Leaving the house for the last time had been difficult enough. "The will says we have to offer it to the employees first."

"And accept any reasonable offer they make," Wendy reminded me.

"Well, 'reasonable' covers quite a lot of territory, Wend."

"I suppose so."

"Dad's insurance policies will pay for Mum's upkeep until about 2020. She's okay at The Limes. You and I don't have to be greedy."

She thought about it. "No. It's a good idea. I'd prefer it to go to his workers."

"All right, let's do that, then. Get in touch with them, tell them to make us an offer. I'll go along with whatever you decide."

"All right." There was a pause. "We're doing the right thing, aren't we?"

It was a long time since I'd heard my sister sounding quite so unsure about what to do. I imagined that at the other end of the line was the plump happy teenager I'd left behind somewhere.

"We're doing the best thing for everyone," I said. And I couldn't help reminding myself that I needed the money.

Seventeen

Eric and Lisa were almost human again in the first few days after I got back. They were kind and thoughtful. It was a little unnerving. One night they took me out to an expensive Chinese restaurant in Cockfosters and we had the sort of relaxed, cheery evening that most normal people manage now and again. I even found myself having a half-interested conversation with Lisa about her job with a brokerage house in the City. They were just gearing up for a move into Docklands, and I listened to her fairly mild horror stories about packing up and measuring the new offices and fitting the new computer system.

I let myself be wined and dined. They were only doing it because they thought they had to. Getting the bereaved out of the house, back into society. I deliberately drank very little because I knew that if I didn't I would start to get abusive.

For a couple of days afterwards the atmosphere in the house was quite good, but Lisa's eternal forced friendliness started to irritate me, so I stopped talking to her. She must have said something to Eric, because he stopped talking to me, and a week after I got back from Nottingham everything was back to normal and I knew where I was again.

I hadn't been able to face going to the office, but after a fortnight of mooching about the house and going for long walks which usually didn't take me past the nearest pub, I thought I should go in, if only to check the post.

Rain was scouring the streets of Bloomsbury when I came up out of Russell Square station. A dozen or so people were sheltering just inside the station, waiting for the rain to stop, but I just stepped out into it and trudged off towards the office.

It was getting on for two o'clock when I finally reached the top of the stairs, dripping and miserable, and faced the little handwritten sign on the office door. There had been two fat piles of post just inside the street entrance, and there was a yellow padded envelope leaning up against the office door. That was always happening; couriers and delivery men just left stuff on the landing if there was nobody in the office. I was amazed it wasn't knee-deep in parcels. I picked up the envelope, unlocked the door, went inside, and the phone started to ring.

I walked through to Harry's room, dumped the post on the desk, and picked up the phone.

"Ramsay?"

"Hello, Bob," I said, sinking carefully into Harry's chair.

"Jesus Christ, Ramsay, where have you been? We've been worried about you."

I smiled. I never had got round to calling Martin and Bob to tell them what was going on. "I had some trouble at home. I had to stay in Nottingham for a while."

"We thought you'd gone and done a Harry on us."

I tore open a couple of envelopes and looked inside. Invoices. I threw them over my shoulder. "I know. I'm really sorry, Bob."

"What sort of trouble?"

I opened another couple of envelopes. Bills. They followed the invoices. It was amazing how quickly I had adopted Harry's attitude to creditors. "My father died."

"Oh." There was an embarrassed silence on the other end of the phone. "I'm sorry. I didn't know."

I picked up the padded envelope and hunted about in one of the desk drawers for Harry's letter-knife. "How on earth were you *supposed* to know, Bob?"

She ignored the question. "How are you?"

"Oh, surviving," I said, levering the staples out of the envelope with the paper-knife and flicking them across the room. "You?"

"Do you want me to come over?"

"I've only come down to pick up the post and make sure nobody's robbed the office."

"But you're back in London for a while now, right?"

"For good, as far as I can make out." I upended the envelope and a videotape fell out, bounced on the desk and fell onto the floor.

"Well, look, call me in a couple of days and the three of us can have a drink together, OK?"

"OK."

"I mean that, Ramsay. No finding excuses not to come out, all right?"

"All right, Bob."

"Or I'll send Martin round."

I laughed. "I'm shaking in my socks. I'll call you. I promise."

When we'd hung up I leaned down and picked up the videotape. It was an ordinary E30 VHS tape. It wasn't labelled, there was no invoice with it, and no return address on the envelope. In fact, there was no writing at all on the envelope.

I sighed and turned on the television and the video and slotted the tape. Weeks after his disappearance, stuff Harry had ordered was still coming in, even though I hadn't the first idea what to do with it. I picked up the little remote control and pressed Play and then started to go through the rest of the letters.

The video must have been playing for a minute or two before I glanced up from the post to see what it was, and my heart sank.

The camera was panning across the wreckage of Bank Junction. The Royal Exchange, its DIG FOR VICTORY banner hanging limply across the front, passed from one side of the screen to the other. I swore and picked up the remote to switch it off. I'd had enough of the Bank Junction bomb to last me the rest of my life. Then I sat bolt upright in the chair.

The camera had panned further across, to the corner of Poultry, and standing there was a plump young man with fair hair and an ill-fitting suit. He was holding a cumbersome-looking ciné camera to his eye and he was filming the crews clearing the rubble.

I paused the tape and leaned in close to the screen. My God, *it was Mr Sierpiński*! I couldn't see his face properly because his camera was in the way, but I knew it was him. Somebody had actually filmed him filming Bank Junction. I let out a little hysterical laugh. There he was, the bastard, taking the footage that he'd use to make his hoax film and rip me off fifty-odd years later. Amazing. I should really get a copy made of this and send it to him.

I re-started the tape. The viewpoint swept around the scene again, then began to advance towards the corner of Cornhill, and that was when a vague unease came over me. There was something wrong with this footage, something I couldn't quite put my finger on.

At the corner of Cornhill there was a pillarbox, its top painted with white gas-reactive paint which was supposed to change colour if the Germans staged a gas attack. The scene wobbled, jerked, and was suddenly stable again and—it was in *colour*! It was colour film. I'd never ever seen colour footage of the Bank Junction bombing. That was what was wrong. It simply hadn't struck me that this shouldn't be in colour.

I was glued to the screen by now. I presumed that the cameraman had balanced the camera on the rounded top of the pillarbox, and now I saw why. He stepped out from the edge of the shot and moved sideways until he was more or less in the centre of the screen.

He was wearing a thick dark blue coat with an astrakhan collar, and a blue pinstripe suit under that. He had a homburg on his head that made him look a little like Tony Hancock, and slung over one shoulder on a length of string was the cardboard box for his gas mask. He looked solemnly into the camera and waved, then he moved forward, reached out, and the picture wobbled alarmingly and disappeared in the snow of blank tape.

The blank tape went on and on. I didn't rewind the tape or stop it. Even when it ended and the machine spat the cassette out, I still sat there, open-mouthed.

Eighteen

A few days before Christmas, Wendy sent me an invitation to stay with her and Andy for the holiday. It seemed like a nice thought, but Wendy had a certain way with invitations, and this one was phrased in such a manner that I knew she didn't expect me to accept, so I made an excuse and stayed in London.

With the invitation were a number of documents that needed my signature. My father's employees had finally come up with an offer for the company; I imagined small-business loans being negotiated for, insurance policies being cashed in, life savings removed from building societies. It still didn't come to very much. I read the documents, then I signed them and put them in the post back to Wendy. I sat and thought about it, and convinced myself I had a clear conscience.

Eric took Lisa to Antigua for Christmas and New Year. I stared at him in disbelief when he told me where they were going. Previously, Eric's most adventurous holiday had been in Aviemore, and he'd come home early from that because he'd broken his ankle on one of the nursery slopes. Now he was off to Antigua. He was metamorphosing faster than I could follow, turning into one of the corporate androids who had come to the party. It was like *Invasion of the Body Snatchers*. I actually fantasized that he had become one of the Pod People. One drunken night after he had left, I became terrified of falling asleep in case I woke up the next morning and found myself just like him.

On Christmas morning I roasted a chicken-quarter and some potatoes and I made some Yorkshire puddings and boiled some carrots and Brussels sprouts, and early in the afternoon I sat in the kitchen and looked at my Christmas dinner and started to cry.

Later in the afternoon, on an impulse, I got the Brianmobile out of the garage and drove down into town. There were more people out on the roads than I'd expected, but it wasn't busy. I was finding driving a lot less stressful these days, I'd noticed. Either I was getting used to it or a fortnight or so of being driven around Upper Silesia by Witek had cured me of my fears.

We hadn't had a white Christmas, but it was cold. I'd turned the heating off when I'd left the office a few days before, and so the air there was freezing. I turned on the lights and stood at the front door gazing around Harry's little kingdom. Lonesome Charley Productions looked like the tomb of an untidy Pharaoh. It smelled musty and unused.

On top of Sophie's desk was the heavy glass paperweight I'd looked for on the morning I'd thought the office had been burgled. I picked it up. It was almost spherical, with a flat place on the bottom so it wouldn't roll off a desk. Embedded inside was a spiky abstract form in red and blue glass, advertising some prescription medicine. It was the kind of thing that medical reps give to doctors. Harry had bought it at a car-boot sale.

I sat on a corner of the desk and pulled my coat tighter about me. The whole office had been furnished from bankruptcy sales and fire-damage sales and car-boot sales, and I felt as if I had come from the same source.

I'd picked up the post from downstairs, the last deliveries before Christmas. I went through the envelopes without much interest. There were some letters from Harry's various film sources around the country, a reply from an old folks' home in Hertfordshire where I remembered pinning up a request for reminiscences back in September, about a thousand years ago. Martin and Bob had sent me a Christmas card. It was home-made and featured a cartoon of Santa Claus being buggered by one of his reindeer. Bugger Christmas. Right.

I hadn't been into the office more than half a dozen times since I'd got back from Nottingham, and even then it had been only to pick up the mail and make sure the place hadn't burned down or been burgled. I wasn't sure why I bothered. Half the time I thought I must be going daft.

I stood Bob and Martin's card on the desk, looked up, and saw Page standing in the doorway. We looked at each other for a couple of seconds, then I said, "It's polite to knock, Detective Sergeant."

He grinned. "I rang you at home and you weren't there so I thought I'd pop down here on the off-chance."

"Because I look like somebody who hangs around deserted offices on Christmas Day, right?"

"Something like that."

"I could have gone up to Nottingham, for all you knew."

"Oh, I tried that other number you gave me too. Was that your sister who answered?"

I sat back in the chair. "Was she rude?"

He nodded.

"That was Wendy. Pull yourself up a chair, Detective Sergeant. Fancy searching the office again?"

Page pulled one of the visitor chairs over and sat down. He was wearing a thick grey pullover, jeans, and a heavy-looking old leather biker's jacket scuffed at the elbows and across one shoulder. "I hadn't heard from you for a while," he said.

"Why, Sergeant," I said, gathering the mail together, "I didn't know you cared."

He put on his sardonic policeman's expression. I think they show detectives videos of *Inspector Morse* until they get that expression right. "I was going to tell you what we've decided about Mr Dean and Miss Trze—uh . . ."

"Sophie."

"Yes. Well, it looks as if the two of them have run off together."

I waited, but he didn't say anything else. "Is that it?"

He shrugged. "No obvious business worries, no history of violence, no enemies. We've no reason to believe either of them is in any danger. We're at a dead end."

I folded my arms across my chest. "So you're just going to stop."

"I didn't say that. The file isn't closed until we know what's happened to them, but we haven't the manpower to keep actively looking."

I nodded. "So this is what I pay my council tax for, is it? It looks as if they've run off together. Brilliant, Detective Sergeant. *I* could have told you *that*."

"If you could have told me that, why didn't you?" he asked, leaning forward on his chair.

I looked at him and shrugged, and he smiled and sat back.

"Fancy a drink?" he asked.

"I don't know." I was a little startled. "Is anything open round here today?" Page grinned and took a half-bottle of Scotch out of a pocket of his biker's jacket. "Aha," I said. "Right. I'll get some glasses."

The office drinkware collection comprised one glass and four mugs. I washed the glass and a mug out in the sink in the little lavatory across the landing, and when I came back Page poured us both hefty measures.

"Merry Christmas," he said, raising the glass.

"Absolutely," I said, raising my mug.

"So," he said, relaxing back in his chair, "is your sister usually so rude?"

"She can be a bit of an acquired taste," I said. "You're a policeman—surely you're used to people being rude to you."

"Ah," he said, taking another drink, "there's rude and there's rude."

I nodded. That was my sister.

"She sounds as if she's still pretty upset about your old man."

I looked at the mesh of cobwebs decorating one corner of the ceiling. "I don't think *upset's* quite the right word."

"Oh?"

I looked at him. "Oh, it's complicated."

"I've got all day."

And so I told him about Wendy. And then I told him about my father and my mother. I talked for ages. We finished the whisky. At one point I thought the lights had suddenly got brighter, but looking at the windows I realized it had got dark outside.

"I don't think he ever really hated us as such," I said. "He was . . . *indifferent*. It was as if he thought that if people didn't bother with his problems he wouldn't have to bother with theirs."

Page nodded. He had his feet up on the desk and the chair tilted dangerously back on two legs. He was wearing a pair of hiking boots.

I picked up my mug and drained the last few drops of whisky. "He was never an easy bloke to live with, but after my mother got sick he just sort of withdrew. He didn't want to be any trouble to anybody and he didn't want anyone to be any trouble to him." I shook my head. "It drove me bloody mad."

"Did you ever talk to him about it?"

I screwed up my eyes and tried to concentrate. "It wasn't something you could talk to him about. There wasn't much you *could* talk to him about and feel that he was interested."

Page took his feet off the desk and his chair thumped down onto all fours. He leaned forward. "So he brought you and your sister up on his own?"

"Oh, no. Not our Brian. No. Mostly it was uncles and aunties and neighbours." I tipped my head back and looked at the ceiling. "Dad was *there*. He cooked, he cleaned, he did the washing. He hated mess, my Dad. He couldn't trust anybody else to tidy it up properly so he did it himself. But as to bringing us up? No." I looked at him. "If there was ever something important to do with school we had to take it to Auntie Roz over in Broxtowe, or Uncle Tommy in Aspley, or Mrs Murray next door." I sat there staring into space, thinking that I hadn't said goodbye to Mrs Murray when I finally left. "All the kiddie stuff that parents deal with, you know? Wendy broke her wrist playing netball at school once and Mrs Murray took her to hospital and sat with her while she was waiting to be X-rayed and while she had her arm plastered. My dad didn't turn up until all his employees had gone home and he'd locked up the factory."

Page got up and went over to the windows and tried to look out. He scratched experimentally at the dirt on the glass, then gave up and leaned back against the windowsill with his arms crossed.

"I suppose we both reacted against it differently. Wendy became some kind of zealot, once she was old enough. She wanted to take care of him, hated to share him with anyone. She was the one who was looking after Dad." I sighed. "Of course, that suited her because now there was a reason why she couldn't leave Nottingham and live her own life." I looked across the room at Page. "She's a great mum, you know. The best in the world. A great wife, loves her husband to death. But it's to excuse the fact that she thinks she was too inadequate to be a success on her own terms. Is this making any sense?"

"Actually, no," said Page.

I shrugged. I should have known better than to try and explain my family to an outsider.

"What about you?" asked Page. "How did you react?"

"Me? *Ha!*" I spread my arms. "Am I not Timothy, son of Brian? I did exactly what he did. I got indifferent."

"To your old man?"

"To lots of things." I folded my hands in my lap. "Do you think a psychiatrist would be any help?"

He looked sad. "I think it's a bit late for that now, don't you?" he said gently.

I picked up the glass paperweight and stared at the spiky shape inside. "I do miss him, you know?" I said. "He was the most irritating old bastard on God's green earth, but I miss him irritating me."

"That's not quite the same thing as missing him," Page pointed out.

Maybe not, but maybe it was a start. I looked at my watch. It was half-past seven and something had occurred to me.

"I keep forgetting," I said. "I'm driving."

Page looked at the empty bottle. "Oh no you're not," he said.

I shook my head. "That's what I mean. I drove down here; I shouldn't have been drinking at all." Something else occurred to me. "How're *you* going to get home?"

"I was going to ring for one of the duty drivers."

"Can you do that?"

He shrugged. "Not really supposed to, no," and we both laughed. "Can I drop you off?"

"Are you going to North London?"

Page shook his head. "Penge."

I had to laugh again. "You live in Penge?"

He looked affronted. "What's wrong with that?"

"Nothing." I'd never been to Penge, but it struck me as being so stereotypically commuter-belt that it was hard to imagine anybody I knew living there. "No, I'll call a cab. I'd be taking you miles out of your way."

"It's no trouble," he said, still a little annoyed that I'd laughed at him living in Penge. "And it's cheaper than a cab."

"No, it's OK. I can imagine what the neighbours would think if I turned up in a police car."

"OK. Can I use your phone?"

Page's driver turned up suspiciously quickly, as if he had been parked just around the corner. Or maybe the Met's duty drivers are just very efficient. I don't know how these things work.

We shook hands at the downstairs door. "Give me a ring sometime," Page said.

"If people find out I have a detective for a friend, that's my social life up in smoke," I said, but I liked Page. He was good company and I didn't get the feeling he was judging me the way Eric did.

After Page had gone back to Penge I sat looking round the office, thinking. I didn't feel remotely drunk, but I knew that the moment I got the Brianmobile out onto Southampton Row there would be a blue flashing light behind me. There was no way on earth I could pass a breathalyser test. I rang for a taxi.

While I waited, I unlocked the safe, took out the tape, and put it into the video. I perched on a corner of the desk and watched the scene of Bank Junction come up on the screen again. I'd lost count of the number of times I'd watched it now, but every time I saw it I got more and more pissed-off.

It was his ego, I realized. He couldn't be satisfied with just cleanly *disappearing*. He had to show me how sodding clever he'd been, how wonderful he was.

I ran the tape forward to where he put the camcorder on top of the post-box, and I sat and watched Harry Dean step into shot and wave to me from January 12, 1941. I blew him a raspberry. Or possibly I blew myself a raspberry for being so monumentally stupid.

The morning after reading the manuscript, I had been convinced that Mr Sierpiński had conned us out of a large amount of money. I was ill and hungover, and I was upset at having been made a fool of.

But Harry hadn't been upset. It hadn't occurred to me at the time, but it occurred to me now. The Harry I thought I knew would have returned from Poland in a rage and all but decapitated me, but the Harry who returned from Poland had sent me home instead, and later told me not to come back to work until I was feeling better. He hadn't even been annoyed, and I'd been feeling so shitty that I hadn't noticed. Christ, he'd sent me to make *photocopies* of the manuscript and I'd been so full of flu that I'd done it without wondering why he wanted copies of a fake document.

The first thing I did when I recovered from seeing the tape was to search the office. All the copies of Mr Sierpiński's manuscript and Sophie's translation had gone from the office safe. I hadn't thought to check when I came back to work. I phoned the bank and discovered the deposit box Sophie had opened had been closed again a few days later and everything in it removed. A few days later. Busy Tuesday . . .

It was insane, but here I was on Christmas Day evening watching live camcorder tape of Harry Dean prancing about in the Blitz. There was only one answer. Mr Sierpiński had spun a loopy tale about the persistence of violent historical events, and it had been true and Harry had accepted it. While the police and I ran about like idiots looking for him, Harry had bought a camcorder and gone to get live footage, actual *verité* tape of the Blitz for his film, stuff that nobody had ever seen before.

What happened to him after that, I didn't know. Maybe he got too close to a lump of falling German high explosive. Maybe he decided to sit in the audience at the Café de Paris and capture Snakehips Johnson's last performance. And he'd taken Sophie with him. Taken her to see the Blitz, the way another generation of Englishmen had taken their women to see India.

I had this picture of him dragging Sophie from one bombing to another, filming them all. I thought of him emerging occasionally to buy new tapes, lantern-eyed and crazy, camcorder virtually welded to his hand. I read the papers, just in case he turned up. I had a lot of questions to ask him.

Harry believed, Sophie believed, and, after thinking hard enough about it for long enough, I believed too. I'd almost told Page about it, but I'd thought he would have arrested me on the spot.

For a couple of weeks after I first saw the tape I walked through the City, haunted the yuppified ghosts of the docks, took buses through the West End, trying to connect myself with Mr Sierpiński's Secret, looking for those places where the Blitz, because of the Luftwaffe's violence, was still going on. I wandered around Bank Junction for ages, trying to hear German bombers overhead. Nothing happened.

I re-read my copy of the manuscript dozens of times. There had to have been a page somewhere that told the reader how Mr Sierpiński had entered the villages; there had to be some technique, some way in, something he stumbled on. Otherwise *everybody* would have been doing it. Sophie must have left it out of the translation, and later told Harry what it was. There was nothing, no clue, to tell me how to follow them. Most people, faced with someone they love leaving them, can at least make a stab at following. Sophie had gone somewhere I could not.

I tried to get in touch with Mr Sierpiński but he didn't answer the phone or reply to my letters. I couldn't afford to go over to Poland and see him, and finally his son returned all my letters, unopened, with a note saying his father had died. I actually cursed his memory for what he had done.

I looked at the photos on the walls and thought about the Blitz, my father, Sophie, the film, in no coherent order. It all seemed jumbled up together, a tapestry of losses. There didn't seem to be very much left now. No father, no home, no job, no Sophie.

Down in the street, the taxi sounded its horn. I turned out all the lights, locked up, and went downstairs.

Back at home I reheated my dinner and opened a bottle of wine. Later I put on a James Bond video and fell asleep before the end. It was Boxing Day before I woke up, stiff-necked, on the sofa. I sat for a while, staring into space, thinking. Then I got a pencil and a notepad and started to write down everything I would have to do.

Part Four

Harry at the Palazzo

Nineteen

1

"You're not serious," Ron said.

"This film is the only thing standing between me and the dole queue, Ron," I said, leaning forward across the table. "I've rarely been more serious."

He sat back and stared at me. "Are you out of your mind?"

"Harry screwed things up enough for me," I said. "He's not going to put me out of work as well."

Ron lit a cigarette and looked away from me. We were sitting in his favourite pub, and it was awful. It was somewhere in the maze of streets between the Goldhawk Road and Uxbridge Road, just west of Shepherd's Bush. I didn't think I'd be able to find it again, though it was unlikely I'd ever want to. At the far end of the bar, on a patch of floor bare of carpet, three greasy youths with guitars and a drumkit were going through a soundcheck which consisted entirely of repeated renditions of a tune I thought might once have been "Louie, Louie".

"Well?" I said.

Ron looked at me blankly for a moment, then raised his eyebrows.

I sighed. "I'm going to finish this film, Ron, whether you're involved in it or not."

He took a drag on his cigarette, shook his head, and went back to watching the band.

I was starting to get frustrated and annoyed. "Good Christ, Ron, are you afraid of money or something?"

"It wouldn't be the same," he said without looking at me.

"Same as what?"

"Same as Harry."

"Oh, for heaven's sake." I sat back on my rickety stool and rubbed my eyes. "Of course it'll be the same. It's a film about the Blitz—how different *can* it be?"

He looked at me. "Harry was a filmmaker."

"No he wasn't. He never shot a foot of film in his life."

Ron ignored me. "Harry was a real bugger when it came to paying, but he had passion, artistry, a sense of purpose. You're just an office boy. Go and get me some stills, check out the obituary columns of *The Times* from June 1940, check something out at the library. The office boy."

I wasn't sure what disturbed me more, his description of me or the idea of Harry as an artist. "Harry's gone," I said.

He snorted. "With that tart."

Of course. The whole of Western Civilization had known about that. Except me. "Don't you want this film to be made?"

"Rather that than piss away the chance to make something decent."

"I'm astounded." I slapped my thighs, picked up my glass and took a swallow of beer. I waved the glass at him. "You're not the only rostrum man in London, Ron."

He shrugged.

"I can't believe this," I said, shaking my head. I really wanted to shout at him, or walk out of this smelly dark pub, but Ron had been working on Harry's film, on and off, for two years, and I needed someone who knew what was going on. "Look," I said, "I'll put you on a salary. A proper salary."

That seemed to get him thinking. He stubbed out his cigarette, lit another one, and blinked at me through the smoke.

"And if you want to do other work while you're working for me, that's fine," I said while I thought there was an advantage. "How about that?"

He stood up. "I'll call you," he said, and walked out, leaving me there with the band.

"OK." I said. "Great."

I had spent the first three weeks of January renegotiating the television contract. The enterprise grant and the small business loan and an Arts Council grant Harry had never bothered to mention were safe because they were paid into the company account, but the television contract was with Harry himself rather than Lonesome Charley Productions, and without Harry there was no contract.

Harry's relationship with the television people was, to put it charitably, unconventional. I'd never really understood it, and from the few phone conversations I'd had with them I got the impression they didn't either. I wondered if, like me, they had inherited Lonesome Charley Productions and its film about the Blitz from someone who had once understood the deal but who no longer worked for them.

A number of faces in the commissioning department went pale when I told them what had happened, and I didn't see a conspicuous display of confidence when I told them I intended to finish the film, either. I didn't feel all that confident myself, but I managed to talk them into a new contract, mainly because I promised to do it more cheaply than Harry had, and at least I offered them half a chance of getting something for the money they'd already spent.

Lonesome Charley was still under a cloud. Everywhere I went, news of Harry and Sophie's disappearance had arrived ahead of me, along with the news that the office boy was running the business now. Most people found it amusing, and it irritated me no end. I had to answer everybody's questions about the disappearance, and that irritated me too. I told them I had no idea where Harry and Sophie had gone, and it was almost the truth.

It took me forever to get back to the office. I kept just missing buses, and Ron's favourite pub was about as far from a Tube station as it was possible to be and still be in Central London. I set out to walk, cursing Ron and London Transport in roughly equal proportions. Then it started to rain.

I was soaked to the skin when I got back to Bloomsbury. My feet hurt and my back ached. I'd walked most of the way.

I climbed, dripping, up the stairs. The card was still pinned to the door at the top; I glared at it while I unlocked the door.

Inside, nothing had changed. There were files and letters and cassettes strewn everywhere. Cobwebs dangled airily from the corners of the ceiling. The windows had become so dirty it was almost impossible to see out of them. I looked around my little kingdom and then I yelled "*Bollocks!*" loud enough to be heard by Antonio, six floors down in the sandwich bar.

2

"Oh, my," Ruth said when she saw the office for the first time.

"I know," I said. "It's sort of—"

She turned to me. "It's *filthy.*"

"Yes. That was the word I was looking for." I sighed. "Filthy."

She looked outraged. She kept looking at the mess as if she couldn't quite believe what she was seeing.

"I keep meaning to tidy up . . ." I said lamely. Then I gave up. "All right, Mrs Wolfe, I'll be honest with you. The man who used to run this company has disappeared. The police think he ran away with his secretary. The place has been this way since before he left. I'm trying to carry on his work, and I can't cope on my own. How about it?"

Ruth crossed her arms across her chest. She was in her early fifties, dressed in an expensive business suit, and an agency on Holborn had sent her to me in response to my plea for a secretary.

"Well," she said, "if the rest of your business is in this much of a mess, I think I've arrived just in time."

Ruth was trying to get back into the job market after her children had grown up and left home. She said she came from Finchley, but I knew that God had sent her to me.

On her second morning, she turned up wearing jeans and a plaid shirt and carrying a plastic bag stuffed with dusters and bottles of Mr Sheen, and, after looking at me and tutting gently, she started to change my life. After watching her clean the office for about ten minutes, I went to help her.

I kept Harry's room as my office, but Ruth and I moved all the videos and audiotapes and photos into the middle room. I ordered some shelving from Homebase, and together we got everything up off the floor and desks and onto the walls and into filing cabinets. I'd always suspected there was floor, but in parts of the office I'd never been sure. We cleaned the windows; it took us all one afternoon. I looked out when we'd finished. I hadn't realized we were so high up. She was not impressed with Antonio's coffee, and arranged to have the office coffee-maker repaired by a friend of her late husband.

By the Wednesday of her first week it was like working in a new office. I asked her to marry me and she almost fell out of her typing chair laughing, so I gave her a raise instead.

3

I kept going. There were people to see, things to do. I was hanging onto the film like grim death because it was the only solid thing I had left and Lonesome Charley was the only home I had. I felt I had to focus on the things I understood, otherwise the things I didn't understand would just knock me over.

So I renegotiated the contracts. I pored over every note and scrap of paper Harry had left behind. I read his script over and over again. I ran his tape of the uncompleted film dozens of times, recutting it in my head. First thing to go was the list of obituaries. I began to see that I might be able to put something together with the material we already had.

Ron moved into the office two days a week. I gave him the middle room. Ruth didn't like him, mainly because he seemed to be smoking from the moment he arrived to the moment he left, but I knew that without him I wasn't going to get anywhere.

Together, Ron and I went through every bit of tape and every letter we had. We dealt the photos out on the floor and stood on the table looking down at them, picking out the ones we wanted to use and then arguing with each other about why we wanted to use them.

I spent hours in the Imperial War Museum's library reading about the Blitz. I haunted second-hand bookshops looking for eyewitness material. I went up to Colindale day after day to read contemporary newspapers, hunting for a Shape to put on the film. It wouldn't be the Shape that Harry had been carrying in his head, except maybe by coincidence, but it might get the film finished. I tried not to think about what I would do after that.

The Northern Line was in chaos—a security alert at Burnt Oak or something—and it took me forever to get back to Bloomsbury. When I reached the office I found Ruth and Detective Sergeant Page sharing a joke.

"Hello, Tim," he said, getting up and shaking my hand. He had a solid, firm, dry handshake.

"Colin." After two hours trying to get back from Colindale, my own handshake was probably less than firm and dry. "News?"

"Just a social call."

"OK. Ruth, could we have some coffee?" I would have made the coffee myself, but Ruth was a coffee snob. She wouldn't let me use the coffee-maker and she had brought in a grinder and little bags of very expensive beans. If she wouldn't marry me, maybe she'd adopt me . . .

We went through into my office and sat down, and Page looked appreciatively at the shelves and the new filing cabinets I'd bought. "This place is a lot tidier than the last time I saw it," he said.

"Ruth has had a calming effect on Lonesome Charley Productions," I said.

He laughed. "So I see."

"Is this important or did you just want to criticize my office-management style?"

Page shook his head. "No—like I said, I was driving past and I thought I'd pop in."

Ruth appeared with the coffee, put the cups on the desk, and left again. I spooned sugar into mine and said, "I wasn't aware the Met did an after-care service."

He gave me that sardonic look. "You know it's not that. We charge for that." He picked up his cup and looked around the office. "How's business?"

"It is less than ideal."

"I'm sorry to hear that." He actually sounded as if he meant it. He sipped his coffee and smacked his lips. "This is really nice coffee."

"Ruth buys it. Out of her own money. She thinks I need a coffee education."

Colin laughed. "Do you?"

"I'm being educated all the time, these days."

He put his cup down on the desk. "Are you really going to go ahead and finish Mr Dean's film?"

"I actually don't have any choice. If the film doesn't get made I'm going to owe a lot of people a lot of money which I don't have. Yes, it's irrational. Yes, I'm probably out of my mind. But I'm going to try."

Page smiled and picked up his cup again and said, "I'd be interested to see it when it's finished," but I knew he was only humouring me.

Ron was only humouring me, too, but at least in his case it was for the sake of the salary I was paying him. I didn't think Viren believed I could finish the film either, but he let us use his editing suite and helped me cut together a rough new version to show the television people.

After I showed it, there was a long and embarrassing silence in the viewing room. Nobody was willing to look directly at me. I rewound the tape and ejected it from the machine. It hadn't been *that* bad, surely.

It turned out that it wasn't; it was just a lot less like a finished film than the commissioning people had expected. Actually they thought it looked quite promising. Not quite promising enough to give us more money, but not quite worth abandoning either. On top of that, it was the first time they had seen any product at all from Lonesome Charley, and at least the evidence that some work was being done in Bloomsbury must have reassured them slightly.

I virtually waltzed back to the office and gave Ruth the day off.

On the other hand, I was starting to learn that life doesn't give you a break. The morning after my modest success with the television people, Eric came into the kitchen at breakfast and sat down at the table.

He sat there for quite a while, puffing on his cigar while I ate my toast and tried to concentrate on the quick crossword in his *Independent*.

After a while he said, "Look, Tim."

I looked up. "Hi, Eric. Didn't hear you come in."

He glared at me, but he had decided to be decent so he didn't say anything nasty. Instead he said, "Look, you know things haven't been going too well recently . . ."

I put my pen down. "How long have I got, Eric?"

He suddenly looked surprised and relieved in about equal measures. "Well," he said, refusing to look me in the eye, "let's be civilized about this. A month's notice is usual, isn't it?"

I shrugged. "You tell me. I've never been thrown out of anywhere before, Eric." For about a tenth of a second I felt guilty about making him feel awkward. Maybe less than a tenth of a second.

"I'm not throwing you out," he said. "This was always an open-ended arrangement."

I put my elbow on the table and leaned my chin on my fist. "Was it, Eric? How was that?"

"Well . . ." He sat back in his chair and waved his cigar. "You know . . ."

I shook my head. "I have no idea, Eric. I'm not rich."

He glared at me again. His glare had come on in leaps and bounds; it was actually quite intimidating now. Maybe Lisa had been giving him lessons.

"You're impossible to live with," he said. "You're rude—when you can be bothered to grunt more than a couple of words at me—you're untidy, you won't do any washing-up, your rooms are like pigsties, and you're nasty to Lisa."

"I only asked her if she enjoyed that porn tape I got for you," I protested.

He leaned forward. "You asked her if it gave her a wide-on."

"I never realized she was such a shrinking violet."

"You really upset her, and I think you did it deliberately, to upset me."

I looked at my toast. It was probably cold by now. I'd missed my train, but I was late for the office anyway. "This is Lisa's doing, isn't it?"

He looked bemused. "What?"

"All this. Throwing me out."

"I'm not *throwing* you out, Tim. I'm giving you your notice."

"She's never liked me."

"You've never given her much reason to like you."

"Did it?"

"Did it what?"

I looked up and grinned. "Give her a wide-on?"

"Can't you take anything fucking seriously?" he shouted.

"Of course I can. Say something fucking serious."

He looked at me pityingly, all trace of awkwardness gone. "Grow up, Tim," he said.

"Why?" I yelled. "Why, for Christ's sake? What in God's name is *wrong* with not growing up?"

Eric shook his head. "If you're not prepared to be mature about this . . ."

"What? If I'm not prepared to be mature about this, what? You'll hack me to death with the butter-knife? You'll have daddy's chauffeur come round and duff me up? You'll devastate me with your sparkling wit? What, Eric?" I'd been expecting this for weeks and I had been determined to be cool about it, but the whole thing had quickly run out of control; I was aware that I was unloading my anger at Harry and Sophie onto Eric, and I couldn't stop myself. Mainly because I was rather enjoying it.

He got up. "You had a month," he said. "Now you've got two weeks." He looked at me and shook his head. "I used to think you were OK, but I don't think you're fit to live with other people."

"Oh, not pity!" I cried. "I can stand anything but that!"

He shook his head again. "You're an idiot, Tim."

"At least I'm still human."

"One week. I should really thump you one."

"I'll be out by Friday. And try it if you feel lucky."

He snorted, stubbed out his cigar, and left the kitchen with a great deal more dignity than I felt sitting there.

4

I knew what Sophie would have been telling me. Self-destructive, Tim. Deliberately self-destructive. You had to cast yourself as the wronged party, so you taunted Eric into throwing you out and now you can feel happily hard-done-by because nasty Eric is throwing you onto the street. Now you can feel sorry for yourself without feeling guilty about it.

Yes. Right. And what happened to *your* sense of responsibility, darling?

It was almost eleven before I reached King's Cross. I decided to give up on the morning, went down to Covent Garden instead, and had a coffee and an omelette in Boswell's. It was still too chilly to sit outside and watch the tourists heading for the Piazza, so I took a booth right at the back and had a look at the *Guardian* crossword.

The first edition of the *Standard* was just arriving in the newsagents' as I walked back to the office. I bought a copy, and copies of *Time Out* and *Loot*, intending to spend the afternoon phoning the numbers in the accommodation pages. OK, Sophie, I hadn't given any thought to what I would do when Eric asked me to leave, but now he had, and I was dealing with it.

The stairs up to the office seemed a lot steeper than I remembered them from the previous day, and my legs felt heavy and tired when I reached the top. I pushed open the door and said, "I'm really sorry, Ruth. I had some unexpected business." And then I stopped. Ruth was sitting stiffly at the typewriter, a nervous look in her eyes. Actually, for the first moment when our eyes met it was a look of sheer panic, and I felt my heart skip. Ruth was usually one of the most unflappable people I'd met.

"You've got visitors, Mr Ramsay," she said, jerking her head towards my room. "Mr and Mrs Delahunty. They said they'd wait in your office."

I relaxed. From Ruth's body language I'd expected the worst kind of bad news. I rubbed my eyes. "It's Mr and *Ms* Delahunty, Ruth. They're brother and sister. And they're friends."

"All right." But she looked at me as if wondering how I chose my friends.

I walked through the office and stopped at the door of my room. "Get out of my chair, Delahunty," I said.

"Swivel needs oiling," Martin said, getting up. Over the time I'd known him his Mohawk had evolved into an alarming foot-high coxcomb that he waxed and varnished into a series of sharp spines. No wonder Ruth had been nervous. It was a miracle she hadn't phoned the police.

"I like it that way," I said. "I'm sentimental like that."

Bob got up from the visitors' chair and gave me a hug while I shook Martin's hand. "Hi, Ramsay. How's it hanging?"

"Well, it's still hanging. I suppose we have to be grateful for that." I sat down behind the desk and looked at them. "It's good to see you, boys. I mean it."

"Careful, Bob," said Martin. "I think he wants to shag you."

"Or you," said Bob, grinning. "I'm serious, Tim. How are things?"

"Well, I don't want to shag either of you." Which wasn't quite true; I still harboured fantasies about Bob. I'd never had sex with anyone taller than me. "Things are all right, I suppose."

"You've cleaned the place up," Martin said.

"Ah, I have Ruth to thank for that. Without her I'd still be wading through Harry's rubbish."

"Still no word?" Bob asked.

I shrugged.

"But *why*?" she said. "Why did they both run off like that?"

I shrugged again.

"Look," Martin said, reaching into a pocket of his combat jacket. "We've got something you might like to see."

"I might have known this wasn't a social visit."

"We haven't seen you for a long time," said Bob. Her eyes had never left my face. "We were worried about you."

"Bob was, anyway." Martin took a videotape from his pocket. "I was more curious than worried. Bloke brought us this yesterday. Wanted to know if we were interested."

"What is it?"

He went over to the video and slotted the tape. "We're not sure. But we *were* interested. It cost us nearly a grand." He switched on the television.

Superficially, the scene that appeared on the screen was the same as the photo on the office wall: a smoke-filled sky above a battered wall of shops and offices, St Paul's dome rising above the railway bridge over Ludgate Hill, hoses all over the road in the foreground, people running everywhere damping down still-smouldering buildings. It was all very familiar. Except I had never seen this particular scene in colour before.

"Not another one," I groaned.

"You what?" Martin asked.

I put my head in my hands. Harry was just rubbing my nose in it now.

"Look," Bob said slowly. "Look, we've all seen film before, and we've all seen stuff that's been shot straight onto video, and we've all seen tape-transfer, and we can tell the difference." She looked awkward. "This just doesn't look *right*, Tim."

"And that's apart from the fact that we've never seen colour footage this good from the early 'forties," Martin said.

I picked up the remote control and ran the scene backwards and forwards again. "It's not film," I said. "It's video. Camcorder footage."

"Bollocks," Martin said.

"It's from Harry. A live dispatch from the Blitz."

Martin and Bob looked at each other, then at me. I sighed.

We took the Story on tour. We started in the pizza restaurant, then moved on down to the new pub on Holborn Circus, then up to Burger King. I'd never actually told the Story to anyone before, and I hadn't realized just how long it was, or how ludicrous it sounded. I was glad I hadn't told the police any of it.

"If I didn't know you, Ramsay, I think I'd be phoning for the men in the white coats by now," said Bob.

"I think we should phone them anyway," Martin said.

We were back in the office, sitting round Harry's old desk with tins of Coke and packets of cheese-and-onion crisps. The Delahuntys ate more than anyone I'd ever met before; I suppose it came from being so tall.

"I've got my copy of the manuscript here," I said, opening a bag of crisps. "You're welcome to look at that."

"But not the film," Bob said.

I shook my head. "Harry took the video and the film with him. Or at least he put them somewhere safe. I don't know."

"What about this mate of his?" asked Martin. "The one who did transfer for him."

"Viren must have watched it with him, I suppose," I said. "But there's no reason to think he noticed anything unusual about it." I frowned. "At least, he's never said anything about it."

"*You* noticed something unusual about it," Martin pointed out.

"I thought the old man was trying to con us," I said. "I just assumed it was faked. I don't know. Maybe Viren did see something. Go and ask him. No." I rubbed my eyes. "Don't go and ask him. It's probably best if we keep this between the three of us."

"Well, I'm happy if people don't think *I'm* a nutter," said Martin, opening his second tin of Coke.

"I'd quite like to read the manuscript, Tim," Bob said. "But you've got to agree it's pretty far-fetched."

"Yes, I know," I said miserably. I got up and opened the safe and took out the first tape. I ejected Martin and Bob's tape, slotted Harry's, and let them watch as he showed us just what a clever fellow he was. I blew a raspberry when he waved; I was doing that every time I watched the tape now, in lieu of punching him.

Afterwards, the Delahuntys just sat and stared at me, wide-eyed. Bob recovered her voice first. She said, "Um . . ."

"Jesus Christ," Martin said.

Bob waved at the screen. "I don't understand," she said. "Is he tormenting you or something?"

Bless you, Bob. "You paid a thousand pounds for this thing, right?" I nodded at the tape they had brought, and Bob nodded back. "It's obvious. He's run out of the money he was carting about with him in that bloody suitcase."

"Right," Martin said. "Obvious."

"What about the bloke who brought you the tape?" I said.

"He works for a little company up in Mill Hill," Bob said.

"Bob followed him," said Martin.

That sounded promising. Anyone who could let himself be followed by a six-foot-four-inch bald woman wearing black denim dungarees and oxblood Doc Martenss either wasn't very good at shaking off pursuit, wasn't very observant, or didn't care much either way. "Do we know them?" I asked.

"FilmSafe," Bob said. "Capital F, capital S. All one word. They're new. I checked."

"Any connection with Harry?"

"Not that I could see. The owner's a chap called Nathenson. Mid-twenties, not long out of college."

"How do you know all this?"

She grinned. "I went in and asked, dimbo. Gave him our card, said I was drumming up business." She saw the look on my face and her grin went away. "Was that a bad idea?"

"I don't know." I stared at the television. "I don't know what's a good idea and what's a bad one these days. If this FilmSafe mob is in touch with Harry and word gets back to him that a tall bald woman's been into the office . . ." I shook my head. "Doesn't matter, Bob. It's too late to worry about it now."

"You think I should have worn a wig, then?"

I thought about it. "Have you got one?"

"Oh, yes. Lots."

Martin had been looking from Bob to me and back again. He'd decided to believe the whole thing was an elaborate hoax until someone proved otherwise. "The two of you are actually into this, aren't you?" he said incredulously. "You're enjoying it."

"I'm not enjoying it particularly, Martin," I said.

"Oh, *I* am," said Bob, smiling cheerfully at her brother. "This is the most interesting thing I've heard in weeks."

Twenty

1

"Well, what do you think?"

Ruth stared at the television screen, pouted, bobbed her head from side to side in an agony of indecision.

"You only have to say yes or no, Ruth," I said, taking the tape out of the video recorder.

"Well . . ." She looked at me. "Do you really want to know?"

"Of course I want to know. I wouldn't have shown it to you otherwise. Look." I sat down again. "The television people just sort of ummed and ahhed. They didn't say what was wrong with it and what was right with it. They were noncommittal. I just thought you might have some ideas."

Ruth looked from the television to me and back again. She was sitting in my chair behind the desk; I was sitting on the other side on one of the paint-spattered old kitchen chairs. She opened her mouth and took a breath as if she were going to say something, then seemed to think better of it.

"Ruth," I said, "you've watched documentaries on telly before, yes?"

She looked at me and nodded.

"And you know what you like, yes?"

She nodded again.

I sighed. "So what do you think?"

Ruth thought for a while. "It needs a narrator," she said.

"It needs a what?"

"There—I knew you'd be angry."

"No. No." I shook my head. "I'm not angry, Ruth. It just . . . never occurred to me." I sat back. A narrator.

"It's all very well, all those people talking," she said, "but you really need somebody to tell the story."

I nodded. A narrator. It would mean writing a narration, of course, but that couldn't be too hard, could it?

"In fact," she went on, "I know somebody who might be able to do it for you."

"Tim?"

I sighed and put down my slice of toast. "OK, Eric, you got me."

"It's been a couple of weeks now, and—"

I looked up. He was wearing his office suit and tie, his office gold cufflinks, his new office haircut. He looked like an alien lifeform. "I've been . . . occupied," I said awkwardly.

"I noticed." He pulled up a chair and sat down opposite me. "Anything I can help with?"

I shook my head. "I don't think it's anything your life has prepared you for, Eric," I said wearily.

He was quiet a moment, analysing my statement for sarcasm and enmity, and when he didn't find any he just looked confused. I actually felt ashamed at how I'd let our relationship fall into sniping and ugliness. We'd had some good enough times together.

"I'll need another week or so," I said. "I haven't managed to find anywhere else to go yet."

"Take whatever time you need," he said, still looking confused. He'd come into the kitchen expecting another row and I was just too tired to argue. "Are you sure I can't help?"

I nodded. "It's OK, Eric. Just another week and I'll be gone."

It was about eleven o'clock before I finally made it into the office. Ruth wasn't there yet. Today was a Thursday, and she did voluntary work at an old folks' day centre in Barnet on Thursday mornings. I sat in my chair with my feet up on the desk and ran the tapes one last time, trying to decide what to do. Finally I picked up the phone and dialled Martin and Bob's number.

2

"Something inconspicuous," I said.

"What?" said Martin.

"I said to get something inconspicuous."

Martin looked around the inside of the car. "So?"

"Something with a little less chrome might have been appropriate," I said. He shrugged.

"And bright pink might not be considered exactly inconspicuous."

"Oh, stop moaning."

"Lastly, I'd like to point out that a bright pink Lincoln Continental may not be a common sight on Mill Hill Broadway."

"You're lucky we're helping you at all, you crazy bastard."

"So that's what I meant when I said, 'Get something inconspicuous.'" We'd been sitting in the car for over an hour and I was getting bored. Starting an argument was the only interesting thing I could think of doing.

"Boys," Bob tutted from the back seat.

I reviewed the situation. I was sitting in a large, pink American car covered in chrome, with a tall bald woman and a tall man with spikes on his head. I had been sitting there for half the morning. My chances of remaining unnoticed were around zero. I would count the morning a success if nobody called the police to come and look at us.

Martin punched at the tape player on the dash and the car began to thud as if someone were hitting it very slowly with a huge rubber mallet. I didn't know what the tune was, and the volume was up so high I couldn't tell anyway, but if it lasted very much longer every shopkeeper in Mill Hill was going to be standing on the pavement to see what was making the noise. Of course, by then I wouldn't care. By then I would be in a concussion-induced coma. I poked around on the front of the tape player, and it spat a cassette into the footwell. Martin glared at me.

"Here he is," Bob said calmly.

I looked across the road. FilmSafe, Limited, was between a bookshop and a branch of Robert Dyas. A short young man with shoulder-length brown hair was just closing the door.

"Is that the bloke who brought you the video?" I asked Bob.

"No, he was younger. Red hair. No, that's young Terry."

"Aha." Even though he might be older than his colleague, Mr FilmSafe was nevertheless younger than me. He was wearing a charcoal-grey suit, plain white shirt, and a red tie with a silver tieclip. He didn't spare the most conspicuous car in the universe a second glance as he walked past on the other side of the road. Maybe Martin had been right. Maybe the bloody thing was so obvious it was invisible.

Ruth actually knew him. Her late husband, Joe, had been in the same Masonic lodge as Nathenson's father, and she had reacted with great indignation at the slightest suggestion that young Terry might have been doing anything untoward. Terry was a nice boy. He worked hard, he was turning a modest profit, he hadn't embarrassed his family. A son like that was rare these days.

The family lived in Hampstead Garden Suburb, their house a half-timbered mansion all but hidden behind huge conifers. Martin had driven us past it on the way up to Mill Hill, and every head on the street had turned to watch us until we'd gone.

Terry was walking back towards the station. I opened the door. "Okay. If I'm not back in twenty minutes, go to your office. I'll call you there later."

"Great," Martin said. As I started to walk along the pavement, I heard the car start to thud again.

I stayed a respectful ten yards or so behind Terry and on the other side of the road, but he wasn't really paying any attention to his surroundings. He crossed over in front of me and went into a newsagents'. I dawdled at the window of a furniture shop until he came out. He didn't bother to look at me, just turned right and headed on towards the station. For about half a minute more I pretended to be fascinated by a three-piece suite in the shop window, then I followed him.

The M1 goes right over Mill Hill on a great sweeping flyover that also carries one of the main railway lines between London and the North. To get to Mill Hill Broadway station I had to follow Terry under the flyover and up the stairs. I'd taken the precaution of buying a six-zone travelcard when we arrived earlier in the morning, just in case, and I was six feet behind him coming up onto the platform.

We caught a southbound train, and I got a seat at the far end of the carriage from him. The morning rush was long gone, and it was unlikely enough people would get on to block my view of him when he decided to get off.

The train swept through Hendon and Cricklewood and West Hampstead without stopping. At Kentish Town, I craned my head up over the seat in front of me so I could get a clear view of the doors, but Terry stayed in his seat.

After Kentish Town the train went underground for a few minutes, then emerged at the King's Cross Thameslink station. Terry got off. I followed him.

I stayed a few yards behind as he went down the steps into the complex of King's Cross Underground station, along the long tunnel to the Piccadilly Line, and onto a southbound train.

We were at Leicester Square before he made his move. I waited until he was at the door until I got up, and I was on the platform just as the doors closed behind me. Terry was going towards the exit.

I worked my way through the throng until I was two or three people behind him on the escalator; I wanted to see which way he went when we reached the surface. He was still blissfully unaware that he'd been followed from Mill Hill. This was a piece of cake; I felt a new vista of career opportunities open before me as a private detective if the bottom fell out of the independent film-production business.

As I came through the gates in the ticket hall, I saw Terry turn right at the entrance to the station. I hurried outside and just caught sight of him in the crowds. He was moving purposefully but without any hurry; he looked like a man going shopping or off to his favourite restaurant to meet a friend for lunch.

I followed him up the Charing Cross Road, and crossed over a few yards behind him at Cambridge Circus. As we moved further into Soho, garish neon signs started to appear advertising books, mags and videos. I supposed at night it was all lit up and looked kind of alluring in a seedy sort of way, but during the day it just seemed sad and shabby. A little group of crusties was sprawled on one street corner in a confusion of khaki parkas, knee-length jumpers, Doc Martenss and yard-long pseudo-dreadlocks, passing a plastic bag and a tin of glue to each other. It occurred to me that, if Eric had no idea about the seamy underbelly of society, I wasn't all that far behind him.

I'd heard that Soho was becoming gentrified again, with pavement cafés and delicatessens, but all I could see were sex shops and clubs and litter. It didn't seem the sort of place a nice young lad like Terry would go, but it might be the sort of place Harry would arrange to meet somebody and pass over the fruits of his camcorder.

Terry eventually stopped in front of a shop with a mirrored front window and a curtain of purple-and-green tinsel hanging in the doorway instead of a door. He pushed the tinsel to one side with his arm and went inside, and after a moment so did I.

"You're kidding," said Bob.

"Cross my heart and hope to die."

"What did he buy?"

"I couldn't see properly." I was keeping my voice down because I didn't want Ruth to hear me and blab all to Terry's folks. "It looked like *Vampire Suckers* or something."

"Yuk. It's crap," Bob said.

I looked at the phone. "You know it?" I said, surprised.

"Bucharest, 1982. The Romanians made some truly crap porn in the 'eighties. Underground stuff. It's dubbed into English really badly."

"I hardly think he's likely to be bothered about the dialogue, Bob."

"Yes . . . well. It's supposed to have a political message. The vampires are supposed to be the Ceaucescus or something. It isn't even very horny, from what I can remember. How much did he pay?"

"Forty quid."

"Mm." I heard her suck her teeth. "Silly sod. Probably had a really horny cover, yes?"

"I suppose so," I said cautiously. From what I'd managed to see, surreptitiously, the cover had featured a large erect penis being swallowed by a pair of ruby-red lips, from the corner of which a drop of blood was running.

"Gets them every time. With half these tapes the cover's the most pornographic thing about them."

"This is all very interesting, Bob, but I've got an appointment in a couple of minutes."

"OK. So, no Harry."

"No Harry." I'd followed Terry and his purchase back out of the shop, back to Leicester Square station, and back up to Mill Hill and FilmSafe, and then I'd had to retrace my steps all the way into town for my meeting with Ruth's friend.

"Right. Well, we must do it again sometime."

"Maybe. Look, there is one more thing, Bob."

"Fire away."

"You don't know anybody who's got a couple of rooms to rent, do you?"

She was quiet for a couple of seconds, then she said, "I might do. I'll call you."

"Only, I've got to move out by the end of the week."

She chuckled. "Had a row with our landlord, did we?"

"Something like that."

"OK. Don't worry. I'll call you later." And she hung up.

"Well," I said, putting the phone down. "Hasn't *this* been an interesting day so far."

Ruth's friend was actually the daughter of a friend, or possibly the daughter of a friend's cousin—I never found out. Her name was Ann.

"I've been acting for about two years now," she said, looking very young and uncomfortable sitting across the desk from me. She had jet-black hair and a very pale face and her eyes were very wide.

"Anything I might have seen you in?" I asked. It occurred to me that she was maybe a bit overawed at meeting this Leading Independent Filmmaker, and I was trying to repay the compliment by remaining professional, even though I'd never interviewed anyone for a job before.

"I've done a couple of walk-ons in *EastEnders* and *The Bill*," she said. "Just in the background, you know. Nothing . . ." Her voice trailed off and she looked around the room. When she looked at me again she seemed completely despondent. "Mrs Wolfe says you're looking for a voiceover artist."

"I haven't really decided yet, Ann."

"Only it's something I really want to get into," she said. "There's tons of money in voiceover."

I couldn't argue with her there because I didn't know any different. "So you've never done voiceover work before."

"I've done some auditions," she said sadly. "Nobody's ever picked me up, though."

"Well—"

"I just need one chance, Mr Ramsay."

"Tim—"

She was half off her chair and across the desk. "Just one chance, Tim. Just to show I can do it."

"OK." I held up my hands to ward her off and she sat back down. "OK, Ann. I think what you should do is make me a tape of yourself reading something. Doesn't matter what, an article from the *Standard*, anything, and I'll listen to it. All right?"

She nodded.

"OK."

Back in the front office, I got Ruth to give Ann some money from petty cash to cover her travelling expenses and then I showed her down the stairs to the front door.

"Well?" Ruth asked when I came back.

"We'll see," I said coolly, just for the sake of mischief, but I already knew. Ann Radley had the most beautiful voice I'd ever heard. We could do this. We really could. All I had to do now was write the narration.

3

In the end, it was ridiculously simple. Bob phoned me, gave me a phone number, and four days later I was living somewhere else. Eric had the decency to offer me his hand when I loaded up the car for the last time, and I managed to overcome my embarrassment and shame long enough to shake it.

Raj and Zoran lived just around the corner from Bounds Green Underground station. They were friends of friends of Martin and Bob's. Their house was in something less than ideal shape: plaster was slowly cracking off the kitchen ceiling and the weird red-and-green flock wallpaper in the hall was peeling away from the wall in what appeared to be one huge sheet. Raj and Zoran had tried to stop it by stapling it to the wall, but the paper wanted to go its own way and tore away from the rusting staples and fell flopping forward. The back garden, onto which my bedroom window looked, was a mass of overgrown grass and weeds. A leather armchair sat at the bottom of the garden, near the rickety fence. I asked Raj about it, but he didn't care. All he and Zoran cared about was having a good time.

Two days after I arrived, we had a party. About a hundred people turned up and packed into the house, the overspill staggering out around the front door. The living room was a solid mass of bodies heaving to music from the sound system. People were sick in the garden, groped each other in the bedrooms upstairs, and the police were called twice because of the noise.

The next morning I wandered hungover into the living room and found fifteen people sprawled unconscious on the floor, and I wondered if Eric hadn't been right after all. Maybe I *was* too old for all this.

The next weekend, we did it all over again. We still hadn't finished tidying up from the previous party. The police called three times and we had two arrests.

This time when I walked into the living room the next morning I discovered that someone had smashed all the front windows and made a spirited attempt at levering the fireplace away from the wall.

An hour later I gave a rather confused and ill Zoran and Raj a month's rent in lieu of notice and did what I should have done in the first place.

4

"Look at it this way," I said. "Harry's not using the place and the company's paying his service charges and his cleaner. At least this way I get some use out of it."

"Mm." Page looked dubiously around the kitchen.

I picked up a plate of sliced beef, scraped it into Harry's huge carbon-steel wok, and started to push it around in the hot oil. "It's just been sitting here empty all this time," I said.

Page selected a piece of sliced red pepper and crunched it. "Mm."

"Look, for Christ's sake stop saying 'Mm' like that all the time. And stop eating the vegetables."

"Fruit," he said.

"What?"

"Pepper's got seeds. It's a fruit."

"Thank you. I'm learning something new every day." I shovelled pepper and spring onion and shredded lettuce into the wok and stirred them about. "I'm here legally. Mortimer says so."

"Mm."

I sighed and turned to him, spatula in hand. "Someone had to look after the fish."

Page raised an eyebrow and glanced through the archway into the living room. "Have you got any beer to go with this?"

I waved the spatula at the fridge. "In there. Sol or Budweiser, take your pick."

He opened the fridge door and peered inside. "And you seemed so keen on North London," he murmured.

I laughed and started to ladle the stir-fry onto two plates. "There's bread or rolls in the bin over there," I said. "Get the butter out of the fridge while you're there, will you?"

We put our meals on trays and took them through into the living room. We settled down on the sofa with the trays on our knees, and Page complimented me vaguely on my cooking. Then he nodded towards the corner of the room nearest the windows and said, "I suppose you've got a good reason for having that."

I looked at the traffic cone I had put in the corner. Despite resolving several times to stick it in someone else's wheely-bin I'd never quite done so, and when I'd moved it had seemed important that the cone come with me. I didn't know why.

"It was here when I moved in," I said. "You'll have to ask Harry about it." I put a forkful of stir-fry into my mouth.

"Mm," said Page, who had been the first person into the flat when Mr Pahlavi had given up the key and who presumably couldn't remember having seen a traffic cone in that corner. "Mm."

"Are you ready?"

He gave the cone a last look, then he nodded. "Yes—go ahead."

I pointed the remote control at the video, pressed a button, and Tim Ramsay's film about the Blitz started to roll.

I felt as if the move into Harry's flat had been some kind of good-luck charm. Away from the chaos of Raj and Zoran's house, and surrounded by dozens of history books, it had taken me just over a week to write the narration for the film. It was a simple chronological history of the Blitz, from the first bombs on September 7, 1940, to the all-clear at dawn on May 11, 1941, which marked the end of the Blitz.

I'd added a postscript about the "baby Blitz" in 1944, and done a few paragraphs about the V1 and V2 which let us use some footage Harry had found in Wigan and the reminiscence of an old chap from Bermondsey who'd been a postman at the height of the V-weapon attacks. I'd had to resist the urge to include the footage Harry had sent from the scene, so to speak. It would have had a nice symmetry to it, but I was sure somebody would notice there was something wrong with those particular bits of film.

I'd also had to resist the urge to rename the company Motley Crew Productions, because that was what we finally wound up with. Ron knew some people who could do us cheap footage of the Blitz bombsites today. Viren made a phone call and got somebody to do the dubbing as a favour to him. Before I knew what was happening I had a production crew who were all working off favours for each other. Everybody knew everybody else. It was like some weird underground association of independent film people. We did the whole thing to bits of Vaughan Williams's *Job* and Sixth Symphony because Ruth liked them and happened to have CDs of them at home.

Everything was on a shoestring, everything was ad hoc, but as the film came together I started to feel exhilarated, almost giddy. I hadn't believed it myself, but we were getting it made.

I'd kept the narration as spare as possible, but using it imposed a framework on the film which hadn't been there in Harry's version, and Ann Radley's gorgeous voice hung the whole thing together as if she'd been doing historical documentaries all her life. I loved it—I couldn't stop watching it.

When the tape had finished, Page nodded and said, "I didn't think you could do it, you know."

I slurped Budweiser straight from the bottle and smacked my lips. "I know, Detective Sergeant. I know."

He smiled. "All right, you can tell me you told me so."

I put my bottle down on the floor by my feet and said, with great relish, "Detective Sergeant Page, *I told you so!*"

They aired the film just ahead of the programming for the fiftieth anniversary of D-Day. There were a quite a few World War Two documentaries on television that week, and I don't think that hurt us at all. The reviews were very kind, and for a couple of weeks afterwards I got letters from some of the old people whose voices and words we had used, telling me how much they'd enjoyed the film. That actually meant more to me than the reviews.

I gave Ruth and Ron bonuses. I asked Ann to stay on as a researcher, but within forty-eight hours of the film being shown she had received three offers of voiceover work, each of them for five or six times the pathetic salary I had paid her. She said that any time I needed her voice for another film she'd be there for me, gave me a hug, vigorously French-kissed me, and was gone towards her new career. I rather envied her.

There hadn't been much time, what with finishing off the film and getting the narration dubbed, to keep an eye on young Terry and FilmSafe. Martin and Bob had occasionally asked one of their less conspicuous friends to spend a day on watch, but the only reports that came back to me were of business meetings, trips to see the bank manager, the odd expedition to Soho, and lunches with his fiancée, Angela. I did toy briefly with the idea of blackmailing him by threatening to mention his little Soho trips to the lovely Angela unless he told me where he'd got the Ludgate Circus tape, but I rather thought I'd be wasting my time. My heart wasn't in it, anyway.

I had tried not to think about what I was going to do when the film was finished, and in the last couple of frantic weeks of production I hadn't thought about it at all; but now I did have to think about it, and things didn't look good.

There was no more television money; the grants and stuff had been for just the one film. Ken Numata knew somebody who might be able to sell the film to an American television company, but nothing had come of that yet. I had spent almost the last of the money getting the rights to use the Vaughan Williams music. Lonesome Charley was virtually penniless. I paid Ron a one-off retainer, more as a goodwill gesture in case I needed him again than anything else, and put Ruth on part-time. My share of the money from the sale of my father's firm came through about a fortnight after we finished the film. It was a pretty substantial chunk of money, but it was my money, and I intended to keep it separate from the company. I wasn't going to use it to buy so much as a postage stamp for Lonesome Charley.

I cast around half-heartedly for new projects. Dunkirk had been done. Stalingrad and Kursk had been done. I thought there might be something in the Fall of Poland or the Battle of Britain. Both of them had things to commend them. I could do the bulk of the research for the Battle of Britain right here, and there was tons of archive film available. On the other hand, I didn't think anybody over here knew very much about the Fall of Poland, Witek would do all my research for me for not very much money, and I'd heard there was a lot of old footage surfacing in Russia that had been impounded by Soviet troops and was going for a song. I determined to start researching both. I joined a library and staggered back to the office carrying a shoulder-bag packed with reference books and histories. They passed the time.

It occurred to me that the disposal of Harry's flat would provide me with a large chunk of ready cash. I thought about that for quite a long time. I didn't know if it was mine to dispose of, legally speaking, but I knew it would give me a huge amount of pleasure to have Harry finally come out of the villages and find he didn't have anywhere to live. On the other hand, it would mean I would have to find somewhere else to live, too, and I was starting to rather enjoy St John's Wood.

The D-Day commemoration came and went. I taped the other documentaries and studied them to see how they were put together. It never occurred to me that Lonesome Charley would do anything except World War Two documentaries. That was what we did; that was who we were.

The film came out on video, in a deal I knew nothing about until one of the television people phoned one day to tell me negotiations were at an advanced stage. The royalty on that would never make me rich, but it kept us ticking over. Lonesome Charley limped along. I kept looking at the accounts and wondering how long it would be before I was forced to dip into my inheritance to keep the damn thing going. Four to six months, I thought; and once I started spending my own money on the company I might as well just kiss it goodbye. I decided our next project would be Poland, and took all the Battle of Britain books back to the library.

In the late summer evenings, I sat in the office with all the windows open and the sounds of traffic and birdsong coming in from outside, and I wrote an outline of the Polish film I wanted to make. I was just getting ready to pitch it to the television people when the Americans phoned and my life changed again.

Twenty-one

1

"Well?" Ed asked.

I rubbed my eyes. "Mr Farraday—"

"Ed." He was small and so thin I had thought at first he must have some terrible disease. "I call you Tim, you call me Ed. OK?"

"Ed. Right." I looked at the copy of the script that lay open on my knees. "Um. Well, there are some inconsistencies."

"Warren." Ed waved his cigarette at me. "Warren, doesn't he have a beautiful accent?"

Warren, the executive producer, was busying himself with the room's mini-bar. "I guess," he murmured. He was as thin as Ed but about two feet taller; he looked like a retired basketball player, and nothing ever impressed him.

"Beautiful accent," Ed said again, shaking his head and beaming at me.

I smiled uncertainly.

"Inconsistencies. Right?"

"Yes. Right." I wasn't sure whether he was taking the piss or not. He hadn't stopped smiling since I'd come into the room. When he was really happy he looked like an escaped lunatic. I turned a page in the script. "Er, you have Lily and Ben meeting in Piccadilly Circus. She tells him to meet her under Eros." I glanced up.

Ed was nodding enthusiastically. I knew I was on dodgy ground here because Ed had a writing credit on the script. "Well, um, Eros wasn't there during the war."

Ed's smile dimmed a fraction.

"The statue was taken away and put in storage," I went on. "There was a sort of box-thing over the top. The government told people Eros was still underneath, but he wasn't." I reached down to the briefcase by my feet. "I've got a photo of it—"

"Tim," Ed said gently. "Tim." He sounded like one of my old teachers when I got something wrong in class. He climbed out of his chair and walked over to the window. The sliding door was open and I could hear the noise of the traffic fighting its way round Hyde Park Corner eight floors below.

Warren turned from the mini-bar with a miniature of vodka in one hand and a glass in the other. He stared levelly at me as if calculating how much I was planning to rip them off for. I was beginning to be rather unnerved.

"Tim." Ed stood silhouetted against the bright sunlight coming through the window. "When Americans think of London, what do they think of?"

I thought about it. "The Tower?" I tried.

He nodded and jabbed his cigarette at me. "Right. The Tower. Beefeaters. Cockneys. Buckingham Palace. Saint Paul's. Piccadilly Circus. *Eros.*"

Any residual guilt I might have had about sending Mr MacDonald and his family off in the wrong direction, all those months ago, blew away like a light mist. "So," I said, "you're saying Americans won't know it's Piccadilly Circus unless we have Eros there? Even though it really *wasn't* there?"

He nodded firmly and gave me his escaped-lunatic smile.

"So." I looked at the script again, entirely out of my depth with these two maniacs. "Why not have them meet on the steps of St Paul's? Or by the Tower?

Ed stopped smiling, and I realized instantly why he did it all the time. When he wasn't smiling he looked about seventy years old.

"Only my opinion, of course," I said hurriedly. I looked at Warren but he was still regarding me as if I were a vacuum-cleaner salesman.

Ed lit up his smile again, just a touch. Now he looked only about sixty-five. "Word to the wise, Tim, eh?"

"Absolutely." I sat up straight to show I was paying attention.

He came back to the chair. He twitched up the cuffs of his trousers, sat down, and crossed his legs. It was a beautiful manoeuvre; I would never have got it right in a million years. I'd have fallen over the chair.

"You're the script adviser, right?"

"And historical consultant, yes. That was my understanding."

"And we already have writers, right?"

I could see where this was going and I put up my hands. "You're right, Ed. Not my place to tell you how to write your film. Absolutely. I'm really sorry."

He inclined his head to show that my apology had been accepted. "OK, we'll say nothing more about it." He switched the smile up to normal intensity. "So. What did you think of the script?"

"It's great," I deadpanned without a moment's hesitation.

They were making an historical romance set in London during the Blitz; something to do with a brave American airman falling for a simple British shopgirl during wartime. Which, I discovered, was just about possible. On August 3, 1940, a contingent of Canadian troops had arrived in Britain, and among them were some Americans who had volunteered. One of them could have been a flint-jawed air ace, I supposed.

The Americans had seen our film while Ken Numata's friend had been trying to sell it to the networks and wondered if I'd fancy being script and historical adviser on theirs. I'd said I'd give it a try. I had no idea what a script and historical adviser did, but I'd had no idea how to make a documentary about the Blitz either.

I had been given to understand that Hollywood, like everywhere else, was feeling the pinch financially, but maybe I just hadn't understood that everything is relative. The Americans proceeded to hurl fabulous amounts of money at me.

By this time I had read the script and knew my name was going to be up there on the credits of a true dog.

"I think I just had a meeting with the Mafia," I said.

"Oh, rubbish," said Ruth. "How did it go?"

I put my briefcase down on one of our new padded visitor chairs and shrugged. "I got the feeling that if I criticized their film I'd wake up tomorrow with a horse's head in my bed."

She got up and went over to switch the coffee-maker on. The coffee-maker was her pride and joy; the Americans had paid for it with their first advance. It looked like a piece of modern sculpture and made coffee so good that Antonio downstairs had threatened to sabotage it.

I sat down on the edge of her desk. "I mean, Hollywood people aren't *really* like that, are they?"

"I don't know," she said, spooning grounds into the coffee-maker. "Miss Delahunty called while you were out." Ruth could never quite bring herself to call her Bob.

I picked up a little stack of post and looked through it. "Did she say what it was about?"

"No. She says she'll call you at home tonight."

I shook my head. "I've seen John Carpenter being interviewed, and he wasn't like that."

"What *are* you talking about?" she asked, looking over her shoulder.

I put the letters down. "You don't suppose they're just a couple of con-men, do you?"

Ruth turned back to the coffee machine and muttered, "Paranoid."

"No, really. Ed said my accent was beautiful."

She looked over her shoulder again and raised an eyebrow. Ruth thought I sounded irretrievably working-class. She'd told me dozens of times to put on a posher voice when I answered the phone.

"Really," I said. "Americans only say that in films or jokes, don't they?"

"Their money is real, Tim," she said, switching on the machine and returning to her desk. "Just keep telling yourself that. Their money is real. What is it now?"

I was frowning at her desk calendar. "Do you know what today is?"

"It's Tuesday."

"Mrs Wolfe," I said very seriously. "It is exactly a year since I came to work for Lonesome Charley Productions."

"Well, then," she said, sitting down at the IBM. "After we've had coffee you can take me out for lunch to celebrate."

I smiled. "It would give me no end of pleasure."

She waggled her fingers at the typewriter. "And then we can go to a computer shop and you can buy me a word processor to replace this bloody thing."

2

A whole year. Jesus. I closed the door behind me, dropped my briefcase in the hall, and walked through into the living room. I said hello to the fish and sprinkled some food into the aquarium. I took off my jacket and dropped it on the floor and flopped onto the sofa. A whole year, and here I was living in the boss's flat, with American lunatics paying me unlikely amounts of money for the privilege of ignoring my advice.

I got up and went over to the drinks cabinet. It hadn't started out as a drinks cabinet; it was a chest-high cupboard with intricately carved doors. I thought it might be an antique, but I hadn't yet got up the courage to ask an expert to look at it. Harry had filled it with bottles of Scotch and brandy and a four-pack of John Smith's. I'd drunk the bitter on my first night in the flat, and kept replacing it with more John Smith's. It had become the traditional drink at Chez Ramsay.

Where had he got all this from? I opened a tin of beer and leaned back against the cabinet. A flat this size, in this part of London, must have cost him a fortune, even without the furniture. The sofa alone was worth more than he had ever paid me as an employee, and yet he'd regularly quibbled me down to the last ten pence of my expenses and then refused to pay them anyway. Page's and Little's investigation of Harry's business affairs had turned up some independent money, some modest investments, but nothing to explain this apparent wealth.

The effect Mr Sierpiński's film had had on him must have been apocalyptic. It was impossible to tell what he'd taken with him, but it was obvious he'd left in a hurry. His wardrobes and drawers were still full of clothes. He'd owned a lot of pairs of corduroy trousers, and a large number of sweaters and cardigans, but only two suits. There were perhaps half a dozen empty hangers in the wardrobe to indicate what might have gone into his famous suitcase on Busy Tuesday.

There must have been a serious streak of voyeur in me. Even before I had unpacked all my stuff I had wandered about the flat with the delicious sense of walking through someone else's life and being able to look anywhere I wanted without fear of them bursting in on me.

I had gone through all Harry's cupboards and drawers. In one drawer I found a stack of yellowing letters that turned out to be from Harry to his father. They had return addresses from places like Hong Kong and Vancouver, San Francisco and Dubrovnik. I spent one evening drinking Harry's Scotch and reading what he had written about all the places he had been to while he was at sea, but halfway through I started to feel rather sad. I thought that if Harry had these letters now it must mean that his father was dead. I put the letters back where I'd found them and didn't disturb them again.

There were signs of Sophie everywhere. There were two toothbrushes in the bathroom, two half-full bottles of different brands of shampoo, a bottle of Anaïs-Anaïs on the dressing table in the bedroom, seven bras and pairs of panties in one of the drawers, four skirts and a dozen blouses in the wardrobe. Among Harry's videos of television sitcoms, science-fiction films and his small collection of mild porn were films by Kieslowski and Wajda, Agnieszka Holland's *Europa, Europa*, Skolimowski's *Moonlighting*. There was a four-volume English-Polish/Polish-English dictionary on the bookshelf, and a beautiful Polish-language Bible.

For the first couple of nights I slept on the sofa because I couldn't bring myself to use the bed they had used. Then I realized that, while the sofa was comfortable enough, it wasn't a bed, and moved into the bedroom.

I pitched my empty beer tin towards the waste bin in the corner and took another out of the cabinet, and the phone rang.

"We've got another one," said Bob.

It was very impressionistic, a helter-skelter rush through a night lit by flames.

"Very nice," Bob said, bending over to look in the aquarium.

The view jogged and jiggled. Burning buildings swept by, flashes of figures aiming hoses at the flames. I blew a raspberry, out of habit.

"I told him it was crap," she said.

"Mm." Once you'd got over the sheer *impossibility* of having camcorder footage of the Blitz, it was painfully obvious that Harry was the world's worst cameraman, trying to film everything at once and hardly managing to film anything at all. Maybe I should show this to Ron Booth and everyone else who thought Harry Dean had been a real filmmaker. "What did you do?"

"I offered him two hundred." She came back to sit beside me on the sofa. "He wanted a thousand, like last time."

It seemed Harry was running up the Strand with the camera at his side. The whole sky was lit with flame. The view was bouncing around so much I could hardly get a good enough look at the buildings to work out where he was.

"FilmSafe again?" I said.

Bob nodded. "The red-haired bloke. His name's Chris; he's young Terry's cousin or something. He came in about ten minutes before I phoned you."

Something occurred to me. "Could he be doing this off his own bat?"

"What?"

I waved the remote at the television. "Maybe Chris has a deal with Harry that Terry doesn't know anything about. Maybe we've been following the wrong person all this time."

Bob picked up her bowl of ice cream and shook her head. "He asked me to make the cheque out to FilmSafe."

A cheque. I almost laughed, with my Harry Dean-educated hindsight. This sort of stuff should only have been sold for cash. Cheques bounce, or get stopped. We were dealing with innocents here. "Do you think they know where it's coming from?"

Bob shook her head. "Harry would be crazy to tell them it's live footage. Chris said it was from some old bloke who was with the ARP, and that it had been treated to look like video. That's probably what Harry told them."

It was a plausible enough story. Until you sat down and wondered what an Air Raid Precautions officer had been up to, attending bomb strikes with a ciné camera rather than doing his job. Maybe Terry and Chris hadn't bothered to sit down and think about it. It smacked of a Lonesome Charley explanation, something Harry had made up on the spur of the moment. It might have been better to say the footage was from some recently rediscovered Mass Observation archive, but that had obviously not occurred to Harry. I paused the tape.

There was a little church on the screen, its interior lit by an intense, unlikely light. Flames were pouring out of every window in its tower. It looked like some kind of surreal lighthouse. I'd seen it before.

I got up and went over to the bookshelves and took down one of Harry's reference books. This one was packed with photos and dates of Blitz bombings. I couldn't understand why he hadn't taken it with him—it would have made a handy guidebook, where he was.

"St Clement Danes," I said, carrying the book back to the sofa and showing Bob the photograph. It was almost identical to the picture on the screen. "May 10, 1941."

She shivered slightly. "It still gives me the creeps."

It had stopped giving me the creeps. Now it just irritated me. "Why does he need more money?" I said. "You paid a grand for the last one. He could make that go a long way in the early 'forties."

"He couldn't *use* it in the early 'forties, though," she pointed out. "He'd look a bit foolish slapping a pound coin down on some bar, wouldn't he?"

"Mm." I started the tape again and St Clement Danes roared in flame. The camera was jiggling so much it looked as if Harry was dancing on the spot.

"He'd have to go to antique shops and coin collectors and buy old money," Bob went on. "White fivers, old pound notes, shillings, half crowns, that sort of thing. Stuff he could use in the villages. That stuff's not cheap, you know."

"What did this Chris bloke say when you wouldn't pay him any more?"

She grinned and slurped a spoonful of melting ice cream. "He wasn't a happy bunny."

"But he sold it to you."

"Well, obviously."

"And?"

Her smile broadened. She looked deliriously happy. "He said he could get us something better."

"Did he?"

"He said he'd bring it in tomorrow evening."

Bob and I looked at each other. We both grinned.

3

"He didn't expect you not to pay the asking price," I said. "If Harry's still in the villages, Chris wouldn't have been able to set up an emergency meeting with him."

"So unless little Chris has a stash of tapes, he must have a meeting arranged with Harry sometime today to pick up more footage," Bob said.

I shook my head. "He hasn't got any more tapes. Otherwise he would have said he'd bring one round to you this morning, not this evening. No. He's meeting Harry today."

Bob sighed. "You know, I've lost count of how many times we've been through this."

"Right." I squirmed in my seat to try and get some blood moving in my body. "Sorry."

We were crammed together in the front seats of a little blue Fiat Panda across the road from FilmSafe. We had been there for three hours. A friend of Bob's had kept an eye on Chris last night, and I had picked him up when he left his flat in Clapham this morning for the long, long journey up to Mill Hill. This time I'd brought a book to read on the way. Bob waited for me outside FilmSafe in case Chris didn't go for his meeting with Harry on his way to work. When I arrived in Mill Hill she was sitting in the car wearing a long brunette wig and holding a flask of coffee and a paper bag of lukewarm croissants.

"I hope you're right about this, Ramsay," she said. "I really do. Martin thinks I'm out of my mind. I shan't tell you what he thinks of you."

"I never thought to thank you properly for all this," I said.

"No," she said. "You never did, did you?"

I stared across the road at FilmSafe's offices. "I'm not even sure I'm doing the right thing. I mean, what's the point?"

"Ah," Bob said, as if she knew something I didn't.

"Oh, bloody hell," I said. "Chris is supposed to be young Terry's office boy, right?"

"That was the way I understood it," said Bob.

"So why isn't he out and about? Jesus, Harry had me running all over London. What do Terry and Chris get up to in there?"

"You should learn to be more patient," she said, and, just to prove her right, Chris came out of the office and set off towards the station.

"OK." I took my book out of the glove compartment and opened the door. "I'll call you." I got out.

Bob held up her mobile phone and waved it at me. I patted my coat pocket to make sure I had mine. I leaned into the car and kissed her on the forehead. "Thanks, Bob."

She looked amused. "Don't let him get away."

It was almost a re-run of my day following Terry. Chris and I took the train down to King's Cross and then the Piccadilly Line down to Leicester Square.

He was a cinch to follow. His hair was such a startling shade of ginger that it was easy to spot him in a crowd. He was wearing jeans, white sneakers, a black teeshirt and a bright blue-and-green checked lumberjack shirt. Even walking up Shaftesbury Avenue he stood out like a sore thumb among the shoppers and tourists. Added to that, he was making no attempt to try and shake off pursuit. I could see how Bob had managed to follow him back to FilmSafe; he wasn't paying any attention at all.

The two of us wandered along without much urgency. He stopped in a couple of bookshops and I went in behind him. He bought a Ken Hom cookbook in one shop and a big coffee-table book about Matisse in the other. He never noticed me, a few paces away. It was too easy.

I followed him across the Charing Cross Road and then down High Holborn. As we reached the junction with Kingsway I was getting cocky and standing right beside him. I was looking the wrong way when the lights changed, and when I noticed this he had already reached the traffic island in the middle of the road.

I ran to follow, but the lights for the southbound lanes had changed by the time I got to the island, and I nearly went under a bus. I had to stand like an idiot on the wrong side of the road while I watched Chris disappear into Holborn station.

When the lights changed again I ran across and dashed into the station, knowing for sure I'd lost him. Even if I guessed which platform he'd headed for, the chances were that he'd be on a train and gone before I could get there. But as I ran into the booking hall Chris was still standing at the ticket barriers. He was putting his ticket into one of the gates and the illuminated sign on top of the gate kept flashing up SEEK ASSISTANCE. I veered off towards the ticket machines and started to feed coins into one of them.

One of the station staff came over and spoke to Chris. He held up his travelcard and said something. The guard looked at it, then took out a master-card and put it through the gate to let Chris pass. When I saw the top of Chris's head disappear from view on the escalator I turned from the ticket machine and followed him, leaving a free ticket for whoever had been next in line at the machine.

I was about ten feet behind Chris as he reached the bottom of the escalator and headed for the Central Line platforms. He walked past the entrance to the westbound platform, went down the stairs to the eastbound, and walked along to the end of the platform. I wandered up close to him, but not too close. He was reading the advertising posters on the wall across the track. I shook my head. A typically Lonesome Charley go-between.

When the train pulled in a minute or so later I got into the carriage behind Chris's and watched him through the windows between the carriages as we pulled out of Holborn.

It takes about half a minute to go from Holborn to Chancery Lane. Chris moved aside to let some people get off, but he stayed on the train. The beeper sounded and the doors closed, and we moved off again.

The next station was St Paul's. Chris got off, and I followed him through the station and up onto Newgate Street. He turned left and walked down Paternoster Row into St Paul's Churchyard. As I came round the corner into the churchyard I caught sight of him going up the steps of the cathedral, and I hurried to catch up.

I'd thought he was perhaps going to catch a bus on Cannon Street, on the other side of the cathedral, but when I reached the top of the steps I saw him standing a few yards away.

He was facing me but he wasn't paying any attention. He had one hand in his trouser pocket; in his other hand was a small brown-paper-wrapped package. He was talking to someone. Between us was the line of columns that stand in front of the entrance to St Paul's. Whoever Chris was talking to was standing between two columns, out of my line of sight. I tried to look like a tourist, gazing about, blending in with the other tourists. There was a little group of Germans sitting on the steps just below me, arguing noisily and taking photographs of each other. I tried to look as if I belonged to them while I edged closer to Chris.

"She said it was crap," I heard him say. "She only gave me a hundred."

Whoever he was talking to said something, I didn't quite catch what. I was moving from column to column now, trying to look inconspicuous.

"I told you," Chris said. "No."

I was only two columns away from them now. I edged round one and saw the end of a suitcase protruding from behind the next.

I marched around the remaining column and just had time to see the surprised look on Chris's face as I grabbed Harry by the front of his coat and yelled, "*Hello!*"

I hadn't really thought about what I was going to do next. Harry looked startled for a moment, then he reached out with one hand, took me by the lapel and *pulled* me and everything *blinked.*

I looked around me. Some tourists screamed and scattered away from us. Something was different . . . Then there was a huge *boom.* I felt the concussion in my stomach, up through the soles of my feet. The buildings around us seemed to vibrate.

"Bishopsgate, April 25th, 1993!" Harry shouted at me. "Is this what you want?"

I looked at him. I said, "Harry—" and he *pulled* again and suddenly it was night and everything was quiet. I heard a bus coming up Ludgate Hill towards us. My stomach turned over, but I didn't let go of Harry. I looked at him and there was another huge bang, this time further away.

"St Mary Axe!" he screamed in my face. "April 10th, 1992! Is *this* what you want?"

I said, "Harry—" again but the world blinked into light once more. And blinked again into darkness, and again into light, but this time it was red-hot light. "Do you want *this*?" Harry shouted. "Do you?" He jerked my lapel again and the sun came back. "Do you want to see the Great Fire of London?" Jerk. Blink. "Do you want to see the fucking *Big Bang*?"

"Harry!" I shouted. "He's ripping you off!" Jerk. Blink. "Harry!" Jerk. Blink. A wave of furnace-heat rolled across us. "Bob paid him two hundred for that tape of St Clement Danes!"

Jerk. Blink.

Harry said, "Whoops," and the world blinked a couple more times and came to rest. "How much?"

"Two hundred," I panted. "*Jesus*, Harry."

He put his suitcase down on the step beside him. "What about the Ludgate Circus one?"

I looked about me, my head spinning. It was daytime again, a warm summer day. All the buildings around the cathedral seemed wrong. Old-fashioned cars and buses were going up and down Cannon Street. On the other side . . .

"Well?" Harry demanded.

I suddenly realized I was gaping. "A thousand," I said in a weak little voice. "Harry . . ."

"The little shit!" he shouted. "He said she gave him four hundred for it! I'll kill him!"

"Harry," I said. If I hadn't still had a hand buried in the front of his coat, I would have fallen over. "Where's Paternoster Square gone?"

"There," he said, pointing.

The road up Ludgate Hill divided at the cathedral and ran around both sides, instead of stopping at one side for the modern pedestrians-only precinct. Cars and buses were driving up the hill and going off on both sides of us, which was definitely not what I was used to.

"No!" I shouted, feeling that I was losing my reason. "Where's Paternoster Square *gone*?"

"Oh." He waved a hand vaguely, finally understanding what I was getting at. "Not there yet."

The precinct and the modern row of shops and offices on St Paul's Churchyard were gone, replaced by Victorian buildings. There were still shops on the ground floor, but now they had awnings outside them. The bland 'sixties development of Paternoster Square had been replaced by a tide of ugly buildings washing right up to the cathedral. People in 1940s dress were walking by, looking curiously at us as we stood there on the cathedral steps holding on to each other's coats.

I tried to swallow but my throat was dry. I said, "Where . . .?"

Harry smiled and looked up, and I heard a sound I had only ever heard on news-reel film before, the sound of air-raid sirens starting up. Harry looked at me and tipped his head to one side. A few moments later I thought I heard the sound of thousands of aircraft engines.

"Oh no," I said.

September 7, 1940, was a warm, sunny Saturday. It's said that around four o'clock that afternoon Göring and Kesselring stood on the cliffs of Cap Gris Nez and watched the bombers of the Second Air Fleet form up and head for London. I have no idea if that's true, but I do know what happened next.

The first wave of Heinkels and Dorniers, with their fighter escorts, came in from the east, up the river. They dropped their bombs on Woolwich Arsenal. Wave after wave of bombers came in.

In the evening the night bombers came and, using the fires started by the first attack as markers, started bombing again.

In those days, in Fire Brigade terminology, a fire that needed the attendance of thirty pumps was a big fire. By midnight on September 7 there were nine fires in East London rating over a hundred pumps. Woolwich Arsenal was a two-hundred-pump inferno. The firemen who fought the fires there were incredibly brave. Woolwich Arsenal was full of boxes of live ammo and nitroglycerine.

The devastation was unbelievable. The fires set the wooden blocks in the roadways alight. During the brief "all clear" around seven that evening, Bow Road and the East India Dock Road were choked with vehicles carrying people trying to get away.

In the docks, the warehouses burned. The firemen had to deal with conflagrations the like of which they'd never imagined. There were rum fires, pepper fires, paint fires, rubber fires, tea fires. By one o'clock on Sunday, September 8, the London Fire Brigade had discovered that sugar, floating in liquid form on the Dockland basins, burned as well.

Rotherhithe, Bermondsey, Poplar—the whole East End seemed to be on fire. Support was called in from fire stations a hundred miles away, and it still wasn't enough. Some of the fires in the East End burned for almost a week. And it was only the beginning.

I'd seen the photos. I'd watched the film. I was listening to it happening. I stared wide-eyed at the new world Harry had dragged me into.

Harry grinned and *pulled*, and the world blinked one more time. The noise of the German bombers and their bombs and the anti-aircraft batteries along the Thames Estuary was cut off.

"Oh, God," I said.

"Are the fish all right?" Harry asked.

Twenty-two

1

"It's not time travel, Tim," he said. "This isn't really 1940. It's a recording." He stopped and looked back. "Tim."

We had walked from St Paul's to Holborn Circus. I was standing on the pavement with my mouth open. I'd recognized hardly any of the buildings on our walk here from St Paul's, but then I didn't know that area very well. I did know Holborn Circus well, though, and it was as if I were in a different city. The only familiar thing here was the statue of Prince Albert on his horse in the middle of the junction.

On the other side of the road, occupying the entire block between Leather Lane and Hatton Garden, where I was used to seeing the big bronze-glass building that had W.H. Smiths and Dixons and Boots on its ground floor, were the four buildings, each of them slightly different, that made up Gamages.

"Jesus," I said. On all sides of me pedestrians in 1940s-style clothes were passing by, glancing inquisitively at me. Almost all the men were wearing hats and loose-fitting suits. The women were wearing heavy, drab dresses, thick stockings and sensible shoes. Most of them wore hats too. I stared at them and they stared back. They all had that air of not-quite-reality that I'd noticed in the newsreel footage I'd watched at Lonesome Charley. I thought about those two immense bangs I'd heard as Harry dragged me here, the two massive IRA bombs that had hit the City. A recording . . .

Harry came back and took me by the arm. He'd got his cardboard-box-on-a-string out of his suitcase before leaving St Paul's and slung it over his shoulder. There was no gas mask in it, but that didn't matter because Harry knew the Germans never tried a gas attack on London; it was just for camouflage, like his baggy blue pinstripe suit, and his dark overcoat with its astrakhan collar, and his homburg. He was sweating slightly in the warm afternoon. I looked at him and thought for a moment that he was starting to take on the same air of unreality as everyone else here.

"Are you going to embarrass me?" he asked quietly, trying to get me moving again.

"I'm going to do more than fucking embarrass you," I said.

He shook me gently by the arm. "Don't swear. The people here will notice it."

"Oh?" I watched the cars and open-topped buses waiting at the lights opposite Gamages. "Am I supposed to give a shit?"

He looked about him at the pedestrians going past us, touched the brim of his hat to two pretty girls. "Not that it matters," he said. "A lot of these people have been dead for fifty-odd years."

"Why didn't you tell me?" I said, refusing to move.

Harry sighed. "Would you have believed me?"

"I believe you now." I glared at a couple who were going past gaping as if I'd just stepped out of a flying saucer . . . only of course they'd not have heard of flying saucers, and wouldn't for another ten years or more. "Why are all these people looking at me?"

His face took on a grumpy, long-suffering expression. "You swear too much."

"Sod off."

Harry folded his arms across his chest. "You've got an earring; you're wearing jeans, a combat jacket and a sweatshirt with a picture of Frank Zappa on the front; and your hair's too long. And these people have never seen a pair of red-and-blue trainers before."

"Well, excuse me for not dressing for the occasion."

He shrugged and looked at me. "Maybe we can pass you off as an American. Most of these people have never met an American."

I pulled my jacket shut selfconsciously. "Shit." I suddenly felt defenceless and alone. I'd been more at home in Poland.

"Actually," Harry said, "I think you're dealing with this quite well."

I looked at him. "A recording?"

He nodded. "Sort of. You're not in 1940. You're in . . . oh, I don't know what it is. A bit of 1940 that never went away."

"Harry."

He shrugged again. "When did you figure it out?"

"When I saw the tape you left outside the office."

Harry looked sad, as if I'd disappointed him.

"Oh, so I was supposed to just work it out from available information, was I?" I shouted. "You disappear and I was just supposed to guess straight away?"

He tugged my arm again. "Let me buy you lunch."

I shook my arm free. "Are you *insane*?"

Harry took hold of my sleeve again. "It'll all look better once you've got some food inside you."

"No meal on earth is going to make this look better."

"Don't shout," he said, a pained expression on his face. "You're attracting attention."

"But they're all *dead*!" I yelled in his face. "What does it *matter*?"

"Let me buy you lunch," he said again.

I looked around me. "Is there a Burger King or something near here, then?"

It was Friday, September 6, 1940. Tomorrow, Göring and Kesselring would stand on the cliffs in France and watch the Blitz begin. Tomorrow night the Surrey Docks would be an inferno. By Monday morning Holborn would be impassable because of the rubble choking the streets.

"Here," Harry said, tugging my sleeve.

We went down a little alleyway off Holborn, and emerged in a tiny courtyard. Facing us across the court was a building with a little red-and-white wooden sign over the door.

"The Palazzo," said Harry. "My favourite restaurant."

"I'm not hungry," I said. "I'm angry."

He tugged my sleeve again. "I know. Come on and have something to eat. Did you have breakfast?"

I thought of the tepid croissant I'd washed down with unsweetened coffee in Bob's car in Mill Hill. "Yes."

"Don't be stubborn," he said like a firm but fair parent. "You're a stranger here."

"No I'm not," I said, staring at the front of the little restaurant.

"Oh yes you are." He beamed mildly at me. "You've read the books and you've seen the film. That's not the same thing. Now come and have some bloody *lunch*, will you?"

He urged me across the court and pushed open the door of the restaurant. A breath of warm air scented with coffee and garlic and bolognese brushed my face.

"Just a coffee," I said.

"And minestrone," Harry said, ushering me through the door. "The Palazzo does the best minestrone in Northern Europe."

The Palazzo was smaller than Harry's living room. A dozen or so tables stood crammed together with hardly any room to get between them. Most of them were taken, but one, by a window looking out onto the courtyard, was unoccupied.

An extremely old man wearing morning-dress, a wing collar and a black bow-tie shuffled towards us. "Table for two, is it, gentlemen?"

"That's right," Harry said, grinning like a maniac. "For myself and my American friend."

"Stop it, Harry," I muttered under my breath.

The old waiter led us slowly over to our table. The lapels of his tailcoat were stained with food and his shoulders were covered with dandruff. I was so mesmerized by him that I almost didn't notice the stares I got from the other diners.

"Can I take your coats, gentlemen?" he asked.

Harry took off his coat and handed it over. I started to do the same, but I remembered I had the face of Frank Zappa on my chest and held my combat jacket closed with one hand. "I'll hang onto mine for the moment, thanks."

The waiter bowed slightly, seated us, and went off towards a dark little cubby-hole at the back of the restaurant that contained a lot of hanging coats.

"Well," Harry said, settling back in his chair and smiling. "Here we are, then."

"Yes," I said, glaring balefully at him. "Here we are, then. Except by Monday *here* won't *be* here any more, will it?"

He shrugged sadly.

"By Monday *here* will have been bombed to buggery, won't it?"

He nodded. "You have to understand—"

"Oh, shut up, Harry."

Another waiter came painfully towards us with a little basket of bread rolls and two tiny saucers with a postage-stamp-sized pat of butter on each. He looked even older and more decrepit than the one who had met us at the door. He was completely bald and his tailcoat was in a terrible state, stained and threadbare. As he put the bread on the table I noticed that his thumbs were stained with what appeared to be bolognese sauce. Harry poured himself a glass of water from the jug on the table.

The Palazzo didn't appear to have started life as an Italian restaurant. It looked like someone's old living room. The walls were panelled with very dirty, very greasy wood, marked here and there with slightly lighter patches where the original fixtures and fittings had been removed. There were shelves of raffia-covered Chianti bottles and big dusty conch shells, and on the walls there were bits of fishing-net, complete with green glass floats, and framed prints of sunlit rocky bays. The door to the kitchen was open, and I could hear someone cursing in very rapid Italian.

Harry ordered two minestrones with coffee and cakes to follow, and the waiter wrote it down on a little pad that he had to hold right up to his face so he could see what he was writing.

I watched him make his way slowly back towards the kitchen and said, "Is this the place old waiters go to die, or something?"

"More or less," Harry said soberly. "They all live in flats above the restaurant."

I looked up at the smoke-stained ceiling. "Oh."

"This place takes a direct hit at about half-past two on Monday morning," he went on as if he were discussing a film he'd seen. "No survivors."

"Harry."

He shook his head. "You're really taking it very well, Tim."

"I should kick your head in, Harry Dean."

"Why?" He looked innocently affronted. "What on earth for?"

I waved a hand at the restaurant. "For leaving me stuck with Lonesome Charley Productions and just buggering off without a word."

"I thought you'd know where I'd gone."

"How?"

"The old man's film. The manuscript . . ."

"I thought they were fake!" I almost shouted. "I thought he'd ripped us off!"

He sat back and made urgent little placatory motions with his hands. "All right, I should have said something."

"Bloody right you should have," I said in a quieter voice, suddenly aware that everyone in the place was looking at me. "I've been going mad with worry."

"Oh, come on—"

"I've had the police looking for you," I hissed. "What do I tell them now? 'It's OK, officers, I've found Harry. I had lunch with him in 1940 just the other day'?" I sat back and grabbed a bread roll.

"Well, obviously you can't tell them that," he said. He saw the look on my face and held his hands up. "I was wrong. I apologize. But what if I'd left you a letter? 'Gone to see the Blitz. Love, Harry.' What would you have told the police then?"

I tore a piece off my roll and popped it in my mouth. I'd been dreaming for months about what I'd do if I finally caught up with Harry Dean, and none of my dreams had included lunch in an Italian restaurant in 1940. Or in a recording of 1940. Or whatever the bloody hell this was.

"The Blitz hasn't started yet," I said.

"Not till tomorrow, no," he said. "I popped us back a day."

"So how can this be a village? Mr Sierpiński said that only violent events formed villages."

He nodded. "He didn't describe it properly in the manuscript. It's like dropping a stone into a puddle. The ripples go off in all directions. The villages seem to form outwards from the event, in time as well as in space. If the event's violent enough, you get a village that starts a day before the event. Sometimes several days. That was how the old man was able to film the Bank Junction event before it happened. Down in the East End the Blitz village goes all the way back to the beginning of September." For a moment his eyes had a faraway, pained look. "I'm learning all kinds of things here."

"Well, bully for you."

Our waiter came out of the kitchen and started his long trek towards our table with two plates of minestrone soup. He was holding them in such a way that both his thumbs were immersed in the soup. I watched him, spellbound, willing him on. I thought that if I told him to go somewhere else on Sunday night, he wouldn't have to die when the Luftwaffe destroyed his home. None of the waiters would have to die. I could tell them all to get out before the bombs fell.

Harry shook his head. "Won't work."

I looked at him. "What?"

"Won't work. Won't change anything. He's already dead."

"Have you learned to read minds here as well?"

He smiled. "I thought the same thing when I first came into the villages. Save lives. Nice thought. But everybody who's going to die during the Blitz is already dead, Tim."

"He wouldn't die *here*, though, would he?" I said.

"But what would be the point, Tim?"

"Does there have to be a point?"

"I'd say so. You could save this old chap, but the next time the loop repeats he'll get killed just like he was in 1940. What are you going to do? Stay here forever, saving him in each repetition?"

The waiter finally arrived, laid our plates down, and departed, leaving a little drop of minestrone on the tablecloth from each thumb.

"First principles," Harry said, holding up his hand. "One"—he folded down a finger— "this is not the past. It's a loop of time that keeps repeating, that's all. The outside world is still there. In the outside world all these waiters have been dead for over fifty years."

"How do you know this isn't the past?" I said. "Mr Sierpiński could have been wrong."

"Because, if it was, anything we did here would change the present," he said. "And it doesn't. I've been experimenting, and nothing changes in 1990s London."

I felt a wave of cold go up my back. "You've been *experimenting*?" I almost shouted. "I *live* in 1990s London, Harry."

He looked primly at me and folded back another finger. "Two, nothing you do here makes a blind bit of difference. You could come in here and machine-gun everyone in the place, and tomorrow, or the next day, or the next, the loop would just start to repeat itself again and all these people would be back where they were when the village was created."

I felt a bit light-headed, although I couldn't tell whether it was because of the bizarre situation I found myself in or the idea of Harry Dean holding himself up as the world's expert in what was probably a completely unimagined branch of physics. "All right," I said.

"Three"—another finger—"you can't take anything out with you that was here when the village was created. I know. I've tried."

"I'll try to remember that."

"Four, try to think of the villages as concentric spheres. If you have more than one village on a site, they nest. I can stand right here and pop you forwards to the end of the Blitz, or back to the Great Fire."

"Or the Big Bang," I said, remembering what he'd said on the steps of St Paul's.

"I haven't tried that yet," he said with a little grin. "But it should be possible, theoretically."

"Five," I said, "how do you get in here?"

He smiled and put away his hand. "Eat your soup before it gets cold," he said, and picked up his spoon.

I looked down and took the edge of the tablecloth between my thumb and forefinger. It had started out with a pattern of red-and-white squares, but now it had faded and the edge was worn from too much washing. There was a little patch in the middle of the table, not quite under the water jug, where it had torn and then been stitched up.

Harry looked up. "What?"

"It's so bloody *ordinary*, isn't it?"

He raised an eyebrow.

I looked around the restaurant. "I mean, this is incredible. 1940. But it's . . . *shabby*." I looked at him.

He shrugged. "It's no more shabby than things in realtime. What did you expect? Narnia?" He waved his spoon at me. "Eat your soup. It's very good."

I dipped a piece of bread roll in the soup and ate it. I picked up my spoon and started to eat.

"Are you sure Chris was ripping me off?" Harry said.

I nodded, still eating. He was right. The soup was very good.

He scowled. "I thought I could trust him."

"His boss must be in on it," I said. "Bob made the cheques out to the company."

Harry shook his head and muttered, "Bollocks. I just gave him five more tapes to sell."

"How do you do it, Harry? Was it in the manuscript? Something in the film?"

He smiled and kept shaking his head.

"Did the old man tell you how when you went to see him?"

He had finished his soup. He gazed at me and smiled beatifically. I sighed. Our waiter was making his way towards us with coffee and cakes. He was shaking so much that half the coffee was going into the saucers, but he came across the little restaurant with an unshatterable dignity. He laid the plates and cups and saucers on the table, removed our soup plates, and launched himself back towards the kitchen.

I watched the waiter go for a long time before turning back to Harry. "I finished the film," I said, spooning sugar into my coffee.

He smiled mildly at me. "Thanks."

I stared. "Is that all you can say?"

Harry looked around the restaurant. "What else do you want me to say?"

I leaned towards him. "I thought you'd be pleased."

He shrugged. "Well I'm not *upset* or anything . . ."

I sat back and picked up my coffee cup. "You rotten bastard," I said.

"Shh." Harry put a finger to his lips and looked furtively about him. "Language."

"Fuck off."

He pursed his lips disapprovingly and crossed his arms across his chest and glared at me, but it was nice to wipe that soppy smile off his face for a few moments.

I said, "I've worked my bollocks off for the past eight months to get your fucking pet project on the telly, and all you can say is 'thanks'. Jesus, Harry."

He picked up a cream bun and bit into it. Then he took a sip of coffee while he waited to see if I had anything else to say. Finally he put his cup down and shook his head. "I'm sorry, Tim."

"My God. An apology from the Lord and Master. Thank you, Lord and Master; I'm not worthy."

"Don't be sarcastic, Tim."

I waved my own cream bun at him. "I think I have every right to be sarcastic. I think I have every right to slap you to within an inch of your miserable life for what you did to me."

"You didn't have to finish the film, Tim."

"You gave me the bloody company! I had no choice!"

"Don't be silly. Of course you did." He sipped some more coffee.

"Yes. I had the choice between finishing the film and being declared bankrupt before I was twenty-six. Thanks a lot, Harry. Big choice."

He sat back and watched me. "Did they screen it?"

"Yes, they screened it." I nodded. "Oh yes, they screened it. And we got some pretty bloody good reviews too."

"You didn't use the obituaries, though, did you."

"Of course I didn't."

Harry sucked his teeth and shook his head sadly. "I knew you wouldn't."

I stared at him, unsure whether to be really angry or not any longer. "It turned out really well," I said. "Viren and Ron Booth helped."

He inclined his head. "They're good lads."

And then we just sat there looking at each other, the first flood of my anger gone. I sighed and said, "*Why*, Harry?"

He reached into an inside pocket of his jacket and took out his wallet, and from the wallet he took two pieces of paper and put them down on the table in front of me. I looked down at them. They were almost identical, except one was yellow with age and sealed in a little plastic envelope, while the other one was crisp and new. I picked them up.

They were cuttings from the letters page of a newspaper, cuttings of the same letter. The older one was creased and worn, and the bottom had been torn off, along with the name and address of the writer, but I only had to read half a dozen words before I knew what it was. His name was on the new cutting. Jacek Sierpiński. It was the letter he'd written to *The Times* after he'd discovered the villages.

I looked up. "No," I said.

"Yes," said Harry.

I looked towards the door, my heart sinking. "*No.*"

"My old uncle worked on *The Times*," he said. "He must have brought that one home with him and given it to my Dad." Nodding at the older cutting. "I saw it once when I was ten, and I found it again when I was clearing the house after my Mum died. I got the other one about two months ago, in 1941."

My head hurt. He'd been jumping about like a grasshopper, from one village to the next, from one part of a village to another. I rubbed my eyes.

"I only saw it once when I was a kid," I heard Harry say, "but I never forgot it."

I picked up the yellowed cutting in its plastic envelope and waved it at him. I was going to shout as well, but all I could do was shake my head.

"I know you think I'm crazy," Harry said, "but it's true, Tim. I found it, and it's true."

"There must have been some other way. Couldn't you have just gone up to Colindale and looked it up?"

He shook his head. "It never went into the paper. My uncle only had it because he worked at *The Times*. They set it in type and then they decided to take it out again. It's a crank letter; I'm amazed they even thought about publishing it."

I looked at the two letters. "Did you see your uncle?"

"Hm?"

"When you went to *The Times* to get this one." I held up the new cutting.

Harry smiled approvingly, as if I had come on satisfactorily in his absence. "I took him to the Cheshire Cheese on Fleet Street and bought him a pint. You have to understand, Tim."

"What?" I said. "What do I have to understand?"

He put his elbow on the tabletop and supported his chin in the palm of his hand. "I never forgot that letter, Tim," he said in an almost dreamy tone of voice. "Oh, I didn't think about it every day, but I didn't quite forget it either. I'm not one of those people who believes in flying saucers and crop circles." He tapped the yellowed old cutting with his fingernail. "But I got a funny feeling when I saw this, and it never went away."

I crossed my arms and frowned at him.

"So," he said. "Here I am, pushing fifty. I'm making a film about the Blitz, but to be honest with you I don't know how I'm going to do it."

"I'd noticed."

He smiled. "I should never have gone to sea. My Dad wanted me to. He was Old Navy, on corvettes during the war. I made it all the way to the dizzy heights of Chief Petty Officer and he was really proud, but I hated practically every minute of it. I couldn't just pack it in, though, because he'd have made my life an even bigger misery than it was in the Navy."

I nodded. I could sympathize with that.

"I first had the idea for the film in Singapore, oh, twelve or fifteen years ago," Harry said, a faraway look in his eyes. "Met this old chap in a bar one night. He'd been with the anti-aircraft battery stationed in Hyde Park, came out East to the rubber plantations after the war. He told me all these stories about the Blitz, and I must have spent fifty quid buying him drinks just to keep him talking. I was hooked. I thought maybe I could write a book about it, but when I tried it was hopeless."

"So you decided to make a film instead?" I asked, smiling incredulously.

He nodded. "Of course, I didn't have any more idea about how to make a film than I had about how to write a book, but I sort of made it up as I went along. I was going to make a film about the Blitz when I left the Navy. It kept me going."

"And then you discovered that thinking about it was different to actually doing it."

"Well, at first it was pretty straightforward." He picked up his cup and sipped some coffee. "When I came ashore I set up Lonesome Charley and approached the television people with the idea and started to gather the material I thought I needed, and then it just sort of"—he looked up into a corner of the ceiling—"stalled." He stared levelly at me.

"You should have told me all this a long time ago, Harry," I said. "You never wanted to finish the perishing thing. All you wanted to do was keep listening to the stories."

He shrugged. "Maybe. I don't know. I was almost fifty and I just seemed stuck. Couldn't go forwards, couldn't go back."

"And then you saw the old man's film."

Harry laughed. "There was something about it, you know. The chronology of it. First the crater, then no crater, then the crater again. I didn't see any splices, and it looked like original stock, though people have been faking film for years. But it reminded me of that old cutting. He wrote about the Bank Junction bomb, and about going back again and again and filming it. It's no wonder they locked him up." He took his chin off his hand and gestured in the air. "You know when you get a feeling that something is just *right*?"

I sat there trying to come to terms with the idea that I was sitting in the Palazzo chiefly because Harry had had a menopausal whim triggered by a few yards of old ciné film and a newspaper cutting.

"I knew it was him," Harry went on. "I knew it was him and that it was all true."

"But you had to go to Poland and check."

"Of course. I didn't want to make a fool of myself."

"You didn't mind making a fool of me, though."

He looked at me. "I was in a hurry," he said.

"Sure," I said.

"I really was," he insisted. "All that time stuck in that fucking office, and suddenly I had something marvellous in the palm of my hand. What would you have done?"

"I'd have left a note."

The rapt expression was leaving his face. "I've apologized for that already."

I sipped some coffee but it was cold. I put the cup down on its saucer and said, "What about Sophie?"

2

I looked at my watch. I had to do it furtively because nobody else on the train had a watch that told you the time in LCD digits and lit up when you pushed a button. It was half-past six on a Thursday evening in August 1995.

Or it was nine o'clock on an evening in late November 1940. I honestly didn't know what to believe any more.

I leaned forward across the aisle of the carriage so that Harry could hear me over the racket of the train, and I said, "Sophie."

He smiled and nodded.

"I didn't come here for you," I said, ignoring the looks I was getting from the other passengers.

He kept smiling.

I sighed and sat back. We were on a Central Line train. Harry had paid the bill for lunch with a huge white five pound note, collected what appeared to be a colossal amount of change, and we had left the Palazzo and walked on up Holborn. I was developing a survival technique: I was ignoring everyone and everything around me and only paying attention to Harry. Every now and again I made the mistake of looking at the buildings or the people and I entirely lost the thread of the conversation.

At Holborn, Harry had done his little trick of grabbing me by the lapels and everything had blinked again and suddenly it was dark and sirens were wailing in the sky and we'd jumped forwards almost two months. The waiters at the Palazzo were all dead. The Blitz was just getting into its stride.

As far as I understood it, the Blitz had effectively made the whole of the East End, the City and the West End one huge village, into which were embedded sub-villages surrounding actual bomb-sites. You could go into the larger Blitz village and revisit the individual bombings over and over again, to your heart's content. There were smaller villages surrounding bombings further west, in Westminster and Chelsea and so on. People kept looking at me as if I were an alien.

We went down into the Tube station. I'd followed Chris here only a few hours earlier, but now it was transformed. The wooden escalators were back, the glazed tiles on the walls, the 1940s posters, the slim tulip-shaped Art Deco lamps on the escalators.

We caught an eastbound Central Line train, just as I had earlier in the day when I'd been following Chris. The train was clean and old-fashioned and somehow quaint, just like the people on it. It wasn't crowded. Nobody came through the carriages mugging passengers. Nobody threw up over their neighbour. Nobody exposed themselves to a homeward-bound typist.

"This is not in the least bit funny," I said, leaning forward again. He hadn't stopped smiling. He looked like a rather seedy Buddha. "It's your right to have whatever weird kind of mid-life crisis you want, but you can't drag Sophie along."

"Oh?" he said. The train started to slow. "Our stop."

I looked up. We were at Liverpool Street.

The last time I had seen Liverpool Street station it had been a marvel of modern architecture, all glass and tubular steel. We came up the stairs into a dark labyrinth of brick and tile and flagstones and the incredible smell of steam engines. A cold wind blew off the platforms and under the station canopies. The end of November 1940. My God, it was all true . . .

"You mustn't think badly of Sophie," Harry said beside me as I looked at the hissing, smoking engines. He put his hands in his overcoat pockets and rocked back and forth on the balls of his feet. "We were together before you even came for your interview. She really thought it was rather sweet when you told her you loved her."

"It was nice of her to mention it to you," I said, wanting to punch him.

He took one hand out of his pocket and put it gently on my shoulder. "I know there's no logic to any of this, Tim," he said. "You're too young to understand that there's rarely any logic to anything."

"What have you done with her?" I said.

Instead of answering he tugged my arm and led me back down to the Underground. I was trying to imagine a bit of film and a newspaper clipping that had changed my life before I was even born. Harry had believed in the villages ever since he was a little boy, and as soon as the opportunity had presented itself he had gone looking for them. I wondered what I would have done in his place.

I stood beside him on the Underground platform thinking about what he had said, and of course he was right. There was no logic to anything. Sometimes things happen that just don't make sense, but they happen anyway.

The westbound train arrived and we got on. I sat beside Harry feeling miserable.

"I'm living in your flat," I said, somewhere between St Paul's and Chancery Lane.

"Pardon?" He leaned sideways to hear me above the noise of the train in the tunnel.

"I said I'm living in your flat."

He thought about it, then he nodded. "Don't overfeed the fish."

"How did you manage to afford to buy it?"

"I didn't. It was my uncle's. He left it to me when he died."

Of course. Almost everything in Harry's life came to him second-hand and cheap. "So where are you living now?"

"You can live practically anywhere you want," he said. "London's full of properties up for rent or for sale."

"Don't tell me you're surprised."

Harry shook his head. "Half these places belong to people in the armed forces. A lot of them belong to people who didn't come back from Dunkirk."

I rubbed my eyes. It was all starting to get too weird for me again.

We got off at Holborn. Up above, the raid must have been in full swing. The platforms were packed with people. Half of them seemed to have brought their life's possessions with them. There was a line of three-tier bunk beds along the back wall of the platform, but there just weren't enough of them to accommodate the sheer numbers of people down here. Somewhere down towards the end of the platform someone was singing. The smell was appalling: a mixture of damp cloth, urine, faeces and disinfectant.

"Nobody mentions the smell," Harry said as we stepped between prone bodies. "Did you ever notice that? Nobody seems to remember the smell. There was usually a bucket or two down the end of the platform, with a blanket to curtain them off from everybody else, but nobody remembers the smell."

I was trying not to tread on somebody's face as I went by.

"And nobody mentions the hardship," Harry went on as if the sheltering hundreds weren't here, as if we were walking through a zoo and commenting on the animals. "If you speak to them, all they talk about is the Blitz Spirit. Their Finest Hours. Nobody tells you about being stuck down here for hours on end in the smell and being scared to death and going home after the All Clear and finding a pile of rubble where home used to be."

"I've heard people talk about their homes being bombed," I said.

He shook his head. "It's not the same. It's romanticized. The old folk who did tapes for Lonesome Charley talked about it as if it was the best moment of their lives, the *defining* moment." We reached the exit. The escalators had been turned off and more people were sitting on the steps, huddled in their coats. I could hear the bombs now, down the throat of the escalator, a dim thump-thump-thump. It was the scariest sound I had ever heard.

"The Blitz Spirit is a load of bollocks," Harry said, staring at the ranks of bodies that mounted up towards the ticket hall far above. "The truth is, everybody was just scared." He looked at me. "Did you put that in the film?"

"I think I mentioned it," I said, suddenly feeling a great compassion for all the frightened people in all the Tube stations and shelters in London tonight. I thought that if I'd had this experience before I'd completed the film there would have been a subtle change of emphasis in the finished product.

Harry shook his head again and began to pick his way along a side-tunnel packed with people.

"You didn't believe it was *fun*, did you?" I said, following.

He waved a hand at the sheltering bodies. "To hear these people talk," he said.

My God, I thought as I tried to keep up with him. The Blitz had *disappointed* Harry. He'd come looking for the Spirit of the Blitz and he'd discovered it had been a retrospective thing, that people had looked back on it and said, "That wasn't so bad. Adolf will have to try harder than *that*." He'd come here looking for community, for a populace with a single purpose, and all he'd found was a city full of scared people. It occurred to me to ask him if he hadn't listened to any of the tapes that Sophie and I had made, but then I realized he had listened to all of them, subconsciously looking for the clue that would lead him to the writer of that letter to *The Times*. And all those voices had told him about the Spirit of the Blitz. Nobody had ever said anything about the smell.

He turned and caught the front of my jacket as I reached him. I tried to watch his feet, his body language, as he *pulled* me and the sheltering people vanished.

"I need you to do me a favour," he said.

It was early morning as we walked down Kingsway. Harry had a little crowbar in his suitcase that he had used to break the lock on the grille across the entrance at Holborn station. We passed a patrolling policeman who touched his helmet as we went by towards the Aldwych.

"You have to understand a place," Harry said. "Its language, its history, the people. I think that's part of it." He swung his suitcase as he walked.

"Is that all?" I said.

He shook his head. "No. No, it's not. I think it helps, though. A sort of sympathy for the place you're going."

At the foot of Kingsway we turned left and walked along the curve of the Aldwych and the front of the Law Courts. After we passed the bottom of Chancery Lane we were on Fleet Street. I was glad there was a moon because there were no street lights. I'd managed to forget all about the blackout, I was so confused. Then I remembered that they called this a Bombers' Moon, and I wasn't quite so happy about it any more.

We walked a little way along Fleet Street before Harry abruptly turned left and walked down a little alleyway. I went on for a few feet before I noticed he was gone, and had to retrace my steps.

"This'll do," Harry said from the other end of the alleyway.

"Sophie," I said. I was tired and upset and too many weird things had happened to me today. I just wanted to find Sophie and go home.

"You've got some strange idea that I took her away against her will," said Harry. "That's not what happened."

"I love her, and I've come to take her home," I said, feeling ludicrous the moment I said it. "If you want a fight about it, that's fine."

We looked at each other from either end of the alley. He was just a vague shape against the barely lighter courtyard behind him.

"I'll tell you where she is if you'll do me a favour," he said.

I thought about it, reckoning I had already done Harry Dean enough favours to last a lifetime. This was what the whole day had been about, of course. The Palazzo, the trip to Liverpool Street to see the trains, the guided tour through Holborn station at the height of a raid—all to soften me up. It was impossible to accuse Harry of not taking advantage of a situation.

"All right," I said.

I saw his head nod. "Come here, then."

Twenty-three

"I always work alone," Fitch said.

"I know," I said. "You keep telling us."

"Shh," Bob hissed, looking nervously about.

"Relax," said Fitch. "Nobody's going to hear us. And if they do they won't pay us any attention."

He was probably right. Even at this hour of the morning there was quite a lot of traffic on Mill Hill Broadway and soaring across the skyline on the flyover and from the Barnet Bypass at the other end of the road. From the main road in front of the parade of shops I could hear a group of drunks shouting and singing as they made their way towards the station, and on the other side of the motorway an express thundered northwards. Nobody was going to hear our humble whispers over that racket. I wondered how anybody managed to live here with all that noise.

I looked down the alleyway and imagined policemen crouching in the darkness behind bins and piles of discarded cardboard boxes. "Is this going to take long?"

Beside me, Fitch shook his head sadly and said, "Amateurs." He was holding a tiny little torch that hung from his key-ring; its beam picked out the lock on FilmSafe's back door in a circle of light about the size of a five-pence piece.

"Don't look," he said.

"What?" I said, looking.

He sighed. "It's bad enough I have to drag you two about with me," he said. "I don't want to give away trade secrets as well."

"Oh. Sorry." I looked away.

"OK," Fitch said almost immediately, and opened the door.

"Jesus, that was quick," said Bob, and made to step inside.

Fitch grabbed her arm. "Wait here," he said, and went into the back of the shop.

Bob and I waited outside, nervously looking up and down the alley, alert for the slightest sound. The drunks seemed to have stopped a few doors further down. There was laughter, some angry shouting. I willed them to go away; the last thing we needed was a passing patrol car to see them and decide to stop.

"All right." Fitch's voice barely reached us. "Don't step on the doormat."

We went inside, stepping over the mat, and I pushed the door shut behind us. Fitch had taken a thick blanket from his bag and fixed it over the single window so that no light could get out; he'd folded his jacket up and put it along the bottom of the door to the front of the office for the same purpose. There was a click and a neon tube blinked into life above us, and we all stood looking a little foolish in the middle of the room. There was a shelf of videotapes on one wall, and three video recorders and a television linked together in one corner. Bob was opening the drawers of a desk that stood across another corner.

"Alarms?" I said.

He snorted. "I'd be ashamed if those alarms were on any office of mine." He was a tall, unnaturally pale man, a friend of a friend of a friend of Martin's, and everything he did had what I thought of as a professional grace. He was calm and unhurried and the only thing that seemed to bother him was that Bob and I were here too.

"Well," said Bob. "Now that we're here . . ."

"Right," I said. "We want videotapes. Little ones that go in camcorders," I added for Fitch's benefit, but he just seemed bored. "And any copies." I pointed at the safe in the corner of the room. "That looks like a good place to start."

Fitch walked over and stared down at the safe and shook his head. I heard him say, "Jesus," very quietly. He squatted down in front of it and ran his gloved hands over the handle and the lock. "Don't look."

I looked away, and when I looked back the door was open. "Fuck," Bob said. "How does he do that?"

"Trade secret," I said, kneeling beside Fitch.

Inside the safe were a cashbox, some legal documents, and about two dozen camcorder cassettes. I took the cassettes out. None of them was labelled.

"OK," I said. "We take all of them."

"Fine," Fitch said, tugging the cashbox out and poking a long thin steel needle into its lock.

"What are you doing?" I said.

He looked at me and raised an eyebrow. "Let's at least make this *look* like a real burglary, all right?"

"It *is* a real burglary, isn't it?" He tipped his head back slightly and regarded me past the tip of his thin, straight nose. I met his eyes for a moment, then I said, "OK. Bob, unplug the videos."

She looked up from the desk. "What?"

"They're going to know they've been burgled anyway, Bob." I stopped. It sounded as if the drunks outside had started to fight. I heard a crash, running feet, then more shouting. "Fuck."

"What about the machines?" Bob said, standing behind the desk.

"We're taking them. Check the tapes on that shelf, see if there are any more copies there." Fitch and I looked at each other. "What do we do if the police come?" I asked, nodding out towards the street.

He smiled. He had a gentle, sad face. He looked as if nothing ever surprised him any more. "They're hardly going to be wondering if there's a burglary going on, are they?" he said.

"They might check."

He shook his head. "Don't panic."

"All right." If he wasn't worried, neither was I. "All right." I looked down at the pile of tapes in front of me. "And see if there's an adaptor around here somewhere," I said to Bob.

We got the tapes, Fitch got the video recorders and the money from FilmSafe's cashbox. We waited until the sound of the drunks went away, then we left. Fitch tidied up his blanket and his jacket. The last thing he did was take a jemmy from his bag and put a series of splintered marks on the door and the frame.

"All the police see is the obvious," he said in that sad way of his. "They haven't the time or the manpower for anything else," and I knew those splintered marks were his insurance. The police knew him, and knew he wouldn't use brute force to open a door. They'd see those marks and just figure someone had broken it open, and that young Terry hadn't locked his safe properly. They'd see the missing video machines and the empty cash box and reckon kids had done it.

We split up. I walked back to the Brianmobile with the tapes. Every step of the way I expected a policeman to leap out of the shadows and arrest me, but nothing happened. Bob went back to her car, parked a few streets away. Where Fitch went, I have no idea.

I had to stop once on the Finchley Road to be sick, but otherwise I got back to St John's Wood without incident. I was dreading seeing somebody in the block, but I got to the flat without bumping into anyone. I closed the door and leaned back against it and sighed a huge sigh of relief. Just over a year ago, I had been a directionless young graduate. Now I was an independent filmmaker, I was the boss of my own company, I was living in a sumptuous flat, and I had just burgled an office in Mill Hill. Amazing. I dashed into the toilet and was sick again.

I started to wash my face before I realized I was still wearing the thin rubber gloves that Fitch had given us earlier in the evening. I stripped them off and put them in the kitchen bin. Then I took them out, balled them up, and put them in my coat pocket.

The clock in the living room read half-past two. I still had about an hour. I unzipped my bag and took out the pile of videotapes we'd taken from FilmSafe. There were fifteen of them. Harry had said he'd given Chris seven: the two that Martin and Bob had bought, plus five more on the day I'd interrupted the meeting at St Paul's. I fumbled one at random into the VHS adaptor Bob had found in the office, switched on the tv, and slotted it into the video.

The picture that came up was of a young blonde woman sucking a large erect penis while being fucked from behind by an Arab-looking chap with a tattoo on his arm. I stared, then fast-forwarded the tape for a while before I remembered what I was supposed to be doing. I popped the tape out.

The next one had a man on a bed with two women. I popped the tape out and threw it over my shoulder, slotted the next one.

Burning buildings. A crazily bobbing viewpoint. Bingo. I took it out, put it to one side.

I had the fourth one in the machine when the doorbell rang. In this one the Arab-looking man had been secured to the head and foot of a bed by his wrists and ankles with handcuffs. A white-haired woman whose torso had been squeezed down to a fraction of its normal volume by a leather basque was gently whipping his thighs with a riding crop.

"You got here then," said Bob.

"Come on in," I said. "The late show's on."

Bob took one look at the telly and said, "Home-made." The man on the bed had a huge erection by now. He was twisting and turning against the restraint of the handcuffs, grinning broadly. The woman peeled off her latex panties and straddled him. The camera suddenly did an extravagant sweeping pan. "Crowd goes wild," Bob said. "A thousand horny punters get motion sickness." She tutted and said, "Derivative."

"I don't imagine you can get too creative," I said.

"You'd be surprised." She turned away from the screen. "Does this kind of thing turn you on, Ramsay?"

I bent down to the video and ejected the tape. "I don't have time."

I parked the Brianmobile on a meter in Shoe Lane and we walked down to Farringdon Street and across the road to Ludgate Circus. It was very quiet, so still that I could hear the buzz of the streetlamps high above us. I thought it was weird, it being so noisy out in Mill Hill but so quiet here in the middle of London.

"Take me with you," Bob said.

"Where?"

"Into the villages," she said. "Take me with you. You owe me."

It was true, I did owe her. Unfortunately, tonight was not Bob's lucky night. "I'm not going in. I don't know how. Harry's coming out."

"Shit," she muttered.

We walked up Ludgate Hill. The cathedral was illuminated by powerful blue-white lamps mounted on the buildings around it; it looked as if it were being illuminated by daylight coming in from another dimension. Huge and pale, it rose above us the way it must have risen above the Londoners who saw it being completed. I'd hardly even noticed it was there after seeing it the first once or twice. It occurred to me that there was a lot of London I had just taken for granted.

At the top of the hill we walked across the cathedral forecourt and stood squinting up at St Paul's. Trust Harry to have a clandestine meeting in a place that was lit up like daylight.

"Well?" called a voice behind us.

We looked round and there was Harry, with his homburg and his entrepreneur's coat and his cardboard box on a string, standing back in the shadows near the corner of Ave Maria Lane. We walked over to him.

"Hello, Bob," he said, touching the brim of his hat.

"You have a lot to answer for, Harry Dean," said Bob.

"I don't doubt." He looked at me. "Did you get them?"

I held up the seven camcorder cassettes, wrapped in brown paper and tied with string, as per instructions.

"The copies?"

"There's no way to tell if we got all the copies," I said. "We took what we could find. You can't use full-size VHS tapes in that camera anyway. I'll wipe them."

He nodded and took the package. "Teach them to try and rip *me* off," he muttered.

I took another package out of my coat pocket. Two fresh powerpacks and a charger for the camera and seven hundred pounds in white fivers and pound notes circa 1940. Bob had spent a whole week touring antique shops and currency collectors looking for them; they'd cost me a fortune.

Harry took them. "You won't see me again," he said.

"Unless you need something," I said.

"That's OK, Harry," Bob said sourly. "You're welcome."

"Where's Sophie, Harry?" I said.

He shook his head. "I don't know."

"You bastard!" I yelled, and my voice echoed up and off the facades of the buildings around us. "You said you'd tell me if I got those tapes back!"

Harry was looking disingenuous. "I really don't know, Tim. She said there was something she wanted to see in Poland."

I felt my shoulders slump. "Where?"

"Poland," he said again. "She just said there was something she wanted to see in Poland."

"And you simply let her go?" I said very quietly.

He spread his arms, one hand holding the tapes, the other holding the money and the batteries. "How was I supposed to stop her? She didn't want to see the Blitz."

"*I* want to see the Blitz," Bob said, stepping forward, but Harry just smiled and shook his head, seemed to set his feet deliberately, and was gone.

"Fuck," said Bob.

"Oh, you *bastard*," I said, staring at the place where Harry had been and trying to deal with the news that Sophie hadn't gone with him at all, that she had set out on some journey of her own.

We stood there in silence for a minute or so, then Bob turned to me and said, "What now?"

I took a deep breath and sighed. "Let's go home."

On the way back to the car I took out the balled-up rubber gloves I'd worn to burgle FilmSafe and I shoved them into a pile of boxes and rubbish bags on the pavement outside a shop.

"Coffee?" Bob asked.

"Mm." I went through the flat turning the lights on. Bob went into the kitchen. I switched on the television and the video and slumped down on the sofa. It was gone four o'clock in the morning and I didn't feel remotely tired.

All the other camcorder tapes from FilmSafe's safe had turned out to be pornography, enacted in a bewildering variety of combinations and situations. Five of the VHS tapes were copies of the Bank Junction and St Clement Danes footage; the rest had been copies of the pornography on the tapes from the safe. The last one we'd looked at, the one in the machine now, involved a long-drawn-out sequence that started with a woman masturbating on a sofa and added people in ones and twos until the whole screen was a heaving field of flesh and pubic hair. I picked up the remote control and turned the sound off, afraid of bothering Mr Pahlavi next door with the screams and moans coming from the set.

"Do you think it's blackmail?" I asked as Bob came in with two mugs of coffee.

"What?"

I nodded at the tv. "Do you think Terry's blackmailing all these people?"

Bob laughed. "You're such an innocent, Ramsay. I told you: this is home-made porn."

"Really?"

She nodded. "Young Terry probably handles distribution and copying."

I waved my hand at the set. "You mean these are all real people? I mean, ordinary people? I could bump into them on the bus or something?"

"It's possible," she said.

"Good grief."

"Ramsay?"

"Mm?" It was hard to tear my eyes from the screen. Lisa would have loved all this. She and Eric would never have come out of his room.

"Have you got any condoms?"

I looked at her. "What? No."

She sighed. "Well, thank Christ I brought my own."

Daylight was brightening the curtains when she said, "You've got to find her, you know."

I snuggled up against her side and said, "Who?"

"Don't pretend to be a prat. You know who I mean."

"I'm not pretending," I said, nuzzling against the curve of her breast.

"Yes you are." She sat up. "You've changed a lot since I first met you."

I grinned lasciviously. "One night with you," I said.

Bob crossed her arms over her breasts and looked down at me with an annoyed expression on her face. "That day you came into the office with Harry's invoice. Remember that?"

"Oh, don't remind me." I pressed my face to the mattress in embarrassment.

"You were such an idiot then. You looked like a rabbit caught in a car's head-lights, all alone in the big bad world."

"All right," I said, struggling upright and punching the pillow into shape behind me. "All right, I'll buy it. How am I different now? I'm still an idiot. The world is still weirder than I can cope with. I'm living in a city where housewives make their own hard-core videos and you can go and eat in 1940, for Christ's sake."

"You still love Sophie."

"No." I hugged her, trying to pretend I hadn't heard the name. "No, I don't."

"Ramsay. Ramsay, look at me."

I looked at her. There was an expression on her face that I couldn't read, and my heart went out to her in something beyond love, beyond sex, beyond lust. Something incredibly precious had happened to me here last night, something too valuable to articulate.

"Last night you burgled somebody's office just so Harry would tell you where Sophie was," Bob said. "You broke the law just to find out if she was all right."

"She said she didn't believe me."

"So?"

"So what am I supposed to do?"

She shrugged her shoulders. "I don't know. I don't think you're supposed to just give up, though. You've got to prove it to her."

"She's in *Poland*, Bob," I said gently. "Not just in Poland, but a bit of Poland's history. Have you any idea how *much* violent history Poland has?"

Bob shook her head.

"And, even if I did find out where she is, how can I follow her?"

"You'll find a way." She smiled.

I lay back against the pillow. "This isn't going to happen again, is it? Last night, I mean."

Bob shook her head. "I'm opposed to long-term relationships, Ramsay. Hey, are you crying?"

I rubbed my eyes. "No."

"Jesus. Nobody ever *cried* before."

"Can we still be friends?"

"What?" She looked surprised. "Of course we can still be friends. Fucking hell, the only thing that's different is that now I know how pathetic your cock is." She laughed, and I thought I could see a wet shine in her eyes too.

"Can we do it one more time?" I asked. "Before you have to go?"

She smiled at me. "OK. I'd like that."

"I love you, Bob," I said.

Bob's smile widened into a huge grin. "I don't believe you," she said, leaning over me.

Twenty-four

1

The first thing Mr Rutkowski said to me was, "*Dzień Dobry. Jestem* Jacek Rutkowski." After he had said it a woman's voice said, "*Kto to jest?*" and then there was a silence, during which I was supposed to say, "*To jest* Jacek Rutkowski." Then she said that as well.

The Rutkowskis lived in a large town that could have been Warsaw or Kraków or Poznań or any large town in Poland. Their flat must have been huge, because it housed not only Jacek and his wife Marta but additionally their three children, two pairs of grandparents, and a lodger who was from Canada. There was also a dog called, for no apparent reason, Balicki. From the drawings of him, Balicki seemed to be that type of mongrel which Poles call "multidog".

Marta cooked. The kids went to school. Jacek worked in an office. The grandparents had a plot of land in the country and they were always out there planting vegetables or pulling up weeds or chasing away moles with a broom, which as far as I knew was an original solution to the problem of mole infestation but made for funny drawings.

The Canadian was great fun. His name was Robert, and he was a true innocent abroad. He was continually getting lost and having to ask directions to the hotel, the post office or the railway station, and the people he asked for directions all had the same clear, regionless, classless accent as the Rutkowskis. I was starting to think of it as BBC Polish.

Each lesson was accompanied by a booklet with vocabularies and illustrations. Jacek had a little goatee beard. Marta was large and jolly. Robert was blond and vaguely untidy and eerily resembled Kurt Cobain. He always had a rucksack over one shoulder, even when he was in the flat. Each booklet covered a different subject. The Town. The Country. The Kitchen. The Grocery. Then there were little excursions. The Rutkowskis somehow managed to cram the entire family into their Little Fiat and motored off to Sopot on the coast. The children splashed in the Baltic. Robert got lost in Sopot and had to ask for directions to the beach.

I was fascinated by them. It was like a weirdly sedate soap opera. Even after I had gone through the baby-lessons and graduated to long lists of nouns and verbs and complex sentences, I kept going back to the well thumbed booklets for another fix. I loved the Rutkowskis. They had never suffered through Communism; Marta had never queued for anything; Jacek had never worried about his job. The only one of them who seemed to suffer any misfortune was Robert, and that was only because he had no sense of direction.

"I think it's unhealthy," said Ruth.

"Sorry?" I said, looking up at her and taking off my headphones.

"I said I think it's unhealthy," she repeated, nodding down at the booklet on my desk. Lesson Thirty: The Swimming Baths. "You're obsessed with those people."

"It's just the same as *Coronation Street*," I protested.

"It is *nothing* like *Coronation Street*," she said huffily. Ruth was an avid fan of the Street, from way back when Albert Tatlock was still alive. "You sit there listening to those tapes and giggling, did you know that?"

I waved my hand at the booklet. "Robert—"

"I don't want to hear about Robert," she said. "I hear far too much about Robert as it is. What about work?"

"This *is* work, Ruth," I said, slightly affronted and a little embarrassed. "I'm getting ready for my trip."

Ruth pursed her lips and made a rude little noise. Her grandmother had been born in Lublin just before World War One and had never had a good word to say about the Poles in general. She still thought I was going to Poland to research a film. If I'd told her the real reason she would probably just have resigned.

"What about that?" she asked, nodding down at the long white envelope sitting beside my coffee-mug.

"What about it?"

"Don't you think you should open it?"

Ruth was having one of her I-want-to-pick-a-fight-about-something days. I picked up the envelope and turned it over in my hands. It had a couple of fifty-cent stamps on it, and a franking mark that said it came from the Federal Bureau of Investigation, Washington DC.

"The postal service is notoriously unreliable," I said to her. "It's entirely conceivable that this letter actually arrived after I left for Poland."

"The postal service is not *that* unreliable," she said.

"Of course it is." I put the letter back down on the desk. "Now what you could do is nip along to the travel agents' on Dean Street and pick up my tickets. Do some shopping while you're on Oxford Street. Have lunch. Put it all on expenses."

"You're a sexist pig, Mr Ramsay," she said. "And you've forgotten there's no more American money coming in." She smiled and turned and walked away. "But there's a nice coat in C&A I've had my eye on for a while. Thank you."

I sat back and watched her go. I owed Ruth so much that a coat from C&A would go only a fraction of the way towards paying her back. She'd kept me sane and stable when everything was coming down around my ears. She'd been a mountain of calm when we were finishing Harry's film, had brought the velvet-voiced Ann Radley into my life, had generally fussed me back from the brink in a no-nonsense Yiddisher Momma sort of way. I was going to miss her.

The Americans had spent almost the entire summer asking my advice and then ignoring it. My contract required me to be on call twenty-four hours a day to answer queries about historical accuracy, and I wound up taking urgent and often nearly incomprehensible phone calls from Ed Farraday at all hours of the day and night. I was once summoned to a script conference at his hotel room above Hyde Park Corner at three o'clock in the morning, and when I'd driven over there and parked the Brianmobile and got up to the room I found everybody fast asleep among a snowdrift of torn pages of shooting script.

I spent hours and hours in the little corner of Pinewood Studios that the company had hired for interior scenes. On one of the lots outside they had built Ed's vision of a 1940s East End street, which didn't look very much like the photographs I had found for him of real East End streets from the period. When I told Ed that it was too wide, too clean and too neat, his smile vanished and he reminded me yet again that he already had writers, and I put my hands up and agreed with him and shut my mouth.

About halfway through the filming I got word from the police in Nottingham that Johnny Bowman had been arrested breaking into a chemist's shop in Berwick-on-Tweed, having dropped out of sight after kicking the living daylights out of me. He'd been brought back to Nottingham, where, tough-guy that he was, he had almost immediately named the rest of his partners in crime and then confessed to an impressive catalogue of muggings, robberies and burglaries. It seemed he'd worked harder since leaving school than a lot of my former classmates.

I went up to Nottingham for a couple of days to give evidence, and when he was sentenced to eight years' imprisonment he didn't look too upset. Maybe that was what he'd wanted all along. I came back to London with a definite sense of having tied up one of the last loose ends of my life.

The making of Ed's film grew more and more surreal. For Lily and Ben's historically incorrect meeting Ed had built at Pinewood a largely inaccurate replica of Piccadilly Circus, but he'd decided to dress Aldwych Underground station as Piccadilly Circus station to film footage of her going to the meeting, cutting in reverse shots of the Pinewood set.

We filmed for two days at Aldwych. I knew Aldwych had been used by lots of film companies as a location even before it was permanently closed to the public, but it did have some small drawbacks when it came to masquerading as Piccadilly Circus. I mentioned to Ed that Piccadilly Circus station, unlike Aldwych, is entirely underground, and he just waved a hand and shushed me.

After that I just concocted any old bullshit and it made no difference, although when Ed asked me what colour pillarboxes had been in 1940 and I told him they were canary yellow I did detect a glimmer of a harsh look from Warren.

I did all the groundwork I needed to do on the Polish film. I reestablished contact with Witek and advised him that, as soon as I was free, I was coming to see him with a lucrative proposition. I bought Polish-language tapes and books and listened to them on my Walkman in the office. In the clubs and associations I practised my Polish on old gentlemen who had served alongside Sikorski and Anders, on dispossessed counts and countesses, barons and baronesses, and one ancient, almost senile but still unbearably dignified ex-cavalry officer who thought he had known my grandfather, though he was never certain.

It was amazing how much Polish I actually remembered once I started to work on it. My grandmother had insisted on speaking nothing but Polish around the house. She did it to annoy my father, who refused to learn a word of the language, but it was incredible how much of it had stuck in my head, and once I had more than a nodding acquaintance with the Rutkowskis it all started to fall into place.

At the end of principal shooting, Ed favoured me with an unnaturally firm handshake and a mind-boggling severance cheque. Warren looked as if he still thought I had ripped them off, and if he had ever bothered to ask me about it straight out I would probably have agreed with him.

I did another couple of weeks of preparation, then made arrangements to fly over to Poland to begin the groundwork. Two weeks before I was due to fly out I was sitting in the office with a mug of Ruth's coffee and a Danish when I spotted a half-page article in the *Independent*.

Ed Farraday had been found, stark naked and dead, in the living room of his Malibu beach house. The house was, apparently, an Aladdin's Cave of pharmaceutical enjoyment, and Ed's business affairs were in such a state of chaos that the Internal Revenue Service had thrown up their hands in despair.

"I told you they were the Mafia!" I announced to Ruth, storming into the outer office waving the torn-out page of newsprint.

Ruth read the article and tutted and said, "Poor man."

"'Poor man'?" I cried. "Look there. Look, they're talking about Warren. 'Warren Burke, alleged confidante of the Gambino Family.'"

Ruth just shook her head and said, "Poor man," again. Tragedy, in Ruth's eyes, transcended any criminal connections.

The letter from the FBI arrived a week or so later; it must have taken them that long to unravel Ed's connections far enough to get to me.

I picked it up again, reached over, opened the safe, and put it inside, on top of the two letters from the I.R.S. that Ruth knew nothing about. I closed the door and spun the combination. I'd deal with the letters if I came back from Poland. I knew what they wanted: they wanted to talk to me about my business dealings with Ed and Warren, and though I was pretty sure I was entirely blameless I knew that if I started a correspondence with them I'd be stuck here for weeks—particularly if someone managed to connect me to the newspaper headlines of the day after Harry and I had met. I was famous. Forty German tourists had seen two men vanish into thin air on the steps of St Paul's. The papers had been full of it; it was one of those silly-season stories. A third man had been seen to run away with a brown-paper package and a couple of carrier bags in his hands, and had yet to be found. I'd been more than a little alarmed when I saw the papers, but the story passed quickly. The middlebrow tabloids ran a couple of articles about mass hysteria, the lower end of Fleet Street had some anti-German cartoons, and that was it. A bona fide miracle happening in the middle of London and all it generated was a few pop-psychology pieces and some clumsily xenophobic cartoons. Amazing.

I'd worried for a few days that Terry and Chris would somehow connect me with the burglary at FilmSafe, but the weeks went by and nothing happened. I took the train up to Mill Hill several times and bought local newspapers and scanned them for news of a local company being burgled, but there was nothing. Harry had told me he hadn't mentioned Lonesome Charley in his dealings with the FilmSafe boys, and I didn't think Chris had got a good look at me as I lunged around the column on the steps of the cathedral. I'd vanished into thin air in front of forty tourists and then I'd gone on to burgle somebody, and I'd got away with it.

I put my headphones back on and went back to the Rutkowskis' visit to the cinema. Robert was lost again, poor bugger.

2

"Mama?"

She was sitting in the same chair as last time, wearing the same dress. Even the early autumn sunlight was the same. It was as if I'd just stepped out of the room for a moment. She looked round and said, "Daddy!" in Polish.

I closed the door behind me, crossed the room, and sat down on the end of the bed. She watched me with bright, smiling eyes.

"Oh, Daddy," she said, "I've missed you so much. Are the Germans all gone?"

It was the first time since she'd gone into The Limes that I'd been able to understand what she was saying. It gave me an odd, creepy feeling in the pit of my stomach.

"All gone," I said.

Her face lit up with childlike joy. "So we can go home now, yes? Oh, please, Daddy!"

I took one of her hands in mine. "Of course we can. But—" I looked away, and when I looked back she was almost bouncing up and down with happiness. "I might not be able to come and see you for a long time."

Her smile dimmed a fraction and she tipped her head to one side.

"I'm going to Poland," I said, looking at the floor. "A friend of mine is in some kind of trouble and I'm going to try and help her. I don't know how long I'll be gone." I looked into her eyes. "I'm not even sure if I'm coming back. I'm sorry."

We stared at each other for a long moment, then she said, "Will I be able to go riding again?"

I sighed. "Would you like that?"

"Oh yes! Mama and Piotrusz can come riding with me."

I nodded. It was amazing: now I understood what she was saying her body language suddenly made perfect sense. She was five or six years old and she was talking to her Daddy. Piotrusz was her elder brother, my Uncle Peter, who had died of pneumonia shortly after my grandfather sent the family to England in the spring of 1939. All those years, and I hadn't understood anything . . .

"And you can come too, and you can wear your uniform." Her voice dropped conspiratorially. "I heard Mama say you're the handsomest man in the world when you wear your uniform. She's so proud of you."

I reached out and ran my hand over her hair. "I'm very proud of her too, my love. I'm proud of all of you."

She suddenly looked concerned. "Oh, don't cry, Daddy. We're going home. You should be happy."

"I'm crying because I *am* happy," I said gently, wiping my eyes with my fingertips. "Shall I brush your hair now? Would you like that?"

"Oh, yes, please."

I took the hairbrush from the bedside table and I spent the rest of the afternoon gently brushing her hair while she told me about the forests and the snows and the horses of the childhood she had never really had. And when the nurse came in and said it was time for my mother's nap I helped put her to bed, and I sat beside her until she fell asleep. Then I kissed her on the forehead and went downstairs to phone for a taxi to take me back to Nottingham and the next train back to London.

Part Five

Sophie in the Villages

Twenty-five

1

If I was going to be objective—something I had more or less stopped bothering to try to do—I supposed a number of fairly surreal things had happened to me since I had first walked into Lonesome Charley's offices, but they all paled into insignificance when I first read about what happened in the German border town of Gleiwitz on August 31, 1939.

In early August 1939, Admiral Canaris, head of the Abwehr, received an order from Hitler himself to deliver to Himmler and Reinhard Heydrich, the head of the SD, a hundred and fifty Polish uniforms and some Polish small arms.

At about the same time, Heydrich briefed a young SS-Sturmbannfuhrer named Alfred Helmut Naujocks on something code-named Operation Himmler. Naujocks was charged with staging a fake Polish attack on the radio station in Gleiwitz, during which a Polish-speaking German would broadcast an appeal for Poles to rise up against the Germans. This "provocation" would provide Germany with the pretext to invade Poland.

The operation at Gleiwitz was not the only one planned, and in order to provide "evidence" of Polish provocation a number of inmates from Sachsenhausen were to be made available to Operation Himmler. Dressed in Polish uniforms and given lethal injections, their bodies were to be riddled with bullet wounds and left at the sites of the "incidents". The bodies, these dead men whose names I was never able to discover, were code-named Canned Goods.

I knew all this stuff because Naujocks gave himself up to the Americans in 1944, and a year later he was spilling his guts at Nuremberg. He said Canned Goods were condemned criminals, and he said Heydrich made one available to him for the Gleiwitz operation.

Naujocks went to Gleiwitz and hung around for a few days. At noon on August 31 he received the code-word from Heydrich to carry out the attack. The attack was mounted at eight o'clock that evening. The radio station was "seized", a speech was broadcast, and the body of Canned Goods was left behind as evidence.

At dawn the next morning German guns opened up on the Polish fortifications at Westerplatte, the first shots of World War Two, although I thought of Canned Goods as the first of its millions of dead.

September 1 was a lovely late-summer day, by all accounts. German forces poured across the border into Poland. Somewhere along the way they paused briefly to kill my grandfather.

Fifty-five years later, the border had shifted. Gleiwitz was now in Poland and Witek and Julia lived there.

Perspective. Sympathy.

Sophie once told me she thought British people's attention spans, in terms of history, were rather limited. She accused us of having an island mentality and of not caring very much about our own history, let alone the history of Europe. She and I had days like that sometimes.

Looking out of the window I could see the early-evening lights of Berlin, far, far below. I had started to understand what Sophie had meant.

I was trying to look at Central Europe the way she had, from a perspective of shifting borders and fluid allegiances, a Central Europe that had been conjured up out of the tatters of the Habsburg Empire. Nothing ever changes in Britain. It's been the United Kingdom for ages. Poland has been its present size and shape only since Yalta. Over its history, it's been all sizes and shapes. Between 1795 and 1989 it had only about twenty years of real independence, and for extended stretches it hasn't existed at all except as a kind of conspiracy.

The whole of Polish history seemed to be composed of periods of peace punctuated by massive periods of catastrophic strife. To Western eyes, Poland has always been a victim nation, one whose people are brave, romantic, fond of their drink and pathologically unable to govern themselves. And at times I think any or all of those things were true.

But that's a narrow view, and it ignores the fact that in the late seventeenth century Poland was the largest state in Europe. In 1683 the army of Jan Sobieski broke the Turkish siege of Vienna. When the siege was over the Poles just went home. They didn't take part in the peace negotiations between the Sultan and the Habsburgs. It was as if they weren't particularly interested.

A hundred years later, Russia, Prussia and Austria simply partitioned Poland out of existence. They melted down the Polish Crown Jewels and destroyed books and documents on a massive scale. They were determined that history would record the Poles as being incapable of governing themselves and that Poland had never been a sovereign state anyway. They were so successful that most people west of Berlin don't realize that in 1610, after receiving full crusading status from the Vatican, King Zygmunt III's forces occupied Moscow. Not bad for a little victim nation.

It was hard to imagine living in a culture like that, and trying to imagine it, these past few months, had made me feel more and more provincial.

Dinner arrived. New potatoes, a slice of ham, a tiny little sausage, a bit of lollo rosso and a radish. I unwrapped the plastic knife and fork and I ate the sausage and one of the potatoes. I looked out of the window again, but Berlin was gone.

Canned Goods. The name had given me a peculiar shiver when I'd read it. The deception had taken place practically next door to Sophie's home town. Could that have been it? I pushed my dinner aside and put my nose to the window. Some lights, far below, fought their way up through wisps of cloud and then vanished again. We must be over Poland already, I thought. It was only an hour or so from Berlin to the border by train. I strained my eyes and tried to see the lights through the cloud. Canned Goods.

Canned Goods was dead, had been dead since the end of August 1939, and Harry had said you couldn't take a person from a village if they were part of it. But would that matter to somebody who wanted to save World War Two's first combat casualty?

I had a list of dates and incidents that ran to three A4 pages. Battles, wars, invasions. Operation Himmler was on the list, but so were the Warsaw Uprising of 1944 and the Siege of Częstochowa of 1655. Every bad thing that had ever befallen Poland was on my list, and I believed Sophie was somewhere in one of those conflicts. Reading it made me feel sad and a little afraid. I had tried to empathize, to work out where she might be, but I had failed. I might guess that an English person would go to the Blitz, or the Civil War, or the Battle of Hastings, but how could I guess what a Pole might feel worth visiting?

In that last couple of days in London I had done the rounds of the Polish associations and clubs again, asking members where they would go if they had the chance, trying to get a handle on it, trying to second-guess Sophie, but it was hopeless. Everybody had a different destination. One old chap had even quite fancied seeing the Siege of Vienna, and refused to countenance any event which took place on Polish soil.

I'd been able to narrow it down a little from Harry's information that Sophie had gone to Poland. That wiped out all the events that had taken place in areas that were now in Belarus and Ukraine, but it still left far too many possibilities. I found myself despairing. Then I found myself on the Friday evening BA flight to Warsaw anyway.

Okęcie, Warsaw's airport, had just had a massive overhaul, and it looked like Heathrow's little brother. It was clean and airy and efficient. My bags arrived on a proper carousel rather than on a tractor-cart, and I zipped through Customs and Immigration without a hitch. Out in the Arrivals area, a stranger was holding a piece of card with RAMSAY written on it. I recognized the piece of card first: it was the little sign Witek had been holding the evening I arrived at Kraków. It took me a moment longer to recognize the person holding it.

"So you still need my help, English boy?" he said when I reached him.

"I hope you've got a better car this time, Witek," I said, handing him one of my bags.

He laughed and shook his head. "Idiot English boy. Who can afford a new car?" His English hadn't got any better, but everything else about him was different. He'd had his hair cut and shaved off his big moustache, and that would have made him look ridiculously young if he hadn't lost weight as well. The last time I'd seen him he'd been painfully thin; now he was skeletal. His hair was brushed straight back from his forehead, and there were big purple smudges under his eyes.

"Julia not feeding you?" I said.

"Julia has left me," he said, leading the way towards the doors.

That pulled me up short. "I'm very sorry to hear that, Witek," I said in Polish. "Really I am."

He stopped and turned and looked at me, frowning. "How long have you been able to speak Polish?" he asked.

"I've been having lessons," I said.

"You still have an accent." He turned away. "Come on."

We drove into the city in silence. Witek's Little Fiat was making an alarming noise which suggested some vital part of the engine was about to erupt from the boot. He had hung one of those cardboard air-fresheners shaped like a Christmas tree from the rear-view mirror. I wondered if I should have brought him a pair of furry dice.

His driving hadn't changed. He drove at every intersection with a barely con-cealed snarl on his lips, and as the huge Stalinist-baroque tower of the Palace of Culture loomed up ahead of us I found myself gripping the dashboard whenever we approached a set of traffic lights. Trundling to my doom in an ineffectually whining hairdrier. A Lonesome Charley sort of car, I thought.

"Something funny?" Witek asked in Polish.

"No," I said, wiping the smile off my face. "Absolutely not." It *was* sort of funny, though. The Lonesome Charley-mobile. Driven by the faithful Witek, carrying his master the Green Pillock to yet another fucked-up appointment with Destiny . . . No. On second thoughts, maybe it wasn't that funny after all.

"It is Russian, of course," Witek said, nodding at the Palace of Culture, all lit up like a big fat stone spaceship. "A gift from the workers of the Soviet Union to the workers of Poland."

"Those blokes must have really hated you," I said. It was, without a doubt, one of the ugliest, most out-of-place buildings I had ever seen.

"There was some debate a few years ago about what we should do with it now the Communists are gone and the Soviet Union is a bad memory," he said. "Do we knock it down? Do we erect some facade over it? Do we ignore it? Who knows?"

"Paint it pink," I said.

He glanced across at me. "What?"

"Paint it pink. That way it'll be so obvious nobody will be able to see it. Trust me. I know about these things."

He made a face and shook his head. "The one good thing about it is that you can see it from practically all over Warsaw, so you can never get lost."

"Better street signs. That always helps in these situations."

He looked at me again. "Are you on drugs, English boy?"

"I'm high on life, Witek. That and your driving. And my name is Tim." I grinned at him.

Witek sighed. "I knew you were crazy the first time I met you and you tried to speak to me in Polish."

"My Polish is much better now, though, isn't it."

"Not perfect. How did you learn?"

"The Rutkowskis taught me," I said with a certain amount of pride. "Robert helped a lot, of course."

He shook his head. "Crazy."

"And Balicki too."

"You're not paying me enough," he muttered.

"OK. Have a pay rise. I'm loaded, Witek. Things have changed. I'm a Leading Independent Fil—hey!" To my horror, he had taken both hands off the steering wheel and raised them to his face. Mistaking it for a suicide attempt, I grabbed at the wheel, but he had already put his hands down and steered us back into the correct lane. I slumped in my seat, panting. "You mad *prick*, Witek!"

"I bet the Rutkowskis didn't teach you to swear like that," he said mildly.

"No," I said, holding my chest. It had actually been the old lad who had thought he'd known my grandfather.

"Listen," he said, driving a little more carefully as we rounded a traffic island. "You don't go around Warsaw telling everybody how important you are and how much money you have. This city is full of criminals. Russian mafia, Polish mafia, god only knows who else. You'll wind up kidnapped or dead and I'll have to sort out the mess afterwards."

"Your concern strikes me speechless, Witek."

He snorted. "If only it did."

My heart-rate falling back to something like normal, I said, "Did you find Marcin?"

Witek nodded. "He works for a company that makes surgical tools. They have offices here and in Kraków. Once a week he takes the express and comes up here to deal with business for two days. Then he goes home."

"Where is he today?"

"Here. He arrived this evening."

I smiled, imagining the look on Marcin Sierpiński's face when I saw him tomorrow.

"Good," I said. "Very, very good, Witek."

2

"It's extremely important," I said.

Behind her desk, the secretary shook her head again. I turned around and walked away, fuming. Then I stopped and walked back and leaned on the desk.

"I'm from London," I said, looking her in the eye. "I'm here to see Mr Sierpiński on a matter of extreme urgency. I have an appointment."

The secretary looked down at her desk diary. She was drop-dead beautiful. Her hair was expensively feather-cut and her skin was that peculiar orange sun-tan colour that comes from close proximity to large amounts of money. "Mr Sierpiński is not here," she said once more with a degree of patience which I would have found admirable at any other time.

"All right," I said. "I lied. I don't have an appointment. But I *have* come from London, and it *is* very important that I speak with Mr Sierpiński."

She looked up at me and shook her head with an expression of immense regret on her face. She was incredible, entirely unflappable. I wondered if Ruth would mind if I head-hunted her.

"I'll wait," I said, going back to the line of padded bench-seats along the opposite wall and sitting down.

"He isn't here, Mr Ramsay," she insisted.

"Do you have a name?" I asked, crossing my legs and my arms in what I hoped was an emphatic gesture.

"Danuta," she said, without missing a beat.

"Well, Danuta," I said, "I'm an old friend of Marcin's from London and I have a really hot deal for him, so I think you should just push the button on that little box on your desk and tell him I'm here."

Danuta looked at the intercom, then at me, and smiled. "I've already asked if Mr Sierpiński is in the office, Mr Ramsay. He's not here."

I glared around the reception area of Zapmed, SA. There was hessian on the walls, sturdy pile-carpet on the floor, a Swiss Cheese Plant in one corner. In a glass-fronted cabinet by the door was a torturer's delight of shiny surgical instruments produced by the company, from scalpels, saws and drills to things whose purpose I didn't dare guess at. I looked at Danuta again. She looked younger than me and was infuriatingly professional. I knew that Marcin Sierpiński was somewhere in the office, and she knew I knew, and she would go through this game quite patiently until either I gave up or she had to call the police to remove me.

"Would it make any difference if I told you I thought you were quite magnificent?" I asked her.

She smiled and shook her head.

"What if I told you that Marcin Sierpiński was an informer for the SB during Martial Law?" The SB were the secret police.

Danuta shook her head again, that same private sad smile on her face.

I stood up. "Fuck it, Danuta, you're too good for me," I said, and I meant it. I'd been there for three-quarters of an hour and I'd got no further than her smile.

I went over to the desk, took a piece of scrap paper from a neat little pile she kept at her left hand, and borrowing a pen I wrote, "Marcin Sierpiński, I want to talk to you about villages and I will make your life a misery until I get what I want. Love, Tim Ramsay." I handed the note to Danuta. "Will you make sure Mr Sierpiński gets this?"

"I'll be sure he sees it," Danuta said, a little furrow digging itself down into her forehead as she read the note.

"Private joke," I said.

She smiled. She had a lovely smile.

I went to the door and pulled it open. "I've lied to you almost constantly since I came in here," I admitted, "but I meant it when I said I thought you were magnificent. Zapmed don't deserve you."

As I stepped through the doorway and let the door close on its spring, I heard her say wistfully, "I know."

The ground floor of Zapmed's building was occupied by a bank. Their common foyer was huge, scattered with bench seats and plant displays and unreliable-looking men who would tell you that they were giving a good exchange rate on any Western currency. Actually, their exchange rate was the same as the bank's; they just didn't charge the bank's commission. They didn't have the bank's overheads, of course. As I walked towards the door one of these men, dressed in a cream-coloured linen suit, his wrists weighed down with gold chains, got up from his seat and came towards me with a floppy wad of złotys clutched in his fist. From the way he backed away from me, I think the look I gave him put him in fear for his life. I was in that kind of mood.

"I don't see why it's so important to speak to him," Witek grumbled, obviously slightly alarmed at the temper I was in on my return to the hotel. Maybe he thought he was the only person who was allowed to be fiercely annoyed. He was in for a disappointment.

"It's very important, Witek," I said. "Fucking important." I sat down on the end of the bed and put my face in my hands. I hadn't come from London thinking this would be easy, but I'd at least thought it might be *straightforward*. "Shit." I looked at him. "I'm sorry, Witek."

He shrugged. "For what? It's only your first day, after all."

I sighed. "Yes."

Witek had booked us both into the Warszawa, a large, anonymous-looking hotel in the centre of town, five minutes' walk from the Palace of Culture. My room was a bit spartan but it was comfortable and clean. It looked out across a courtyard of pitched roofs to the windows of the kitchens in the other wing of the building. I had my window open and the smell of cooking cabbage drifted into the room.

"You should go to Zakopane," he said.

I smiled. "Where the rugs come from, right?"

"Rugs," he snorted. "Skiing, English boy, that's what Zakopane is for. Poles go to Zakopane to ski. Those that don't go to Zakopane go to Sczczyrk, but the skiing's not so good there. Julia and I—" He stopped. He hadn't yet got out of the habit of saying "Julia and I". I felt sorry for him in spite of the miseries he'd put me through the last time I was here. "You're different," he said finally.

"It's been commented on," I said, thinking of Bob and wishing for an aching moment that I'd decided to stay in London.

He shook his head. "I mean really different."

I'd told him the barest bones of what had happened. Harry had left and given me Lonesome Charley. I had finished the film. He'd never asked what had happened to Sophie . . .

"How well do you know Zosia Trzetrzelewska?" I asked.

He looked at me as if the question only confirmed how confusing my transfiguration, such as it was, had been. "Why?"

"She never spoke much about her life here," I said, and as I said it I realized it was true. Apart from the odd occasion, Sophie had only ever talked in generalities about Poland. The food is better, the people aren't so rude, the weather's more reliable—that kind of thing. "You were at college with her, weren't you?"

He nodded. "Her and her husband."

All of a sudden everything seemed to change gear. I could hear my heart beating. I could hear the blood rushing through the veins in my ears. I could hear the cooks talking in the kitchen. The whole hotel seemed to come alive around me like a vast noisy animal. I could hear a couple arguing in a room a dozen metres down the corridor. For a moment I actually thought I was dying.

"Husband?" My voice was an almost inaudible squeak.

Witek nodded as if the whole world hadn't become a huge sounding-board. "Mirek." He shook his head. "A wild lad, Mirek. Wild and clever."

"Husband," I said again.

He looked at me, then he shrugged. "Of course, Zosia was wild in those days too. Every night a party, you know?" He smiled. "Good times. I miss them, sometimes. Things were so uncomplicated then." His face took on a wistful look. "We all seem to have married badly, now I think about it."

I suddenly felt sick, all kinds of scenarios cartwheeling through my mind. I swallowed and said, "Children?"

Witek seemed to come out of his reverie. "Oh yes. Little Franek. I'm his godfather." He looked sad. "Not a very good godfather, as it turns out."

"Oh," I said.

We took a tram. I felt as if the world had stopped being quite real. Warsaw took a terrible battering during the war, much worse than London. After the Uprising, Hitler ordered the city obliterated, and he pretty much got his wish. I once read that, after D-Day and with the Allied forces pushing through France, Hitler had given a similar order to the German general in command of Paris, but the general just didn't have the heart to destroy such a beautiful city. Warsaw hadn't been so lucky.

The New Warsaw that grew up in the age of Stalin and Kruschev had a sort of faceless, generic Iron Curtain look, but the Poles set about rebuilding the Old Town using paintings allegedly done by Canaletto as guides because the original town plans had been destroyed. So modern Warsaw became a painstaking reconstruction of the old, surrounded by the new. The modern part looked like an elaborate film set, an eye-bustingly exact recreation of a Communist town for a director a whole lot more demanding than the late Ed Farraday. I watched it all go by and wanted to be back home with Bob and the things I understood.

"He was a complete bastard, of course," Witek said as he fed our tickets into the punch attached to one of the upright handholds in the tram.

"Yes," I said, bereft.

"He only wanted a wife for the social status," he went on, handing me my ticket. "He beat her, you know."

I looked at him.

"As soon as he could, he went off to the West."

"West?" I said, dazed.

Witek nodded. "Berlin, I heard. Then Paris. Then maybe Madrid, I'm not sure."

I crushed my ticket slowly in my fist. I felt my heart begin to levitate. "Paris," I said. The world began to snap into focus around me.

"Zosia divorced him, oh, four years ago, I think," Witek said, his brow furrowing as he tried to remember the date. "Yes. Four years ago in December. Just before she went to England." He looked out of the window. "Bad times."

I wondered what Witek would do if I kissed him. The tram skirted the edge of the Old Town, and I watched all those old buildings go by that were really less than fifty years old, and I smiled. I had the same feeling as I'd had when Ann Radley first came to the office, the feeling that I'd set myself some ridiculous task but that I could do it, that it was within capabilities I hadn't known I had. Of course, I still had no idea how I was going to get what I wanted, but now I felt as if I *could* get it, somehow. I just needed an hour alone with Marcin Sierpiński.

3

"This is very silly," I said.

"It's my car, and I'm not going to have some bastard stealing it," said Witek with an edge of determination in his voice that I hadn't heard before.

"Anybody who stole this thing would need psychiatric treatment, Witek," I said.

"It's your bloody stupid idea, anyway," he told me under his breath.

I sighed. "Just watch the road and don't crash your bloody precious car."

My search for that elusive single hour with Marcin Sierpiński had foundered on Danuta's absolute insistence that he wasn't in the office whenever I turned up. Harry would have loved her. Marcin had told her he didn't want to see me, and she wouldn't let me see him, no matter how often I turned up, no matter whether I brought her flowers, or chocolates, or the package of a hundred Rothmans that I'd bought duty-free for Witek. I could have arrived outside with a Lamborghini all wrapped up in pink ribbon and Mr Sierpiński would still not have been available. I tried for two whole days and got nowhere, and by that time I thought I was more than a little in love with Danuta, with her feather-cut and her sunbed-tan and her expensive Italian business suit. Zapmed seemed to be doing all right in the New Poland, and I thought it probably had a lot to do with Danuta.

The previous evening, after spending all day running into the immovable object that was Danuta, I had had this idea to catch the same train that Marcin got on his return home from his visits to Head Office, just barge into whatever compartment he was in, sit down beside him, and make him talk to me.

Witek knew roughly what time he got back to his office in Kraków after his trips to Warsaw, and from that it was fairly straightforward to work out which express he caught from Warszawa Centralna. It all seemed pretty simple to me.

Unfortunately, Witek refused to let me go alone, which left us with the sticky problem of what to do with his car. So here we were driving through the suburb of Ursynów, about as far from the centre of Warsaw as it was possible to get and still be in Warsaw, looking for the flat of his widowed second cousin, who had agreed to look after the car until Witek could come and collect it. I was more than a little furious, and more than once I had offered to buy the bloody car, just so we could stay at the Warszawa and be handy for the station tomorrow morning. But no, Witek had to have his car.

"I waited five years to get this car," he said angrily. "You don't understand how things were, bloody English boy."

"You can buy another," I said as the blocks of flats went by. "Jesus Christ, Witek, I'm your employer."

A determined expression set on his face and he didn't answer. I sat back in my seat, wondering numbly if I was fated with the Lonesome Charley way of doing things or if I had simply been that way all along. Maybe Harry was right. Maybe nothing was logical. Maybe the whole world was like Lonesome Charley, ad hoc and chaotic. Fuck it, all I wanted to do was *talk* to Marcin Sierpiński.

Witek's cousin Bronek was about forty years older than us, a little, leathery old man who wore a pair of trousers from one suit and the jacket from another. His flat was three rooms and a kitchen and a bathroom right at the top of a tall block overlooking a grubby, anaemic-looking park. Bronek loved me the moment he saw me. His father had escaped from Poland at the outbreak of the war, leaving his wife and son behind to survive as best they could. Bronek's father had flown with the RAF, and after the war had made a bigamous marriage with a girl from Prestwick.

Bronek told me all this with a barely controlled enthusiasm. How he didn't remember his father at all, how his mother had died of a broken heart, how there was a huge, unknown Scottish side to his family, how one of his half-brothers ran a restaurant in Largs—and would I deliver a parcel to him when I went back to England?

When Bronek had fed us, and given us vodka, and exhausted his stories about his father and his Scottish family, he started to tell us about fishing. Bronek loved fishing.

That night, trying to get comfortable on the spectacularly unyielding sofa-bed in Bronek's living room, I thought about Sophie and her husband. I didn't blame her for not saying anything to me about Mirek, though it made me a little sad to think she hadn't felt we were good enough friends to confide in me.

The flat's heating was turned up to equatorial levels; I was sweating like crazy. I flopped over on my back, kicked the duvet down to the end of the bed and lay staring up at the ceiling. Ten or fifteen floors down, I heard somebody singing in a gorgeous, husky, but undeniably drunk voice.

I thought there had always been that sadness about her, as if something secret had hurt her once. Looking back through the knowledge that she had been married, it seemed obvious now. It had been more than a little alluring at the time, but I had never stopped to think that that sadness might have cost her something.

All I had to do was see Marcin Sierpiński tomorrow and everything would just work out all right. I had it all planned out. Sophie would have been proud of me.

4

"Why not?" I said.

"He can't drive," Witek said in a small, abashed voice.

I gazed around the living room, at the furniture pushed against the walls to make space for the sofa-bed, at Witek and Bronek standing side by side in the doorway. They didn't look like cousins. They looked like slightly seedy fantasy characters, a wizard in a denim jacket and a fishing-mad dwarf who couldn't come to the station with us and then drive the wizard's car back to the safety of the dwarf's garage.

"Fucking *hell*, Witek," I said in English, looking at my watch. "The train leaves in forty minutes!"

Witek and Bronek looked at each other.

"If he can't drive, what does he have a garage for?" I demanded.

"It was available," Witek snapped. "You don't say no to something like that just because you can't drive."

"Oh my God." I looked out of the window, certain I was going to be completely demented by lunchtime.

"He keeps his fishing equipment there," Witek told me. "And some furniture."

I turned from the window. "Well, get somebody who *can* drive it, then!" I almost shouted.

The cousins had a quick whispered discussion, then Witek said, "Bronek says there is nobody trustworthy. He says the car would be stolen, even if he came with us."

"Doesn't he have any friends who can drive the thing back?" I said, barely resisting the urge to tear my hair. "No, don't answer that. Let me buy the car, Witek. Go on. I'll give you a thousand quid for it. That's—" I tried to do the sums, gave up. "It's *lots* of złotys. You can *buy* a new one."

Witek looked at the floor and shook his head.

I took a deep breath and forced myself to be calm. "All right. So how do we get to the station then?"

Of course, when we went down to the taxi rank at the end of the street there wasn't a single car there.

5

"I never treated her properly," Witek said.

"That's your fault, Witek," I said, staring out at the countryside whipping by beyond the window.

"I know, I know," he said morosely. "I should have treated her properly."

I rested my temple against the window and closed my eyes. The express was hurling us south through the Golden Autumn that the Polish tourist brochures mention so often, through huge birch forests, past farms where big horses pulled huge flat carts with lorry tyres on the wheels, across hectares of fields planted with some crop I didn't recognize whose thin green stems and feathery violet-blue heads made the fields look as if they had a thin layer of blue smoke hanging over them.

The train didn't stop until Katowice, where we had to change—didn't even seem to pass through any towns, just punched southwards. There was an extraordinary feeling of velocity on this train that I'd never come across with British Rail, and it still wasn't fast enough. We were still one train behind Marcin.

"We should have found out where he was staying," I said without opening my eyes. "Gone to see him there. Really put the pressure on."

"I can't be expected to do everything," Witek said.

I crossed my arms and snuggled up against the wall of the compartment. "Not your fault, Witek. Forget it."

It was, of course, all Witek's fault, but it was pointless blaming him any more. We'd wound up catching a bus into town from Ursynów, and by the time we'd got to the station Marcin's train had already left and we had to kick our heels for a couple of hours until the next one.

It was only after we had been on the train for an hour or so that it occurred to me we should have gone to the airport straight from Ursynów and flown to Kraków. I could have been waiting for Marcin at the other end when his train arrived. That would really have put his nose out of joint.

I hadn't much warmed to Marcin when I met him at his father's flat, but now I was developing a healthy loathing for him. He knew why I was here. That was the only explanation I could think of for his unwillingness to see me. He knew I wanted to talk about the old man's Secret.

"Julia loved the car," Witek said tentatively.

"Oh?"

"I can't give it up."

I was tired of this. The story of the collapse of Witek's marriage, as Witek told it, had a cast of thousands, and both he and Julia, depending on which version he told, was the villain. Julia was a bitch, he was a bastard. She hated him, he loved her; he hated her, she loved him. Her parents were to blame, his parents were to blame. The government was to blame. It was as if he were trying to cover every angle of something he didn't quite understand. Myself, I thought Julia had left him because he was simply impossible to live with, but I kept my opinions to myself as Witek told the story over and over again.

"I never loved her, you know," he said.

I fell asleep.

It was dark when we finally got off the Katowice-Kraków train. Witek had bought half a dozen bottles of beer from the Piwo Man who had just been getting onto the express at Katowice as we got off, and had proceeded to drink them all by himself on the hour or so's journey to Kraków. We left our compartment with the empty bottles arranged in a neat line on the floor.

"Go home," I said to him on the platform at Kraków. "I'll be all right."

"I am your employee," he said, blinking at me.

I nodded. "And as your employer I'm ordering you to go home. Go on, Witek. Get some sleep." I looked down at the bags by my feet. "I'll be fine."

He looked at me, and for a moment he seemed like some inexpressibly sad hunting dog waiting for its master's next command. I wondered how on earth I had ever been afraid of him. And then, finally, I realized just how complete his collapse had been.

"Oh, Jesus Maria, Witek," I said, and I put my arms around him. "I've been a real bastard to you."

"You are my employer," he said into my shoulder.

"No." I stepped back and held him at arms' length. "No. I'm your friend. And I promise that when all this is over I'll explain it all to you." He looked at me as if he hadn't understood a single word. "I can't tell you now, but when I have what I want we'll sit down and have a drink and I'll tell you, OK?"

The expression on his face changed and he pushed me away. "Don't patronize me, English boy," he said. "I'm all right." He burped. "I'm going home now."

I tried a smile. "OK. Take care, Witek."

He looked as if he were about to burst into tears. He turned away and started to walk unsteadily back down the platform to catch his train home. I thought I heard him mutter, "I could have fucking driven back." He never looked round, so I picked up my bags and walked away.

All the way to my hotel I tried to rationalize it to myself by thinking that Witek had become caught up in forces too great for him to understand, but I still wound up feeling like a bastard. I told myself I only wanted Sophie, and that nothing else mattered. I still felt like a bastard.

At the hotel I ordered a plate of sandwiches and a bottle of Wyborowa from room service. I was so tired after the pantomime in Ursynów and the train journey that I was drunk after the third glass. I reflected that I had used Witek the same way I had used Eric, as a means to an end. Eric had provided me with rent-free accommodation and food for three years, and Witek had been ready to do whatever I told him. What was the difference? I went to bed feeling like a bastard, and I woke up feeling the same way the next morning, except in the morning I had a hangover too.

Twenty-six

1

I knew I was finished the moment I stepped into Zapmed's Kraków office. Behind the desk sat a secretary with feather-cut hair and a solarium tan. I stared at her.

"My name's Ramsay," I said when I got over the shock. "I'm here to see Mr Sierpiński."

She smiled that same sad private smile that Danuta had smiled in Warsaw. "Mr Sierpiński isn't here," she said.

"That's Mr Marcin Sierpiński."

She smiled again and shook her head. "I'm sorry, but he isn't here at the moment. Can I make an appointment for you?"

I shook my head. Maybe the Poles were cloning the perfect secretary. Maybe they'd latched onto the next growth industry and any day now they were going to flood the world with copies of Danuta. Maybe "Danuta" was just a trademark.

"I know when I'm beaten," I said to her, and I swear she smiled as if she knew exactly what I was talking about.

Out in the Market Square, I watched a group of Hare Krishnas wind their way singing and dancing among the groups of tourists gawping at the Sukiennice. The tourists ignored them, but the Poles stopped and stared. I stopped and stared too. I'd seen the Krishnas on Oxford Street dozens of times and they'd looked completely out of place *there*. Here they looked as if they had broken through from another dimension altogether.

I walked over to one of the cafés on the edge of the square, bought a coffee, and sat outside in the autumn sunlight watching the world go by. Considering that every plan I had made in the past week had collapsed in an embarrassing heap, I felt calm and in control. I was a Leading Independent Filmmaker, in Poland to research my new project. I still felt like a bastard for the way I'd treated Witek and Eric, and I wondered if the feeling would ever go away.

Maybe all the best ideas come when you feel relaxed, because I looked at my glass with its coffee grounds cooling in the bottom, and I took out my wallet and removed the slip of paper with Marcin's home phone number on it that Witek had given me, and I smiled.

"Hello?"

"Oh, hello. Is that Mrs Sierpińska?"

"Yes it is."

"Oh good. My name's Ramsay. I've just arrived from London, and I need to speak to your husband."

"Oh?"

"Yes. I'm from Lloyds of London, and it seems your father-in-law took out a certain amount of life insurance when he was in Britain during the war."

There was a silence at the other end of the phone. Then she said, "How much?"

I tried to put on a vague bureaucrat's manner. "Well, it's something I should speak to your husband about, really, but the policy has been sitting in our office for over fifty years now, and we recently heard of your father-in-law's death." I had no idea what I was talking about. I was making the whole thing up as I went along. "It is a matter which, you will understand, we would like to clear up as soon as possible."

"I understand perfectly," she said.

"Could you perhaps get your husband to call me?" I gave her the name and number of my hotel. "It is not a *huge* amount of money, but it may be of interest."

"I'll tell him you called," she said.

I left the telephone kiosk in the foyer of the hotel and went upstairs to my room, and fifteen minutes later the phone rang.

Marcin Sierpiński and his father hadn't been much alike; the old man had been small and round and alarmingly moustached. Marcin was short and stout and neat, a little nervy where his father had been almost cosmically calm.

We met at a café on the Market Square. Marcin was wearing jeans and one of those denim jackets lined with sheepskin that everyone seemed to wear and I had wanted to buy the last time I was here. He had a glass of coffee and a plate of cakes in front of him when I arrived.

"Marcin," I said, walking over to him.

He looked at me but he didn't get up. There was a hard, angry look in his eyes. "Sit down," he said. His English was excellent.

I sat and smiled sunnily at him. "Nice to see you again."

At any other business meeting with a Pole there would have been five or ten minutes discussing the weather, our families, the most recent government, before we got down to business. Marcin wasn't in the mood for all that.

"Go home," he said. "Leave me alone, and go home."

"No," I said.

He shook his head and I realized he was almost vibrating with fury. "I spend two days at our office in Warsaw," he said, "and each day you are there asking to see me. You come to the office ten, fifteen times each day." He reached for his glass, but his hand stopped halfway. "And when I come home, finally, my wife tells me that a man from Lloyds of London has called to say he has brought us a huge amount of money."

"I said it *wasn't* a huge amount," I said.

His hand finally made it to the glass, but instead of picking it up his fingers curled through the handle of the little silver glass-holder and stayed there.

"She tells me I must go and see the great Mr Ramsay, of Lloyds of London." He looked at me. "I am seeing you now. And I am telling you to go home."

A waitress came over, and I ordered a glass of tea and a pastry. When she had gone again, I said, "I have a problem, Marcin, and only you can help me."

He stared blankly at me.

"A friend of mine has gone missing," I said. "I think she might be in some kind of trouble." I realized I was fiddling with the sugar-bowl and I folded my arms and sat back. "I'm pretty sure she's gone into a village somewhere in Poland."

Marcin's blank expression didn't change.

"Come on, Marcin," I said, "don't tell me your father never told you about the villages."

He lifted his glass, took a sip of coffee, and put the glass back down on the table. He nodded. There was a sour expression on his face. "He told me. It was all I ever heard from him. His great Secret. The greatest moment of his life."

My tea and pastry arrived. I smiled at the waitress and watched her until she was serving another table, then I said, "I need to know how to get into the villages."

Marcin didn't seem angry any longer. Now he just seemed sad. He shook his head. "No."

"I'll pay."

He shook his head again. "You people honestly think you can come to my country and buy whatever you want."

"That's not true."

"It is, it is." He shrugged, as if it were something he hated but had no power to change.

I leaned forward. "I know I didn't buy the only copy of your father's manuscript, Marcin. All I need is an hour with it, that's all."

He seemed to think about this for quite a long time, but finally he said, "I can't let you. It is something which I must protect."

"What?" I said, surprised.

"I must protect this Secret."

"Why, for Christ's sake? What does it *matter*?"

He was looking at me: I was a very, *very* stupid student. "What would happen if the ultra-nationalists got hold of this secret? What would they do, hm?" He tilted his head to one side and I saw the angry look return to his eyes. "Would they run day trips to the Siege of Stalingrad? Take coachloads of tourists to help defend Berlin in 1945? 'You too can replay key periods in history.' 'The experience of a lifetime.' 'Dresdenland'—history as a theme park." He scowled. "I want nothing to do with it."

I thought about it. Put that way, it did make Jurassic Park sound like a kiddies' playground. There were fortunes to be made here. "It might not be that bad."

He looked at me pityingly. "Of course it would. How would you like to see a couple of hundred neo-Nazis charging around the streets of 1940 London armed with Uzis?"

"It doesn't have to be like that."

"Or some sociopath with an AK47 having a weekend break at your Battle of Naseby? Would you like that?" He leaned forward across the table and lowered his voice. "You can do *anything* in the villages, Mr Ramsay. You can murder, rape, have sexual contact with farm animals, and it doesn't change a thing, because the people there are not real people. The villages are the places where maniacs can indulge their blackest fantasies." He sipped some more coffee and looked seriously at me. "You could go to your Battle of Hastings armed with an automatic rifle, shoot William the Conqueror and put the Normans to flight, and you wouldn't change history because you wouldn't be *in* 1066. You'd be here, now, watching 1066 happening. And when the loop ends, the event starts again. William comes ashore, the battle takes place again, just the same as it always was."

"So why does it matter?"

He waved a hand at the window and the crowds walking through the Market Square beyond. "This is the largest mediaeval market square in Europe," he said. "Look at it. Full of foreigners with cameras. That is what would happen in the villages. Imbeciles with cameras and guidebooks, or weekend soldiers wanting to see if they're equal to the great armies of history, or crazy people who want to assassinate Hitler or Churchill or Stalin." He watched the tourists and shook his head sadly.

I rubbed my eyes. "Marcin, look. All I want to do is find Sophie. I know she's here somewhere, I know she's gone into a village. I need to know how to follow her. I'm not going to tell anybody else."

He shook his head again, not looking at me.

"I have to see the original of your father's manuscript, Marcin. He wrote about how he got into the Blitz villages in London, but Sophie didn't put it in the translation I saw. I've got to know how your father did it."

One more time, Marcin shook his head. "I burned it."

It was all I could do to stop myself lunging across the table and grabbing him by the ears. I tried to keep myself from yelling, and my voice emerged as an almost-inaudible squeak. "You did *what*?"

"Burned it." He looked at me. "I burned it."

I sagged back in my chair. I didn't know what to say. We stared at each other.

Finally he said, "It was mine, to do with as I wished. It was part of my father's estate, which I inherited."

I broke off a piece of pastry with the edge of my fork and popped it into my mouth, sipped my tea. Marcin sat calmly watching me. It was the kind of calmness I had previously associated with his father, a kind of fatalistic stillness. I wanted to punch him.

"Did you read it?" I said.

He tipped his head to one side and raised his eyebrows.

"You did. You read it. Of course you did." I dropped my fork on the table. "You know, don't you? You know how to do it."

"Sit down, please."

I was halfway out of my chair. I sat down. "Fucking hell, Marcin," I said between clenched teeth. "I want to *know*."

He shook his head.

"Please."

He shook his head again. "And you can't make me."

I uttered an incoherent little noise and slapped the table hard enough to make the cutlery jump.

"And behaving like a baby will not change my mind," Marcin said, unimpressed.

"You have no right to do this, Marcin," I said quietly.

"I do," he replied, just as quietly.

I looked down and saw that I was gripping the edge of the table with one hand so hard that the knuckles had gone white. I said, "You have no right to endanger someone's life for the sake of some vague ideal."

"It is not a vague ideal," he said. "And, if your friend is in danger, she chose to endanger her own life."

"I can't believe this," I said. Sophie was gone. She would be like Harry, popping in and out of villages, looking for whatever it was she wanted, living on the outside only as long as she had to. I'd lost her because the calm, certain man on the other side of the table hated tourists. "You *twat*," I said quietly.

"I congratulate you on your grasp of Polish," he said, standing up. "But I would suggest you put it to better use."

I wanted to get up and follow him out of the café, preferably shouting at the top of my voice. But I suddenly felt very tired. I'd learned Polish, studied the country's history, watched Polish films, listened to Polish music. I'd spent months getting ready for this, the way Harry said I had to be ready, and it had all been a waste of time because Marcin Sierpiński hated tourists. I sat and watched him walk between the tables. He never looked back once as he pushed the door open and stepped out into the bright cool autumn sunshine.

2

That was it, then. Marcin had burned the manuscript, and, if he'd bothered to read it at all, he wasn't going to tell me how his father had gone into the villages.

I went out into the Market Square and sat on the steps at the base of the statue in front of the Sukiennice, watching the tourists Marcin hated so much wander about happily and innocently, chatting to each other, taking photographs, pointing out interesting things. I leaned back against the statue's plinth and hugged my knees. I thought about Sophie and wondered what I was going to do now.

I knew what I was going to do now. I got up and went back to the hotel and phoned Witek.

The next morning, I hired a car and picked Witek up at the station, and we did a long tour of his contacts. We drove out to Wielicka and Mylenice and Kalwaria Zebrzydowska, and everywhere we went there was a welcome waiting for us. In every house and every flat there were smiling Poles ready for us with the table set and cakes and coffee waiting, and once a full three-course meal with barszcz and breaded pork cutlets and potatoes and poppy-seed cake. It was wonderful hospitality, and it wasn't just because I was an English filmmaker visiting with Money. It was hospitality because that's the way Poles treat their guests, and it was very nice. It did a lot to improve my mood.

Witek, on the other hand, seemed unusually subdued. I decided this was because I had insisted on driving. I'd never driven on the Continent, and it took a little getting used to, but I was in no hurry.

"Are you all right?" I asked at one point on the road from Wadowice to Zator, when he'd been staring out of the passenger window for twenty minutes or so without saying a word.

"Hmm?" He looked at me. "Pardon?"

"I asked if you were OK."

He seemed to take a long time making his mind up. Finally he said, "Yes, I'm OK."

I glanced over at him and for a moment I saw a look on his face that I couldn't quite identify. For a fraction of a second, I thought he looked furious with me.

"Well, we've done all right today," I said, a bit unsettled.

"Mm."

"You've been a great help, Witek. I couldn't have done it without you."

He grunted. "Of course you could."

It was true, though. Witek had collected dozens of names and addresses of people who might have bits of film relating to the German invasion. Everywhere we had gone, cupboards had been opened, attics turned upside-down, ancient projectors dusted off for the film-show after the coffee and cakes. I'd watched hours of footage already today, some of it on stock so degraded as to be unusable. It was incredible. The countryside seemed to be a vast archive. It was even more incredible that all these people had just stood there with ciné cameras while their country was overrun. I watched tanks roll silently across bedsheets pinned to walls, shuffled through foot-high stacks of photographs, listened to stories of German bombing and occupation. I knew why Harry hadn't wanted to stop listening to the stories, why he hadn't wanted to stop collecting material. It was almost narcotic. But it didn't stop me thinking about Sophie.

"What about her mother?" I asked after we had passed through Zator and the road had dog-legged towards the northwest.

"Eh?" Witek had been staring out of the window again.

"Sophie's mother," I said. "In Zabrze."

He was looking at me again with that weird expression on his face. "What about her?"

"Maybe I should visit. While I'm here."

He sniffed and shook his head. "She wouldn't see you. She hates Zosia."

"Why?"

Witek shook his head and went back to looking out of the window.

"Because of the marriage?" I said. "The divorce?"

"You wouldn't understand," he said without looking at me.

"I could try," I said, but he just sat there and wouldn't say anything, so we drove on in silence.

"What happened to the little boy?" I asked after another couple of kilometres. "What was his name?"

"Franek," Witek said to the passing scenery. "He's with Mirek."

"In Paris?"

He nodded.

"Sophie just let him go?"

"No, imbecile." He glared at me. "She didn't 'just let him go'. She spent weeks in court trying to get custody of Franek."

"And?"

He turned his glare towards the windscreen, a look of disgust on his face. "Mirek knew the magistrate."

"Shit," I said.

"Yes," he said bitterly. "Shit."

After Zator, signs started appearing at the side of the road telling us of the decreasing number of kilometres to Oswięcim, and other signs giving the German rendering of the name. Auschwitz. Auschwitz-Birkenau. Signs in several European languages told us we were driving through green hills towards the heart of the Nazi madness.

I hadn't really meant to do this. After our last stop in Wadowice, Oswięcim was just on the way back to Gliwice, where I planned to drop Witek before driving back to Kraków. All my life I had thought of myself as English, when I thought about it at all. But my mother's family had been Polish, and two of her cousins had gone into Oswięcim and not come out again. When I was young, it was just a scary story my grandmother told me, although looking back I realized now that she was deadly serious, that she was passing on a piece of oral history to me, something that shouldn't ever be forgotten. I could, after all, have chosen a different route around Witek's list of contacts. I could have bypassed Oswięcim altogether.

We drove into the little town, over the river, and I swung the car into the car park of the camp. There were a couple more cars already there, and an Orbis tourist coach.

"I won't go in," Witek said as I put on the handbrake and undid my seatbelt. "Why not?"

He glared at me. "Why? Why? Why?" he shouted in English. "Always with you it is 'why?'!" He crossed his arms and stared straight out through the windscreen.

"You don't have to come," I said. "We don't have to stay here at all. We can drive home now."

He snorted.

"I had family here," I said, suddenly feeling stubborn. "I owe them."

"What do you owe them, English boy?" he said harshly. "You can't help them now."

I looked out of the window at the buildings on the other side of the car park, and wondered if the simple weight of human suffering that had taken place here would be enough to form a village. I thought of rampaging through the camp in 1944 with an AK. I thought of taking a small nuclear device in with me and wiping the filthy place off the face of the earth. And then I thought of the village's loop coming to an end and beginning again, and Auschwitz reappearing, untouched, and for a moment I saw it the way Marcin would have seen it. Auschwitzland. I shuddered.

"OK," I said, doing my seatbelt up again. "You're right. I don't need to see this."

"No, you don't," Witek agreed, and for the rest of the journey back to Gliwice neither of us said another word.

It was getting dark when I finally got back to Kraków and handed the car over to the hire people. I walked to my hotel and sat on the bed in my room staring at the walls. My back and shoulders hurt from all the driving I'd done. I lay back and stared at the ceiling, thinking of Oswięcim and knowing that, despite what I had told Witek, I did need to see it, because I would have to include it in the film. I'd have to go there one day without him. I twirled the dial of the radio by the bed back and forth, looking for the World Service, but the only foreign radio station I managed to pick up sounded Czech. I listened to the Czech station for a while and they played some rather jolly folk tunes. I fantasized beating the Secret of the villages out of Marcin Sierpiński. I fantasized kidnapping his children and ransoming it out of him. I fantasized blackmailing it out of him by setting him up in a compromising situation with three or four prostitutes. I fantasized going to him on my knees and begging him to tell me. I fantasized going home and forgetting about the whole thing and getting on with my life. Nothing worked.

The music stopped and the Czech DJ favoured me with some high-speed patter. I lay back again and put my hands over my eyes. Boy meets girl. Boy loses girl. Girl vanishes into another dimension. Boy listens to Czech radio. Shit.

The phone rang. I sat bolt upright and grabbed the receiver, imagining all kinds of wonderful changes of heart. "Marcin?"

"Is that Mr Timothy Ramsay?" asked a strongly accented voice in English.

"Yes? Who is this? I speak Polish."

"Ah, good," the voice said in Polish. "My English isn't very good. I understand you're interested in tourism."

"What? Who are you?"

"We are also interested in tourism." The person on the other end of the line sounded in his twenties and his Polish had an odd, unidentifiable accent. "We run a tourism business."

"Look, I'm not—"

"I understand you wish to visit historical Polish villages, is that true?"

"Listen, I don't know how you got my numbe—"

"Historical Polish *villages*, Mr Ramsay."

I took the receiver from my ear and looked at it. Then I put it to my ear again and said, "What?"

"We know what you want. We can help you. Please meet us in the Sukiennice in fifteen minutes."

"Who are you?"

"Patriots," he said. And he hung up.

I didn't wait fifteen minutes. I put my shoes back on and went straight out into the square.

Tourists were everywhere in the brightly lit square, moving singly or in pairs or in large groups with a guide loudly describing the history of the buildings they were looking at. I watched them as I walked across the square, trying to see Marcin's point of view. I wasn't much fonder of tourists than he was, but that wasn't the issue. I didn't want hordes of tourists flooding into the villages either. All I wanted was Sophie. I thought of Auschwitzland and the image still made me shudder.

The clock of the Mariacki Church struck the hour, and high up in the tower a lone trumpeter started to play his mournful *hajnal* tune, just as he did every half-hour throughout the day. I paused to listen until the trumpeter stopped in mid-bar to commemorate his predecessor, killed by a Tartar arrow while trying to raise the alarm sometime back in the twelfth century.

History. I looked up at the tower, thinking. There was a village here. Several villages, nested one inside the other as Harry had described, going back centuries. I had a sudden sense, a sense I had never had in London, of history continually going on around me.

I took a deep breath and tried to let the feeling grow. All around me violent events were still going on, unseen. I stood very still. Mr Sierpiński had found the Secret by accident; it couldn't be *that* hard. Unlike Warsaw, Kraków had emerged from the last war almost entirely unscathed, but it had a long, long history of strife and occupation, had been invaded half a dozen times—and each time a village had been created. Sophie could be in any one of them, right here in this square. I tried to imagine the square as it had been during the German occupation. I tried to force myself into the villages that must be here. Nothing happened.

"Excuse me?"

I realized I had been holding my breath. I exhaled, looked round. A young man wearing jeans and a scuffed leather flying-jacket was standing beside me.

"Mr Ramsay?"

I could feel the villages receding from me. I thought I had been close to them, but it was probably my imagination. I glared at the youth.

"My name is Oskar Matzerath," he said.

"You're kidding."

He smiled. "It's not my real name, man. I didn't mean to startle you."

"I was . . ." I looked around the square again, suddenly unsure exactly what I had been doing. "I was thinking about something. Are you the person I spoke to on the phone?"

Oskar nodded. "A friend of mine happened to overhear your conversation in the café yesterday. He seemed to think I might be of help to you."

"How?"

Oskar reached into a pocket of his jacket and took out a little white rectangle. "My card," he said, holding it out to me.

The card said, "Patrioci." The Patriots. "Tour Guides." The rest of the card was taken up by an engraving of two postage stamps. One showed a Warsaw church I recognized from the guidebooks. The other stamp had a picture of the same church in ruins after the Germans had finished with it. Before and after. I felt my heart perform a vertical take-off. I looked up at the youth. "I could probably tell you more about the history of this place than you could tell me."

He grinned. "But could you visit it?"

I took a deep breath. "You can do this?"

Oskar nodded.

"Why haven't I heard about it?"

He shrugged. "It's a discreet tour. For the connoisseur. You understand?"

"I understand. But I need proof."

He looked at me blankly for a moment. Then he laughed. "You want a demonstration?"

"I would appreciate it."

Oskar looked thoughtful. "We haven't been asked for a *demonstration* before."

"You're being asked now."

He put his hands in the pockets of his jacket and looked slowly around the square, sucking his teeth. Then he looked back to me. "You'll have to pay for this as well, you know."

"Quite honestly, I'd have been disappointed if you hadn't said that, Oskar."

He nodded. "OK. Do you know Częstochowa?"

"I can get there."

"Good. Get there tomorrow at midday. I'll meet you at the station." And he started to walk away.

"Hang on," I called. He stopped and looked over his shoulder. "Can't we do it here and now?"

He smiled. He had a nice smile, the innocent smile of a child, open and uncomplicated. "There wasn't time to check you out properly before, Mr Ramsay. I have to do that now."

"Why, for heaven's sake?"

He gave me a slightly pitying look, as if he thought I hadn't quite connected with the real world just yet and it made him sad. "Tomorrow, Mr Ramsay." He walked on a few more steps, leaving me standing there.

I looked about me. "Bollocks," I said. When I looked again, Oskar had vanished into the crowds.

Twenty-seven

1

It did occur to me, as I caught the rickety little local train at Kraków station the next morning, that I was being more than slightly foolish. I'd never seen Oskar before in my life; it was more than probable he was some kind of con-man, even if he had chosen a literary alias. Oskar Matzerath was the vertically challenged narrator of *The Tin Drum*, which I'd had to wade through during O-level German. On the other hand, he hadn't looked particularly dangerous, and he did seem to know what he was talking about.

Or maybe he didn't. Maybe he'd just overheard Marcin and me arguing in the café and caught just enough to work out that I was interested in "villages". Maybe I was about to be shown some fine examples of Polish rural life, at an inflated price.

Then again, there was the little card in my pocket with its before-and-after stamps, which seemed significant. And Oskar had seemed to understand when I asked for a demonstration . . .

Oh, bugger it. If Marcin had burned the only other copy of the manuscript I might as well see if Oskar was the real thing. And, it struck me as the little train rattled out of the city, I really only had myself to blame. I hadn't had the wit to ask Harry where he'd put the copy of Mr Sierpiński's manuscript that I'd brought back with me.

He was waiting outside the little station at Częstochowa, a big fat leather satchel slung over one shoulder. I tried not to show the relief I felt. I'd half expected him not to be there.

"Well," I said, "do I pass the tests?"

Oskar lit a Golden American and exhaled a cloud of smoke. "You're an interesting man, Mr Ramsay."

"Tim."

"Are you researching a new film, Tim?"

"About the Fall of Poland," I said, impressed he'd managed to find out that much about me already.

He grinned and looked about him. "Not a very popular subject around here, I'd have thought."

"I won't make the Germans the good guys," I told him. "Promise."

Oskar beckoned me and started to walk away from the station. "A documentary," he said.

"It's what I do," I said, falling into step beside him. "And you seem to know an awful lot about my business."

"It isn't easy, being a Patriot," he said, squinting off down the street as if searching for possible danger. "You have to be careful all the time, man."

"Why?" I asked, honestly amused.

"If some people knew about half the things we know . . ." He shook his head and made a little tutting sound.

"Like what?"

He just made that little tutting sound again, and I had to look away in case I burst out laughing. We walked on towards the hill on which Jasna Góra, Częstochowa's fortified monastery, stood. The monastery had been under siege twice in its history, but the moment Oskar asked me to meet him here I knew what he had chosen for his "demonstration". In the mid-seventeenth century the country was going through yet another of its periodic incursions, this time from the Cossacks, the Muscovites and the Swedes. Eventually the Polish-Lithuanian Commonwealth simply folded up, and Lithuania was signed away to Sweden; but during the invasion there were a few centres of resistance, and most famous of all was Częstochowa.

Oskar had walked me quite a long way, all the time glancing sharply about him to make sure we weren't being followed. It made him look so comically conspicuous that I had to work hard at not laughing. "We call this *Dom Częstochowa*," he said. "Częstochowa House," he added in English.

"Right," I said. We were walking up a broad, tree-lined avenue, and at the end I could see the narrow wedding-cake tower of the monastery. Then I realized what he had said, and it made no sense. "What?"

But he had put on a spurt of speed and was a couple of yards ahead of me. I had to run after him, and suddenly we were at the bottom of the hill and I could see the verdigrised rooftops of the monastery above the brick fortifications. There were people moving about on the ramparts. To be honest, I had expected something a little more austere. Without the pollution-blackened tower it would have looked more like a Mitteleuropean stately home than a place of worship.

The trees opened on both side of us, and to our left a path cut diagonally up the hill. Oskar was already halfway up the path, and I had to trot to follow him, past temporary stalls selling some of the most awful religious kitsch I had ever seen.

"Lots of pickpockets here," Oskar advised over his shoulder. "Be careful."

I zipped up my jacket and put my hands in my pockets to protect my keys, and jogged in his wake.

As I reached him, Oskar said, "In 1655—"

"I know the story, Oskar," I said.

He laughed. "I'm a tour guide, man."

"I'm not paying for a tour guide right now," I said, walking up the path beside him. "I'm paying for a demonstration."

He shrugged and looked at the tourists walking up the hill with us. "You know all about Chmielnicki, then."

"Yes, I know all about Chmielnicki, thanks." I actually rather liked Bohdan Chmielnicki, even though everything I had read about him—apart from Sienkiewicz's portrait of him in *With Fire and Sword*—had painted him as more than slightly unlikeable. A member of the landed gentry allied to the Cossacks, he had, in 1654, in order to resolve his own personal grudges and greeds, placed himself under the protection of Muscovy in return for his military assistance against the Commonwealth. The following year the Tsar Alexei invaded Lithuania, while Chmielnicki's Cossacks moved into Poland.

The Poles appealed to the Swedes for help against the invaders, and the Swedes, exhausted by the Thirty Years War, decided to get themselves a piece of Poland while they still could. The Poles must have thought they were fighting *everybody*.

"In the normal course of events, Kmicic would be here showing you this," Oskar said as we walked through the gateway into the monastery. "But Kmicic is sick. I don't dare let him out until he's well again."

I looked at him, on the verge of asking who the hell Kmicic was, but the name sounded familiar even though I couldn't work out where I'd heard it before.

The place was crowded. Częstochowa is one of the most holy places in Poland. It houses the Black Madonna, a picture supposedly painted by Saint Luke. At the height of the siege, the Poles had gone to pray to the *Czarna Madonna*, and the Swedes had given up and gone home, so the story went. Well, if I was prepared to believe in the villages . . .

"It's about time," Oskar said, checking his watch and grinning broadly. "Shall we . . .?"

The chapel looked like Wembley on Cup Final day. People were shouldering each other out of the way for one of the twice-daily unveilings of the Black Madonna. I'd never seen anything like it. Oskar grabbed my wrist and dragged me through the crowds towards the front of the shrine, and then we stood, side by side, waiting, shoved and buffeted by the people around us. I was almost pushed over, and would have fallen if Oskar hadn't held me up.

The time came, and all around me arms went up holding cameras. Over the ornate altar there was a heavily decorated silver window-frame set high in the wall, covered by a golden screen. The screen began to slide away from the painting beneath, and I remembered Sienkiewicz's *The Deluge*. The hero of that had been here during the siege. I hadn't been able to make it all the way through the book, but the film—in two parts because the book was in two fat volumes—had been part of my Polish studies back in London. Daniel Olbrychski had played the hero, leader of what I could only describe as a bunch of superannuated Hell's Angels redeemed by an act of immensely foolish bravery later on in the film when he destroyed a Swedish cannon. I remembered that the hero of *The Deluge* had been called Kmicic, and I turned my head and stared at Oskar.

"You first went into a village in Gdańsk, didn't you? When it was Danzig," I said loudly over the singing that had broken out in response to the Black Madonna's appearance.

Oskar looked at me.

"I've read *The Tin Drum*," I said. "That's what you saw the first time you went into a village. The gunfight at the Polish Post Office. That's why you call yourself Oskar Matzerath." In the midst of the unveiling of Poland's most holy relic, I elbowed my arms free and grabbed Oskar by the shoulders. "You name yourselves after characters in books, don't you!" I said gleefully into his face. I did a little dance on the spot and almost shoved over a camera-wielding tourist. "Jesus Maria!"

"So what if we do, man?" Oskar grumped.

"I'm sorry, Oskar," I said. "I got a bit carried away."

We had left the chapel and were walking through the monastery. Here and there, monks had set up trestle tables and were blessing holy medals and trinkets with long brushes dipped in holy water. I had already walked too close to one of them and had my right sleeve inadvertently blessed.

"It's part of being a Patriot," said Oskar, still irritated. "You take a name associated with the first house you go into." He looked defiantly at me. "I like Günther Grass."

"Hey, me too," I said, putting my hands up. He snorted and we walked on another few yards. "What was it like? The Polish Post Office?" *The Tin Drum* described the shootout between Poles and German troops at the Polish Post Office in Danzig in the days immediately preceding the war. As Grass described it, it was the Polish equivalent of the Alamo.

"Not like the book," he muttered.

I grinned and followed him. Right up until the moment when I'd figured out the business with the names, I had still half-believed that Oskar was some kind of con-artist. Now I knew he wasn't. Nobody would have bothered to make up anything quite so loopy and adolescent.

"You stick to the house you first saw," Oskar said when I caught up with him. "I do Gdańsk, Matejko does Kraków, Kmicic does Częstochowa. Well . . ." He seemed about to add something, then changed his mind. He shook his head and looked at the flagstones as he walked.

"How many of you are there, then?"

Oskar shook his head again. "You already know too much about our organization, man."

"You make yourselves sound like the Secret Service."

He nodded. "Only more secret."

"Oskar," I said, "since I left university I've met a lot of strange people, but you are without doubt one of the strangest."

"I have to be, man," he said soberly. "I'm on the run all the time."

"Who from?" But he had put on a sudden spurt and I had to run to catch up with him.

"If you do Gdańsk," I said, hurrying beside him, "why aren't you there now?"

Oskar snorted. "Somebody has to do the organizing. You wouldn't believe how much fucking organization a thing like this takes."

"I'm prepared to try," I said, but Oskar didn't seem inclined to explain.

We were walking along a narrow alleyway between two of the buildings. We were some distance away from the main tourist areas of the monastery. Two priests went past us, heads down, deep in conversation, but I couldn't see anyone else.

"Here," said Oskar, coming to an alcove in the wall. "In here."

The alcove was just big enough for the pair of us if we stood with our noses almost touching. Oskar fumbled in his satchel and pulled out a big wad of folded cloth. "Put this on."

The cloth came unfolded as he handed it to me. It was a big hooded cloak. I had to step out of the alcove to put it on, and while I did so Oskar took another cloak from his satchel for himself.

"The place we're going is very dangerous," he said. "The people don't speak any kind of Polish you would understand. Stay with me and do everything I say."

"You can save the tourist lecture, Oskar," I said.

"You're paying for the demonstration," he said, beckoning me back into the alcove, "you get the lecture. Come here. Stand very still." He reached out and took my hand. "Hold on very tight and close your eyes," he said. "The transition can be disorientating."

"I know."

Oskar let go of my hand and looked at me.

"I've seen it before," I said. "In London."

He glared at me. "You said you wanted a demonstration."

"I know it works," I said, taking his hand. "I want to know if *you* can do it." I looked out of the alcove. "And if you *can* do it, I suggest you do it now."

It happened so quickly that I missed it. Oskar grabbed the front of my cloak with his other hand, and jerked me towards him, and a wave of icy air settled about me.

I said, "Did—?" and there was a long roll of thunder that was answered a second or so later by a series of eardrum-smashing explosions. I smelled smoke and shit and horses. I swallowed. "I presume we've arrived."

"Don't speak," he said. "You'll sound like the Man From Mars to the people here, even if you talk in Polish."

I nodded, stepped backward out of the alcove, and my feet shot out from under me. The ground hit my back and knocked the wind out of me, and the next thing I knew Oskar was standing over me and shaking his head. I turned my head and saw about four inches of snow covering the flagstones.

"Idiot," Oskar said very quietly. "Get us both killed."

"Sorry," I whispered. I pulled myself to my feet and stood brushing snow off my legs and cloak. The little alleyway we had walked down to reach the alcove didn't look very much different from a couple of minutes ago, but something had definitely changed. For all the dirty smells, the air seemed cleaner, fresher. When Dom Częstochowa had been created, Southern Poland's mind-boggling pollution was still three hundred years or so in the future. I walked down to the mouth of the alley, and stopped, my mouth hanging open.

People in incredible costumes were running about yelling in an incomprehensible language. Several incomprehensible languages. There were men in tunics with hip-high leather boots and huge hats with long feathers tucked into the brims. There were men in leather clothing and bits and pieces of armour. Monks with swords and flintlock pistols. One huge man with an incredible moustache seemed to be dressed entirely in sheepskins.

"I told you to stay with me!" Oskar hissed behind me.

The noise was unbelievable. People yelling, horses neighing, muskets and pistols firing. Where a couple of minutes ago there had been only tourists wandering around aimlessly, now extravagantly dressed people were running with great purpose. I saw five men carrying another man whose legs had been blown off above the knees. Blood was pulsing weakly from the stumps into the filthy slush on the flagstones. I felt my eyes go wide with shock. It hadn't been like this in the Blitz. The Blitz had been disconcerting, but it had been familiar. It had been something I knew about. This was something entirely outside my understanding.

Four olive-skinned men in black leather clothes, their huge-brimmed hats sporting immense plumes, strode past the mouth of the alley. They all looked at us as they went by, and I tugged the front of my cloak shut so they wouldn't see my jeans and Barbour jacket and roll-neck sweater. One of them nodded to me and I nodded weakly back, and they were gone.

"Spanish mercenaries," Oskar murmured at my shoulder. "Satisfied?"

I took a deep breath and stepped forwards. "No."

"Oh, Jesus Maria," I heard him mutter as he followed me.

It really was a miracle the defenders had survived. The place was in chaos. Nobody seemed to be organized, nobody seemed to know what to do. I pulled up the hood of my cloak and carried on walking. There was something I needed to see.

The smell was almost solid, even in the cold air. It was burned gunpowder and burning wood and shattered stone and scorched meat and unwashed bodies. The stones underfoot were slick with a mixture of slush and blood and ordure. I kept going, and Oskar kept up with me, muttering under his breath.

People were constantly getting in my way. I shoved them aside. They had swords and flintlocks, and I thought the whole bunch of them wouldn't be worth anything against a couple of people with M16s. This was it. I was finally here. This was what Marcin Sierpiński had been afraid of, and I knew what he meant. History as spectacle. Dresdenland. Anybody who knew how could come here and just *indulge* themselves. Grenades. Landmines. Wire-guided anti-tank missiles. Suitably armed, I could single-handedly give this place to the Swedes on a plate. Oskar grabbed my shoulder but I shrugged him off.

Finally I reached the walls of the monastery, and stopped. The flagstones were littered with broken bodies and shattered cannon. I walked right up to the wall and put my hands flat on the parapet. I was barely aware that I was panting.

The modern town of Częstochowa was gone. At the bottom of the hill there was a forest. It had once been closer to the hill—I could see stumps dotted here and there where the besieging army had cut the trees down.

And there they were, between us and the trees: the Swedish guns, dug into a complex system of earthworks and embrasures. Beyond the cannon I could see a small town of tents. Smoke rose up from thousands of cooking fires. Small figures moved unhurriedly about between the tents. I had the same feeling I'd had in Warsaw, that I was looking at a very detailed film set. I thought that if I'd known how to do this in London I could have taken Ed Farraday to the East End and shown him what it was like in 1941. Christ, we could have *shot* the film in 1941 . . .

"Are you satisfied now?" Oskar said in a whisper, and there was an edge of panic in his voice.

I nodded. "Oh yes," I said. I looked around me, just in case Sophie was there, but I couldn't see her. I smiled at Oskar. "And now you're going to teach me how to do it too."

2

"Have you ever seen a snuff movie?" asked Oskar.

I wondered about the implications of that. "Not unless they really killed all those people in *The Terminator*. Have you?"

He ignored the question. "This is the tourist equivalent of a snuff movie."

I thought it was a rather apposite comparison, considering what I'd just seen. I shuddered and drained my glass.

We were sitting in what must have been the roughest bar in present-day Częstochowa. All around us large men with scarred knuckles and misshapen faces were playing the game of drink-yourself-senseless. Most of them looked like fair-ground boxers on their day off, but three of them had politely vacated a table for us when we walked in and bought a bottle of cheap vodka and the use of two glasses. Either there were hidden depths to Oskar or he came from a family of renowned psychopaths.

"I want to be a Patriot," I said.

Oskar shook his head.

"I can pay."

He shook his head again, and his face was an icon of wounded forbearance. "You can't buy your way into the Patriots, man," he told me, filling my glass up again.

"I'm not going to set myself up in competition with you, Oskar."

Oskar sat back and stared at me for a moment. "Only a Patriot can go into the houses."

"Somebody must teach new Patriots how, surely."

"You have to have the aptitude, man."

"Jesus Christ, Oskar!" I said. Two of the big, violent-looking men turned their heads to look at me, decided I wasn't worth the effort, and went back to their conversation. "I want to learn," I said in a quieter voice.

"Ask your friend in London."

"You're not still upset about that, are you?" Obviously, he was. "He won't tell me. I asked him."

"So ask him again."

I sighed. I drained my glass and held it out for another refill. The vodka was at room temperature and tasted horrible. I wondered how I could bear to drink it.

"Just out of interest, why do you call them 'houses'?" I asked.

"Ah." He shrugged, clearly happy to have moved on from the subject of my wanting to join the Patriots. "It's the Germans."

I paused a moment, wondering if I'd misheard. "What about the Germans?"

Oskar waved a hand in the air. "They started it. You know, 'Berlin Haus', 'Dresden Haus', that sort of thing."

Dresdenland. I suddenly felt cold. "The *Germans* do this too?"

He nodded. "There's a bunch of punks and anarchists in Potsdam, they do tours. The punks and anarchists are OK, you know?"

I leaned forward. "Oskar, how many people know how to do this?"

"Well." He looked around the bar and lowered his voice. "I just hear rumours, you know?"

"I love rumours, Oskar."

He shrugged again. "Well, there are some people in Prague, there's a man in Bratislava, the German boys, us. There's a boy in Turin who says he does tours, but I never heard of anyone who could confirm that."

I put my head in my hands. "Jesus Christ." I felt like Eric, aware of drugs and pornography going on around him but completely unable to connect with it. It was the world that Marcin Sierpiński had been afraid of, and it had already happened.

And he'd burned the fucking manuscript anyway. I leaned down and rested my forehead on the scarred tabletop and groaned.

"And of course the French are making a fortune," said Oskar. "D-Day House."

"If everyone's doing it," I said, sitting up, "why won't you teach me too?"

He just shook his head, crossed his arms, and looked at me.

"OK," I said, pulling out my wallet and removing an obscene wad of Polish currency. "How much?"

"Hey, hey," Oskar said quickly, smiling nervously and pushing the money away. "Hey, man."

"It's good money," I said. "I've got dollars. Sterling. Swiss Francs. Anything you want."

"I know, man, I know," he said, still smiling and making discreet pushing motions with his hands. "Just put it away, eh? This is not the right place to let people know you have money, all right?"

I looked around the bar, but nobody seemed to be taking any notice of us. I waved the money under his nose. "Yes or no, Oskar?"

He seemed undecided for a moment, then his nerves got the better of him. "OK, OK. Yes. Just put the money away."

I put the money away.

"Jesus Maria," he murmured, looking around the bar. "Let's hope we get away from here alive."

I looked around the bar too. After Częstochowa House, it seemed rather pedestrian.

The potential of the villages, or the houses, or whatever you wanted to call them, had started to scare me. I was aware I had lost my mind for a moment in Częstochowa, that the only-just-graduate who had walked up the stairs to Lonesome Charley Productions all that time ago would have run as fast as he could in the opposite direction and not stopped until he found something he could understand. I, on the other hand, the Leading Independent Filmmaker, had just walked through it all without worrying about being blown to bits or shot or beaten to death by a Spanish mercenary. Was this what growing up was all about? Or was I just crazy?

Oskar and I parted at the station. As the train pulled in he thrust a piece of paper into my hand.

"Call this number at seven minutes past five tomorrow afternoon," he said. "Use a public telephone. Don't be early, don't be late."

I looked at the piece of paper. "You're joking."

He was looking at the other passengers boarding the train. "It's necessary, man. Trust me. Paranoia is part of a Patriot's life."

I put the slip of paper in my pocket. "I'm getting a bit tired of hearing about the many facets of a Patriot's life."

"Get used to it," he said. "You're going to be hearing a lot more in the next couple of days."

3

I made the call the next afternoon from a public telephone in a restaurant on Floriańska Street. I presumed this was what John le Carré called a "call-box-to-callbox routine", a pantomime to ensure the conversation wasn't being bugged.

The phone at the other end rang once before the receiver was picked up, and Oskar's voice said, "The train to Chorzów leaves in fifteen minutes. Call me from the station when you arrive."

I said, "Oskar—" but he had already hung up.

I went outside and stood in the street with my hands in my pockets. Paranoia might have been part of being a Patriot, but it was really starting to annoy me. In fact, I was so annoyed that I didn't notice the car pulling up beside me until it had stopped and the passenger door opened. I must have been particularly annoyed not to notice, because Floriańska was a pedestrian-only street.

"Timothy Ramsay?"

I looked round. A tall, very good-looking man with dark-brown hair going grey at the temples was standing beside the car. He was wearing a short padded jacket and jeans.

"Mr Timothy Ramsay?" he asked again.

I scowled, thinking this was another of Oskar's paranoid tricks. "What do you want?"

"Police," he said, giving me a moment's glance at an official-looking pass before putting it back in his jacket pocket. "Could you come with us, please?"

"What for?" I said, suddenly remembering all of Witek's warnings about mafia gangs and kidnappings.

He looked sadly at me, and to be honest he didn't appear any more threatening than Oskar had. "My superior would like to ask you some questions," he said in nearly flawless English. "You may be able to help us in a criminal matter."

"Do I have a choice?" I asked, wondering what my chances were of outrunning him.

"If you're worried, we can go to your hotel and you can telephone my superior."

"I'd like that," I said, thinking at least I might stand some kind of chance at the hotel.

He nodded. "All right." He bent his head inside the car and said something to the driver, then he straightened up and closed the door. "Shall we?"

We walked in silence back down Floriańska to the hotel, where the policeman showed his identification to the girl in reception and asked for the use of a telephone. The girl slid the phone to me along the reception desk as if she thought I was an international criminal. The policeman dictated the number and I dialled.

The phone at the other end didn't seem to ring. A gruff voice suddenly said, "Yes?"

"I'm Tim Ramsay," I said.

"Why aren't you here now?" the voice demanded.

"This may sound paranoid, but I was afraid I was being kidnapped," I said, starting to get annoyed again.

"Don't be stupid," said the voice. "Get over here right now. I want to talk to you." And he hung up.

"Happy?" asked the policeman.

I looked out through the front doors of the hotel. The policeman's car was waiting outside. "Oh, sure," I said, thinking that a telephone call to a number I'd never heard before didn't prove anything at all.

We drove for ten minutes or so, through streets I was unfamiliar with, until we came to a big old building with a number of blue-and-white police cars parked outside. I looked at the cars and breathed a discreet sigh of relief.

My policeman and I went in, and I was left sitting on a wooden bench in a corridor while he went to find his superior. I could hear a drunk singing away somewhere in the depths of the building, but otherwise it was eerily quiet. It occurred to me that, no matter where I went, I always seemed to wind up listening to singing drunks. Maybe it was the same drunk, stalking me across Europe and singing "Come into the Garden, Maude" in any number of Continental languages. I stared at the opposite wall and wondered if I was becoming unhinged.

The policemen who walked past me along the corridor spoke to each other in hushed voices. I looked at my hands folded in my lap and reasoned that at least I hadn't been kidnapped by criminal gangs. I'd only been kidnapped by the police.

My policeman came back down the corridor with a much older man: tubby and with a magnificent mane of snow-white hair. He was wearing an ill-fitting grey suit and there was a fat manila folder under his arm. He stopped at a door just along the corridor and opened it, then beckoned to me.

Inside was a room almost bare but for a heavy, dirty table and three chairs. My policeman sat down on one of the chairs and indicated one on the other side of the table. The older man stood beside him and regarded me with steady pale-blue eyes as I sat.

"I am *Pułownik* Sochocki," he said in English. "This is Major Nowak."

I was flattered. A full police colonel and his sidekick. "I would like to call the British Consul," I said in Polish.

Sochocki pulled up the third chair and sat down beside Nowak. "I shall be delighted to let you, Mr Ramsay," he said, lighting a cigarette. "But first I must ask you why you are in Kraków."

"I'm here on business."

He shook his head. "You have been seen associating with antisocial elements of the population." He flicked ash from his cigarette onto the floor.

I leaned forward. "This is more like it, Colonel. This is what I *expected* a police state to be like."

The colonel looked at Nowak, who if anything, now I took a proper look at him, seemed at least as tired and confused as I felt. Nowak sighed. "Poland is not a police state, Mr Ramsay."

"Prove it."

"You have been seen in the company of one Povilas Vysniauskas, a Lithuanian criminal," Colonel Sochocki told me. He opened the folder on the table and looked down at it.

"I don't know who you're talking about," I said, but I kept a carefully straight face. I'd thought Oskar's accent was strange, but after my Polish language tapes, with their Polish version of Received Pronunciation, *everybody* here had a strange accent.

"This criminal Povilas Vysniauskas is currently under investigation in connection with a number of murders in the Kraków area," said Sochocki, carelessly flicking more ash while he read the file. "Five tourists known to have associated with him have been found dead in the past two years." He looked up, tipped his head to one side and watched to see what my reaction would be.

"I wasn't aware I had met any Lithuanians," I said mildly. And all of a sudden I had the strangest feeling that the colonel and I had met before, somewhere.

"You were photographed with him in the Market Square two days ago," said Nowak. "And at Częstochowa yesterday." We looked at each other and he nodded apologetically. "It's true. I've seen the pictures."

"He said his name was Mirosław," I said to Sochocki, picking a name out of nowhere while I struggled to remember where I knew him from. "He said he was from Sosnowiec."

"Mirosław." Sochocki wrote the name down in his file. "No surname?"

I shook my head.

Sochocki gave me one of the most level and scary looks I had ever seen. "Are you telling us the truth, Mr Ramsay?"

"I have no reason to lie, Colonel."

He looked at me a moment longer, then he turned to Nowak. "Call Sosnowiec. Arrange for photographs to be circulated. Make arrangements for surveillance of the railway station."

"Why don't you just arrest this man?" I asked, trying to put an edge of innocent concern into my voice. "If he's as dangerous as you think he is, should he be running around?"

"No evidence," Nowak said pointedly.

Sochocki sighed and rubbed his eyes. "Our enquiries," he said, as much for Nowak's benefit as mine, I thought, "are still continuing. We are not a police state, Mr Ramsay, no matter what you might think. We cannot just arrest a man any longer." He sounded as if he regretted the passing of the Good Old Days, when he could arrest anyone he felt like arresting.

"What did this 'Mirosław' want with you?" Nowak asked.

"I'm researching a documentary about Poland during the last war," I said. "He must have heard about it; he rang me at my hotel and said he had some archive film which might be useful to me."

Sochocki and Nowak looked at each other, then Sochocki made a note in the file. "And was it?" he asked without looking up.

"Pardon?"

"This archive film. Was it useful to you?" He looked at me and nibbled the end of his pen thoughtfully.

"No." I shook my head. "Complete waste of time. The film was degraded, useless. Somebody had been keeping it in a cowshed or something."

"Did he threaten you?" said Nowak.

"Not at all. He was charming." I watched Sochocki write "charming" down and said, "Was I really in danger?"

"We have good reason for thinking so," said Sochocki, capping his pen and putting it into the breast pocket of his jacket. "It may be that you have had a lucky escape, Mr Ramsay." He stood up. I stood too. "I shall want to speak with you again. Major Nowak will take you back to your hotel." He put out his hand.

I looked at his hand. "I know you from somewhere," I said. I looked at his face. "Are you the one who's been following me about?"

Sochocki narrowed his eyes. He frowned at me. Then he sat down and took his pen out of his pocket and opened the file. "Well," he said. "*This* is interesting." He wrote a couple of words. One was "train".

"Oh, bollocks." Me and my big mouth. I sat down as well. Sochocki had been one of the people standing around the body on the railway lines in Kraków, the last time I'd been here. He was the one who had watched me throw up down the side of the train.

He looked up from the file and smiled brightly, an expression which seemed somehow incongruous.

"Was that one of the murders you're talking about?" I asked.

"Yes." He smiled again. "Imagine my interest, Mr Ramsay. You are seen associating with a suspect in the matter of five murders, and now I recall seeing you simply sailing past me on the train last year when the third of those murders was discovered."

"Small world," I said.

"Not *so* small."

"Last year I was here to buy a piece of film for my former employer. LOT and British Airways had some sort of argument and I couldn't get home by air. That's the only reason I was on that train."

"But you were here in Kraków."

"In Gliwice." I watched him write the word "Gliwice" down.

He capped the pen again and clasped his hands in front of him on the tabletop. "I love coincidence, Mr Ramsay," he said mildly. "Such a wonderful phenomenon."

I stared at him. "I do hope you're not suggesting I have something to do with these murders, Colonel."

"Were you planning to deny it?"

"I'm planning to bet what little money I have that there are a dozen tourists in Kraków right now who were also here at the same time as me last year."

"A dozen suspects." Sochocki smiled at Nowak, then at me. "That sounds almost like a luxury. Ah." He closed the file. "In my own life, there have been a number of unfortunate coincidences, Mr Ramsay," he said, standing again and holding out his hand to me. "Not least the coincidence of being born a Pole. Do you know much Polish history?"

"Yes."

"Then you will understand the unfortunate coincidence of being born a Pole. Particularly in the past seventy or so years."

It seemed that I had got away with it. Whatever "it" was. "What should I do if Mirosław gets in touch with me again?"

"Call me immediately," he said as we shook hands. "And on no account must you go anywhere with him alone. Do you understand?"

I nodded, imagining the number of ways I could kill Oskar. "Absolutely, Colonel."

Nowak's driver took us back into the centre of town and dropped me outside the hotel. As I got out of the car, Nowak handed me a card with a telephone number on it.

"We're desperate to catch this bastard, Mr Ramsay," he said in English. "Call this number if you see him again."

In the dim light of the overhead bulb in the back of the car, Nowak looked worn out. I realized that they expected me to help them trap Oskar, to set myself up as bait. Sochocki was very good, I had to admit. He hadn't recognized me until I'd mentioned seeing him somewhere before, but he'd bounced right back with all that stuff about the unfortunate coincidence of being Polish, about my accidental witnessing of the third body. He'd meant to soften me up so I would volunteer myself in order to clear my own name.

"I'll be in touch, Major," I said, getting out of the car.

"No," he said. "*We'll* be in touch. Goodnight, Mr Ramsay."

Twenty-eight

1

The next morning I woke to find that a folded piece of paper had been pushed under the door of my room while I was asleep. Written on the piece of paper were a telephone number and a time.

I sighed and sat down on the end of the bed, suddenly wondering if it was worth it. Back in London it had all seemed reasonably straightforward. Highly irrational, perhaps, but straightforward by its own internal logic. Now, Sophie seemed to be receding from view behind a screen of Patriots and policemen. At least Oskar's paranoia made some kind of sense after yesterday's visit to the police station, though I had trouble believing he was involved in murder.

Everything was becoming just a little too complicated, and I found myself half-considering packing up and going home on the next flight.

Part of the problem was that I was having trouble knowing what to believe. It was as if every person I met told me another part of a huge and very unlikely story. Marcin Sierpiński wanted to keep tourists out of the villages; then Oskar told me hundreds of people all over the world were going in every year; then Colonel Sochocki told me Oskar was mixed up somehow with the deaths of five tourists. I stared at the wallpaper. Why hadn't the police just arrested him instead of following us about and taking photographs? Surely even the suspicion that he was responsible for five deaths would have been enough to pull him in for questioning? Was this the way the Polish police worked? Or just the way Sochocki worked? Or was there another part of the story that somebody had yet to tell me? Too many questions. All of a sudden it all seemed too serious, too real.

Bollocks. I put my hands to my face and the urge to go home came over me again. I thought of Sophie saying, "I don't believe you," and I got up and started to get dressed.

The first thing Oskar said was, "Where the fuck were you, man? I was going to meet you on that train."

"I was arrested yesterday," I said.

There was a silence, then he said, "Everyone should try it at least once. Did you enjoy it?"

"By Colonel Sochocki, and the hunky but sad Major Nowak."

Incredibly, I heard him laugh at the other end of the line. "Nowak is all right, actually. But for Sochocki, man, law-and-order is an obsession, you know?"

"I got that impression." I was standing in yet another café, my luggage at my feet, passport and ticket in my pocket. "They had photographs of us in Częstochowa."

"They have lots of practice, photographing people."

"I got that impression too, Povilas."

There was another moment's silence, then he said, "Oh, that's not fair, man! I *hate* that!"

"I don't care what your real name is, Oskar. I'm going home."

"You're what?"

"I'm going home. I've had enough of this. I'm not getting anywhere. I want to go home. I just thought you should know."

"But you wanted to learn how to be a Patriot!"

I shook my head and looked around the entrance of the café. A young couple pushed by me on their way to the cloakroom. "I give up, Oskar," I said. "It's all just too weird for me."

"What about my money, man?" he shouted. "You haven't paid me for the demonstration!"

"I'll have it wired to you."

"No good, man," he said firmly. "Cash only. No banks."

I looked at the telephone. It was bright orange. There was one just the same in my old hotel room. Standardized. One model fits all. Sophie once said that a few years ago trying to telephone Poland had been like trying to telephone the Moon.

"The police say you're responsible for five murders, Oskar."

The silence this time was so long I thought he had put the phone down and run away. But finally he said, "Oh?"

"Is that all you can say? 'Oh?'" I pressed the earpiece harder against the side of my head. "I tell you the police are after you for five murders and all you can think of to say is 'Oh?'"

"I didn't think it was *murder*," he said.

I had no idea what he meant by that. "OK," I said. "I'm going now. Have a nice life, Oskar."

"No! Wait! Wait, man. It's not the way the police think. I can explain. And you still owe me the money."

I almost hung up, but finally I said, "All right, Oskar. I owe you money and you owe me an explanation. How do you want to do this?"

"OK. OK, do you know Gliwice?"

"Sure."

"Right. I'm going to give you an address. Be there at six." And he gave me the address. Then I had to ask him to give it me again because I was sure I'd misheard him.

"You promised me an explanation," I said. "And I'd like it now."

"It's a secret life, being a Patriot," Oskar said.

"That's not an explanation," I said. "Is it, Witek?"

For the first time since I'd known him, Witek looked sheepish. He shrugged and looked at the tabletop.

"Because my life would have been much less complicated if you'd just *told* me," I went on.

"I needed the money, you bastard," he said, looking up and glaring at me. There were red spots of anger and embarrassment on his cheekbones. "You think the world owes you a favour, but some of us have to work for our living."

I rubbed my eyes. We were sitting around the table in Witek and Julia's flat, the table at which I had eaten so many meals while I waited for Marcin Sierpiński to let us know that his father was well enough to see me. This, of course, was Oskar's version of a safe rendezvous. I was here visiting my old friend Witek. Oskar had been here when I arrived with my presumed police tail, and he would stay here, or in one of the other flats in the block, after I had gone and until he felt it was safe to slip away.

Oskar and Witek started to argue in low voices and I just let them. At least this explained a number of things. Witek must have mentioned me to Oskar, and Oskar must have been following me when I went to meet Marcin, and had overheard our argument in the café. By the time we'd gone out for our day trip, Witek had already known I wasn't really in Poland to look for film, which explained his sullen mood.

"All right." I held up my hands. "This is getting us nowhere." Oskar and Witek stopped arguing and looked at me. I ran my fingers through my hair and stared at Oskar. "Murders," I said.

Oskar started to fidget. He knitted his fingers together and looked down at the floor. "You have to understand, man. We take people into some dangerous places. Second World War places, mediaeval places. Violent stuff. There's no nice houses. At least I've never seen one."

No Golden Summers to revisit, no times of blessed peace. The villages were created by the violent release of energy, and the events they captured were all violent. "OK," I said. "I'll take that for granted."

He took a deep breath and looked at me. "Some people, man, they think it's just a game."

"Are you trying to tell me you *are* responsible for those deaths?"

His face twisted up. "Only as far as being their guides. They were accidents, man. They didn't listen, didn't stay with us. We know the houses. We know where every shell and rifle bullet and cannon ball is going to hit." He shook his head. "But they just went charging off, like you did in Częstochowa House. They didn't *listen.*"

I supposed it made sense. With an ordinary guide, if you wandered off on your own maybe the worst thing that could happen would be you'd get lost. Not in the villages, though. Oskar was right; I'd done it myself. I sighed.

"So we leave them where they fall," he said. "And when the house comes to an end and starts to repeat they just . . . pop out."

"Last year they found a body on the railway line in Kraków," I said. I watched Witek and saw his shoulders hunch up towards his ears as he remembered putting me on the train. "Was that one of yours?"

"I told you man, it's not our *fault.*"

"Was it?"

Oskar nodded sulkily. "The Australian. Only Australian we've ever had, and we have to go and lose him." He looked at the window. "Stupid bastard."

"What happened to him?"

All of a sudden a surge of energy seemed to seize Oskar. He flapped his arms and yelled, "He ran out in front of a fucking tank! What do you *think* happened to him?"

"To be honest with you, Oskar, I'm afraid to guess any more."

The energy left him as suddenly as it had appeared. His shoulders slumped and his hands flopped down on his lap. "He was trouble right from the start. I should never have let him go into the houses. He wouldn't wear period clothes, wouldn't listen to advice. He was taken into the 1943 house and he simply . . . ran out in front of a German tank. Nobody knows why. Maybe he got a little crazy, I don't know. And the fucking thing just . . ." He held his palm out flat in front of him and ran his fist along it. "Never even slowed down."

"And you left him there."

"Oh, come on." His look told me I was the world's biggest idiot. "If the stupid bastard wanted to commit suicide by jumping under a Panzer—and pay for the privilege—am I going to argue? If there's an accident, all the Patriots have instructions to leave their clients where they fall. Those are my standing orders. I'm more interested in live Patriots than dead tourists." He shrugged moodily and went back to looking at the floor.

I looked at Witek and raised an eyebrow, and he just shrugged as well. Oskar glanced up. "I've got something to show you, man."

We left Witek's flat and went up four flights of stairs to the top floor of the block. Oskar stopped at one door, rang the bell, and then knocked twice. Then he knocked twice and rang the bell. There was the sound of locks and bolts being undone. Witek looked embarrassed and turned away.

The door opened and a burly, bearded young man peered out. He stared at Oskar, then at Witek, then at me.

"He's from England," Oskar said to the bearded man. "It's OK."

We went inside, and the bearded man closed the door behind us and locked and bolted it while we stood in the narrow hallway.

When he was done, Oskar said to him, "Canned Goods, this is Tim Ramsay."

I felt a tingle go up the middle of my back. Canned Goods and I shook hands, and I wondered how the hell a few gunshots could release enough energy to create a village. Canned Goods, I presumed from his name, was the Patriot who took people to see the start of World War Two, the incident at the radio station in Gleiwitz. I flashed a glance at Witek, a thought occurring to me, but he was already walking down the hall.

"How is he?" Oskar said.

"Asleep," said Canned Goods. "Sobieski's with him."

Oskar sighed and shook his head. "Two people, man. Two people all the time when he's asleep. How many times do I have to tell you?"

"We have families, prick," Canned Goods said, glaring. "Responsibilities."

Oskar pulled himself up to his full height and tapped Canned Goods lightly on the chest. "We're Patriots, man," he said. "We look after our own. OK?"

Canned Goods just snorted and pushed past us. Oskar and I exchanged glances and followed him.

The layout of the flat was exactly the same as Witek and Julia's, except this one was filthy. Every room was untidy, and it stank of beer and inexpertly produced meals and, strongest of all, sweat. The kitchen was a mess. Witek was standing at the sink, looking out of the little window.

At the end of the hall, where Witek and Julia's bedroom was in their flat, Oskar stopped at a closed door. "Just be really quiet, man," he said. "That's all I ask of you, OK?"

I nodded, and he pushed open the door.

The smell inside the room was incredible, a stench of sweaty tension. A camp-bed had been set up under the window, and there was a blanket-wrapped shape lying on it. Beside the bed, a tall, thin middle-aged man with bags under his eyes looked up from a tattered copy of *Penthouse*.

"Kmicic," Oskar said quietly, nodding at the figure on the bed. "He would have taken you to Częstochowa House if he wasn't ill."

"What's wrong with him?" I whispered, staring at the gently breathing shape.

Oskar's face became a map of concentration. "You have to understand, the houses are like those Chinese balls. You know? One inside another?"

"They nest," I said. "Yes, I know."

He nodded. "But in the centre of all of them there's one *huge* fucking house."

I thought about what Harry had said to me on the steps of St Paul's. "Big Bang House."

"The houses, it's kind of the way you look at things," he went on. "Like those computer pictures? Look at them one way and they're just a lot of garbage, but cross your eyes and there's this three-dimensional picture right there?"

I nodded, wondering if these lunatics had already been here while I was sitting downstairs waiting to see Marcin Sierpiński's father.

"The houses are like that. Once you have the trick, it's dead easy. And the more you do it, the easier it gets. Kmicic says everything produces a house. Any release of energy. He says if you get sensitive enough you can go to a house that was created by a loud argument."

I was lost. "So?"

Oskar inclined his head at the camp-bed again. "So Kmicic is so sensitive he can go into a house that's been created by a person's *heartbeat*, man. But it's done something to him. He started doing it in his sleep."

Oh, Christ. "And you're afraid he'll fall all the way through to Big Bang House?"

"It's OK when he's awake—he can control it. But he can't stay awake for ever. So we have to keep somebody with him when he's asleep, and if he goes in they follow and pull him out."

"Jesus, Oskar," I said in my normal voice, and he hissed and put a finger to his lips. The figure on the bed stirred but didn't wake. Sobieski, the one with *Penthouse*, glared at me. I held my hands out in front of me and put on an apologetic expression.

"Go home," Witek said quietly behind me. "There's nothing here for you, English boy. Only grief."

I turned and looked at him. "No, Witek. There's something for me here, and I'm going to tell you what it is."

We went back down to Witek's flat and sat around the table again, and I told them an abridged version of the Story. I watched Witek as I explained to them what had been in the materials I had bought from Mr Sierpiński, but he just sat looking at me with a sad expression on his face. I told them about Harry and Sophie's separate disappearing acts, about tracking Harry down, about our day out in the Blitz villages. Witek stared at the ceiling and shook his head. In contrast, Oskar started to get animated when I told them about the Blitz, and I knew he was thinking about opening a London branch of the Patriots.

When I'd finished we all sat looking at each other. Then Witek got up and went into the kitchen and put the kettle on. I could see Oskar was still thinking about the tourist possibilities of Blitz House, so I went into the kitchen too.

"Do you know where Sophie is?" I said.

Witek was taking tea-glasses out of a cupboard. He shook his head.

"Can you make a guess at where she is?"

He shook his head again. "Tim—"

"Doesn't matter, Witek. Everything's forgiven. Let's just tell each other the truth from now on, OK?"

"You weren't exactly honest with me, man," Oskar reminded me, coming into the kitchen. "You never said anything about Zosia."

"I apologize, Oskar."

"And of course that makes everything all right," he grumbled.

"OK!" I shouted. They stared at me. "All right," I said more quietly. "Let's proceed from first principles. Sophie is here somewhere, probably in a village, and I want to find her. You're going to teach me how to get into the villages, but I need to know where to look. Any ideas?" Nobody said a word. "You must have some idea, Witek. You know her better than I do."

He sighed and put the glasses on the wooden worktop, balanced a strainer over one and spooned granulated tea into it. Oskar leaned against a cupboard and crossed his arms.

I said, "Witek, how long have you been a Patriot?"

He shrugged morosely, and for a moment he reminded me of Viren's shop assistant. "Four years?" he said, nodding towards Oskar for confirmation.

"Five," Oskar said.

"Five years," Witek said to me.

"So you already knew about the villages? The houses? When you first met me?"

"Of course."

Lovely. I'd been riding around Poland with the answer to at least half my problems sitting by my side. "Witek," I said gently, thinking of our last day trip, "are you the Patriot who takes people to Dom Oswięcim?"

He nodded, and I felt my stomach come up into my mouth. "And people *want* to go there? See it when it was still running?"

Witek looked at the ceiling again. "Sick people," he said in English. "Sick people want to see Auschwitz House."

"Jesus." No wonder he drank so much. No wonder he had wanted to get away from Oswięcim as quickly as he could. "I'm sorry, Witek."

"You don't understand," he sneered without looking at me.

"A Patriot goes everywhere," said Oskar with a ludicrous amount of pride, considering one of his guides was in imminent danger of visiting the Big Bang and another must have been driven half-crazy by the things he had seen.

"You," I said to him, "can shut up about what it means to be a Patriot."

Oskar looked affronted. "It's business!" he shouted. "People want these things! I don't force people to go into the houses, and I don't force people to become Patriots." His face was purple and he was almost levitating with rage. "We're organized, we support each other. Kmicic couldn't survive without us."

"He wouldn't be *in* that state without you, Oskar." I raised my hands. "OK, boys. This is getting us nowhere. There's something here that Sophie wants, and I need to know what it is."

Oskar walked to the window. There was a drone of engines in the sky, and looking through the gap in the net curtains I saw four parachutes blossom, one after the other, against the overcast. Every afternoon, regular as clockwork: you could set your watch by the local skydiving club.

"They had a flat," Witek said. "Zosia and Mirek. In Bytom."

2

"It was stolen from Bronek's garage," Witek said vengefully as we left the block and walked towards the railway station. "Some bastard pulled the garage doors off and drove away with my car."

"Don't worry about it, Witek," I said. "They can't have got very far." We looked at each other, and he made a brave attempt at a smile.

"It was because of the Patriots that Julia left me, of course," he said after we'd been walking for a couple of minutes. "She hated everything they stand for."

"I'm almost with her on that one," I told him, looking casually over my shoulder to see if I could spot any police tail, but there was nothing obvious.

He waved his hands hopelessly in the air. "It was the money!" he said in a loud voice. "So much money!" He jammed his hands into his coat pockets so suddenly I thought he was deliberately trying to burst the linings. "She never understood. As a Patriot, I made five times as much money as she made at the hospital. Without it, we would have starved."

"You could have tried an honest job," I said gently.

"Ach." He spat into the gutter. "Now you sound like her. Tell me, what sort of honest job can I get? I am a translator in a country where every fifth person is a translator. An English teacher in a town where every street has two schools of English. A tourist guide in Kraków." He snorted. "Honesty."

"So how did you survive under the Communists?"

"Hah! The Communists. Under the Communists, we were not *allowed* to be unemployed. They made jobs for us. Twenty people would work on a production line where five could have done the work just as efficiently." We stopped at a traffic crossing and waited for the green light. "I'm afraid, you know? Shall I tell you what I'm afraid of?"

I nodded.

"People in Poland today tell me that things were better under the Communists," he said, launching himself across the street as the light changed. "And I'm afraid that one day I will start to believe it."

I followed him, and as we reached the opposite pavement I said, "Something's been bothering me."

Witek grunted. "Everything bothers you. If the train is late, that bothers you."

I frowned. "Have we had this conversation before?" I asked.

"Unlikely, isn't it?"

"It's just . . ." I shook my head. "Doesn't matter."

"What were you going to ask?" We had crossed the bridge near Witek's flat, and were nearing the tram stop.

"I was just wondering why you call yourselves the Patriots, that's all. I mean, Oskar isn't even Polish."

Witek gave me the same Tim-is-an-imbecile look that Oskar had given me earlier. "It's the name of an American football team, isn't it?"

"Is it?"

He nodded. "New England Patriots. New York Patriots. Chicago Patriots. Something like that. Oskar likes American football."

"An American football team," I said. "I see." I was in the hands of madmen.

3

Bytom was a dreadful industrial town about half an hour's bus-ride from Gliwice. You couldn't get there directly from Gliwice by tram because there was a viaduct between them which had been under construction or repair for about a decade. You had to take a tram, then a bus, then another tram from Zabrze. I'd done this journey before, but then it had been fun. Now it wasn't anything like so amusing.

I'd ridden through Bytom often enough the last time I was here, and it hadn't improved since. It was dirty and smelly and run-down, the pavements were uneven, and there was a black crust of pollution on all the buildings, even the newer Communist-built blocks on the edge of town.

Sophie and Mirek's flat was in one of the newer blocks, a slab of dirty-yellow plonked down in the middle of a few dozen acres of filthy sandy soil. A solid band of graffiti encircled the base of the building, and in places the yellow cladding had been broken away to expose the prefab panels underneath. The balconies were festooned with aerials, laundry and satellite dishes, and all the stairwell windows were broken. It made Witek's block look like Trump Tower.

"We always had to wait," Witek said, leading me up the stairs. "You would put down your name and wait five years and one day you might get a car. You would put down your name and wait ten years and one day a flat might become available. This was the way we did things. When your car finally arrived, it might not be the colour you wanted. It might not even be the *car* you wanted. But you took it, because a car is better than no car, even if it's not the one you wanted."

I stopped on one of the landings and looked out between filthy shards of glass. A maroon Fiat Polonez was driving down the street. I thought I had seen it before, as we waited at the tram stop in Gliwice.

"It was the same with a flat," Witek went on without me. "Oh, there were always ways to speed things up. If you had an aged relative, you could get them to move in with you and rent out their flat to a friend. Officially, your friend wouldn't be living there, of course, but it would do until their own flat came through."

"Witek," I said, catching him up, "this is *horrible*."

He looked about him. "I know," he said.

"I can't believe that Sophie lived here."

"I know," he said again, as if I'd just revealed some deep character flaw. "Wait here." I stopped and watched as he went up the last few steps and pressed a doorbell. The door opened, but because of where I was standing I couldn't see who had opened it. Witek and the person in the flat had a short, quiet conversation, then there was a brief pause, after which a hand emerged holding a bunch of keys, which Witek took, nodding profuse thanks. The door closed, and he beckoned me up.

We ascended another two flights, above the flats, and came to a heavy-looking metal door. Witek selected a key from the bunch he'd been given, unlocked the door, and pushed it open.

Beyond was an enormous dusty space that must have run the length and breadth of the block, just beneath the roof. There was a click, and a line of low-wattage bulbs came alive down the middle of the ceiling, casting weak pools of light on scattered piles of furniture and boxes.

"Attic," said Witek. "The flat we stopped at was Zosia's. It still is, as a matter of fact. Mr Pawluk, who is there now, kept her furniture because he couldn't afford any of his own. But the rest is here." He pointed at a modest stack of boxes. "There."

"I still have to learn how to get into the villages," I said without moving from the doorway.

"I know," he said sadly. "I'll teach you." He turned and put a hand on my shoulder. "We have a lot of work to do. Come on."

"I have a theory that once upon a time everyone knew how to enter the houses," he said, sitting crosslegged on the floor beside the boxes that contained Sophie's life. "But gradually the knowledge, the aptitude, was lost."

"Mm," I said, opening the flap of another box and looking down on the books packed neatly inside.

"The classical image of Hell, for instance, could just as easily be an interpretation of the house which contains Earth in its early volcanic state. Fire, brimstone. Unbearable heat."

"Forget it," I said. "Nobody could survive that for long enough to come back and tell people about it. There was no air to breathe."

Out of the corner of my eye, I saw him scowl, but he went on regardless. "The houses are as much about theory as practice," he said. "You have to understand that. It's not like putting a key into the ignition of a car. As Oskar said, it's all about the way you look at the world."

"And the way you move," I murmured.

"What?"

I looked up from the box. "Harry and Oskar both moved in a certain way. They put their feet in a certain position. Aligned their bodies a certain way. I never got a good look."

Witek snorted. "For fools. Does Kmicic do all this when he's asleep? As soon as I met him I knew all that nonsense with the body was worthless. All it does is give the mind something to focus on."

I sat back on my heels, thinking. "So how could you discover it by accident?"

He shook his head. "I don't think you could."

"So how did *you* discover it?"

"I didn't. Oskar taught me."

"And who taught Oskar?"

Witek rubbed his face. His hand left dusty streaks on his cheek. "Another Patriot. And one before him, and one before him, I suppose. I told you. People have *always* known how to do it."

I thought about it. And an awful realization crept over me. I'd thought it had been an accident. All this time, I'd been presuming that Mr Sierpiński had been walking down the street in London one day, and chanced to get his body just *so* and found himself at an undamaged Bank Junction. But that was stupid. I'd presumed it when I had flu, and I hadn't bothered to think about it since. Even if it happened by accident, it would have happened to other people too . . . .

Oh Jesus . . . "So somebody must have taught old man Sierpiński how to do it."

He looked thoughtful for a moment, then nodded. "I suppose so."

"So there were people in London doing it in the 1940s."

He looked disinterestedly around the attic. "Perhaps he learned it here, before he fled to England."

I shook my head. "No. It was the Great Secret he learned in London. He kept calling it that." I looked at him, and I suddenly thought of Mr Pearmain's story, of the ghost of Dr Johnson stepping suddenly out of thin air in front of him. It hadn't been a ghost. It had been a tourist, in the equivalent of local costume, maybe for the

Great Fire village. "Jesus Christ, Witek. There were Patriots in London." My eyes widened. "Maybe there still are."

He nodded again. "Why not?"

I had a sudden image of Harry Dean bumping into a tour-group shepherded by the British equivalent of Oskar, toting cameras and semi-automatic weapons and all the paraphernalia that Marcin Sierpiński had been so worried about. And if there had been Patriots in London, why not Patriots in Rome, Paris, Guernica . . .? I slumped back against a pile of books and they slid across the dusty concrete.

"Anything?" Witek asked, completely unconcerned.

"What?" I was still flummoxed by the idea of a world-wide secret society that had survived for decades, visiting and revisiting the sites of disasters, completely ignorant of its various branches. "Oh. No."

He picked up a book. *A Child's History of Poland.* I'd flicked through it. Some of my old books had still been in the attic at home when my father died. I'd looked through them while I was clearing the house and realized what a little bugger I'd been with books: every page was covered with wax-crayon scrawlings, drawings of Mummy and Daddy—and later Wendy—in the margins, figures coloured in so energetically they were almost obliterated.

Sophie's books weren't like that. Apart from being almost thirty years old they were as good as new. Not a mark on them. There was no sign she'd even opened them. A single pencil-mark in *A Child's History* might have given me some kind of clue, but there was nothing.

"Can we get all this stuff back to your flat?" I said. "There's too much to look at now."

He looked at the books, the boxes, the pile of Sophie's junk, and he nodded unenthusiastically. "I have a friend with a van."

I'd been wrong all along. But Marcin Sierpiński had been catastrophically wrong. Dresdenland wasn't just a possibility: it had been happening for years. Certainly since the 'forties. Almost certainly longer. Centuries maybe. I'd actually stumbled onto one of the Secret Things that conspiracy theorists believe in, a hidden agenda operating just below the level of normal life. The next time I saw that bastard Sierpiński I planned to tell him exactly what was going on.

"How did you become a Patriot?" I asked.

Witek scratched his head and looked around the attic. "Oskar knew one of the guides I worked with at the Wawel. He came and had coffee with me one day and told me about the houses."

"You didn't believe him straight away, did you?"

"Of course not." His withering stare was a flash of the old familiar Witek. "No, he offered to show me."

"And he took you to Oświęcim to show you?"

He nodded, and I suddenly felt terribly sorry for him. He'd been recruited specifically for Auschwitz, of course. That had been Oskar's intention all along, to find somebody desperate enough to help him open up a new tourist destination, one that most sensible people would avoid like the plague. And I knew that on his worst days Witek could have been arrogant enough to agree to take it on.

"You know the police are probably outside," I said.

He waved a dismissive hand. "They see you and me carrying some boxes out to a van. It's research material, isn't it?"

I looked at the piles of books. "I suppose so." Half-buried under one pile was a stubby furry leg. I pulled it out and held it up. It was attached to a little teddy-bear. Its fur was worn down to the cloth in places, and it had only one eye, but there was a bright red ribbon tied in a bow around its neck, a more recent addition. I held it to my nose and sniffed, and imagined I smelled the faintest ghost of Anaïs-Anaïs. I got to my feet and put the bear in my pocket.

"What do the Patriots call you?" I asked.

Witek didn't bother to get up. He squinted up at me and said, "Nothing. I couldn't bear to take a name." And then he said, without the slightest trace of irony, "I'm the Patriot With No Name."

I sighed and put my hand down to help him to his feet.

Twenty-nine

1

"Ready?"

I fixed my feet, aligned my body, tried to alter the way I perceived the world. "Go."

The world blinked.

I blinked too. The buildings across the street looked almost brand-new, bright and sharp, not dirty and worn. The modern street-signs were gone. One sign with the street's name had appeared on the building directly opposite us. It was in German.

Witek let go of my hand. "Now do you see?" he asked quietly.

A tank with a black cross painted on its side went past the doorway. Behind it was a truck carrying German infantry. I shook my head. "Sorry."

"Oh, for Christ's sake." He grabbed my hand. "It's easy." The world blinked again and we were back in the entranceway of Witek's grandmother's building in Gliwice.

"I'm sorry, Witek."

He stared and me and shook his head hopelessly. "You will never learn," he said in English.

"If it's any consolation, I can't 'see' those 3D computer pictures either."

He tugged my arm and we walked down the steps into the weak cold afternoon sunlight. "Forget computer pictures," he said as we walked down the street. "Forget standing in a certain position. Forget what Oskar says. *I'm* teaching you. Listen to *me*."

"I have been."

"No, you haven't."

Witek claimed to have learned how to be a Patriot in three days. We'd been at it over a week and I still couldn't go solo. I couldn't even see what he was getting at in all his lectures about seeing the world a little differently. It all sounded like New Age stuff to me. I looked at the world with my eyes wide open, my eyes half-closed. I tried to imagine the villages we were going to. Nothing worked. If Witek let go of my hand and told me to follow him I'd just find myself standing there on my own until he came back to berate me for being too stupid to learn.

"I'll have to go with you," he said angrily. "It's the only way."

"No, Witek."

"You'll never learn to do it alone."

"I've got to. What's Sophie going to think if I turn up with you in tow?"

We reached the bus-stop and Witek stopped and crossed his arms. "You're not going anywhere, English boy." He glared at me, then he said more gently, "Some people just can't get the trick of it. I don't know why—it's perfectly simple. But that's the way it is."

I scowled and put my hands in my pockets. I still had Sophie's little teddy-bear in one pocket. It was fast becoming the mascot of my frustrations.

Apart from my failure to "get the trick" of the villages, I'd had no luck at all with the stuff we had brought back from Bytom. All I had done was put the childhood and young-womanhood of the person I loved under an increasingly desperate microscope.

The various boxes had indeed turned out to contain almost all of Sophie's life. There was a photograph of her, at not much more than a year old, lying on a fur rug and grinning at the camera with all five of her teeth. In another she was serious-faced and wearing her first Communion dress, holding a little posy of flowers; she had on white high-heeled shoes and white socks and she was looking into the camera with a single-minded concentration I recognized.

The other stuff was the same. She seemed to have kept almost all her old school books, and I could follow her schoolwork nearly through to the time she left to go to university. Her handwriting was almost the equivalent of the photographs: I could see her adult handwriting in it, the way I could see in the photos the Sophie she would become, the Sophie I had thought I knew. I sat up late at night at the dining table in Witek's flat and read them over and over again. Sometimes I just traced the hand-writing with my fingertip.

There was a photo of her at some party or other when she must have been about my age. She was laughing into the camera, wild and drunk, wearing a short red dress that probably exposed more cleavage than was proper. She was the single most beautiful human being I had ever seen.

There were letters from her ex-husband when they were courting. I read them, excusing it as research. He pledged undying love. He couldn't live without her. One was so frankly intimate that I folded it and put it back into its envelope, embarrassed, hating Mirek more deeply than I had ever hated anyone or anything in my life.

In a lot of the photographs she was with an older man who I presumed was her father. They were laughing in most of them. She looked happier than she ever had while working at Lonesome Charley Productions. He had the sort of avuncular good-looks I'd sometimes wished on my own father when he was being more than usually distant and difficult. It was obvious they loved each other. There were, I noticed, no photographs of her mother.

Late one night, when Witek had gone to bed after a particularly frustrating day trying to show me how to "get the trick", I tackled the one box we had not yet opened, and found it full of clothes. I pulled out dresses, shirts, jeans, bras, panties, a scarlet-and-black lace suspender belt and white fishnet stockings, and dumped them on the table. Right at the bottom, in a little cardboard box, was a tiny pair of white high-heeled shoes. I put them on the table and sat down and stared at them and considered how stupid I was.

Of course there were still Patriots in London. And just like the Polish Patriots they had accidents with the tourists they were guiding. That was how the two burned bodies had come to be lying in front of St Paul's on the morning of my interview at Lonesome Charley. Tourists who had got just a bit too close to the Great Fire, or had perished in one of the incendiary attacks of 1941. Obvious. I could go home and tell Detective Sergeant Page how they'd died and it would probably make his career. Or he would just laugh at me. I put my hands to my face and rocked back and forth on the chair.

I'd been trying to focus on what Witek called "the thing with the body". Oskar, who had learned the technique from another Patriot, seemed to think an actual physical stance was necessary to get into the villages: body just so, feet just so. Harry seemed to agree. Except Harry had learned how to do it from Mr Sierpiński's instructions, and Mr Sierpiński—if he'd been telling the truth in his manuscript—had learned how to do it in London in 1940, not in Poland.

Mr Pearmain had said something about the ghost of Dr Johnson doing some kind of "shuffle with his feet" before vanishing. It sounded wearyingly familiar now: "The thing with the body." I wondered if there had been some kind of cross-fertilization between the Polish and British Patriots, somewhere along the line.

The stance stuff didn't appear to be necessary: Witek could sit in a chair and just vanish; it was extraordinary to watch. But both the Polish and the British Patriots seemed to have got the same idea. It was sort of unlikely they would develop the same redundant technique independently of each other. Had a Polish Patriot come to London some time in the early part of the twentieth century to spread the word? Oskar spoke of the Patriot tradition in Poland going back at least as far as the middle of the nineteenth century. Had a British Patriot, schooled in visiting the Great Fire, arrived in Kraków in the 1850s as part of the Grand Tour?

Actually, a more reasonable explanation was that it had arrived from somewhere else altogether, from one of the German or French groups of guides Oskar had mentioned. Maybe it was just a weird convention that had spread across Europe during the last century.

I'd spent all this time presuming that only Mr Sierpiński had known how to get into the villages, that he had discovered them accidentally. Then I'd bumped into the Patriots. Then I'd found out that half the world seemed to spend half its time in the villages. It was going on all the time, had been going on for years, would keep going on and on. And *I* couldn't do it . . .

I was still sitting staring at the shoes, completely lost, when Witek came in the next morning.

"You've become sick, my friend," he said gently. "This isn't good."

"Fuck off," I heard myself say distantly.

The shoes were still on the table when we got back from our abortive trip to the villages. I'd cleared all the clothes back into their box and repacked all the books and photos and notebooks, but I'd left the shoes where I could see them every morning and every evening, to remind myself what I was doing, to keep myself going.

I was tired. I was tired of Poland. I was tired of living with Witek. I was tired of the Patriots and the villages, of policemen and dead tourists. My hindbrain kept telling me to give it all up and go home and have an ordinary life. It kept saying to let Sophie have whatever it was she had come back to Poland for. It whispered that if I loved her I could at least do that for her. That was why I hadn't put the shoes away. Maybe Witek was right. Maybe I had become sick.

I heard him messing about in the kitchen, the dull thud of the gas ring of the cooker being lit, the metal-on-metal sound of the kettle being put down over the flame. I went into the kitchen.

"Would Julia know?" I said.

He was preparing glasses and tea. He stopped, but he didn't turn around. "I've asked her."

I wondered what that had cost him in terms of awkwardness and lost pride. "And?"

He shook his head and went back to getting the tea ready. "She doesn't know."

"It's something important, Witek. Important enough to just pack a bag and come back here without saying goodbye to anybody."

"Well," he said, putting tea into the strainer, "Julia doesn't know."

"I've got to talk to Sophie's family, then."

He turned to look at me. "She has no family," he said. "Only her mother, and she won't talk to you."

"Why not?"

Witek shook his head. "This is a personal thing; I don't understand it. Zosia wrote to Julia from England and said that her mother hated her. When Julia went to see Mrs Trzetrzelewska, she refused to let her into the flat."

That must have been why Sophie hadn't asked me to go and see her mother when I was first in Poland. "And you've no idea why?"

"None," he said emphatically.

I sagged back against the doorframe. "Witek, she's all I've got left. Maybe Sophie came to see her when she came back from London. Maybe she explained what she was here for."

"I doubt it."

"But maybe she did." Jesus, I should have done this first. I'd been so determined to see Marcin Sierpiński and learn how to get into the villages that everything else had been blotted out. A Lonesome Charley approach to what I was doing. "I have to see her, Witek."

"Impossible."

"There has to be a way."

He shook his head. "You don't know Zosia's mother."

"*Please*, Witek."

The kettle was boiling; a solid rope of steam was pouring from the spout. Witek sighed. "After this," he said, "you're going to owe me a favour you'll never be able to repay."

2

In terms of ugliness and dirt, Zabrze fell somewhere between Gliwice and Bytom. It didn't look particularly terrible, or particularly great. The buildings were the same buildings you could see all over Upper Silesia: old German pre-war blocks and newer Communist-era blocks, all of them gently falling into disrepair. I never got to see the centre of town, so I never found out if it had the same gentle Old European feel as Gliwice. All I saw were drab pollution-stained tenements; bars and shops with wire screens over their windows; people in shellsuits and denims; the bright day-glo shop signs the Poles seemed so keen on, advertising chemist's shops, optician's shops, meat shops.

It had been a while since I'd thought about Lonesome Charley Productions. I should call Ruth and let her know I was all right, but it all seemed so distant now. Not just the office, but London. England. Eric, Harry, Bob and Martin, Detective Sergeant Page, my father's death—everything seemed to belong to something I'd read in a book or seen in a film, something that hadn't happened to *me* at all. It seemed strange that all of it was still waiting for me back in England. I still had some scars from the beating I'd taken on the night my father died, and when I looked at myself in the bathroom mirror after I'd had a shower I found I could just as easily ascribe them to childhood accidents, they looked so slight and unimportant.

I supposed that I was doing what Sophie had accused me of avoiding. I was taking hold of events, not letting them take hold of me. I was making things happen, instead of just letting them happen and then making the best of them. From the way Sophie had talked, this was the way to live your life. I didn't like it at all.

The tram deposited me at a stop outside an old block not far to the east of the centre of town. I looked at the address Witek had given me, then I looked up at the block.

Witek had phoned her first. Then, when she had refused to speak to him, he had gone to see her. He had gone back, day after day, to talk to her locked door. It had taken almost a month. The autumn was very nearly over, there were already fifteen centimetres of snow on the slopes of Kasprowy, down in Zakopane, and there was a fresh, cutting chill in the air in Zabrze.

It had been a little like waiting for Marcin Sierpiński to tell us his father was well enough to see me. We had practised techniques for entering the villages every day, and I still couldn't do it solo. We popped in and out of half a dozen villages, and once we arrived in one just as its event-loop was ending. It was January 1945, out in the countryside near Auschwitz, site of a skirmish between German troops and the Red Army, and we popped in some hours after the end of the battle while the Russians mopped up.

"It's a sad thing, being a Patriot," Witek said in unconscious imitation of Oskar.

"Tell me about it." We were standing under a tree a few hundred metres from the scene of the firefight, and from that distance only the hats of the Russian officers distinguished them from Germans; it was the sole detail of the uniforms I could pick out.

"So much violence," he said, and the loop ended and we were suddenly back in a peaceful forest. He looked at me. "Little house," he said. "Only fifty or sixty dead."

"Mm." Just in front of us, invisible and intangible, the village was replaying its stored violence again, from the moment of the first shot, the first mortar round. It would probably keep doing it, over and over again, for centuries. Maybe for ever. Anybody who wanted to could go and watch it, if they knew the trick.

We had been a long way from the fight. Maybe I'd overestimated how much energy it took to create a village. If Kmicic was right, the act of switching on a lightbulb would be enough.

Witek's theory was that the formation of villages was a fundamental process in the universe. He reasoned that every release of energy caused them, no matter how small. He thought it was going on constantly at the quantum level, that the universe was leaving behind an immense ghost-image of itself as it aged, a village whose loop would take billions and billions of years to end, if it ever did, and included everything that had ever existed.

If he was right, there was a complete world village somewhere, a place where any portion of history could be accessed by somebody sensitive enough, a loop that hadn't been completed yet. Perhaps all the villages the Patriots went into, all the villages Harry and Mr Sierpiński had seen, were part of the bigger village. I didn't know. I didn't care.

I looked at the address again, then I went up the steps and found her name on the entryphone box that looked to have been newly installed beside the door. I pressed the right button.

"Yes?" a crackly voice asked.

"It's me, Mrs Trzetrzelewska," I said, leaning close to the speaker grille. "Tim Ramsay."

"You're the one the idiot Witold Grabówski told me about?"

"Yes."

The lock on the door buzzed. I pulled the handle and the door swung open.

She was up on the fourth floor. The stairs were freshly swept, and there was new glass in the stairwell windows. On one landing I smelled cooking turnips; on another I could hear a track from a David Hasselhof album; but on her landing there was only silence, and no smell of cooking.

I rang the bell and a voice said, "Who is it?"

"Tim Ramsay."

There was a sound of keys being turned, chains taken off. The door opened. "English?"

"Yes," I said.

She smirked. She was almost my height, and nearly as thin as me. She was wearing a faded print dress and there was a cardigan draped over her shoulders. "You are the one who loves Zosia?"

I sighed. I'd told Witek to use any means of persuasion to get her to see me, but I hadn't said anything about this. "Yes," I said.

"You're an idiot too, then." She had an unsettling habit of not quite looking at me when she was speaking, of looking somewhere off to the left of my head.

"Possibly," I said.

She smirked again. "You'd better come in then."

She moved to one side to let me pass and I stepped into the flat. The first thing I noticed was that the place was in almost complete darkness apart from a faint nimbus of light around the closed curtains. The second thing was that old-person smell I had always associated with my grandmother, and later with my visits to The Limes. I took a few steps into the entranceway and stopped to let my eyes get used to the dimness.

"You can turn on the light," she said, closing the door behind her and relocking it. "I don't bother."

I turned and saw her dim shape moving towards me down the hall. I stepped out of the way and she sailed out into the room beyond without a moment's hesitation, stepping aside before she bumped into tables and chairs. Witek hadn't bothered to mention to me that Sophie's mother was blind.

I felt my way along the wall of the hallway until I found a light switch. I turned it on and the hall filled with light, casting my shadow across the living room. Sophie's mother was already sitting in an easy chair by the window. I stepped into the living room, found another switch, turned on the light.

She turned her face upward as if she could feel the minuscule heat from the bulb. "It's amazing, you know," she said. "You don't miss the light at all."

I wondered if she'd be quite so smug if I rearranged some of the furniture while I was here. I looked around me. The room was neat, as I supposed it would have to be for her to find her way about it. There was a dining table, and a big old television set, and a little tape-player sitting on the floor beside her chair with three neat piles of cassette boxes alongside it. There was a rug from Zakopane hanging on one wall, just as there seemed to be in almost every home I'd seen in Poland. A bookcase against another wall. The furniture was arranged so there were wide aisles, but not so wide that she couldn't touch something if necessary and establish her position in the room.

"So," she said, looking not quite at me. "You're Tymoteusz."

"Tim," I said, pulling one of the dining chairs out from the table and sitting down.

"Tymek," she said. "It's a very old name. I am Anna. I'm sixty-eight years old and I have diabetes. I've been blind for seven years and I am an extremely unpleasant old woman."

I crossed my legs and sat watching her, uncertain how I was going to handle this.

"My cousin tells me I'm unpleasant," she said. "She is seventy years old, and much more unpleasant than me, but she comes to cook my meals and tidy up after me. I have no younger relatives."

"Sophie's in danger," I said.

She tipped her head to one side. "Sophie?"

"Zosia."

"Zosia." She shook her head. "I know no person called Zosia."

"You seemed to know that I was in love with her."

She grinned a horrible, indulgent, directionless grin. "Yes, I did know that. The idiot Grabówski told me. His wife has finally seen sense and left him, I hear."

"Yes."

She settled back in the chair. "I was related to the woman's father. He was an idiot too. The Communists killed him."

"Oh?"

"He thought joining Solidarity at his age would be a wonderful thing to do. The magicians from the SB made him disappear one night. Did you know we had magicians in Poland, Tymek?"

"I'd heard."

Again that grin. "Are you a political man, Tymek?"

"I don't think so." I couldn't actually remember if I'd voted in the last election.

"You've never lived in a country where your politics could kill you, obviously."

"Not unless you can die of boredom, no."

She laughed. On a little table beside her chair were a lighter, a packet of Golden Americans and an empty ashtray. She picked up the cigarettes, took one from the packet, lit it, and returned the packet to the table.

"Is your father alive?" she asked, exhaling smoke and dropping the lighter into her lap.

"He died last year."

"Did you love him?"

"No. I don't think so. Not all the time."

Anna Trzetrzelewska took a drag on the cigarette and smiled. "You hated him, then?"

I shook my head. "No." Then I said, "I don't think so. It's complicated. I'm sorry he's dead. I think."

"I loved my father," she said. "He was the mayor of a town a few kilometres from here. We had a big house and there were always important people about. Was your home like that?"

"No. My father ran a workshop. I don't think he had many friends, but a lot of people came to his funeral."

Anna reached out deliberately and tapped ash into the ashtray. "The Communists would say that I was bourgeois and you were proletarian, then."

"I couldn't say," I told her. "I'm not political."

She nodded and took another drag on the cigarette. "You knew Zosia in London."

"I worked with her."

"And her pimp, the bastard Harry Dean."

"You couldn't call Harry a pimp," I said. "He was never that organized. And Sophie isn't a prostitute."

"She slept with him for gain, didn't she?" She turned her head so that she was looking approximately at me. "Isn't that how you define a prostitute?"

"I don't think you can describe it like that," I said, surprising myself by how much I had mellowed towards Harry and Sophie's relationship. "I think they really loved each other."

"And you love her too."

"Yes."

"And she left you."

"Well, sort of—"

She nodded enthusiastically and snapped another length of ash into the astray. "Because you had nothing to offer her. The bastard Harry Dean could offer her a visa to stay in England. What did you have?"

I looked around the room, trying to think of an answer.

"Correct," she said. "You have nothing she wants, Tymek, so she does not want you."

"She left Harry as well," I pointed out.

"Then she had got everything she could from him," she said airily.

"She's in trouble," I pressed. "She's your daughter and she's in trouble."

Anna shrugged. "So what?"

"So . . ." I cast about looking for the right words. "So doesn't that mean *anything* to you?"

She shook her head. "Absolutely not."

"Why?"

Her sightless eyes fixed me with a look much more scary than I had ever had from a sighted person, even scarier than the one Colonel Sochocki had given me at the police station in Kraków. "My husband and I were very close, Tymek. And we were both very close to Zosia, but she was closer to me." She reached out and touched the ashtray with a fingertip, just to reestablish where it was. "I suppose that's the way it is. My husband used to say that the women in his life were ganging up on him. Is it that way in England?"

I thought of my father and mother, Mr Pearmain and his son. I thought of the photos I had found in the boxes we'd taken from Sophie's attic, none of which included her mother, and knew I would never understand the dynamic of her family properly. I wondered if her mother understood it. I said, "I don't know."

She tipped her head to one side.

"Mine wasn't a typical family," I said.

"OK." She nodded. "Not a typical family. Is your mother alive?"

"Yes. But she's very sick."

"Were you with your father when he died?"

"No. Yes."

She tipped her head over to the other side.

"I was in the same hospital. I was attacked on my way to see him."

To my anger and astonishment, she repeated that horrible directionless smile. "You've had an interesting life, Tymek."

I resisted an urge to walk out. "Zosia," I said. "Your daughter. The one you were close to."

Anna flicked more ash, and this time it missed the ashtray and tumbled off the edge of the table and onto the rug. I kept my eye on it for any signs of combustion.

"He lived for fifteen days," she said angrily, "and she wouldn't come home. Her beloved Daddy. My husband, my Pawel, and she wouldn't come home. I telephoned her. I wrote to her. She wouldn't come home. Because she didn't have her visa yet. Because they wouldn't have let her back into England without it." She was shouting by now, in a cracked, desperate voice. Tears were trickling down her cheeks. "My husband died and she wouldn't come home! She said everything would be all right! Because of that bastard Harry Dean and her fucking visa!" She suddenly put her hand to her mouth. When she took the hand away she said more quietly, "Excuse me."

My eyes widened. "How did he die, your husband?" I asked quietly.

Tears were pouring down her face. She gestured with the stub of the cigarette towards the bookcase. I got up and slid the glass door aside. On the bottom shelf were a couple of leather-bound scrapbooks. I took one out and opened it. Inside, yellowing press cuttings were stuck to the pages like huge ancient butterflies. They all seemed to be about the Zabrze fire brigade. Here they fought a fire in a factory. Here they received a medal from the local Party boss for the rescue of a family from a blazing flat. I flipped forwards. On each cutting the name of Pawel Trzetrzelewski had been underlined in red. I turned the pages until there were no more cuttings, then I reached for the second volume.

I found it at the end, several pages cut from the local newspaper and stuck onto the page. It was a long, long article about a forest fire three years ago, by a man named Roman Balicki. He wrote very well about the wall of fire sweeping through the forests of Upper Silesia. He spoke of villages being evacuated. He spoke of the bravery of the firefighters who went in to try and hold back the blaze. I felt my heart lift off.

"Can I take this with me?" I asked the crying woman in the chair.

Thirty

1

I left the flat in a daze, the scrapbook under my arm. I needed Witek, but today was Friday, and Friday was Witek's day for non-Patriot tour-guiding in Kraków. But I needed Witek very badly.

I needed Witek so badly that I found myself at the railway station buying a ticket to Kraków.

Roman Balicki had been there through almost the whole fire. It had destroyed thousands of acres of forest, emptied dozens of little villages. It had been the biggest thing to hit the area since the Germans rolled in, and not a word of it had been reported in the West.

I read and reread the newspaper articles on the train, trying to get a sense of what it must have been like, the firemen desperately trying to beat back the flames alongside civilian volunteers, often taking ridiculous, suicidal risks. I read the bit about the school again. There was a little hand-drawn map with the article, but it wasn't good enough.

There was a bookshop just off the Market Square in Kraków that sold maps. I bought a detailed map of Upper Silesia, walked on into the Market Square, and sat down at one of the tables arranged in front of the Sukiennice to spread the map out.

"Mr Ramsay."

I looked up. Major Nowak was standing apologetically beside me. He looked down at the map and said, "More sightseeing?"

"Major," I said.

"You seem to have been doing quite a lot of sightseeing recently," he said. "All over the countryside. And Bytom, of course."

"Research materials," I said, folding the map, sliding it inside the scrapbook, and standing up. "Have you been following me, Major?"

"Day and night," he admitted.

I looked around the Market Square and was puzzled to see Marcin Sierpiński standing by the shops along one side. I said, "Your nights must have been pretty boring."

"You have been almost constantly in the company of one Witold Grabówski," he told me.

"I know," I said, frowning in Marcin's direction. "He's my researcher."

"He is also known to be connected to Povilas Vysniauskas. Did you know that?"

I shook my head, still trying to work out what Marcin was doing there. "No, I didn't know that."

He sighed and straightened his shoulders. "Timothy Ramsay, you're under arrest."

I looked around us. The square was full of tourists; I couldn't see anyone who remotely resembled a policeman. I looked him in the eye. "Just you on your own?" I said.

He ignored the question. "You've been lying to us, Ramsay. We no longer believe that your presence in Kraków last year was such a coincidence as you claim. You know more about these murders than you've told us."

"So what now? Rubber hoses? Water torture? Brass knuckles?"

Nowak made a face. "We're not animals. We don't beat people up."

"Don't kid me, Major."

He shook his head. Over his shoulder, I could see Marcin watching us.

"You won't be harmed," Nowak said. "You have my word on that."

Marcin started to walk towards us. He was wearing jeans, trainers and his denim jacket, and over his shoulder he was carrying a big grey leather sports bag.

"Ramsay?"

"Sorry? Oh. Yes. You were arresting me." I sighed. "It really isn't necessary, Major."

"The colonel thinks it is."

"The colonel would." Marcin was coming towards us with an odd single-minded look on his face. He didn't look left or right. He just kept coming.

"I don't want to make a scene," Nowak said.

Marcin was just a few yards from us. He unzipped the sports bag and put his hand inside. Nowak was still talking. I looked at him, then back to Marcin. I reached out and grabbed Nowak by the lapels.

"What the hell are you doing, Ramsay?" he shouted. "Let me go!"

Marcin's hand came out of the bag holding a pistol. He brought it up and pointed it at us.

Nowak was struggling, beating at my hands and trying to get free. I looked him in the eye and shouted, "Shut *up!*"

For a fraction of a second Nowak relaxed. I took a deep breath, planted my feet, tried to remember everything anybody had ever told me about the villages, and *pulled.*

Everything went grey. The square was suddenly packed solid with featureless smudged grey figures in constant smeary motion; the buildings were the only solid things around us, and they looked odd. The modern signs and awnings had become translucent, showing older, similarly translucent signs in layers beneath. Suddenly I knew what Witek had meant. It was a way of looking at the world, of seeing the history behind what was on the surface, like trying to look inside the layers of an onion. All you had to do was look. I tried to force us through into the nearest village, and for a moment some of the figures seemed to gain a little solidity, but I couldn't manage it.

I kept my eyes on the smeary grey figure that I knew was Marcin; it seemed to be pointing its arm at us. There was a faraway popping sound, and a tiny dirty grey smudge emerged from the end of Marcin's arm.

Nowak was screaming. I could hear other people screaming around us. Some of the grey figures were running around; they ran through other grey figures without seeming to notice.

Nowak gave a sudden startled yelp and the grey smudge emerged from his chest and struck me just below the base of the throat. I felt a tug on my skin, another on my back, and then it was gone.

The grey figure that was Marcin seemed to change texture subtly. Then it did it again. I realized he was dropping down through the nested villages trying to find the one we were in. But we weren't in a village; we were somewhere in between, and he couldn't find us. Abruptly he turned and began to move away.

I relaxed and the world snapped back into existence around us. People were screaming and running about and for a moment I thought I caught sight of Marcin's back among the running people, but then the crowd closed again and I lost him. I *knew* he'd read his father's manuscript.

"Jesus Maria!" Nowak said. He was breathing hard. "Jesus Maria!"

I let go of Nowak's lapels and looked round. An elderly woman was lying sprawled on her back on the stone flags of the square behind me. There was a neat little black hole exactly between her eyebrows and a slowly spreading pool of blood beneath her head.

Nowak looked aghast. "What did you do?" he shouted. "What did you do?"

A crowd was gathering around us, but it was gathering at a cautious distance. I wondered what we had looked like while I tried to force us into the next village. Not quite scary enough to clear the square, obviously.

"What did you do, Ramsay?" Nowak yelled at the top of his voice. "What was that?"

I grabbed at his arm and he shied away. I grabbed again and got hold of his wrist. "Do you have a car near here?"

He nodded dumbly.

"I'll tell you in the car," I said. "We have to get away from here." I started to haul him across the square. The crowd parted for us. It occurred to me that I had probably ruined Oskar's tourist business.

"Flat," Nowak said.

I stopped. "What?"

"We have to go to my flat."

"What?"

He looked embarrassed. "I have to change my trousers. I wet myself."

2

Nowak's flat was a short distance south of the centre of town. While he was in the bathroom washing himself, I poked around. The flat was small and untidy. There were a couple of muddy watercolour landscapes on the walls, one of the ubiquitous Zakopané rugs on another wall, the usual sofa-bed and fitted bookshelves. Nowak read a lot of classics, none of them in Polish: Tolstoy, Jane Austen, Dickens. I took down a copy of *The Brothers Karamazov* and behind it on the shelf was a Luger.

"Who was it?" Nowak called over the sound of running water.

"Pardon?" I said, looking at the gun on the shelf.

"In the Market Square. The one who shot at us."

"His name's Marcin Sierpiński." I stood very still, trying to decide what to do.

"You know him?"

I reached out and picked up the gun. It was much heavier than it looked. "He's the son of the man who started all this." I put the book back, started to look behind the others.

"Started all what, Ramsay?"

The Luger's clip was behind *Middlemarch*. I stood with it in one hand and the pistol in the other, trying to figure out how to put them together. It always looked pretty simple in the movies. "I think you're going to have to suspend disbelief a bit, Major Nowak," I called.

"Did he kill the tourists?"

"What?" I fiddled with the clip and one of the bullets popped out and fell on the floor. I watched it roll under Nowak's sofa-bed. "No. No, I don't think so." I popped the rest of the bullets out of the clip into the palm of my hand and pocketed them.

"But you do know more about this business than you've told us?"

"I'm not really interested in your murders, Major."

"So why are you here?"

I put the clip into the butt of the pistol and knocked it home with the heel of my hand. I put the Luger in my coat pocket. "I'm looking for a friend of mine."

The sound of water stopped and Nowak came out of the bathroom. He'd changed into a clean pair of jeans. "Is he involved with the murders?"

"It's a she." Either Nowak was tougher than I'd thought, or he was monomaniacal about these bloody murders. "And you still haven't asked me the obvious question."

He looked at me for a moment, then he went into the kitchen. He came back with two glasses and a frost-encrusted bottle of vodka. "Drink?"

"I had the screaming habdabs the first time it happened to me," I said.

He raised his eyebrows. "Habdabs?"

"Panic," I said in Polish. I walked over to the table and sat down. Nowak sat opposite me and unscrewed the cap of the bottle. "You hardly panicked at all."

He snorted. "I pissed myself. Doesn't that count as panic in England?"

I took one of the glasses and put it in front of me. Nowak filled it to the brim, poured himself the same measure. He lifted his glass and knocked it back in one go. Then he looked calmly at me.

"Major," I said, picking up my glass, "you probably won't believe what I'm going to tell you, but I promise you it's all true."

I told Nowak everything. I left nothing out, from the day I walked out of my last exam knowing I'd fucked up my Finals to what had happened in the Market Square an hour or so ago. I told him things I hadn't even told Martin and Bob. I told him about the night, not too long after I'd moved into Harry's flat, when I had felt so wretched that I had sprayed Sophie's perfume on my pillow and gone to sleep hoping to dream of her. I hadn't told anyone else about that because the next morning I'd thought it was not too far from being completely crazy.

When I finished Nowak poured himself another glass of vodka. He hadn't said a word while I was speaking, hadn't expressed surprise or disbelief. He had sat there like a rakishly handsome carving. I wondered if he was in shock.

"So," he said finally, screwing the top back on the bottle and replacing it carefully on the wet circle the melting frost had made on the tablecloth. "You lied to us."

I looked around the living room. "Well, *yes.*"

He nodded and sipped his vodka.

"Major," I said, "aren't you in the least little bit curious about what I've told you?"

"I hate being lied to," he said calmly. "I hate being cheated, I hate being made a fool of, and I hate being lied to."

"OK, I'm sorry I didn't tell you the truth right away. But you'd have arrested me, or had me thrown out of the country, and I'd never be able to find Sophie."

He sighed and put his glass down. "Yes. Pani Zosia. Your girlfriend."

"She's not my girlfriend."

Nowak shrugged. "To be honest with you, Ramsay, I find your villages easier to believe in than the idea of you coming all this way to find a woman who clearly does not love you."

I felt my shoulders slump. "Do you have a black belt in puncturing people's egos, Major?"

"I do think you are deluding yourself, but it is only my opinion."

"Your opinion."

"And in my opinion, if Pani Zosia—"

"Sophie."

"If *Sophie* had any feelings at all for you, she would not have left London without telling you."

I shook my head. "There was something she wanted really badly. Something here. She couldn't think about anything else."

"Clearly." Nowak pursed his lips. "However, if you believe this quixotic journey will change her mind about you, I think you're in for a terrible disappointment."

"I've been disappointed before, Major," I said, starting to get annoyed with him. "I'll take the chance."

"No one lives happily ever after," he said. "The world just doesn't work that way." He got up and carried the bottle back to the freezer. "Life is a chaotic thing, Ramsay," he called from the kitchen. "You cannot plan your life to some romantic vision."

I slurped the last of my vodka. "I can try."

"We have to go now," Nowak said, coming back to the table.

I looked up at him and smiled. "OK."

"Where are we going?" I asked.

Nowak put the key in the ignition. "We have to tell the colonel about this."

I stared through the windscreen. "Fine."

Nowak switched on the ignition, revved the engine.

"There's just one thing, though," I said.

"Oh?" He looked round. "What?"

I took the gun out of my pocket and rested the muzzle against his thigh. He looked at it. Then he looked at me. "Is that my pistol?"

I nodded.

"How *dare* you steal from me," he said in a low voice.

"I think you're missing the point here, Major."

He looked at the gun again. "Have you ever fired a gun before, Ramsay?"

"Not yet, no."

As tough-guy threats go I don't suppose it was much, but it seemed to do the trick. Nowak sighed and said, "What do you want?"

"Just drive us out of town."

He raised an eyebrow. "Any particular direction?"

"West," I said. "Just drive west till I tell you to stop."

There was a sudden flurry of motion and noise in the back of the car, and by the time I looked round Witek and Oskar were sitting side by side in the back seat.

Nowak made a grab for the gun and I snatched it away and waved it in his face until he sat back.

"One of the Patriots saw you in the Market Square," Oskar said. "You've really fucked up my business, you bastard. Nobody'll trust us now. It'll be all over the news."

"You're all under arrest," Nowak told us.

"Shut up," I said. I glanced over at Oskar and Witek and glared at them. "Just shut up. I'm sick of being followed about by policemen and Patriots and whoever just gets the urge to see where I'm going."

"You still can't do it properly," Witek said morosely. He shook his head. "You'll never learn."

"I was coming to look for you, but I think I've got it straight in my head now. I think I can do it now."

Witek just shook his head again.

"You can't hope to get away with this," said Nowak.

I looked at him. He was very calm. I thought he was more annoyed at me stealing his gun than at me pointing it at him. "You realize you're kidnapping an officer of the law?" he said.

"This isn't kidnapping," I said.

"You're pointing a gun at me and forcing me to go somewhere I don't want to go," he said. "I'd call that kidnapping,"

"It's not kidnapping," I explained, "because you're just taking some well deserved leave and going on a little day trip with some friends. That's all. Now, would you put the car into gear, please?"

I wondered what Eric would think if he could see me now, all grown up and stealing a Polish policeman at gunpoint.

3

We drove through the centre of Kraków and out towards Zabierzów. Nowak kept looking at the gun resting against his leg and I watched him weighing up the chances of grabbing it without the car crashing or me shooting him in the thigh.

After we had been driving for some time I said, "Do you believe in all that stuff?"

"What stuff?" said Nowak.

"What you were saying in the flat. About life being chaotic."

He glanced over at me. "Are you starting to weaken, Ramsay?"

"You should be so lucky. No, keep on driving." I stared out through the passenger window at the fields going by, thinking about Harry standing beside me at Liverpool Street in November 1940 and telling me that things were rarely logical. "No. It's simply that a couple of years ago I was just another graduate. I didn't do very well in my final exams, I owed a lot of money to the student loan people, I didn't have much chance of getting a job. And then one day I saw an advert in a magazine.

I answered the advert, and here I am, holding a Polish policeman at gunpoint." I rubbed my eyes. "It wasn't even the current issue of the magazine; it was two weeks old. I read it in the barbers'."

"So you admit you are kidnapping me?"

"You haven't listened to a word I've said, have you?" I said, looking at him.

"You haven't *told* him, have you?" Oskar said from the back seat.

"Oh, shut up, Oskar."

"Sure," he said huffily. "You're happy now you've got a gun, aren't you?"

Nowak was quiet for a long time. Such a long time that I thought he wasn't going to speak again, and I went back to watching the view. Then he said, "You want to know if I believe life is chaotic, Ramsay?"

I looked at him. "Yes."

He took a deep breath. "Let me tell you a story. I joined the police force in 1979. My father was a policeman, and his father, and his father. Our family has had at least one member in the police force in Kraków at any one time for almost a hundred and twenty years, and when I was old enough there was never any question that I would not join as well."

"I've heard of families like that," I said.

He nodded. "I was a good policeman. Maybe not as good a policeman as Colonel Sochocki, but good enough. And, like a good policeman, when Martial Law was declared I supported the secret police when they went to arrest Solidarity activists. I once even helped to capture a Western spy. It never bothered me, because I was upholding the Law. It might have been wrong, but it was still the Law, and I was a servant of the Law, literally and genetically. Do you understand, Ramsay?"

"Assuming it's possible to be a policeman, genetically speaking, yes." Actually, what he was describing sounded more like Judge Dredd, but I could see what he was getting at. "Take a left here."

He waited until we had made the turn. "Then the Communists fell. For our prime minister we had Mazowiecki, who I believe is a good man, and for our president we had Wałęsa, who is probably an imbecile. Mazowiecki didn't last long. I've lost count of the number of prime ministers we've had since then, but Wałęsa is still president. For the moment." He looked at me. "Does that make any sense to you?"

"Wałęsa is not an imbecile," Witek said from the back seat. "He's a braver man than you'll ever be, policeman."

I hadn't been paying much attention to the news recently, but sometime in the next few days the Poles were going to vote for their president, and things weren't looking that good for Wałęsa. His main opponent, Aleksander Kwasniewski, had been a junior minister in Poland's last Communist government.

"Oh, he's an immensely talented man," Nowak told Witek. "Unfortunately, the only talent he has is for destruction."

"He brought down Communism," Witek said.

"And six Polish governments since then," Nowak said. "The man can't even speak grammatically. Personally, I'm ashamed to have him as my president."

"You should thank God he was in the right place at the right time," Witek said in a loud voice. "Otherwise your orders would still be coming straight from the Kremlin."

"All right," I said before the argument got out of hand. I couldn't speak for the other nations of Central and Eastern Europe, of course, but I thought that only in Poland would you find two people arguing politics in the middle of an armed kidnapping. "That's enough. I can't get my head round Polish politics."

Nowak snorted. "Neither can anybody else. I suspect that's the problem. Anyway, there was a large degree of distrust for the police after the Communists were thrown out. We had to answer for our actions during Jaruzelski's War, which is what we called Martial Law."

"I know."

He sighed. "So there were . . . 'purges' is too strong a word for it, but our records were examined. There were retirements."

"I'll bet."

"Good policemen. Policemen who had served the Law under Jaruzelski and were prepared to serve the Law under Wałęsa. Particularly now, with crime everywhere. We need good policemen."

"I'd like to point out that 'good policemen' like our friend here made Julia's father disappear," Witek said, leaning forward to speak close to my ear. I waved him back with the gun.

"But you didn't retire," I said to Nowak.

"Oh but I did. I didn't even wait for my record to be examined. I resigned. It was a complicated time, Ramsay. You can't imagine it. I fought crime. Occasionally I helped arrest people identified by the State as criminals, but I still fought crime."

"I understand," I said. I wondered if he'd ever spoken about this to anybody else.

"The colonel stayed. He actually dared them to throw him out. But he's too good a policeman to lose, despite having done . . . questionable things. So they let him stay."

"What did you do?"

He shrugged. "I knew English, some French. I became a translator. I translated for foreign businessmen, I translated business documents, I did some work as a tourist guide in the Wawel."

"I know somebody who did that," I said, looking in the rear-view mirror, but I couldn't see Witek's face to tell what his reaction was to finding out Nowak had been a guide too. I could see Oskar's face, though, and it told me his English wasn't quite good enough to follow what was being said. He looked intensely annoyed at being excluded. He was frowning and trying to keep up.

"It was not such a good life," Nowak went on. "Money was very scarce. I struggled. Then one day my office was burgled." He smiled. "There wasn't much to take, but they took what there was. They even stole the steel security gate over my door. I thought on that day that I was at my lowest. And on that day Colonel Sochocki came to see me."

"To offer you your old job back?"

Nowak smiled at the memory of it. "In an oblique way. The colonel is sometimes not very direct. He was working on the case of a missing girl and he thought I could help him. He offered to take me back on a trial basis." He changed gear, a bit more fiercely than necessary. "So I said yes."

"Did you find her? The missing girl?"

Nowak's lips thinned down to a humourless little smile. "Yes, we found her. She'd been killed by a local man. This man had killed twenty-eight other people over the previous fifteen years, all over Poland. He eviscerated the bodies and put them in some hot, dry place, and they mummified. When we broke into his flat we found them all sitting there, like a Christmas party of the dead."

"Jesus. When was this?"

He shrugged. "Three years ago. Why?"

"I never read anything about it in the papers."

"Oh, please, Ramsay, don't insult my intelligence. This is Poland. Who cares what happens here?"

I shook my head.

"The man we caught, the killer. It was my brother, Janusz," Nowak said without looking at me.

I stared at him.

There was another long silence. I heard Witek whispering a translation of the story to Oskar, and I heard Oskar make a rude noise. Nowak didn't seem to notice. He said, "Afterwards, I rejoined the police on a full-time basis. There seemed no other choice." He looked at me. "And that is why I believe life is chaotic, Ramsay. And stupid. And sad." He looked out of the windscreen again. "Mostly sad and stupid."

"*I* could have told you that," Witek said.

I put the gun in my pocket. "I'm sorry, Nowak. I really am."

Without moving his head, Nowak glanced down to make sure the gun was gone. He said, "Give me the gun and let's stop this pantomime, Ramsay."

I shook my head.

Nowak sighed. "Where are we going?"

I sat for a long while watching the countryside go by, thinking about what he'd told me. "We're going to a fire, Major," I said finally.

Thirty-one

1

We drove for a little over an hour. We passed through small towns and large villages. Great arms of forest reached out to close around the road, then opened again to show fields and farmhouses, and once a huge lake on which multicoloured sails danced.

"Tim?"

"Yes, Witek?"

"The old woman told you, didn't she?"

"Not in so many words," I said. "But I know where Sophie is."

"How, if she didn't tell you?"

How indeed? He knew about Marcin Sierpiński travelling all the way from Kraków to Stargard Szczeciński to be with his father when Witek and I visited him, but how could I explain about Mr Pearmain's son taking a day off work to make sure his father wasn't mugged in his own home? Or Harry Dean going into the Navy to please his father, even though he hated it? Or the fact that the Curse of Lonesome Charley had stopped me being with my father when he died? How could I explain that, while I had examined great historical events looking for Sophie, the really important ones are the little events, the ones that don't get into the history books even as footnotes, the ones that affect us most deeply and directly . . .

"I just know, Witek," I said. I looked at Nowak. "I just know."

We passed through a village whose name I recognized from the newspaper cuttings. Beyond it the forest closed in on us again. Patches of it still hadn't recovered from the fire, three years on. The undergrowth had grown back, thick and dense and lush, but the trunks of a lot of the trees looked scorched, and some of them were completely dead, standing in half-glimpsed clumps as we drove by, like signposts into the village only a few people would even suspect was all around us.

I realized that I was the only one in the car who understood what Sophie had done. Because I would have done exactly the same thing. She'd put off coming back to Poland because she thought her father was going to recover. She'd thought there would still be time for goodbyes.

I let Nowak drive on another kilometre or so, then I said, "OK, you can pull over here."

He pulled the car over to the side of the road, put on the handbrake, and turned off the engine. Then he looked at me. "Now what?" he said.

"Get out."

He looked at the trees, then back to me, and for the first time I saw a flash of alarm cross his face. "Why?"

"I'm not going to kill you, Major," I said.

"I wish you'd stop calling me that," he said. "My name's Piotr." He looked at me. "I think we've gone beyond formalities now, don't you?"

I had to smile at that. "OK, Piotr. Well, I'm not going to kill you. I'm going to let you go." The alarmed look came back. I rubbed my eyes. "Nowak. Piotr. I don't want to hurt you, will you please get that into your thick head? Look, you stay in the car. I'll get out. Will that make you happy?"

Suddenly Nowak didn't look alarmed any more. Now he looked suspicious. "What are you going to do?"

"I'm going to let you go," I said.

Nowak's hand scrabbled at his side, found the catch, and pushed open the door. He jumped out and started to run. I got my door open and tumbled out of the car trying to get the Luger out of my pocket. I jumped up and aimed the pistol two-handed over the roof of the car. "Nowak!"

He'd reached the trees. He stopped and put his hands up. Witek, getting out of the back of the car, moved into my line of sight. "Witek, get out of the fucking way!" I shouted. Witek scowled sadly at me and stepped aside. "Turn round you *bloody* idiot!" I shouted at Nowak.

His hands over his head, Nowak turned and looked at me. He gave a little embarrassed shrug.

I lowered the gun and walked around the car towards him. "Major Nowak," I said as I reached him, "I really was going to let you go." I walked right up to him. "But to be honest I'd be happier if I had you where I could see you." I grabbed the front of his jacket.

Nowak's eyes went wide. "Oh shit," he said.

I planted my feet and *pulled*, and all of a sudden the air was warmer and full of the smell of smoke.

I let go of Nowak's jacket and looked around me. Nothing much seemed to have changed. The trees looked the same, the road still curved out of sight behind and in front of us. Nowak's Simca was gone, though, and fifty yards or so down the road a Little Fiat was pulled in on the verge. The only other difference seemed to be the smoke. I looked up. It was billowing above the treetops in gauzy clouds; bits of white ash were drifting down like fat dry snowflakes and the air was full of sooty smuts. That was better: I could do it now. I smiled.

"Shit," Nowak said again. "*Shit.*"

I looked at him. "You didn't believe a word I said, did you?"

He was looking about him and sniffing the air. "*Shit.*"

I tapped him on the chest with the muzzle of the Luger. "I explained everything to you and you didn't believe a single word."

He looked at me. "Are you *joking?*"

"What in Christ's name did you think happened to us in Kraków?"

He leaned his face close to mine and said, "I don't *know,*" calmly and distinctly.

I remembered the strata of belief and disbelief I'd gone through after I'd seen Mr Sierpiński's film and read his manuscript, and I shrugged and looked away.

"Have you any idea what you sounded like with your villages and your Blitz and your bloody Harry Dean? Give me that."

I snatched the pistol away before he could grab it. "I think I'll hang onto this for a while, Major."

He shrugged as if it weren't important any more. "Well," he said, looking at the smoky sky, "is this one of your villages?"

I nodded. "July 1992. I don't know which day it is. The right one, I hope. Otherwise we're in for quite a long stay." Witek and Oskar suddenly popped into existence on the other side of the road. I looked at them and shook my head. This was not going the way I wanted it to.

"And what are we doing here?"

Once again I had to marvel at Nowak's cool. Nothing seemed to faze him for more than a couple of minutes. I supposed that once you found out your brother was a serial killer there wasn't much left that could surprise you.

"We are looking for my friend," I said. "I told you."

He nodded. "Zosia. *Sophie.* And she is here, yes?"

I shook my head. He was incredible. "I don't know. I think so."

"Oh, you think so," he said angrily. "You have endangered my life in the biggest forest fire ever seen in Silesia because you *think so.* Wonderful." He went for a little walk, a couple of paces out, a couple of paces back.

"I didn't ask you to come," I said.

He looked astounded. He leaned his face close to mine again. "Think back two hours or so and try to remember who was pointing whose gun at whom."

"Nowak," I said incredulously, "we are standing in the middle of the most amazing thing that will ever happen to you, and all you want to do is tell me off?"

He stepped back. "I think I have the right."

"All right." I flapped my arms at my sides and walked away a few steps. "All right, Piotr, tell me off." I turned to face him. "Go on, tell me off. I agree: I deserve it."

He sighed and put his hands in his pockets. "Without a doubt, Ramsay, you are the poorest excuse for a man I have ever seen."

"Let's take that for granted. I'm waiting, Nowak. Tell me off." I was really furious with him. Didn't he have *any* sense of wonder? I was proud of the villages, proud that I'd managed to get us into one, and it was all going over Nowak's head.

"Hey, are you OK, man?" Oskar called. Neither he nor Witek had moved since they had dropped down into the village. They both probably thought I was stark raving mad.

"We're all right," I said. "Go home."

"You still owe me money, man," he complained.

"Oh for Christ's sake, Oskar, not now. I'll see you right, I promise. Go home."

He spread his arms. "How, man? We're out in the middle of nowhere."

"Don't you dare think of taking my car," Nowak called. "I know where you live."

Oskar took a couple of steps towards us. "Don't you threaten me, you bastard. If you had any evidence at all you'd have arrested me months ago."

"Oh, you think so?" Nowak said mysteriously.

Tim Ramsey and His Travelling Circus . . . "Boys," I said wearily, rubbing my face, "can this wait?"

Everybody looked at me. I sighed.

"All right," I said. "The two of you can walk back to that village we passed a couple of kilometres back down the road. Get a bus back to Kraków. Hire a car. *Buy* a car. I don't care. I'll pay you back for it."

"He will," Witek said. "He's not in his right mind and he complains all the time, but he'll pay."

That seemed to be good enough for Oskar. He set his feet and vanished, but Witek just stood there looking at me. "You need help," he said.

"It's OK, Witek," I said. I gestured at Nowak. "The police are here."

He looked dolefully at the tall policeman. "He won't be much help to you. Let me take him back."

I shook my head. "The Major is coming with me. He needs a taste of wonder." I was determined to impress Nowak somehow.

Witek shrugged and was gone.

"Such friends you have made in Poland," Nowak commented.

"I've learned to take friends where I can find them, Major," I said.

"I'm sure you have." Nowak had watched everything without any sign of alarm. He looked, in fact, more than a little disgusted. He turned and regarded the trees soberly. "I think if we don't leave soon we may die here. I presume it *is* possible to die here?"

That brought my feet back onto the ground. "Yes." I nodded at the Fiat. "We can take that."

"We are going to add car theft to kidnapping and unlawful possession of a handgun?"

"We are." I waved the pistol. "Let's go."

He shrugged and we started to walk towards the Fiat. "Do I need you alive in order to get back to the real world?"

"Yes," I said, though when the village's loop ended he'd just pop back into realtime along with me and anybody else who happened to be indulging in a little exotic tourism here. It couldn't hurt to link my continuing welfare to Nowak's, though. I said, "Let's—" and Marcin Sierpiński stepped from the trees a few yards in front of us. He was carrying a rifle. He lifted it to his shoulder and pointed it at me. I lifted the Luger and brought its front sight to bear on the middle of his forehead. And then we just stood there.

He must have been following me around for days, must have been on the train from Zabrze to Kraków with me, must have picked up a car in Kraków somehow after he tried to shoot me, followed us out of town and cut through the trees when we stopped and got out of Nowak's car. He must have watched me drag Nowak into the village, and then he'd dropped down through the nested villages looking for the one where we were. Of course he knew how to get in. He'd had his father's manuscript as a guide.

"You lying bastard," I said. "You knew how to do it all along."

"Shoot him!" Nowak yelled. "Shoot him!" I had no idea which of us he was shouting at. Marcin just stood there, pointing the rifle at me.

The Luger was very heavy. My arm was starting to wobble. I said, "I'm getting sick of you doing this, Marcin."

Marcin stared at me down the length of the rifle. He was breathing heavily. I knew he was capable of shooting me—he'd done it in Kraków and Nowak and I had only survived by being not quite in the same dimension as the bullet—but the Luger gave me an edge. Marcin didn't like the idea of being shot himself.

We stood there like idiots, him pointing the rifle at me, me pointing the Luger at him, while the forest burned somewhere not too far to the East of us. I thought of all the ludicrous situations I had ever been in. Surely this one had to top them all. Surely nothing stupider could ever happen to me.

"We're both making fools of ourselves, Marcin," I said. "Put the gun down."

"Kill him!" Nowak shouted.

Marcin and I both looked at him. Before Marcin could shoot him I called his name and he looked back at me. "Lots of people are doing it," I said. "There's a bloody cottage industry going on across Europe to take people into the villages. Are you going to kill them all?" For the first time I saw a flicker of doubt in his eyes. "Hundreds of people have already *been* into the villages," I pressed. My arm was really beginning to hurt. "What are you going to do, hunt them all down?"

Marcin wasn't stupid, not really. He didn't even believe in the wrong things. He didn't really want to kill people, he just thought he had something to protect.

"You're lying," he said.

I shook my head. "The Patriots have taken dozens of people in this year alone. It's a fucking *industry*, Marcin."

I saw his resolve waver. He started to lower the rifle. And that was the moment Nowak chose to decide to be a hero.

Not quite believing anybody could be so stupid, I watched as he jumped at Marcin and made a grab for the rifle. Marcin tried to bring the gun round to shoot Nowak, but Nowak hit him in the face and my right leg was punched away by a giant fist.

2

"Stop complaining. It's only a flesh wound," said Nowak.

"That's easy for you to say," I muttered. "It's not your flesh."

Nowak finished bandaging my leg. He had torn a sleeve off his shirt to bandage the furrow Marcin's bullet had ploughed just above my knee and now he had one long sleeve and one short one. Face smudged with soot from the burning forest, he looked like the hero of a disaster movie.

"Does it hurt?" he asked.

"I feel better already," I said. Actually I felt as if I'd been hit by a lorry. "How's he?"

Nowak looked over his shoulder. Marcin was sitting crosslegged on the road, glaring stonily at us. One of his wrists was handcuffed to the Fiat's bumper. Nowak spat on the ground. "He'll live. Hey, prick!" he called. "The Englishman wants to know how you are!"

Marcin made a rude gesture with his free hand.

Nowak shook his head and went back to tying the makeshift bandage. "You should have shot him."

I'd missed the conclusion of Nowak's fight with Marcin, but at least I knew who he'd been yelling at now. I lay back on the grass of the verge. "I never loaded the gun."

He paused in the middle of tying a knot and looked at me for a long moment. He closed his eyes and scowled as if he had a sudden headache.

"I could have wound up hurting somebody," I said.

Nowak opened his eyes and jerked the final knot of the bandage tight with a great deal more force than was strictly necessary. A bolt of pain shot up my leg and I yelped.

He sat back on his heels and watched me, shaking his head. He looked at his bare arm. "This was a good shirt," he said.

"I'm glad you had it with you. Help me up."

Nowak stood up, reached down a hand, and hauled me up to stand on my left foot. I stood beside him with my hand on his shoulder and gingerly put my right foot on the ground. The bullet had barely touched me, but the whole leg felt bruised, all the way up to my hip. Stabbing pains twitched through the muscles every time I moved, but it was bearable if I didn't put too much weight on it.

"Hurts, does it?" Nowak asked archly.

"Just a touch," I said through gritted teeth. I limped slowly towards the car. "Let's go."

Nowak reached the Fiat ahead of me and slapped Marcin round the head. "We're going for a ride, bastard," he said, bending and unlocking the handcuff on the car's bumper and fastening it about his wrist. He straightened up, dragged Marcin to his feet, and cuffed him round the head again. "How *dare* you point a gun at me!" he barked.

I didn't bother to point out that Marcin had been pointing his gun at me, not Nowak. Nowak had probably had more than enough of people pointing guns at him for one day. I went round to the driver's door and pulled the catch, but the door didn't open.

"It's locked," Nowak said.

"OK." I limped stiff-legged to the edge of the road and found a fist-sized piece of stone.

"What are you going to do?" Nowak said.

"It doesn't matter," I said, loping back to the car. "Nothing we do here matters. I keep trying to tell you but you won't listen." I hit one of the rear passenger windows with the rock and it shattered all over the back seat. I reached inside and popped open the driver's door. It took a bit of doing to manoeuvre my wounded leg into the seat, but once I was in I leaned across, opened the passenger door, and tipped the passenger seat forward.

Nowak bodily bent Marcin over and shoved him into the back of the Fiat. "You can sit on the glass, bastard," he muttered. "Move over. Let me in."

Marcin hitched across the back seat and Nowak got in. I wondered why Marcin didn't just drop down into an older village, or leave the villages altogether. Maybe you couldn't do that if you were handcuffed to something or somebody. Maybe he'd take Nowak with him. It occurred to me that my welfare was no longer linked to Nowak's; Marcin could get him home if anything happened to me. I wondered how long it would take Nowak to spot it too.

"Will you be able to drive?" Nowak asked.

"I'll be OK," I said. I tried the accelerator and winced as a bolt of pain shot up my leg. Well, I'd be OK if we didn't have to stop in a hurry.

Whoever had abandoned the car had left the key in the ignition and had then taken the precaution of locking the doors before buggering off, which was interesting because the last time I had driven a Little Fiat the doors and the ignition had all worked on one key. Whoever had abandoned the car must have had a duplicate set. I suddenly realized I had no idea if the Fiat worked or not. It had to have been abandoned for some reason. I offered a silent prayer, turned the key, and the engine started first time.

Petrol all right, oil all right. I revved the engine and it sounded OK. I had a sudden image of the driver coming back to the road after going into the forest for a piss and finding his car trundling away. Then I thought that you'd *really* have to need a piss to stop in the middle of a forest that was burning down.

It didn't matter. Nothing much I did here mattered. Tomorrow, or the day after, or next week, the loop would end and the car would be back where we'd found it, window intact, just the way it had been when the village had formed. The people who were going to die here were already dead. I had to keep reminding myself of that. It was like being inside a video and being the only person who knew it.

Sod it. There was only one important thing here. I put the Fiat into gear, pressed down on the accelerator, and we moved off.

"Do you have a licence to drive in Poland?" Nowak enquired from the back.

"Is he the murderer?" Nowak asked after we'd been driving for fifteen minutes or so.

"There *isn't* any murderer, Nowak," I said. "How many more times do I have to tell you?"

I heard Nowak slap Marcin round the head again, just on general principles. The poor sod was going to be a mass of bruises before much longer. "So what killed all the tourists?" he said.

I pressed the accelerator again and another spark of pain bolted up my leg. It wasn't so bad now, though; now my leg was starting to go numb. "They had accidents. They went to Częstochowa and got in the way of a cannonball, or they wanted to watch the invasion and got run over by a German tank. Tourists are like sheep—they just bumble about poking their noses into whatever looks interesting. They probably didn't think anything bad could happen to them here."

"What does he want, then?"

I waited for the sound of another slap, but it didn't come this time. "He hates the idea of people touring the past. Isn't that right, Marcin?"

There was silence, broken by the sound of Nowak slapping our prisoner. "Answer him, prick!"

"Oh, stop hitting him, for Christ's sake."

"I'm enjoying it," Nowak said balefully.

"I don't want to talk to you," Marcin said.

I changed gear. Smoke was starting to blow across the road now; the fall of ash was getting heavier. According to the map, the road should start to turn sometime soon and take us away from the fire.

"Marcin wanted to protect the Secret," I said. "He thought I'd go blabbing it all over the place and the villages would be flooded with Japs and Americans with camcorders. The ironic thing is, it's already happened. It's been happening for years."

In the rear-view mirror I saw Nowak look at Marcin. "Stupid bastard," he said.

"I can't understand why you didn't know about the tour groups," I said to Marcin. "Once you believe in the villages they can't be *that* hard to find. All you had to do was put yourself about as a tourist. Was it easier just to ignore them? Or were you planning to kill them off one by one?" There was a huffy silence from the back seat. "Actually, I think you only read the manuscript recently, when you realized it was worth some money. Is that it? All those years listening to your father's stories about the Blitz and the villages, and you just thought they were a load of nonsense. And then one day I turn up to buy those stories. Wow. I bet that made you sit up and take notice, didn't it. I bet that made you think."

"I don't want to talk to you," Marcin said again.

"That's all right," I said.

"No, it isn't," said Nowak in a dangerous tone of voice. "If you want him to talk to you, he'll talk to you."

"Nowak, for Christ's sake!" I yelled. "Marcin didn't kill your sodding tourists! They got killed because they went looking for trouble. They wanted to watch violent events and they got in the way. If Marcin doesn't want to talk to me, that's OK!"

There was a silence from the back seat. Then Marcin said, "I wish you had had this attitude in Warsaw."

I looked in the rear-view mirror. Nowak was glaring at Marcin strongly enough to make him burst into flame. "You shot and killed a woman in Kraków during your attempt to kill us," he said in a low, serious voice. "You won't get away with that."

Jesus. Belatedly, I started to wonder what I was going to do with the pair of them when this was all over. And then I realized I hadn't ever thought about what I was going to do with *myself* when this was all over.

"I never wanted this," I said. "All I wanted to do was find Sophie and take her home." If, I reminded myself, she wanted to come home. I realized I was slumping in the seat; I pushed on the steering wheel and forced myself upright. "I didn't want guns and people hitting each other. I didn't want lies and shouting. I . . ."

"Are you all right?" Nowak asked.

I pushed myself upright again. "Fine."

"You don't look fine. Maybe I should drive."

"I'm all right!" I shouted. I couldn't feel my leg at all now; it was like a block of wood grafted onto my hip. I couldn't move it; I was working all the pedals with my left foot and the car was moving in alternate surges and lurches, accompanied by a nerve-grinding racket of clashing gears.

"If you say so," said Nowak, sounding unconvinced.

The road did indeed curve away from the fire. Vehicles started to appear, parked on the verge. Fire engines, cars, lorries. There were people running about. Wisps and panes of smoke drifted from the trees. I kept going, trying to remember the map and the directions. Not more than a kilometre now . . .

I was worried about getting too far from the fire, crossing the boundary of the village, and popping into realtime. In my present state, I didn't think I'd be able to pop myself back here, let alone worry about Nowak and Marcin. On the other hand, it was a very big fire . . .

I wondered what happened if you popped out of a village while you were in a car. Did you keep the velocity? It seemed too complicated to worry about.

"Ramsay!"

This time it took a real effort to push my weight back against the seat. My body just wanted to crumple forwards and fall asleep. I looked at my hands on the steering wheel and the knuckles were white. I moved my hands and brought us back onto the right side of the road. I looked at the speedometer. We were doing about fifteen kilometres an hour.

"I should drive," said Nowak.

I shook my head, more to clear it than anything else. "You stay back there and look after Marcin, Piotr. Not far to go now."

"He liked you, you know," Marcin said suddenly.

I blinked, wondering if I'd blacked out for a moment and missed the important bit of a conversation.

"My father said you were a good boy. He said you were honest and that you would never be happy."

"He got that bit right," I said.

"He liked Harry Dean as well."

I smiled. "Your father was a rotten judge of character, then. Harry Dean never cared much for anyone or anything but himself."

"And you're different, I suppose." I waited for Nowak to slap him again, but there was no sound of hand hitting head. "He thought Harry Dean was a man like him. A man with a sense of wonder. Harry believed in the villages before he even saw my father's film, you know."

"I know."

"He had a newspaper cutting. It was a letter my father had written to the London *Times* in 1941." I peeped in the mirror and saw Marcin shaking his head incredulously, and Nowak looking at him the same way. "He said he'd been searching for my father most of his life, but he hadn't realized it until he saw the film."

"If it's any consolation, Harry was disappointed with the Blitz." Neither Marcin nor Nowak said anything. I said, "You must have known what your father was selling me. Didn't you try to stop him?"

"You didn't know my father. Nobody could tell him anything. He always knew best. Do you know what he wanted the money for? A piano." Marcin snorted. "He wanted to buy a piano and he didn't have enough money for it. I could have bought him a fucking piano. Two pianos. But no, he had to do it on his own terms and here we are."

"You're kidding," I said. In the mirror I saw Nowak staring at Marcin, and I knew he was thinking exactly what I was thinking. All of this because of a piano . . .

"Was it a good piano?" Nowak asked finally. Marcin gave a little sniff and looked out of the window.

I watched the road. I thought my head was clearing a little. Glancing down, I saw that the leg of my jeans, which Nowak had slit in order to get at my wound, was soaked with blood. A little corner of my mind was astounded that I wasn't panicking at the sight. I couldn't help wondering what kind of damage the bullet would have done if it had hit me properly.

"This is a potentially dangerous thing," Marcin said. "He didn't understand that. He couldn't see past the wonder of it, the miracle of it. To go back and visit old events. Incredible. To my father, the past was not *past*. It was a place he could go whenever he wanted to. He was like a little boy with some wonderful new toy." He gave a snorting little laugh. "He was like the Poles with Democracy. Such a wonderful thing, but how do we use it?"

"Don't worry, Marcin," I said. "I heard someone back home call Poland the only tiger economy in Eastern Europe."

There was a moment's silence from the back of the car, then Nowak said, "Tigers are big cats, yes?" Marcin said something very quickly in Polish, then there was a rapid exchange between them, then Nowak said, "Really?"

"Really," I said. In the mirror, I could see Nowak sitting very still in the back seat. He was looking at me.

"What are we going to do, Ramsay?" he asked.

The school was coming up on the right. I put the indicators on and made a very sloppy turn into the car park. "We are going," I said, "to see an old friend of mine."

I couldn't remember the name of the place; it had been in the newspaper article but when I tried to remember it the name wasn't there in my mind. This had to be right, though. It was exactly the way Roman Balicki had described it. There were only a dozen or so little houses, each with a big allotment behind it, but the school served four or five similar-sized communities in the area and was quite a large place: four one-storey concrete-panel buildings with big windows. There were cars parked every which way in the car park, and police cars, and fire engines, and ambulances, and people everywhere.

We bumped to a halt. I didn't even bother to put on the handbrake. I shook my seatbelt off, got the door open, and fell out of the car.

"Ramsay," said Nowak, standing over me with Marcin still attached to his wrist, "you are very sick."

"That's all right," I said, looking up at him. "This is a hospital. Help me up."

Marcin and Nowak grabbed an arm each and hauled me to my feet. The world greyed-out for a moment, came back.

"This is not a hospital," Nowak said.

"It is today," I told him. "Come on."

Together, the three of us made our way inside, bumping past doctors and soot-stained firefighters in the crowded corridors. At each classroom I made Marcin and Nowak stop for a moment while I looked inside, then we carried on.

We must have made a weird sight: two men handcuffed to each other, supporting a third whose right leg was bloody and all but useless. Nowak had taken out his police identity card and was flashing it in all directions, but none of the people he flashed it at seemed to take any notice of us. They were all far too busy.

"Next one," I said at the doorway of the third classroom. I was feeling light-headed and desperate and there was a near-subsonic roaring noise in my head. This had to be the right day; I wasn't going to get the chance to sit around and wait.

At the fifth classroom, I felt all the pain and tiredness drain away from me. I felt as unreal as the people all around me.

"This one," I said with a little gasp of relief.

The room stank of smoke and burned skin and hair. There were pictures on the walls painted by the children whose classroom this normally was, the kind of thing you see in any school anywhere, but the rest of the room looked like a scene from *M*A*S*H*. The floor was covered with horribly burned bodies. Some of them were screaming; others were just moaning and stirring feebly. A few lay silent and motionless, their faces covered with blankets. Doctors and nurses were stepping over the bodies, bending to minister to the burned, shouting to each other, occasionally shouting *at* each other. All the people in the room who hadn't been burned looked as if they had gone over the edge of exhaustion. According to Roman Balicki, they had worked in this school for almost three days without sleep, trying to save the lives of the injured firefighters. It had been Balicki's last dispatch from the fire, and the paper had printed his name along with the names of all the other people who had died here. There were over thirty names, but only one of them had been underlined in the cutting Anna Trzetrzelewska had given me.

I felt Nowak and Marcin crowd into the doorway behind me. "Jesus Maria," Nowak said quietly.

"Are you happy now, Ramsay?" Marcin asked.

I looked across to the end of the classroom. "No," I said. Nowak put his hand on my shoulder, but I shrugged it off and started to limp between the rows of injured men.

At the very end of the room a man lay on a dirty grey blanket. He was wearing the scorched remains of a firefighter's uniform, and the skin on both hands and one side of his face had actually charred. His hips were an odd shape, and one of his legs bent in an unnatural direction at the knee. His head, hair burned away, was cradled in the lap of a woman who was sitting behind him. I felt an almost electric sense of achievement, of rightness. I had been lied to, exploited, cheated, arrested, threatened and shot. I needed to see a doctor myself, and to be honest I probably needed to talk to a psychiatrist as well, but I'd done it. I'd done the thing I'd set out to do. I took a deep breath and kept going, my heart pounding. I felt the little teddy-bear in my pocket and I took it out and almost crushed it in my fist.

One last chance to say goodbye, to say you were sorry, to say you loved somebody. Who wouldn't?

I could only guess what she'd gone through. When she'd got the news about her father, her visa had expired and she'd been afraid that if she returned to Poland she wouldn't be allowed back into England afterwards. And she had to go back to England because she loved Harry, for all his faults.

So, for maybe the one and only time in her life, she'd behaved like me. She'd let events move her instead of the other way round. She'd told herself that her father was going to get better, that she would have time to come and see him later, when Harry had sorted out her visa and work permit. She'd convinced herself everything was going to be all right.

But she'd been wrong.

And, because she was wrong, she had taken this last chance, come back here to say goodbye, to give a little comfort, waiting for the pain to go away. To torment herself, over and over again, for not having been here the first time.

Hands, terribly burned, reached out and tremblingly picked at the cuffs of my jeans. I shook them off and tried not to look, tried to keep my eyes fixed on the woman at the end of the room, the woman who was talking softly to her father, the woman who looked up, whose eyes widened when she saw me lurching towards her.

My face and clothes were filthy and smoke-impregnated. One sliced-up leg of my jeans was stiff with drying blood and it tapped forlornly against my shin with every step. I must have looked like Retribution itself, sweaty and wild-eyed, loping towards her with her old teddy-bear gripped in its hand.

She didn't get up. Her father's eyes were closed, their lids blistered and weeping. He wasn't conscious but he wasn't quite unconscious either. I remembered that it had taken him fifteen days to die, but that had been in hospital, outside the village, and she wouldn't have been able to visit him there. She'd had to come here, over and over again.

He was moaning softly, his fingers trembling by his sides. He must have been in terrible pain but, according to Balicki's article, the doctors didn't have much more than paracetamol to give the injured. Which, it occurred to me distantly, didn't bode too well for my own chances of medical help here.

I reached Sophie and her father and stood swaying beside her. Waves of pain were thudding in my head. Sophie blinked up at me. Tears were pouring down her cheeks. She was crying with a kind of total surrender, her face twisted spectacularly, her mouth contorted. I wanted to tell her I understood, that it was all right. I didn't know how many repetitions of the village's loop she had already been through, but she looked worn out, right on the edge of collapse. I wanted to tell her it was all right to stop now, that I had come to take her home.

I bent down slightly and waved the teddy-bear towards her. The noise in the room was getting worse; or maybe it was the noise in my head. I could barely stand up.

"*Now* do you believe me?" I shouted.

Acknowledgements

Thanks must go to:

Paul Barnett, for devotion above and beyond, and for then going on to render the manuscript into a form more closely resembling English.

Blotters everywhere, but particularly John Clute, Jane Barnett, Paul Kincaid, Dave Langford, Stephen Marley and Maureen Speller.

David V. Barrett, the mighty Chris Bell, the everso slightly mighty Darryl Smith, Jan Stokes and Irena Valchera, who read early versions of the book. Because all of them had excellent suggestions, the thing is about a hundred pages longer and more than a little better than it might otherwise have been. Any errors in the finished book are mine, not theirs.

I'm also more indebted than I can say to Marta and Tadeusz Michalski, for welcoming me into their family; to Darek and Magda Nowak, who drove us to Kraków one *very* cold day so I could check I'd described the Market Square properly; and to Tomek, for lending me his skiing gear.

And finally, but by no means least, my love to Bogna, who probably didn't realize I was going to spend *quite* so much time typing in the spare bedroom.